RICHARD MATHESON

7 STEPS to MIDNIGHT

FORGE®

A TOM DOHERTY ASSOCIATES BOOK
NEW YORK

7 STEPS TO MIDNIGHT

A Forge Book
Published by Tom Doherty Associates, LLC
175 Fifth Avenue
New York, NY 10010

www.tor.com

Forge® is a registered trademark of Tom Doherty Associates, LLC.

Library of Congress Cataloging-in-Publication Data

Matheson, Richard.
    7 steps to midnight / Richard Matheson.
        p. cm.
    ISBN 0-312-85409-9 (hc)
    ISBN 0-765-30837-1 (pbk)
    1. Impostors and imposture—Fiction. I. Title
  II. title: Seven steps to midnight.

PS3563.A8355A615   1993   93-25509
813'.54—dc20   CIP

First Hardcover Edition: September 1993

First Trade Paperback Edition: July 2003

Printed in the United States of America

0 9 8 7 6 5 4 3 2 1

PART

1

Most of them were wearing digit costumes. One through nine, completely out of order. Others had on letter costumes, caps or lowercase. Plus- and minus-sign costumes. Greater-than and less-than costumes. Parenthesis and bracket costumes. All milling around the stage like sheep.

He leaned toward Wilson, whispering, "How am I supposed to get them in their proper places?"

"Don't ask me," Wilson answered. "You're the director."

"What?" He gaped at the older man. "I thought *you* were."

"Not *this* play," Wilson said.

Chris slumped back with a groan. *I'm the director?* he thought. How could that be? He didn't even know what play it was.

"Come on," he protested. "This is insane. I'm not a stage director. I'm—"

He broke off, wincing, as Wilson grabbed his arm. "Time's a wastin', Chrissie-boy," he said. He held up his wristwatch but Chris couldn't see what time it was. "Now *do* it." Wilson looked infuriated.

"I just don't see how—"

Wilson made an angry noise and lurched to his feet. Chris twisted around to watch him striding up the aisle. He wanted to shout, *I'm sorry, but I'm out of my depth here!*

He didn't though. He looked back at the stage and wondered what he should do. *Time's a wastin', Chrissie-boy.* The words repeated in his mind. He swallowed nervously. How much time did he have?

For the first time, he noticed an enormous clock on the wall of the abstract set. He tried to see what time it was but couldn't make out the hands. He blinked, attempting to focus his eyes, but couldn't do it.

He looked at the actors again. *Were* they actors? They had no faces. Just the digits, the letters, the signs, the parenthetical marks. He peered closely at a group of them. Were they forming a phase function of scattering? he wondered. He stood and started down the aisle. Maybe if he got a closer look.

Now *those* actors were definitely forming the optical thickness of a clearance zone—

"Hey, don't!" he shouted as they began to switch positions. "Stay where you are!"

The actors started laughing as they walked around, changing positions.

"Damn it, stay in place!" he yelled. He started walking more quickly to stop them. He heard the clock on the stage ticking so loudly that the noise oppressed him. "Cut the clock noise!" he demanded. If he *was* the director, by God he'd enforce some discipline!

Suddenly, amazingly, the actors came together in a formula. "Now *that* looks promising!" he cried.

The lights went out. "Goddamn it all!" he raged. "Just when they look like they're getting something right, you turn the fucking lights out?!"

"Chris!" somebody shouted to his left.

He jarred to a halt and thought he saw a figure sitting in the shadows. *"What?"* he asked, impatiently.

"The name of the play," the figure said, "is *Damocles*."

❧ His cheek was pressed against a film of saliva as he slumped across the desk top. He looked as though someone had clubbed him on the back of the head, knocking him forward onto his cluster of papers.

Actually, nothing had struck him but exhaustion. The end result of working seventeen hours after a sleep of five hours following eighteen hours of work after a sleep of three and a half hours following nineteen hours of work . . .

He was thirty-seven but, sprawled on his sheets of penciled figures, in front of the humming computer screen, he could have passed for fifty. Pale. Dark circles underneath his eyes. Threads of white at his temples. Underweight, his shirt like that of a heavier man. Features pinched and tight, his expression one of anxiety.

"Time," he said and sat up.

His half-shut eyes stared at the figures on the computer screen. Wrong, he thought. As usual. He switched off the computer and stretched, wincing at the crackle of his bones. *I'm drying up,* he thought.

He looked at the wall clock. "Christ," he muttered. A memory flickered, a clock on a stage set. Then it vanished. He stood with a groan and stretched again. Why didn't he just have a bed and refrigerator installed in the office? Then he'd never have to go home; he could calculate into oblivion.

He shuffled to the coatrack and pulled down his light blue jacket, slid his arms into the sleeves. He tried to close the zipper but couldn't get it started. MATHEMATICAL WHIZ KID UNABLE TO CLOSE ZIPPER; he saw a headline in his mind. He'd like to see Wilson's expression when he read that.

Grunting, Chris pulled open the door of his office. Weighs too much, he thought. His brain began to calculate the weight; he cut it off with a scowl. *Enough.*

The overhead squares of luminescent light floated back across him as he moved along the hallway. No one else in the department was around. Surprise, he thought. What idiot would work at this time of the morning?

"How do you do," he muttered.

He stared at the place where he'd parked his car.

Too much, he thought. *I work my noodle to the bone till after three A.M. and when I finally leave to go home, my car is gone.*

He turned and looked around the parking lot. Had someone

moved his car? A joke? No, he couldn't see it anywhere. None of the few cars visible were his. He sighed. *Too much.*

Wait a second. His brain automatically sought an explanation. Did he make a mistake, exit into the east lot instead of the west? He groaned and rubbed the back of his neck. As always, it felt stiff.

He made a face then. *Idiot,* he told himself. He looked at the paving, at the slot marks and his name in white: C. Barton.

"Trouble is, C. Barton's wheels are gone," he muttered.

Another weary sigh. Now what? He eyed the distant guard shack. *Now you walk a hundred miles to that shack and say, "My car is gone,"* his brain provided.

"Thanks for the help," he said.

His heels scuffed on the asphalt as he trudged toward the guard shack. He drew in a deep breath of air. He'd never liked the desert by day but at night it wasn't bad. This time of year anyway; the air was cool and fresh. He leaned his head back, looking at the sky. Diamonds flung onto black velvet, he thought. "How friggin' poetic," he mumbled.

He looked back down. Now the guard shack was only fifty miles away. He'd make it by sunrise. "Shit," he muttered. What son of a bitch had taken his car?

The dream was stirred by memory. Actors in number suits? He snickered. How obvious could a dream be? Freud could diagnose it with his brain tied behind his back. Numbers, letters, signs, parentheses and brackets? Kid stuff. And the big clock on the set, Wilson's watch? "Get outta here," he said.

He opened the door of the guard shack and went inside. The uniformed man behind the counter twitched—had he been dozing?—and looked at Chris's badge.

"*Yes,* Mr. Barton," he said as though he knew Chris.

"My car is gone," Chris told him.

"Hmm."

Chris looked at the man's badge. Number 9939. No surprise. Nines always made trouble. He could smell a problem in the works from F. Crain.

"What kind of car was it?" the guard asked.

Is it, Chris's mind corrected; the car's not dead. "A Mustang convertible; blue," he said.

"Hmm," said the guard.

Don't say that again or I'll get testy, Chris reacted. "*Well?*" he asked.

"No car like that's been past here during my shift," F. Crain answered.

Chris visualized his bed, the stacks of books on each bedside table. He was dying to be sacked out in the first and reaching for one of the second. He had no desire to be standing in this shack at almost four A.M., discussing his purloined Mustang with F. Crain, 9939.

No help for it though. "Where do you suppose it *went* then?" he inquired. F. Crain was fifty-seven, two hundred forty pounds, five foot seven inches, he estimated quickly.

"There *is* the back gate," F. Crain suggested.

"I thought they always kept it locked," Chris said.

"They do."

Oh, well now *we're hurtling toward the solution,* Chris thought. Any second now, he'd start to froth and F. Crain would be forced to call for an ambulance. "That doesn't help me find my Mustang, does it?" he said.

"Not really," said the guard.

Oh, Jesus, Chris heard his brain moan haplessly. He struggled for composure. "Listen, Mr. Crain," he said. "The problem is, I've been working for seventeen hours and I'm exhausted. I live eighteen miles from here and I have to get home and go to bed. But I can't do that without my blue Mustang or something to *replace* my blue Mustang."

"Hmm," said F. Crain.

✇ Chris glanced at the dashboard clock as he turned onto the highway. It was almost five A.M. "Gawd," he muttered. He could watch the moon go down as he drove. Or the sun come up. He groaned. His eyes felt like a pair of overheated billiard balls. He had to read, to sleep.

F. Crain had not exactly been a whirlwind of efficiency. Chris had finally been compelled to call Wilson's home, apologize for rousting him from sleep, explain his plight. A grumpy Wilson had instructed the guard to find out which of the people working in the plant was going home the latest and see if Chris could borrow his or her car. He'd have the car returned by the time it was needed and, if Chris's Mustang wasn't found by then, he'd be provided with a rental car until he could purchase a new one. All this information had proved excessive to F. Crain's IQ, and, by the time Wilson had imparted clarity to the guard, Chris could hear him screaming on the other end of the line. *Better him than me,* he'd thought.

A Scotty Tensdale wasn't scheduled to go home until noon so Chris had driven the guard's electric cart to Tensdale's department and gotten the car keys. Crain could not desert his post, of course. National security.

Now he was driving along the highway in Scotty Tensdale's amber Pontiac sedan and hoping that he'd make it to his house before he passed out cold.

The moon was full tonight, casting a silver sheen across the desert. Interesting sight, Chris thought. Stark and oddly menacing, marked by dark outlines and glistening sand. He stared at the highway unraveling ahead, pressing down on the accelerator. Seventy-two. He'd better hold the speed to that; his attention was a little blurry.

Even so, he did briefly try to calculate what might have happened to his car.

He didn't know anyone at the plant well enough for them to play a joke on him. What kind of joke would it be anyway? It couldn't have been stolen. Why bother? It wasn't worth it; there were nicer cars on the lot. Anyway, a car thief wouldn't go to a government plant and try to steal a car from a guarded parking lot.

Some emergency requiring the use of his car? Wouldn't they have told him?

Every possibility seemed blocked by logic. Yet the car was gone.

He had to let it go. His brain was just too muddled. He'd have a go at finding a solution after he'd slept.

Time, he thought. Was that what he'd murmured, waking up? *Why?* Chronology, that's why. Everything separated by time. Him and his bed. Him and the answer to his project. Him and his car.

"For*get* it," he growled. *I refuse to bring it home with me.* . . . R_2 *(x,y,z)*, his brain tried to slip in. He cut it off. *Drop* it, he ordered himself. Wetting the end of his right index finger, he rubbed it over his eyelids, the momentary coolness providing him with the illusion of wakefulness.

He looked at the intersection sign as he sped by it. He should have hung a right and headed for Las Vegas. If he was going to stay up day and night, he might as well enjoy it.

"*Sure,*" he muttered. He wouldn't go to Vegas, that was obvious. He'd go home and take a shower as he always did. Get in his pajamas and clamber into bed. Look to his left, suspense and mystery paperbacks; to his right, science, fiction, fantasy and horror—and wonder which one he would gulp down as a sleeping pill this time.

✥ He had almost passed the man without noticing him. Then his head turned quickly and an impression flashed by him. Old in age and clothes, a baseball cap on the man's head.

By now the car had sped past him; the man's figure was receding quickly.

"Oh . . . *shit,*" Chris muttered. He exhaled loudly, fluttering his cheeks. An old guy stuck out in the desert at this time of night. His foot lifted from the gas pedal and the car began to slow.

Or should I? he wondered. He visualized the old man gabbing at him, driving him insane. He visualized the old man reaching for his groin, a toothless grin on his face. He visualized the old man pulling out a hatchet and burying it in his skull.

The vision faded in a recollection of how the old man had lifted his head, hopefully, as though to say, *Ah, rescue from this dreadful spot.*

Chris groaned and pressed on the brake. All right, all right, he thought. He pulled over to the shoulder, slowed down enough to make a U-turn and twisted the steering wheel to his left. Can't just leave the poor old guy alone out here, he thought.

If only, it would occur to him later, he had never thought that.

2

Chris made another U-turn and pulled up by the old man. Reaching across the other seat, he unlocked the door. The old man opened it, picked up a canvas bag and got inside. "You'll never forget this," he said.

Chris felt a momentary tremor at the words, then shucked it off. The old man looked benign enough. *Hell, it could be Howard Hughes,* he thought. *Hughes didn't really die. And now he's going to give me ninety million dollars for my trouble.*

Repressing a smile, Chris pulled back onto the highway and accelerated as the old man put his canvas bag on the floor. "Been here long?" he asked.

"Hours," the old man answered. "No one wanted to pick me up."

I don't blame them, Chris thought. "Well, that's the way things are today," he said.

Now the old galoot will open up his bag, he thought, *remove a carving knife and reduce me to giblets.* The vision half alarmed and half amused him as the old man responded, "Yeah, nobody trusts anybody these days."

They'll find my remains about a month from now, Chris's vision continued, *and Scotty Tensdale's Pontiac in Massachusetts.* He frowned away the notion. Maybe he should start reading Barbara Cartland.

"Veering," said the old man. "Albert Veering."

"Hi." Chris nodded. "Chris Barton." He wondered where the old man was going. Not that it mattered. He could only take him as far as the entrance to Oasis Village. Then Albert would be on his own again.

"Nice car," the old man said.

Chris thought about explaining that it wasn't his but decided he was too tired for the explanation; Veering might have a brain like F. Crain. He settled for "Thanks."

"What brings you out this time of night?" asked Veering. "Or should I say, this time of morning?"

Say anything you want, Chris thought. "Coming home from work," he said.

"You must be on the night shift," Veering said, "or on the graveyard shift. Except if you were on the graveyard shift, you'd still be working."

As I dreaded, Chris thought; *a blabbermouth.* He pressed down on the gas pedal. *Let's get this over fast,* he thought. "I just worked late," he said.

"At the plant down the highway?" the old man asked.

"Yeah."

"Passed it hours ago," said Veering. "Looks hush-hush."

Chris chuckled at the phrase. "I guess," he said. Obviously, the old man didn't have anything in his canvas bag but dirty underwear and a half-empty bottle of Muscatel.

"All those high fences and gate guards," Veering said. "You in secret government work?"

Chris didn't answer. He couldn't very well believe that this old coot in the baseball cap was a foreign agent. Still, there was the policy. "Nothing secret," he said. "Statistics. Pretty dull."

"How come you have to work so late then?" Veering prodded.

Chris glanced at him. The old man's question grated on him. *None of your fucking business,* he thought.

He repressed the irritation. Hell, the old guy had been stuck out here for hours. He just wanted a little company, that was all.

"Just bad luck," he said.

"Statistics," Veering said. "A lot of details."

"Yeah."

"You a cost analyst?" the old man asked.

"Something like that."

"Defense program?"

Chris had had enough. "Where you off to?" He changed the subject.

"Off to nowhere," Veering said. "Just wandering."

"Sounds good."

"You wandering too?" the old man asked.

Chris glanced at him. What the hell did *that* mean? Maybe the old man *was* a little off.

"Modern man," Veering said.

Oh, Christ, Chris thought. A baseball-capped philosopher. *This has really been my night.*

"Have any personal life?" the old man asked.

Chris felt like saying *What the hell is that to you, you old fart?* But he didn't want to hurt the old man's feelings. He was just being garrulous, that's all. "I work a lot," he said.

"Well, there's the shame." The old man nodded. "There's the pity."

"Hmm," Chris said. *I sound like F. Crain now.* The thought amused him.

"Modern man, so totally absorbed by the mass of details in his existence that he has no time for a personal life."

Jesus Christ, I picked up PBS Al, Chris thought. He didn't have Muscatel in his bag, he had *The Story of Philosophy* by Will Durant. He'd almost prefer a hatchet. Maybe if he didn't respond, the old man would let it go.

The old man didn't.

"Is your life meaningful?" he asked. "Do you have time for anything of consequence?"

Jesus, I am tired, Chris thought. *Why the hell did I pick him up?*

"That's the problem, you see," Veering said. "How to differentiate."

What the fuck is he talking about now? Chris wondered.

"*Reality,*" the old man said. "How do you differentiate reality?"

From what? Chris thought. He sighed, politely quiet. Oh, well, he'd be at the Village soon. Then he could dump Baruch Spinoza and go to bed.

"Is your life real or unreal?" the old man continued.

Chris didn't try to hide his sigh this time. "Real, I assume."

"You *assume*," the old man responded quickly.

Jesus God, he's going to start a seminar, Chris thought. *Give me a break.*

"You *assume* your life is real but how do you *know* it is?"

Oh, God, a shower, a read and a sleep, Chris thought. Maybe he should dump the old guy now, tell him he had to take a left turn into the desert. "I *don't* know," he muttered, unable to disguise the edge of irritation he felt.

"There's a crying shame," the old man said.

Give me a break! howled Chris's mind.

"An intelligent young man like you not knowing what's real and what isn't?" Veering pressed.

"I s'pose," Chris said. How far to the Village? Couldn't be more than nine, ten miles.

"Do you believe your life is organized?" the old man asked.

"Organized?" Chris glanced at him impatiently.

"Everything in place. All the details settled. No surprises."

Relax, Chris told himself. Let him blather. "Well, sure, I know what to expect each day," he said. A little sleep, a lot of work and no solution to the project, his mind completed.

Veering wouldn't give it up. "But do you know what *is* and what *isn't* in your life?" he asked.

You're getting on my nerves, you old bastard, Chris thought. *I pick you up out of the goodness of my heart because you look decrepit and alone in the darkness on a desert highway. And what do you do? Attack me with your Mickey Mouse philosophy.*

"Well?" demanded Veering.

Be patient, Chris ordered himself. He's old. Let him think he's talking sense. "Well," he said, "to the extent that anyone knows what is or isn't real in their lives—"

"Ah!" the old man interrupted.

Chris waited. Nothing happened. That's *it?* he thought. Just *ah?* Not the greatest windup of a philosophical debate he'd ever run across. But what the hell.

"Tell you what," said Veering.

Chris barely managed to control a groan.

"I wager you," the old man said.

Chris looked at him, then back at the highway. "You do," he said.

"I do," said Veering. "I present you with a wager."

To wit? Chris's mind inquired. He felt a gush of pleasure as he saw the distant lights of Oasis Village.

"I wager the security of your existence against your assumption that you know what's real and what's unreal in your life."

Come again? Chris thought. *You what?*

"Are you game?" asked Veering. "Do you accept the wager?"

Chris almost asked, What *wager? I don't know what the fuck you're talking about, you old fool,* then decided to let it go. He'd be home in fifteen minutes. "Sure," he said.

"Don't say it casually," the old man cautioned. "Think about it."

Oh, God, *why did I pick him up?* Chris thought. "Okay," he said. *Never pick up hitchhikers;* he formed a permanent rule for himself.

"You believe, then, that you know what's real in your life and what's unreal. Correct?"

Chris yawned. "Yeah, right."

"And I maintain that you do not," said Veering. He's beginning to sound like a mid-Victorian attorney, Chris thought. "And I repeat—are you willing to gamble the security of your existence on this wager?"

"*Sure,*" Chris muttered. Up ahead, he saw the gateway to Oasis Village. Thank the good Lord, he thought.

"You're *positive,*" the old man said. "You're not—"

"I'm going to have to let you off here," Chris broke in. "I live here."

"*Do you so wager?*" Veering insisted.

"*Okay. Okay.*" Chris started steering toward the shoulder.

"Done and done," the old man said. "You can let me off right here."

Bet your ass I will, Chris thought. He steered onto the highway shoulder, braking.

"Thank you for the ride and interesting discussion," Veering said, picking up his canvas bag.

"You're welcome," Chris replied offhandedly. *Go,* he thought.

Veering opened the door, stepped out onto the shoulder, then leaned back in. In the dimness of the overhead light, Chris saw him smiling.

"*À bientôt,*" the old man said.

He closed the door and started walking, the canvas bag thrown over his shoulder. Chris pulled back onto the highway and drove past him. *À bientôt?* he thought. What the hell was that supposed to mean? He'd never see the old coot again.

As he was driving through the gateway to Oasis Village, it came to him—the definition of *veering.*

To change direction.

He would remember that more than once in the days to come.

3

When he turned the corner onto Oasis Drive East, he saw his blue Mustang.

It was parked in front of his garage. Exactly as he always parked it when he was home.

His mind jumped automatically toward explanation. He'd been so distracted by his work, he'd left it at home. The illogic of that was immediately apparent. How had he gotten to work then? No one else had picked him up. There was no shuttle service between Oasis Village and Palladian.

Which left what? The practical joke again. And who at the plant knew him well enough to perpetrate a joke on him? In a word, nobody.

He pulled the Pontiac into the driveway, parking it beside his car. Was it his car? His mind still sought an answer. These houses were similar in appearance. He must have driven onto the wrong street and approached a house that looked like his but wasn't. With a car parked in front of it that looked like his but wasn't. Farfetched but possible.

The notion was short-lived. Lasting long enough for him to leave the Pontiac, walk around it and look at the Mustang. He always left it unlocked at night. Neighbors told him he shouldn't, there were occasional car thefts in the area. He never paid attention.

Opening the door on the driver's side of the Mustang, he looked inside. The cassette and change box was there across the drive-shaft hump. His cassettes: Mahler, Vaughan Williams, Copland, the *Smithsonian History of Jazz* in three cassettes. Any concept of coincidence was gone. It was his Mustang. And it had been stolen. Taken from the plant and parked in front of his house.

Which made approximately no sense at all.

Still, to be certain—*proof and double proof, the only way*, he heard Uncle Harry say—he opened the glove compartment and pulled out the papers inside. A repair bill from Desert Ford, his name printed on it. The registration slip, his name on it. "Well, goddamn," he muttered.

What the hell was going on?

Backing out of the Mustang, he straightened up and closed the door. Quietly. Immediately it struck him; why had he done that? What caution had impelled him? He grimaced with a sound of self-reproach. There has to be a simple explanation for this, he thought.

He visualized himself a scientist from a fifties science-fiction film uttering those words. He always scoffed when he heard them. Still, there *did* have to be a simple explanation for this. He was in no condition to confront a major enigma at this time of the morning.

He looked toward the house. It was dark and quiet. Was the car thief lurking in there, peering out between the shutter slats, a carving knife clutched in his . . .

"Oh, shit, come on," he berated himself. First, he had imagined Veering with a carving knife, now, some skulker in his house. *You're not paranoid, are you?* he thought.

He walked to the bedroom window and tried to look inside. The drapes were shut. He tried to remember whether he'd left them closed before leaving for work yesterday afternoon. He didn't, usually. But, of course, he must have.

He listened at the window. There was no sound. Why should there be? his mind challenged. "No reason," he muttered a reply.

He was on the front porch when he realized he didn't have the key; it was on his car ring and—

Chris felt a shiver course his back. Where was the car ring, then? If it was in the house, somebody had to have brought it in.

Reason fought uneasiness. All right, someone took his car and put it in the driveway of his house and put the keys inside and then was driven off by some confederate.

Who? his mind demanded.

The front door was locked. No surprise there; he always locked it when he went to work. Still, how was he to get inside now? He frowned at himself for never having thought of it while getting Tensdale's car and driving here.

He walked across the lawn and opened the alley gate, moving along the sidewalk. The house was totally dark. No surprise there either. It was always dark when he returned from work.

He stepped onto the small cement porch by the kitchen door and tried the knob. Locked. Always was; again, no surprise. He stepped off the porch and walked around to the back of the house, to the sliding glass door of the patio. Locked.

He peered into the darkness of the family room, the kitchen beyond. Now what? He shook the sliding door to see if he could loosen the latch.

A minute later, he was standing on the front lawn again, staring at his dark, locked house. And now? he thought. Sleep in the Mustang? The Pontiac?

"Screw that," he said. He looked around for a rock to break a window. But there were only redwood chips skirting the lawn. Groaning, he walked over to the Mustang and opened the door. Pushing the driver's seat forward, he leaned into the back and felt behind the seat until his fingers closed on the putter in his golf bag. How long had it been since he'd played golf? The question drifted across his mind. Another lifetime, was the answer. Why the hell had he bought them in the first place? Wilson, he remembered. Wilson had told him it would relax his mind. Sure. And Wilson was probably the guy whose family owned the golf-ball business.

He walked back to the bedroom window. If he smashed it in, would the neighbors call the police? Anyway, he shouldn't break a front window. Better the small one in the kitchen door. He turned away, then twisted back. The crank window was slightly open. If he could get through the screen, he might be able to uncrank the window all the way and crawl inside. Better than breaking glass.

He was trying to squeeze his hand through the opening when a light went on in the bedroom.

He twitched and made a startled noise, jerking back his hand. He stepped back, staring at the drapes, felt his heartbeat thudding. Wait a second, wait a second, he thought. *Had* he gone to the wrong street, the wrong house? It was possible . . .

He shuddered, remembering his registration slip inside the Mustang, his cassettes. This was his house.

But who was in it?

He felt his muscles tense. Well, he was going to find out, damn it. Striding to the front porch, he pushed the doorbell, hearing the chimes inside playing "Shave and a Haircut, Two Bits." For a moment, his fingers tightened on the putter handle. What if whoever was inside had no desire to see him?

"That's ridiculous," he muttered. He stood impatiently waiting for whoever it was to open the door. This had to be a prank of some sort. A lousy one, but a prank. "Come on," he said.

He heard the sound of a woman's voice on the other side of the door. He couldn't make out what she said. "What?" he asked.

"Who is it?" the woman asked.

He bared his teeth in angry reaction. "Will you open the door, please," he said.

"Why?" the woman asked. She sounded frightened. *Frightened?*

"Because I want to talk with you," he said. "Because you're in my house."

Silence after that. What was the woman doing? He shivered. Did she have a gun by any chance? She'd sounded genuinely upset.

"Are you still there?" he asked.

"You're mistaken," he heard her say.

"What are you talking about?" he demanded. "This is *my house*. That's *my* car in front of the garage with *my* registration slip inside it. Don't tell me I'm mistaken."

Silence again. Now what was she doing?

"Look, are you—?" he began.

"You'd better get out of here or I'm going to call the police," the woman interrupted.

"Good," he said. "I wish you would."

"Who *are* you?" she asked. Her voice was actually trembling. If he really *was* making a mistake, he must sound like a maniac to her.

No, goddamn it! There was no mistake! "My name is Chris Barton and I've lived in this house for twenty-seven months and thirteen days!"

Once more, silence. This was maddening. Chris felt like pounding the golf club against the door and ordering her to let him in.

He tensed abruptly as the door was unlocked and opened enough for her to peer out at him. Chris felt his stomach muscles jerking in. There was a chain on the door.

He didn't have a chain on the door.

God, oh, God, he thought. *Was* he making a mistake?

The woman was in her early thirties, dark-haired, quite attractive. She was looking at him with uneasy disbelief. "You're *who?*" she asked.

He felt like whipping out his wallet, waving it in her face. But there was no chain on his front door and the woman looked genuinely disturbed. "Look," he said. "I don't know what's going on here but— This *is* Oasis Drive East, isn't it?" he added suddenly.

She nodded slightly.

"24967?"

He saw her throat move as she swallowed. "Yes," she said.

Chris felt as though his head had just been covered by a vise that was beginning to compress his skull. "This is my house then," he said, alarmed to hear that he sounded pleading.

"No," the woman said.

"What do you mean, 'no'?!" His voice was shaking. "You—!"

"My husband and I have lived here for more than eight years," she said.

He had read about people's jaws dropping, they were so startled by something they had seen or heard. Now he actually felt his jaw drop, as he stood there gaping at the woman. *Is this what it's like to go insane?* The question whispered in his mind.

His swallow was so dry, he heard a crackling in his throat. "Could I . . . see the living room?" he asked.

She looked at him suspiciously.

"I'm not going to do anything bad," he told her, appalled by the tremor in his voice. "I just—"

He broke off as he saw her gaze drop to the putter in his hand. "Oh," he said. He leaned the club against the porch wall. "Just . . . step back and let me look inside. You don't even have to open the chain."

She gazed at him for several moments more, then stepped aside and disappeared. He pressed his face against the opening and looked inside.

Oh, God, he thought. He stared at what he could see of the living room. The sofa, the chair, the bookcase, the TV, the coffee table, the carpeting.

All his.

"Well?" he heard her ask.

He didn't know what to say. *I'm sorry, lady, that's my furniture? What the hell are you trying to pull off here, lady? Lady, please telephone for an ambulance because my brain has just dissolved?*

The woman began to close the door.

"Wait!" he demanded. But she closed it all the way and locked it. "No!" he cried. He pounded on the wood with the side of a fist. "Open the door!"

"I'm going to call the police!" she threatened.

"Do it then!" he said. He needed outside help, badly.

He heard fast-moving footsteps in the house. "No, don't," the woman said.

Chris drew back quickly as the door was yanked open and a man stood glaring at him. A man about his age, his height, his weight.

Wearing his pajamas.

"Either you get out of here and stay away from us," the man shouted at him, "or you are going to spend the rest of your goddamn life in jail! You understand?!"

4

There was suddenly no gristle in his legs; they felt like rubber. He reached out, clutching, and braced himself against the porch wall. It was redwood and he felt small splinters driving into his fingers and palms. He winced in silence, staring at the man.

"Did you hear what I said?!" the man cried.

"Wait a second," Chris murmured. There had to be an explanation . . .

"I have a gun in my bedside-table drawer," the man said, threatening. "Either you get in your car and drive away and never show your face to us again or, so help me God, I'll blow your head off!"

"You *know* this man?" the woman asked, appalled.

"*Yes,* I know him," the man told her. "I never told you because I never thought he'd have the gall to actually show up at our house."

"Listen—" Chris began.

"I don't *want* to listen!" the man interrupted. "I've listened to you long enough! I'm sick to death of you!"

"I don't even *know* you!" Chris's voice broke uncontrollably.

"*All* right," the man said, nodding once. "That's it." He turned away.

"Chris, what are you doing?" the woman asked.

Chris felt the porch beginning to tilt. "*Chris?*" he murmured.

"Just stay there," the man said across his shoulder. "You have *had* it." He disappeared into the back hall.

"What's your name?" Chris asked the woman weakly. She only stared at him, clutching the edge of her robe shut with both hands.

"What's your *husband's* name?" he asked.

"Chris Barton," she replied.

He had to shake his head; a cloud of darkness flooded upward from the porch at him. He blinked his eyes dazedly. "Now wait—" he said.

He braced himself. *This is insane!* his mind cried out. He fumbled in his back pocket, almost dropping the wallet as he took it out. He opened it and pointed at his driver's license. "Look," he said.

The man came back, a pistol in his right hand. "All right," he said, "you—"

"Damn it, look at my driver's license!" Chris cut him off, enraged and frightened at the same time.

"You think a phony driver's license is going to—"

Chris cut him off again. "Phony?! This is real! *I'm* Chris Barton! Who the hell are you?!"

The man extended his arm, pointing the pistol at Chris.

"Chris, don't," the woman said.

"Get in here," said the man. Chris stared at him numbly. "I said get *in* here!" the man raged.

Chris stumbled in. *This* is *a nightmare, isn't it?* he thought; *I'm still asleep at the plant.* He saw the man gesture curtly toward a chair and, almost gratefully, he sank down on it. The chair he'd sat in hundreds of times, reading, watching television.

"Call Wilson," the man said.

Chris's body spasmed on the chair. *Call Wilson?* There was a pounding in his ears before he heard the rest of what the man was saying ". . . send a security man."

The woman left the room and went into the kitchen, turning on the light. Chris heard her tapping the buttons on a phone and felt dizzy again.

He didn't have a phone in the kitchen.

I'm in an alternate universe, he thought. *I did something wrong. My work. Veering. The wager.* He fought if off. Impossible. This world was real. And there was some explanation for what was happening here. There had to be.

He looked at the man, who was watching him intently. His

pajamas. His slippers too, he saw now. A man claiming to be Chris Barton. *Why?* A plot of some kind?

The notion crumbled instantly. The man was sure enough of himself to have his wife (*Was* she his wife?) call Wilson, ask for a security man.

Oh, no, he thought then. *She's not calling Wilson. That's only a ploy to throw me off some more.*

"What *is* this?" he asked.

"You tell me, you son of a bitch." The man's expression was venomous.

"Listen, no matter what you say," Chris told him, "I've never seen you before in my life and *this is my house.*"

"Jesus Christ, you never let up, do you?" the man said with a humorless smile. "You fucking never give up."

"Damn it—!"

"You're going to jail for a long, long time!" The man refused to let him speak. "No more badgering, no more intimidation. No more terrorizing."

"*Terrorizing?*" Chris stared at him incredulously. "What the hell are you talking about?"

"You'll find out," the man said. He glanced aside as the woman came in. "You reached him?" he asked.

She nodded nervously.

"All right." The man nodded in satisfaction, then smiled at Chris again, a cold, malignant smile. "Just sit there; wait," he said. "Better still, make a run for the door so I can shoot you dead."

Chris stared at him. *So I can shoot you dead?* he thought. Jesus God Almighty, this was worse than any novel he'd ever read.

This was happening.

❧ When the car pulled up outside, Chris felt—despite the insanity of the situation—that something would be settled. For one thing, anyone who looked at it would know his driver's license was authentic. Then again . . .

"Don't move," the impostor instructed him, walking to the front door and pulling it open.

The man who came in made Chris tighten up involuntarily. There was something about him—his thin, pale features, his black suit and hat. Chris watched as he took a billfold from his inside coat pocket and flipped it open to reveal a badge and identification card. The other man nodded. *That you accept,* Chris reacted angrily. *Not mine though.*

He tensed again as the man in the black suit and hat gestured toward the street. "Let's go," he said.

"Not so fast," Chris said.

The man looked at him intently, skin gone taut across his cheekbones. "I can be rough if I have to," he said.

"I'm not leaving until I know what's going on here." Chris wished his voice were stronger.

The impostor made a snickering sound. "He never gives up," he said.

"Listen—" Chris started.

"No, *you* listen," said the man in the black suit and hat. "You're leaving. *Now.*"

"Goddamn it, this is my house!" Chris shouted. "That's *my* Mustang out there! I work at Palladian and just came home to get some sleep! Now, damn it, I want some answers!"

The two men and the woman looked at him in silence. The man in Chris's pajamas looked confused. "Maybe I'm wrong," he said. Chris felt a burst of irrational hope at his words. "Maybe he wasn't trying to terrorize my wife and me. Maybe he's just insane."

"I'm not insane!" Chris pushed to his feet, enraged. "Goddamn it—!"

"Stop shouting!" yelled the man in the black suit and hat.

Chris pressed his lips together, shuddering as the man turned to the couple. "You may be right, Mr. Barton," he said.

"He's not Chris Barton! *I* am!" Chris couldn't seem to stop his voice from shaking now.

He drew back as the man in the black suit moved for him.

"I want to talk to Wilson," Chris told him.

He didn't know what the man did, it happened so fast. Suddenly, his arm was twisted up behind his back, a bolt of pain shooting through his back and shoulder. "Out," the man said through bared teeth.

"Take it easy on him," said the other man. "Maybe he *is* out of his mind."

"Yes," the woman added sympathetically.

"God*damn* it," Chris said, almost sobbing. "This is—"

He broke off with a hollow cry as the man in the black suit yanked up his arm and shoved him toward the door. "You're hurting me!" he gasped.

"I'll hurt you worse if you don't shut up," said the man.

"Take it *easy*," the impostor said. He actually sounded sorry now.

The man in the black suit pulled open the front door and pushed Chris out onto the porch.

Somehow, the putter had slipped and fallen and, as Chris stepped on its handle, it rolled under his shoe and made him lose balance. Abruptly, he was pitching forward, pulling the man with him. The grip on his arm was released as they fell, the man crying out in pain as his knee struck the concrete porch. Chris's head snapped up; he twisted around to see the man clutching at his knee, his face a mask of agony. The man inside the house was looking at him blankly. The pistol wasn't in his hand.

Chris lunged to his feet and leaped onto the lawn, running for the Pontiac. "Stop!" yelled the man in the house. Would he grab his gun and take a shot at him? Suddenly, Chris didn't care. No matter what the risk, he had to get away from there.

Jerking open the door of the Pontiac, he slid onto the driver's seat, fumbling in his jacket pocket for the keys. He pulled them out and, fingers shaking, tried to push in the ignition key. He glanced up, seeing the man come out of the house, the pistol in his hand again. The man in the black suit was struggling to his feet, his face still contorted by pain.

The ignition key slipped in and Chris turned it quickly. The motor coughed on and Chris threw the transmission into reverse. Just as the man reached the car, pistol extended, Chris floored the accelerator and the Pontiac shot backwards on the driveway, bumping hard as it hit the street. He spun the steering wheel so fast, he lost control of the car and it skidded in a three-quarter circle, tires shrieking before he could brake. From the corner of his eye, he saw the man running after him.

He gasped as the pistol was fired and the back window exploded inward. "God," he said. He jammed the gas pedal to the floor and the car leaped forward, bouncing across the curb on the opposite side of the street. Grimacing, he spun the steering wheel and turned back toward the street, grunting as the wheels jarred down across the curb again. He heard another shot behind him but this one missed as the car picked up speed, roaring down Oasis Drive East.

Seconds later, he was turning east onto the highway, accelerating to eighty-five miles an hour. In the distance, he could see a faint glow on the mountain rims. Dawn, for Christ's sake, he thought. He had a sudden image—Veering on the shoulder, thumb raised. He felt a surge of fury. If he saw the bastard again, he'd run him down.

He shook his head spasmodically. No, he mustn't think like that. Reality was not that easily manipulated and something very real was happening; he needed time to find its meaning.

He glanced up at the rearview mirror. No sign of another car yet. They'd be coming soon though. He pressed down on the gas pedal, the speedometer needle jumping up to ninety, ninety-two; the Pontiac shot along the highway. Chris shivered uncontrollably. He'd never driven so fast in his life; what if he lost control?

No help for it. He wouldn't let that man catch up to him. His back and arm still ached. *You son of a bitch,* he thought.

He never passed Veering. Had someone else picked him up? It seemed likely. Who the hell was Veering anyway? Did he have anything at all to do with what he'd just gone through? It was demented to believe that. Still, it had all begun to happen minutes after he'd made that stupid wager. Chris drew in a trembling breath.

Had he already lost the wager?

5

He had to stop and get some rest; he was too exhausted to drive to Tucson. It was better he got off the highway anyway. By now, they'd have phoned ahead. There could be a roadblock waiting. He wondered if he should dump the car and try to get to Tucson some other way. How? Hitchhike? *Sure,* he thought. *Veering and I can ride together in someone else's car.* Veering could present him as an example of the inadvisability of accepting wagers on reality.

His head jerked up, eyes flaring open. Jesus Christ, he'd almost gone to sleep. Now. He had to stop now.

Up ahead, he saw a side road and, slowing down, made a left turn onto it. He drove along it very slowly, partly because of the ruts, mostly to avoid raising a telltale cloud of dust. He was heading northward now. To his right, the glow of sunrise was increasing.

Approximately twenty minutes later, he saw a grove of trees and turned into them, hoping it would keep the car out of sight. He braked beside one of them and turned off the engine, pushed in the headlight knob.

Immediately, he slumped back with a groan. Dear God, he was sleepy.

He was amazed that he didn't fall unconscious right away. His brain would not give up its hold though. It turned over slowly in his head, revolving in sluggish circles.

Trying to understand.

Was there a moment when things had begun to go wrong? A single instant he could recapture?

The moment he had picked up Veering seemed to be the one. Still, there had been one before that.

The moment he'd discovered that his car was gone.

Clearly, the man in his house had taken it. But why? And how in God's name had he gotten into the fenced lot and driven it past the guard? Had he used the rear gate? If so, where had he gotten a key for its lock? Or who had let him in, then out?

He looked down at his identity badge and groaned. For Christ's sake, why hadn't he pointed it out to the man and woman in the house, the man in the black suit? But they must have seen it. Probably regarded it as no more authentic than his driver's license.

He made a sound of pained amusement as he visualized Scotty Tensdale waiting for his car to be returned. It was damned unlikely now.

His mind went back to the old man in the baseball cap. He tried to re-create their conversation in his mind. Had it really been as meaningless and stupid as he'd thought? Or was it actually the cause of—

"Come *on*," he muttered irritably. Shifting across the seat, he lay on his right side, raising his legs and bending them onto the seat. Sleep, he thought. For Christ's sake, *sleep*.

His brain kept turning like a machine in slow motion.

Could it be because of his work? Had he stumbled onto something? *"There are some things man was not meant to tamper with,"* intoned a Van Dyke-bearded scientist in a sci-fi movie. Oh, come on. He twisted irritably on the seat. Life wasn't some damn sci-fi movie. There were spies, yes, foreign agents. But that was equally hard to accept.

"All right," he mumbled. So it was his work. They wanted to find out how far he'd come along on it. Why take his car then? Why all that crap at the house? The couple, the door chain, the kitchen telephone, the man in the black suit? Why not just force his Mustang off the highway, kidnap him and take him some-where; pump sodium pentothal or something into his veins, *ask* him how the project was proceeding?

"Like shit," he heard himself answering.

At which point his brain went dark.

❧ He thought he'd managed to drop off for a few minutes. But when he opened his eyes, it was light.

He looked at his watch. Just past eight. "Gotta go," he muttered, sitting up. *God, I'm stiff,* he thought. He rubbed his eyes and looked out at the grove of trees, then shook himself and opened the door.

It was chilly outside. He stood up clumsily and walked to the tree, urinating on its trunk. He shivered convulsively. Last night, a mathematician in the service of Uncle Sam, he thought. This morning, a homeless fugitive. He tried to find humor in the notion but had difficulty; the best smile he could summon was one of cold irony.

Zipping shut his pants, he looked around. Was that a puddle of water or a mirage? he thought. He walked in toward it.

Bending over, he scooped up a palmful of the cold water, and rubbed it on his face, drying his skin with his handkerchief.

The fingers and palm of his right hand hurt and holding up the hand, he saw that the redwood splinters had infected it. He'd have to find a needle or pin and get them out. Hopefully in Tucson.

Shivering, he returned to the car and got inside. Now he was hungry. He saw an image of a coffee-shop waitress setting down a platter in front of him—sausage, scrambled eggs and rye toast. And a glass of frothy orange juice, a cup of hot black coffee.

"Fat chance," he said. He had to get to Tucson.

He was about to start the motor when he saw a small card on the floor in front of the passenger seat. Leaning over, he picked it up. A single name was printed on it: ALBERT VEERING. Jesus God; a hitchhiker with a calling card? He turned it over.

And shuddered. There were three words written on the card with wavering penmanship.

Are you sure?

He stared at it for almost a minute before reaction set in.

Incensed, he tore the card to shreds, shoved open the door and flung the pieces out; they fluttered whitely to the ground.

"You son of a bitch!" he said, his face distorted by rage. "*Are you sure?*" He made a hissing sound. The old bastard must have had it ready before he'd even been picked up. How many people had he suckered in with that stupid wager, that stupid card?

Chris started the engine and backed out of the grove. Scotty Tensdale certainly kept his car running well, it occurred to him.

He hoped that one day the poor guy would get it back.

▨ For the last hour, he had dreaded that when he drove up to his mother's house, there'd be a line of police cars waiting there. Surely, they'd assume that he might go there; it was one of the most likely possibilities. *How anxious are they to get me?* he wondered.

Then again, it might not be the police at all. Instead, there might be just a single car—a government vehicle with the man in the black suit and hat inside. Chris swallowed apprehensively at the thought of meeting him again. *I hope he broke his goddamn knee and had to be hospitalized,* he thought.

Maybe he should have gone to Wilson's house, it occurred to him. But the man had told his wife to telephone Wilson. Had she really called him or had it been part of the ploy? Jesus God, if *Wilson* was involved in all this . . .

"Come *on,*" he snapped at himself. He was already paranoiac. Now he was approaching certifiable.

He was driving into Tucson when the thought occurred that he might turn himself in to the state police, try to get their assistance. It seemed an obvious thing to do. Why did the idea unnerve him then? Had be really read too many thrillers, seen too many movies? The hero surrenders himself, seeking help, and the authorities he surrenders to promptly turn him over to the bad guys.

"Oh, shit," he muttered. Still, he couldn't make himself accept the notion of giving himself up to the police. He hadn't the remotest idea what was going on but he sensed that it was dangerous, that he had to be careful.

🖾 There were no cars parked in front of his mother's house. Meaninglessly, his brain reversed itself. They wouldn't show themselves out in the open. They could be blocks down, telescopes directed at his mother's house. He suddenly felt stupid for driving directly toward her house in a car that by now had to be totally identifiable.

"*Damn,*" he muttered.

He repressed the urge to press down hard on the accelerator and speed past his mother's house; that would only call attention to him. For a moment, he thought how stupidly he was behaving if there really wasn't anyone around.

Still, he couldn't take a chance. Driving to the corner, he made a slow right turn, eyes searching for any sign of suspicious vehicles or men. *Women, too,* his brain reminded him. "Yeah, sure," he said.

Except for a small boy on his tricycle, the street ahead looked empty. *It's him,* his mind annoyed him. *He's the smallest agent in the world, crack shot, beyond suspicion.* "Oh, shut up," he told his mind. Pulling over to the curb, he braked and turned off the engine. He had to assume there was no one dangerous around.

Getting out, he locked the doors and started for the alley next to one of the houses. Behind him, he could hear the small boy making motor noises as he rode his tricycle. *Now he's taking out his telescopic sight and snapping it onto his long-range pistol. Now—*

"Oh, *stop,*" he said, starting down the alley. If they'd been waiting for him, he'd already be in custody.

He climbed over a low picket fence and started across somebody's backyard. Glancing to his right, he saw an old lady looking out through a back window at him, her expression one of offended surprise. Sorry, Grandma, he thought. He hoped to God she didn't get it in her mind to telephone the police. He turned to her and waved, smiling, then pointed toward his mother's house, lips framing the words, *I'm going* that *way*. Not that Grandma would get a word of it. Still, maybe his benign expression and wave would reassure her.

She only stared at him, expressionless. *She thinks I'm nuts,* he thought, *a lunatic escaped from some local asylum. Don't call the cops, Granny,* he thought. *I'm just a harmless mathematician.*

Reaching the side of the yard, he climbed another picket fence and crossed another yard. No one in that house was visible. He crossed the yard quickly, climbed another fence and moved across another backyard. He could see the back of his mother's house now. *Almost there,* he thought. *Please let me make it.*

He looked in through the back window of her garage, groaning softly to see it empty. She must be teaching; it was a weekday after all. "Damn," he said. How long could he safely wait for her before somebody showed up, checking up on the possibility that he was there? Maybe the old lady was a secret agent too, was already phoning the CIA. Maybe everybody in the world was a secret agent.

What am I going to do? he thought as he turned for the back of her house. He couldn't phone her at the college. They might be watching her; they'd follow her home. He groaned again. He felt so helpless. How could he get out of this predicament?

Whatever it might be.

The key to the kitchen door was under the mat as always. He had to smile. Mom used to keep it there when he was just a boy— and it was still there. Invitation to a burglar, Uncle Harry used to call it. "Oh, come on now, Harry," he recalled his mother's chiding voice as she responded. "You're being paranoiac."

He unlocked the kitchen door, put the key back under its mat and slipped inside the house. Pushing the door shut, he looked at the kitchen and had to smile. Neat as always. Mom was utterly predictable.

He grunted, seeing the coffee pot on the stove. God, let there be a cup left in there, half a cup at least. He moved there, lifting up the pot. There was at least a cup. He turned on the gas beneath the pot and stared at it, smiling again. Somewhere, in a closet or a cabinet, was the automatic coffeemaker he'd given her some Christmases ago. She'd expressed her gratitude for it, then, when he'd left, put it away, preferring this ancient, faithful pot.

In a minute, he got a cup from the cupboard and poured it full of steaming coffee. He drank it slowly, savoring the heavy aromatic flavor. Mom was right. This *was* the best way to make coffee.

He toasted himself a slice of wheat bread, buttering it and spreading on some strawberry jam. Crunching hungrily on it and sipping the coffee, he walked into the dining room and looked at the photographs on the wall. Pop, Mom, Louise and him. All the dogs they'd had: Kate, Ginger, Bart, Ranger. Photographs of the camping trips, of the university. Of teachers at some of Mom and Pop's weekly get-togethers at the house, him and Louise sitting among them like miniature adults, always welcome. Of Uncle Harry with his perennial bow tie and quizzical smile. Of Louise and him at the university special school.

Good days, he thought. Mom and Pop always concerned for their growth, intellectual and otherwise. Opening their minds to "possibilities." Exposing them to science, to culture, to philosophy, to nature. He sighed, wishing that his father hadn't died in the air crash. How much nicer it would be for Mom if she wasn't alone now, if she had his company and could still have fun with him as she did in the old days when they were all together—Pop, Mom, Louise . . .

Louise.

His head jerked around and he looked at the telephone. It would be reassuring to hear a word or two of sanity in the midst of all this. He and Louise had always gotten along well, no rivalry of any kind. Maybe that was because she was five years older than him. Not that he thought they'd have been competitors in any case.

He moved to the phone and picked up his mother's tooled leather address book, opening it to Louise Jasper. He glanced at his wristwatch. It would be about 1:30 P.M. in New Hampshire. He hoped she was there as he picked up the handset and tapped in her number. *Be home,* he thought. *I need a kind word, Louise.*

The handset on the other end was lifted on the third ring and he heard her voice: "Hello?"

"Thank God," he said.

"Chris?" she asked.

"Yeah." He smiled with relief, licking the last of the strawberry jam from his fingers. "How ya doin', sis?"

"Fine," she said. "How are you?"

"A little rattled."

"Oh, God," she said, "is he back again?"

He was confused. "Is *who* back again?"

"That man," she said.

"*What* man?" He felt his stomach muscles pulling in.

"Chris, come on," she said. "Did that man show up at your house again?"

He didn't know what to say.

"Chris, are you all right?" she asked.

He swallowed, tasting the coffee in his throat. "What are you talking about?" he asked uneasily.

She groaned. "Sweetheart," she said. "Did you or did you not call me last night?"

He felt his mouth slipping open.

"Did you or did you not tell me that the man who's been trying to intimidate you and Maureen came to your house last night?"

Chris shuddered and heard the old man's voice repeating in his mind, *"Do you so wager?"*

6

He tightened. *No.* He wasn't going to buy this.

"Chris—?" she started.

"You're telling me you got a call last night and—"

"Chris, what is going on?" Louise demanded.

"What time was this?" he asked.

"Uh . . . about ten-thirty, our time."

The coldness gathering inside him got a little worse. At eight-thirty his time last night, he had been hard at work on the project. Did that mean the man and woman had already been in his house? Speaking to Louise and telling her—?

"Chris, for God's sake," she said.

"Listen to me," he told her. "I don't know who called you last night but it wasn't me."

"What do you mean it wasn't you?" Louise said, exasperated now. "Don't you think I know the sound of your voice?"

"*It wasn't me,* Louise," he said. "Something very strange is going on. When I got home last night—"

"Are you at home now?" she interrupted.

"No," he said. "That man is, and—" He broke off as what she was saying hit him. "Maureen?" he asked. You said me and *Maureen?*"

"I think I better talk to her," Louise replied. "Maybe she can make more sense—"

"*There's no Maureen in my life!*" he cut her off. "What the hell are you talking about?"

There was a heavy silence on the line. Then Louise said quietly, "Who is this?"

The vise was closing on his skull again.

"Oh, my God, you're the man who's terrorizing them," she said.

"Louise, for God's sake—!"

"You listen to me, mister, and you listen good!" she cried. "Get away from them and stay away! There are laws in this country!"

"Louise, for God's sake," he repeated, pleading now. It felt as though the floor was moving under him. "I don't know what's going on but *please*—"

"I'm calling the police now," she said.

He stood there with the handset to his ear, listening to the dial tone. *Reality,* he thought. His shiver was convulsive.

"*What the hell is going on?!*" he cried.

You've been working too hard, you need a rest; another cliché movie line was spoken in his mind. He grimaced in fury. *Yes, I have been working too hard,* he answered the voice. *But I'm not out of my mind.*

Something was being done to him.

He nodded jerkily. His work. Someone out to penetrate the project. Simple and direct: a plot. He tried to hold on to that even though he knew it made no sense whatsoever. If anyone wanted to know what he knew, they only had to pick him up, inject him, hypnotize him, whatever. This insanely intricate cabal was totally unnecessary. Which left him with—

He snapped his head around, seeing a movement from the corner of his eye. A dark blue car had just pulled up in front of the house. He picked up the coffee cup and backed into the kitchen, stepping behind the wall and peering out, his heartbeat quickening.

A man in a gray tweed suit was getting out of the car; he had red hair and a dark red mustache. As the man circled the car and started toward the house, Chris pulled back sharply. Jesus God, what now? he thought.

He started as the doorbell rang, drew in a shaking breath. Thank God he'd parked his car around the corner. He leaned against the wall, feeling the thump of his heartbeat, twitched as the doorbell rang again.

He waited in silence, listening for the sound of the man's car starting up again. It didn't come. What was the man doing? Was he—?

Chris caught his breath, looking aside to see the man moving past the kitchen window. Despite the curtains, if the man turned his head, he'd spot Chris. For several moments, Chris stood, frozen, not knowing what to do. Then abruptly, he stepped back into the dining room, turned right, and moving to the corner, sat on the floor and slumped down so his head was below the level of the window sills.

He swallowed, saw the coffee cup still in his hand and set it down. He looked at his right hand, wincing. Have to get those splinters out, he thought. *Yeah, that's important right now,* his mind snapped back.

He stiffened as he heard the man trying the knob of the kitchen door. What if the man had a ring of keys? What if he could open the door, come in and find him slumping here? Did he have a gun?

Chris pressed his lips together. *Steady,* he told himself. It occurred to him that maybe the man had nothing whatever to do with what was going on. Maybe, for God's sake, after all these years of Uncle Harry's dire predictions, Mom was about to be burglarized.

He shook his head. He didn't believe that. This had something to do with what was going on.

Silence now. He leaned his head against the wall and closed his eyes. What would he do if the man was able to get in somehow? Fight him, try to overcome him? Or just give up? *Okay, that's it, let's find out what the hell is going on.*

He tensed, eyes opening, as the man walked past the windows he was cowering beneath. He looked toward the front of the house and, through the curtained windows, saw the man moving down the walkway. He heard the car door closing, the sound of the motor switching on. The car drove away.

Chris closed his eyes again. *God, I'm tired,* he thought. He hadn't really slept that much. And considering what he'd been through . . .

🎴 "Chris!"

He jolted awake, an expression of alarm on his face, then, seeing his mother looking at him, he uttered an involuntary groan of relief and reached for her; she was kneeling on the floor beside him.

They embraced and kissed. "What are you doing sleeping on the floor like this?" she asked. "Is something wrong?"

He tried to sound amused but failed. "To say the least," he answered.

They stood and embraced again. *Home,* he thought. His mother. He sighed; it felt good.

She brushed back his hair with a gentle touch. "You look terrible," she said. "What's going on?"

He started to answer, then hissed in pain. He'd slept in such an awkward position, his neck was stiff. He rotated it, grimacing. "God," he muttered.

Then he smiled and held her again. It felt so good to be home. He had a fleeting image of himself, a boy, crying hard because he'd skinned his knees falling off a skateboard. She was always there to comfort him.

"Chris, what's happened?" she asked, worried.

He looked at her. In her middle sixties, she was still a lovely woman, almost as tall as he without heels; her gray-tinged hair still mostly brunette, her features firmly cut, her brown eyes deeply intelligent as she gazed at him. "Tell me what happened," she said.

"You sound as though you already know something," he told her.

She walked him to the living-room sofa and drew him down. "Tell me," she said.

He pulled in a long breath and told her everything from the

time he'd woken up in the plant to the man he'd hidden from before. He didn't mention Veering. He wasn't going to allow himself to believe that the old man had anything to do with what was happening.

"What did the man you hid from look like?" she asked when he was through.

Chris described him. "No," she said. "That wasn't him."

Chris tightened. "Has someone spoken to you?"

"A man came to the university and spoke to me between classes," she said.

"What did he look like?"

"Lean," she answered. "Pale. Wearing a black suit and hat."

He shuddered. "He's the one who came to my house last night."

"Oh, no." His mother gazed at him in concern.

"What's his name?" Chris asked.

His mother got up and walked into the dining room; her purse was lying on the table. Opening it, she took out her wallet and, reaching into it, removed a business card. She brought it into the living room and handed it to Chris.

The man's name was Martin Meehan. There was no indication as to whom he worked for; the only thing on the card other than his name was an Arizona telephone number.

"Did he show you a badge?" he asked.

"No." She shook her head.

"What did he say?"

"That you were in trouble and I should make sure to call him if you tried to get in touch with me."

Chris swallowed dryly. The dogs are closing in, he thought. "That's all he said?"

She nodded. "I tried to find out what was going on but he said he couldn't tell me, it was secret."

"Sure." He slipped the card into his shirt pocket, then kneaded at his neck, grimacing. "I wish I hadn't fallen asleep in that position."

"Turn to the right," she told him.

He did and felt her strong fingers begin to massage gently at the back of his neck. At first, the pressure made him hiss with pain but, little by little, it began to fade.

"The thing I don't understand at all," she said, "is Louise's reaction to your phone call. It doesn't make any sense."

"I know."

"She actually said you and *Maureen?*"

"Yes."

"I'm going to have to talk with her."

His eyes were closed now, his neck feeling better. "What should I do, Mom?" he asked her.

"I'm not sure," she said.

"I mean, should I give myself up? Let the police figure it out?"

"Well . . ." She sounded uncertain. "The man said that, above all, you shouldn't contact any authorities. He said it was the worst thing you could do."

"Considering what he did to me, that makes giving myself up to the authorities look pretty good."

She kept working on his neck. "What happened to your hand?" she asked.

"My porch siding is redwood," he told her. "I leaned against it."

"We'll get them out before you go," she said.

He swallowed. "Go where, Mom?"

She didn't reply for several moments. Then she said, "I wouldn't go to the authorities."

He turned in surprise to look at her. "You *wouldn't?*"

She gazed at him inquiringly. "You think it has something to do with your work?" she asked.

"There's no other answer I can come up with," he answered. "That makes any sense, I mean."

She got up and went to get her sewing box and a bottle of Bactine. Returning with them, she started removing the redwood splinters from his palm and fingers. Chris gritted his teeth as she did.

"Is what you do so crucial that . . . ?" She didn't finish.

"That people would like to know about it? Yes," he answered. He hissed with pain. Then he made an amused sound. "Except if they knew how far I was from an answer, they'd be sorry they started all this."

He watched his mother's face. He knew that expression. She was analyzing.

"There's no other factor in this?" she asked.

"No," he said. He hesitated. "Unless . . ."

"What?" she asked.

Chris sighed. He was sorry he'd brought it up. What if Mom put too much credence in it?

"*What*, Chris?" she persisted.

"Well . . ."

He told her about Veering and their conversation. When he was finished, his mother grunted softly. "Curiouser and curiouser," she said.

"You don't really believe—"

"I believe he could be part of this," she said.

Chris looked startled. He'd never thought of that. He'd vacillated back and forth between two possibilities—a plot against him versus Veering's wager. How very shrewd of his mother to join them together.

"But *how?*" he asked. "I mean, how would the two fit together?"

"Both of them have made you doubt your sanity," she answered.

"Of course," he said. It was so obvious. He repressed his overriding feeling that none of it actually made sense. On a lower scale of logic, however, it *did* make sense that all of it was part of one conspiracy—whatever that conspiracy might be and however senseless it seemed at the moment.

"Who would want to *do* all this?" he asked. "And why make it all—"

"*Chris.*" She clutched at his wrist.

Twisting around, he saw that the car had returned.

For a moment, he didn't know what to do. His mother decided

49

for him, pulling him to his feet and walking him rapidly to the kitchen. "Go out the back way," she said. "I'll talk to them and give you time. Where are you parked?"

"Around the corner."

"Good." She kissed him quickly on the cheek. "Go right away," she said.

"You don't think—?"

"After the way he treated you?" she cut him off. "All right, give yourself up to the authorities. But *not them*. Maybe out of Arizona."

He felt hapless and inept as he stared at her. Then she smiled and stroked his cheek. "You're up to anything," she added. "You know that."

He embraced her.

"Be careful now," she said. "Use every skill."

He nodded. "Love you, Mom."

"I love you too. Now hurry."

Their embrace tightened as the front doorbell rang. Chris kissed her on the cheek, crossed to the back door and opened it, glancing back at her. "You'll be all right," she said.

He nodded and went outside, closing the door. He jumped off the porch and ran across the yard, scaled the fence and ran across the next yard. *Man in flight,* he thought. Was that the title of some book he'd read? He scowled.

This wasn't any book.

He crossed another fence and kept on running. Was Mom talking to them now? Was she up to pretending? Or would they sense that she was nervous? Would the antennae of their trade immediately pick up that she was lying?

The old woman looked at him incredulously from her back window. *Yeah, I'm back,* he thought, *mashing down your back lawn; sorry.* He would have been amused by the look on her face if things weren't so grim. This was probably the most thrilling thing to happen to her in a month of Sundays.

He ran around the corner of the old woman's house and started down the alley. Were the men alone or were there teams out searching for him? He kept running, angled across the old woman's front lawn and dashed for the Pontiac. How was Scotty Tensdale going to get home? he wondered. Yeah, like that's important now, he countered irritably.

He unlocked the car as quickly as he could and slid inside. His hands were shaking so badly, he had to use both of them to get the ignition key in its slot. Twisting it, he heard the motor cough to life; *thank* you, Scotty. He tapped the transmission into gear and pulled away from the curb.

Not too noisy, not too fast, he told himself. He drew in trembling breath and pressed down slowly on the gas pedal. The small boy was still on his tricycle. Now he'd pull a walkie-talkie from his overalls and call for backup. *"Thuspect fleeing in maroon Pontiac,"* he'd lisp. *"Agent thixty-thix. Over and out."*

"Oh, *shut up,*" he told his brain.

At the corner, he turned left and headed downtown. Now what? he thought. Where was he supposed to go? He'd really considered turning himself in until Mom had told him not to. That frightened him as much as anything that had happened. What made her think he shouldn't, in Arizona anyway? What difference did it make where he did it? This had to be a federal thing; his work was for the government.

And why did Mom suggest that Veering was part of the conspiracy?

He felt a sense of vague amorphous dread building inside him, his mind jumping back again to the start: his missing car, his talk with Veering, the couple in his house, Meehan manhandling him, the call to Louise, Meehan showing up again with the other man. *Did* it all fit together? And was it all connected to the project? Were they all trying to make him doubt his sanity to prevent him from working on it? If they only knew, he thought.

His brain was already out of sync.

Anyway, he reversed himself once more, why such a complicated plot? Why not just run him off the road and shoot him if they wanted to delay the project?

Is that what they still planned to do?

"God," he muttered. He was really frightened now.

What in the name of God was he going to do?

7

First of all, he needed gas. He'd managed to reach Tucson on the one tankful that Scotty Tensdale had thoughtfully, and unintentionally, provided for him. But now the gauge needle was almost down to zero. There was a Texaco station three blocks ahead; he'd stop there. Should he use his credit card? he wondered. Would it be a clue they could follow?

Hell, they had the only clue they needed, he thought as he turned into the station, a maroon Pontiac with a registered license plate. If he was really going to go on—where, he had no idea— he'd have to dump the car and travel some other way.

He braked by the front pump on the full-service island and got out. Not waiting for the attendant, he unhooked the nozzle on the unleaded pump and pushed down the handle. As the pump started humming, he carried the nozzle to the back of the car.

There he stopped dead, staring blankly at the place where he'd expected to see the gas-tank cover. Then he grunted in disgust at himself. This isn't the Mustang, idiot. Sighing, he returned to the pump and rehung the nozzle as the heavyset attendant came trudging up. "Yessir," he said.

"I thought I had my other car," Chris said. "I'll have to move."

"Yessir," said the attendant.

Chris got back into the car and turned on the motor. *Use your skills,* he remembered his mother's words. *Yes, Mater, right away,* he answered silently, smiling without humor.

He moved the car to the other side of the service island and turned the motor off again. "Is your bathroom unlocked?" he asked as the attendant approached, carrying the nozzle.

"Sure is," the attendant said. "Check under your hood?"

"Under Scotty's hood," he mumbled to himself. "No, that's all right," he told the attendant.

He was halfway to the bathroom when it occurred to him that maybe Scotty Tensdale wasn't all *that* attentive to his Pontiac; it might need oil, transmission fluid, battery water, who knew what else. "Yeah, *would* you check everything under the hood?" he called back. "And check the tires?"

"Yessir," the attendant said. *You and F. Crain should get together for one bang-up conversation,* Chris thought as he turned back toward the bathroom.

He went inside the bathroom and locked the door, flicking the light switch. The room remained shadowy, its only illumination coming from the window over the door. Swell, Chris thought. He moved to the urinal and relieved himself, then washed his hands at the sink, wincing slightly at the tenderness in his right palm and fingers. Had his mother gotten all the splinters out? He hoped so, washing off his face. The cold water felt good on his skin.

He dried his face and hands with two paper towels. His cheeks were getting bristly. Going to look like a proper fugitive soon, he thought. This did not amuse him.

"All right, what now?" he asked the man regarding him from the mirror. "*Quo* fucking *vadis?*"

"*Where can you afford to* vadis?" the man responded.

Chris took out his wallet and checked. Two twenties, a ten, a five, his MasterCard and American Express charge cards. He made a pained face. And the Texaco card sitting in the glove compartment of his Mustang.

"Jesus," he muttered. He'd have to use cash for the gas and there was little enough of it.

He stood gazing at his reflection. It had occurred to him that he could drive back to his house. If the presence of the man and woman had been necessary only to throw him off in the beginning, they might be gone now, the door chain and the kitchen telephone with them. Was it worth a try to find out? It had a definite appeal because it wasn't simply flight, it was a move toward finding out what was happening. And it might be the one place they wouldn't think he'd go.

"Yes, good," he said. That's what he'd do.

When he unlocked the door and pulled it open, the two men were standing outside, waiting for him.

As insane as the idea was, Chris had an urge to hurl himself at them and break free.

But they frightened him the way they stood, faces impassive, looking at him. For all he knew, they were prepared to draw out guns and open fire on him at any instant.

He swallowed dryly, stepping out into the sunlight. Suddenly, he felt very tired, very drained. "All right," he said. In a way, he was relieved. Whatever happened, he'd find out what was going on.

His sense of relief evaporated as Meehan started for him, limping. His *knee*, Chris thought, alarmed. Impulsively, he drew back and bumped against the door. "Leave me alone," he said, remembering the agonizing pain he'd felt when Meehan had twisted his arm behind his back.

Meehan didn't reply but kept moving toward him. Knowing what the agent meant to do, Chris ducked away from him so that Meehan's lunge for his arm missed.

The agent made a snarling noise and shouldered him hard, knocking him back against the door, which flew open. Chris fell back into the shadowy bathroom, catching a glimpse of the man in the gray tweed suit who started forward, saying Meehan's name with an urgent tone.

Meehan didn't stop, but bent over Chris and clutched at his jacket. Chris tried to pull away from him, accidentally bumping his right knee against the agent's injured one. Meehan hissed in pain and jerked back. Chris tried to push himself up and the man in the tweed suit grabbed his left arm, pulling him to his feet. "Take it easy now," he said.

A tone of kindness in the man's voice made Chris relax for an instant. Then, seeing Meehan lunge at him, he tensed again. "Wait a second," he snapped, trying to turn from Meehan, pulling the other man around with him.

"*Hold* it," the other man said.

Then Meehan had his right arm and was starting to pull it up behind him. A bolt of fury struck Chris and he rammed his knee deliberately against Meehan's injured one. With a hoarse cry, Meehan jerked back; Chris turned to the other man. "I'll go with you," he said breathlessly, "but I don't want my arm twisted—"

His voice froze in shock as he saw Meehan reaching under his suit coat. "No," he murmured, shrinking back as Meehan snatched a revolver from a holster underneath his arm.

"Meehan, Jesus!" the other man said. Letting go of Chris, he stepped in front of him. Meehan tried to shove him aside, but the man grabbed Meehan and wouldn't let go. Chris had an impulse to turn and run for his car while the two were struggling but he decided against it. Meehan might shoot him before he reached the car.

He stood, shaken, in front of the bathroom door, watching the two men grapple. "Damn it, Meehan!" the man in the tweed suit said. He glanced across his shoulder at Chris. "Get in your car and wait," he ordered.

Chris needed no further encouragement. Hastily, he walked across the station. "You can't *do* that," he heard the man say to Meehan, and Meehan's tight, infuriated response: "I *want* him, Nels."

Chris got into the Pontiac and closed the door, shaking. The attendant came over, looking disturbed. "What's going on?" he asked. "Shall I call the police?'

"They *are* the police," Chris said. He knew it wasn't true but it was close enough to satisfy the attendant. He swallowed, adding inanely, "What do I owe you?"

"Twenty-seven thirty," the attendant said. "You needed a quart of oil, too."

Chris started to make a groaning sound, then realized it didn't matter; he wasn't going any further anyway. Taking out his wallet, he took out a twenty and the ten and handed them to the attendant. Turning around, he looked toward the rest room. The two men were talking now. Meehan still looked angry but his revolver was put away now. Chris frowned. Wasn't it odd that they were just ignoring him? What was to prevent him from—?

The thought evaporated as he looked at the ignition slot. Of course, what else?

The key was gone.

"Here you go," the attendant said, giving Chris his change.

Chris took it, then turned around again to look at the two men. What were they talking about? And who were they working for? Obviously, they were American. The CIA? Why *him?* The project was important, yes, but he'd done nothing suspect. Anyway, what was happening was far more complicated than just a security investigation.

He stiffened as he saw the two men start for the car, Meehan's expression menacing. What if he simply took out his revolver again and shot him at point-blank range? Chris shudderd. There was nothing he could do about it.

He felt a chill as Meehan walked over to the side of the car he was sitting in and leaned over. Chris saw how white his face was, how dark and lank his hair, how cold his blue eyes.

"I'll catch up to you," Meehan said.

Then he straightened up and turned away. Chris twitched as he heard the door pulled open on the passenger side of the Pontiac. Turning, he saw the man in the tweed suit getting in. "Let's go," the man said, handing Chris the keys.

"Where?" Chris asked.

"Back to your plant," the man told him.

Chris felt confused. Weren't they going to take him to their headquarters? Why the plant? "I don't—" he started.

"Go. Let's *go,*" the man said. He didn't sound as kind now.

Chris started the engine and pulled out of the station into the street.

"You came pretty close to taking a slug there," the man told him.

Chris swallowed; his throat felt dry. "Do you have some kind of identification?" he asked.

The man removed a billfold from the right inside pocket of his suit coat and flipped it open in front of Chris. Chris looked at the badge, then the identification card. The man's name was Gerald Nelson. He felt a shiver convulse his back.

It *was* the CIA.

"Turn left at the corner and keep going north," the man told him.

Chris saw him glance across his shoulder and looked up at the rearview mirror. Meehan was following in the dark blue car. "Is he going with us?" he asked.

"Just drive," the man told him.

Chris said no more. They rode in silence until the car was out of Tucson, moving back into the desert. Then, after Chris looked into the rearview mirror again and saw that Meehan was no longer following, the man named Nelson said, "All right."

Chris glanced at him.

"What's going on?" Nelson asked.

"You tell me."

"Don't get smart," Nelson said. "You're in a lot of trouble."

"*Why?*" Chris asked. "What in God's name have I done?"

"Listen, Barton—" Nelson began.

"Barton?" Chris asked. "You *know* I'm Barton?"

"What's your point?"

"My *point?*" He couldn't believe what he was hearing. "There was a man in my house last night claiming that *he* was Chris Barton but your partner picked up *me.*"

"He's not my partner, Chris," the man said.

Chris felt as though his head were swimming.

"Turn in on that road," Nelson told him. "I want to talk this over with you."

Again, Chris felt a surge of relief at the man's tone; he sounded genuinely concerned. "All right," he said. Slowing down, he turned right into the dirt road and started into the desert. It reminded him of what he'd done early this morning. Would there be another grove of trees? What difference does it make? he thought in aggravation. He was going to find out what everything *meant.* That was all that mattered.

As he drove, he glanced at Nelson. The man was staring straight ahead, his expression grave.

"This is far enough," Nelson told him when they'd driven a little more than a mile.

Chris braked and, at Nelson's order, turned off the motor.

"All right," Nelson said. "Let's hear it; all of it." He cut off Chris by adding, "I only know what Meehan told me."

Chris told him everything he could remember, every detail of his experience since finding his Mustang missing . . . how long ago was it? He looked at the dashboard clock. Jesus, not even ten hours ago?

When he was finished, Nelson looked at him in silence, then grunted. "Interesting," he said.

"Not to me," Chris said.

"That's not what I mean," Nelson told him. "This is not—" He hesitated, looking at Chris guardedly. Then he said, "Well, I can tell you this much. It's not the first time it's happened."

Chris started.

"I've heard this story before."

"You mean—?" Chris stared at Nelson in bewilderment. "Men having their cars stolen and finding them at home, with another man in their house who claims to be—"

"Not just *men*," Nelson interrupted. "Men like you. Advanced scientists, mathematicians."

"How many?" Chris asked.

"That I can't tell you," Nelson said. "Except to say . . . enough to create an ominous pattern."

"But surely . . ."

"What?"

"I mean . . . it's all so *obvious*. If it's being done and you know it's a plot of some kind—"

"That we *don't* know," Nelson responded. He gazed at Chris intently, making him nervous. "You haven't told me everything, have you?" he said.

Chris didn't know what to say. He *had* told Nelson everything.

"You didn't mention Veering," Nelson said. The kindness was

gone from his voice now; his tone was coldly hostile. "You didn't mention the wager."

Chris stared at him dumbly, aware of his heartbeat thudding laboredly. His brain felt muddled. How could Veering be a part of all this? He remembered suddenly that his mother had suggested the same thing. He'd decided against it though. Now—

He started, gasping, as Nelson clamped the fingers of his left hand on Chris's jacket and yanked him close. "*Did* you?" he shouted.

"I didn't think—"

"That's right, you didn't think!" Nelson snarled at him.

Chris saw him reaching underneath his coat with his right hand and a jolt of horror stiffened him. "My God," he gasped.

"You have to die, of course. You understand that," Nelson said.

8

In some demented way, Chris *did* understand. In a moment of total clarity, he knew it was the only thing that made it all comprehensible—that he was valuable to the project and someone wanted the project to fail.

Self-preservation made him grab at Nelson's wrist, pinning it beneath his coat. "Let go," Nelson ordered. "You have to die."

They rocked slowly on the seat, muscles straining. Chris saw Nelson's face getting red as they struggled. He knew that the agent was stronger; soon enough, he'd pull free, snatch out his gun and fire.

"No," Chris muttered, fighting for his life. They wrestled on the seat in a quiet frenzy, almost motionless except for their heaving chests.

The sound of the shot was so loud it made Chris jump back, gasping, releasing his grip on Nelson's wrist.

Nelson was staring at him, looking dazed. Then, very slowly, he looked down at his chest, making a faint sound of disbelief. After a while, his eyes moved up at Chris again. "You . . . bastard," he said in a feeble voice.

Chris flinched as Nelson twisted to the right and pushed open the door. Groaning, the agent tried to stand but collapsed instead. Chris stared at him in mute shock as the agent struggled to his feet and began to weave around, left palm pressed against his side, right hand reaching out as though to signal someone.

Chris couldn't move. He kept staring at the blood on Nelson's coat and shirt, oozing from between the fingers of the agent's left hand as he stumbled around outside, his eyes like those of a blind man. Chris heard the agent's shoes scuffling ovr the gritty sand. Then, suddenly, the man cried out, pitching forward.

And disappeared into the ground.

◈ The vise was on his skull again, his heart pounding so violently it felt as though it would beat its way out of his chest. Chris was sure he was about to pass out. Dark waves pulsed across him. He gulped at the warm air, trying to get enough oxygen into his lungs.

He didn't know how long it had been, but eventually he realized that he wasn't going to lose consciousness. He shook his head and got out of the car, knowing that if it was really true—if Nelson had literally been swallowed by the earth—then Veering would have won the wager and reality, for Chris, would be undone.

Moving on rubbery legs, he circled the car and walked across the sand to where Nelson had disappeared.

He stared down into a shallow arroyo, looking at Nelson's back, praying that there'd be a sign of movement. There wasn't any movement though and, underneath the agent's body, Chris saw blood soaking into more and more dry sand.

"Jesus," he murmured. A killing now. A *killing*.

He jerked up his head and looked around, expecting to see someone rushing at him to arrest him for the murder of the agent. *I didn't murder him,* his mind pleaded with the unseen man. *He was trying to kill* me; *it was an accident.*

Chris covered his eyes with his left palm. Deeper and deeper, he thought. Dear God. Every minute that passed was driving him deeper into this inexplicable nightmare.

After a while, he drew down his hand and looked at Nelson's body again. What was he going to do now? Drive away, try to escape? Take Nelson's body back to Tucson, give himself up to the police?

"*No,*" he muttered. The man had tried to kill him, which meant that the CIA wanted him dead. The thought was chilling. How could he escape the CIA? No matter where he went, they'd find him. He shuddered, terrified. *Goddamn it, what have I done to deserve this?!*

He had to know more.

Bracing himself, he slid down the wall of the shallow arroyo and stopped beside Nelson's motionless body.

He hesitated; then, pulling in a deep, tremulous breath, squatted down. Placing his hand on the agent's body, he tried to turn it over. He could scarcely budge it. *Dead weight.* Grimacing, he bent over and reached under Nelson's body, trying to slide his hand under Nelson's coat to reach his billfold.

He couldn't do it; the man's weight made it impossible. With a faint groan, he straightened up, hissing, teeth bared, as he saw blood on his fingers. "*God,*" he muttered, shuddering.

Just get out of here, he thought. He shook his head. If he did that, he'd be as much in the dark as ever. He simply had to get some answers. Drawing in a quiet breath, he put both hands on the agent's right shoulder and used all his strength to turn over the inert body.

He jerked back with a wince of sickened dread as he saw that Nelson's eyes were open, staring. He couldn't take his gaze off the agent's eyes. They seemed to be made of glass. The stare of a dead man, he thought, lowering his gaze with a convulsive shiver. Reaching down without looking, he felt under the tweed jacket until his fingers touched the top edge of Nelson's billfold.

A hollow cry of shock wrenched back his lips as Nelson's fingers clamped onto his wrist.

Snapping his head up, he saw that Nelson's eyes were looking at him, that his chest was moving faintly with labored breath. He stared at the agent's pain-twisted face. He hadn't seen Nelson reach beneath his coat; he stiffened as the red-haired man raised a .45 and pointed it between his eyes. *I'm dead,* he thought. He closed his eyes abruptly, waiting for the muzzle blast, the blinding pain and darkness.

When they didn't come, he opened his eyes a little, looking at the agent apprehensively. Nelson was trying to say something. His breath was thin and ragged. "Take me . . . Tucson," he whispered. The grip on Chris's wrist tightened slowly and the agent pushed the gun so close to Chris's eyes it made him blink uneasily.

"*Now,*" Nelson ordered in a weak, hoarse voice.

Chris nodded. All right, all right, he thought. Let it be. He couldn't go on anymore; he was too tired and confused. At least he wasn't gong to be killed. Nelson needed his help now.

"I'll help you up," he said.

"*No,*" Nelson muttered. He released Chris's wrist and waved Chris back with his bloody hand. Chris stood up, wavering, almost falling back against the arroyo wall, then regained his balance. He stood, breathing with effort, as Nelson started to get up. The agent made sounds of agony in his throat as he struggled to rise. Chris glanced down at the man's shirt. The left side of it was soaked with blood.

It took Nelson three minutes to get on his feet, shifting the .45 to his left hand and pushing the right one under his jacket to press against the wound; he cried out softly as he did. How badly was the agent hurt? Chris wondered. Would he make it to Tucson? He visualized himself driving up to a hospital with a dead man in his car and a fantastic explanation no one could verify.

"Car," Nelson mumbled.

Chris turned and, leaning forward, clambered up the arroyo wall, shoes crunching on the hard soil. Standing up, he looked back at Nelson. The agent was trying to climb from the arroyo, head down. He could kick Nelson's head, make a run for the car, escape.

He couldn't make himself do it. The agent was badly hurt. He couldn't just leave him here to die. He had to take him to a hospital. Once again, he felt a kind of barren relief knowing that he had to do it. At least he'd find out what was going on.

And how far could he run anyway before they caught him?

Nelson was having trouble getting up to the surface. Chris hesitated, then asked, "Do you want a hand?" Nelson made an impotent, growling sound and Chris looked down at him almost angrily. *I should leave you here,* he thought. *You deserve to be left, you son of a bitch.*

With a final groaning hitch, Nelson got out of the arroyo and pushed himself on his knees, wavering from side to side, his eyes looking as though they were going in and out of focus. Chris felt himself tensing involuntarily. He could kick the gun from Nelson's hand, make a run for the car.

He waited too long. Nelson had struggled to his feet now and was making a feeble gesture toward the Pontiac.

Chris turned and walked to the car, got in and closed the door. He sat motionless, staring out through the windshield as Nelson followed him; he heard the erratic crunching of the agent's shoes as he stumbled to the car. Then he tightened as the passenger door was opened and Nelson dropped down, grunting, on the seat beside him.

Chris looked at him. The agent's expression was frightening, teeth bared, animal-like, dark eyes glaring at Chris. He made a twitching gesture with the .45 which Chris took to mean he wanted to be driven to Tucson now.

"You'd better close the door," he said.

With a moan of pain, Nelson reached out and pulled in the door. It clicked in its frame, barely closing. Chris was going to tell him that it wasn't properly shut, but said nothing as the agent pushed his right hand under his coat again to apply pressure against his wound. "*Go,*" Nelson muttered.

"I have to turn around," Chris said.

"Well, *turn* then," the agent snapped.

"I'm afraid the wheels might get caught in the sand."

"Then look for a *pullout,*" Nelson said through clenched teeth, twisting on the seat in agony.

"All right." Chris started the engine and pulled back onto the dirt road, looking for a place ahead where he could turn around. There was nothing in sight, the narrow road flanked by sand as far as he could see. Was he going to have to drive all the way into the desert with the wounded man? Sooner or later, he'd have to try a turn regardless, or time would run out on Nelson.

"All right, dammit, all right," Nelson said in a pain-thickened voice and Chris looked at him quickly. The agent's breathing was thin and labored. It was like the panting of a dying dog. His eyes had a glaze to them that frightened Chris. "If *I'm* going," he muttered, barely able to speak, "you're going too."

Chris stared at him in shock. *No!* he thought. He looked blankly at the barrel of the .45 as the agent shakily raised it to point at Chris's head.

His body moved before his mind did.

His right foot jumped from the gas pedal to the brake and jammed it down. The car jolted to a yawing stop and, with a cry of agony, Nelson was flung against the dashboard.

Again, Chris moved without thinking, lunging to his right and shouldering the red-haired man as hard as he could, throwing him against the door. Barely shut, the door popped open and Nelson was thrown out onto the sandy shoulder.

Instantly, Chris straightened up and threw the transmission into reverse, pressing down on the accelerator. He saw the agent briefly through the open door, raising his automatic. Chris floored the pedal, panicked eyes looking across his shoulder at the road. He jerked his head down as a pair of shots rang out. He looked to the front and saw the agent falling back into a twisted heap. Oh, God, he *is* dead now, he thought.

So what?! raged his mind. *He tried to kill you* twice, *are you sorry for him?!*

He looked back at the road again, slowing down so he could steer more easily. The anger of his reaction had already faded. He felt sick to be driving away from Nelson, leaving him dead or dying. Still, what else could he do? He groaned in frustration and suddenly twisted the steering wheel to the right. He couldn't just drive *backward* all the way to the highway.

The car bumped across the rutted ground, then stopped as its rear wheels sank into the sand. "Oh, no," he said. "Don't do this."

Face set into a mask of pleading, he put the transmission into drive and pressed down slowly on the gas pedal. The back wheels spun in the sand. "No!" Chris shouted. Goddamn it, was this nightmare ever going to end?!

Easy, easy, he told himself. He felt a trickle of perspiration on his right cheek. *Just control yourself.*

Swallowing, he inched his foot down on the accelerator until the Pontiac began to move. He let it rock back and forth a few times, then pressed down harder on the gas pedal, groaning with relief as the car jumped forward. He turned back onto the dirt road, braked, then put the transmission into neutral and twisted around.

About a hundred yards away, he saw the agent's body still lying in the same twisted posture. He had to be dead now, had to be— Chris swallowed dryly; his throat felt parched. Well, he'd stop at a phone booth anyway and call the nearest hospital. Maybe there was still a chance of saving Nelson's life.

Why bother? his mind demanded cruelly. *The bastard tried to murder you twice.*

"Oh, shut up; just shut up," he told it angrily.

Putting the transmission into drive again, he started for the highway.

9

When he reached the highway six minutes later, he turned left without thinking. Then he began to wonder why he had. Was he going back to Tucson? His sigh was one of weary defeat. What differnce did it make which way he went? They'd find him regardless.

Not yet though, he thought. He wasn't ready to give himself up right now. He had to stop somewhere, rest, try to think. *"Use your skills,"* he remembered his mother's words. Analysis was one of them. He had to get off the road, lie down and rest, then *think*.

A few miles down the highway, he came to a rest stop and pulled in. He stopped and got out, checking the contents of his right trouser pocket. Eighty cents. Enough for one call? Tucson wasn't that far.

First he went into the men's bathroom and relieved himself, then washed off his face. There were no paper towels so he unrolled a handful of toilet paper to dry his face and hands.

He went outside and walked toward the telephones, feeling a little dizzy in the bright sun. Should he just call the police and wait here for them to pick him up?

No, his mind responded instantly. The way things were? The CIA after him? Nelson probably dead? Heroes didn't surrender themselves anyway. They kept on going until—

"Oh, for Christ's sake," muttered. *How many times do I have to tell you?* he demanded of his mind. *This isn't a story, it's reality!*

Reality, he thought as he reached the telephones. Forget that, he thought. He didn't want to get re-entangled in that web of thinking right now.

Should he tell his mother? he wondered. Let her call an ambulance?

No. He didn't want to involve her any more than she was already.

He pulled up the directory and looked up Hospitals in the yellow section. Picking one out, he memorized the number and let the directory flop back. He slipped two dimes into the phone and dialed the number.

The operator asked for fifty-five cents more (thank God it wasn't more) and he put in sixty. "I can't return the overage," she said.

"It's okay," Chris responded.

"Thank you," said the operator.

"You're welcome," Chris replied. Politeness in the midst of nightmare, he thought. Too much for the heart.

Just as the call was answered, Chris saw a figure walking into the rest stop. "Tucson Memorial," the woman's voice said.

"Emergency, please," Chris said. He squinted, looking at the approaching figure. There was something familiar about—

"Emergency," a man's voice said.

Veering.

Chris shuddered violently. "*No,*" he murmured.

"Beg your pardon?" the man inquired.

Chris's throat felt blocked. He wanted to drop the phone and bolt for his car. But he couldn't do it without—

He cleared his throat spasmodically. "There's a man in the desert, he's been shot," he blurted, "on—"

He broke off, wincing, staring at the old man. Had he seen Chris yet? Recognized him?

Then the sign leaped into his mind, he saw it as clearly as though he were standing beside it. "Mesquite Road," he said. "South of the highway a little more than a mile."

"May I have your name, please?" the man asked.

"The man is dying. Hurry!" Chris slammed the handset onto its cradle and broke into a run for the Pontiac.

He looked at Veering as he ran. The old man had seen him now. He had his hand raised. He was *smiling,* the bastard! "Hi!" he called.

Chris couldn't seem to breathe. He raced the rest of the way to the car and jumped in, his gaze darting to the rearview mirror. Was Veering going to reach him before he could leave? *Get in the car with him?*

Chris twisted the ignition key, starting the motor and slapping the transmission indicator to drive in the same moment. He jarred his foot down on the accelerator and, with a squeal of tires, the car jumped forward. Chris twisted the steering wheel around as quickly as he could, just missing a concrete table. The car roared down the exit drive, headed toward the highway.

As he turned onto the highway, he looked into the rearview mirror. The old man was running after him, waving both arms now. No chance, old man, he thought. He pressed down harder on the gas pedal, the car already going sixty-five.

As he sped along the highway, he kept looking back. It wouldn't surprise him, he thought with a shudder, to see Veering racing after him, so fast that he would overtake the Pontiac and, running beside it, pull open the door and jump in.

"Cut it out," he snarled at his mind.

For a while, he actually wondered if he should turn back and pick up Veering, question him. *Was* the old man part of this? How could he be? A transient hitchiker?

Still, Nelson had mentioned him. That was the maddening part. What could the CIA have to do with a man like Veering?

Anyway, he thought, he didn't have the nerve to speak to the old man. What if Veering said something else, making the nightmare even worse?

He realized now that he was driving too fast. For God's sake, he didn't want to be picked up by a highway patrol officer. He eased up on the accelerator, reducing the car's speed to sixty. He'd keep it at that. He had to stop soon though. Mind and body were exhausted.

He had to rest before he could begin to analyze what everything might mean. He trusted his mind to come up with answers if he applied himself to the problem. It always had before.

But first he had to rest.

★　★　★

He drove as long as he could but, by two o'clock that afternoon, he could barely keep his eyes open. He was headed for Los Angeles now. He didn't know why, except that any direction seemed as good as another; he just wanted to put distance between himself and Arizona. He tried not to think about his problem; it wasn't time yet. Anyway, his brain felt progessively more stultified by the hour.

At 2:14 P.M., he pulled up to the office of the Bide-A-While Motel. *That's what I intend to do,* he thought. He went inside and used his MasterCard to pay for a back cabin. It was probably a mistake. The CIA might well have a monitor on every credit card company. By now, surely they had to know that he had only the MasterCard and the American Express. It would be simplicity itself to run him to earth.

Still, what else could he do? He didn't have enough cash; he was exhausted. *Let them find me then,* he thought as he signed the slip.

The woman in the office—tall, lean and as severe-looking as some character in a Dickens novel—made no comment throughout the check-in process, handed him a key, then went back into her apartment. Only later did Chris realized that his unshaven face and the state of his clothes hardly qualified him as a candidate for Guest of the Year at the Bide-A-While.

He drove to the back cabin and parked the car behind it so it couldn't be seen from the highway. This struck him as a little stupid since the credit card would give him away if they were on the lookout for its use, as they must be. Still, one must do the logical thing—hide the car. That's what heroes always do, he thought as he unlocked the door of the cabin and went inside. *Except you're not a hero,* his mind responded. *You're a dumb-ass mathematician in flight.*

Inside, he closed all the drapes, then turned on the table lamp beside the bed. The room was hot and stuffy. He switched on the window air conditioner and stood in front of it until a rush of cool air began. Then, with a heavy sigh, he laid down on the bed and closed his eyes.

★　★　★

✸ Fifteen minutes later, he opened his eyes. It seemed incredible that he hadn't fallen asleep yet. He felt exhausted. Yet every time his brain started to do a slow backward somersault into blackness, it seemed to right itself again like some enervated but determined acrobat.

He looked at the small TV set on the bureau across from the bed. Maybe there was something on the news, he thought. He labored to a sitting position and dropped his legs across the edge of the mattress. Pushing to his feet with a tired groan, he walked over to the bureau and pulled the power button on the TV set. It took almost fifteen seconds for the picture to appear. He twisted the channel selector to see what was available.

What was available—clear enough to be seen, at any rate—was Channel 8. There was a quiz show in progress. He moved back to the bed and stretched out on it, nudged off his shoes and heard them thump on the carpeting.

"No help from the audience, please," the quiz show host requested.

I could use some help from the audience, Chris thought. The audience or anybody else. Wasn't there a single person he could turn to for—?

Gene, his mind interrupted itself.

He opened his eyes. *Yeah,* he thought. Of course. They'd gone to college together, been friends for eleven years. Good, he'd call Gene later; after he got some sleep.

No, call now, his mind insisted. *Oh, for Christ's sake, give me a break,* he pleaded. His mind was a pursed-lipped pedant staring him down. *Now,* it demanded.

With a groan of surrender, Chris sat up again and reached for the telephone on the bedside table. Actually, it made sense to call now, he allowed. If he slept too long, he'd miss Gene at the paper and he didn't remember his home number, nor was it listed.

It seemed to take the stony-faced woman in the office half an hour before she gave him a surly "Yes?" on the line.

"I want to call *The Tucson Herald,*" he told her. "I don't know the number."

"How can I *call* it then?" she asked.

Jesus, was her life that bad? he wondered. "Information," he replied as politely as he could.

"I'll get you Information," she said.

God, she sounded truculent. Well, he could almost posit her life: alone, no strokes, lonely in this godforsaken spot. His smile was humorless. Instant fantasy, he thought. He was good at that. But he couldn't be that far from the truth, considering.

"What city?" asked Information.

"Tucson," he said. "*The Tucson Herald.*"

The woman gave him the number and he memorized it. Thank God his mind possessed that ability, tired or not.

After a while, the office-woman's voice said, "Yes?" again. *Jesus, lady, I am sorry I am ruining your afternoon,* he thought. He gave her the number and she grunted.

"*The Tucson Herald*, good afternoon," a young woman's voice answered. *About a thousand percent more cheerful than mine hostess,* Chris thought. "Gene Wyskart, please," he said.

"Thank you," the young woman said. She sounded as though she was on the verge of breaking into laughter. It must be great to enjoy life that much, he thought. Obviously, the fabric of her existence was not unraveling like his.

"Newsroom," a man's voice said.

"Gene Wyskart, please," he said.

"Who's calling?" the man asked.

"Chris Barton."

"Right," the man said in much the same tone as the quiz-show host. Now he'd take what was behind the second door and Veering would step out, chortling.

Chris closed his eyes and groaned softly. His brain was out of control again. It drifted and babbled when that happened. It had been drifting and babbling for some time now. Was it possible he was going insane? Insanity, no doubt, seemed very logical when it actually took place.

Silence on the line. It disturbed him. He could imagine anyone answering his call now. Gene. Veering. Wilson. The other Chris Barton. His mother.

"Chris?" said Gene's familiar voice.

Chris shuddered with relief. "*Yeah*," he said.

"You shouldn't be calling me," Gene said.

Oh, that I do not understand, Chris thought. He felt a groan coming on. *That I absolutely do not understand.*

"You hear me?" Gene asked.

"Yes, but why?" he demanded.

"Because they can trace a telephone call, what else?" Gene told him, sounding almost angry.

Oh, God, not him as well, Chris thought. Was there *anybody* not involved in this?

"Look," Gene said, "the best thing for you to do is get out of the country."

"Out of the *country?*" Chris felt as though the walls were closing in on him. "What are you—?"

"Listen, *Chris,*" Gene cut him off, "there's no time to explain; they could put a tap on this line at any moment if it isn't on already. Just do what I say. Get out of the country. I mean it, pal. This is serious."

"Gene, for Christ's sake, what are you *talking* about?!" Chris demanded.

"Not now," Gene said. "Do you have enough money to—?"

"I don't have any money at all," Chris broke in.

"Where are you then?"

Chris hesitated.

"Damn it, *hurry,*" Gene told him.

"The Bide-A-While Motel on Highway Eight."

"All right," Gene said.

"Now, will you please—?"

His mouth fell open. Gene had hung up on him.

"Good God," he murmured. He put down the handset and fell on his side on the bed, drawing up his legs. He sobbed now. He was afraid and confused and lost. What was *happening?* Each new shock was like a needle jabbing at his brain. Please, he thought. Some answers. Some meaning. *Please.*

With that, his brain turned off like a bulb and he felt himself tumbling down into a deep, black pit.

He didn't know how long he'd slept when his eyes opened momentarily and he found himself staring groggily at the television set. Disney's *Alice in Wonderland* was playing on it. He saw the bustling rabbit looking at his watch while he sang, "I'm late! I'm late! For a very important date!"

His eyes fell shut and he was falling deep into the pit again.

He woke as though drugged.

The TV set was still on. A local talk show. A man in a red ten-gallon hat was talking about his personal barbecue sauce that had bourbon in it.

Chris looked at him with half-opened eyes for almost a minute. Then he stood and weaved into the bathroom. Turning on the cold water in the sink—it was lukewarm at best—he rinsed off his face. It helped to wake him.

He soaped his hands and washed them, then his face, rinsing it off again. He stared at his reflection in the cracked mirror above the sink. He looked haggard, water dripping from his nose and chin. *I look fifty,* he thought.

He wondered if the hospital had found Nelson; found him in time to save his life. He had enough problems without a death to worry about. Not that it was his fault Nelson got shot. He had only been defending himself.

He shivered and reached for the bath towel, grunting at the size of it. A bath towel for a dwarf, he thought.

He went back into the bedroom and sat on the bed while he finished drying his face and hands. "Yessir," the man in the red cowboy hat was saying, "this sauce will make those ribs of your'n stand up at attention." He chuckled happily.

Chris got up and turned off the set. *Alice in Wonderland* on a local TV station? The thought occurred to him. *I thought the Disney Studio didn't allow that.* He yawned. Well, it had to be Veering. Sure, even Disney reality succumbed to him.

Get out of the country, he thought.

He frowned. *Goddamn it, that's ridiculous. I'm not going to leave the country.*

Still, what *could* he do?

People were after him. People who wanted his life.

He tried to think. The man in his house. Had that woman really called Wilson? No, that made no sense at all. Wilson would know that something was wrong. He wouldn't cooperate by sending a man to—

Chris's eyes went out of focus, into thought.

Unless Wilson was a coconspirator.

But *why?* Chris shook his head angrily. That was implausible. Wilson knew nothing about this. They'd done it all by working *around* Wilson. Around his mother; clearly, she'd been fully as perplexed as he was.

What about Louise then?

Chris shivered. That was something he couldn't fathom. It was an element in the puzzle that didn't fit. That *was* Louise he'd talked to, wasn't it?

He sat in rigid concentration. Was it possible they—whoever in the screaming hell "they" were—had taken over Louise's house—put someone else on the line with him? Someone who sounded like Louise but—

"Oh . . ." Chris twisted his shoulders in aggravation. *Christ Almighty, I know my own sister's voice, don't I?*

Which brought him inevitably back to total confusion again.

"I've got to get out of here," he mumbled. He looked at his watch. 7:21. He'd slept four hours anyway. If there was a cordon closing in, he'd better clear out before it caught him.

He went outside, unlocked the car door and got inside; the interior was hot and close. He switched on the motor and let it run, turning on the air conditioner. Would Scotty Tensdale ever get this car back? he wondered.

He turned on the car lights now, put the transmission into gear and backed out from behind the cabin.

As he drove past the office, he saw the woman in the doorway, looking at him. Was she suspicious? he thought. He tried to drive slowly so she wouldn't think he was trying to make a getaway.

He turned left onto the highway and headed west again. Where *was* he going? he wondered. Were there authorities *anywhere* he could safely surrender to? He wasn't sure there were, not now. Which meant flight. Out of the country? *Sure,* he thought, *with what—twelve dollars in my pocket, credit cards as obvious as bombs?*

Later, it struck him as bizarre that, precisely as he was thinking that, he drove underneath a highway light and, glancing to his right, saw a large white envelope lying on the other seat.

He cried out hollowly and jammed down so hard on the gas pedal that it made the Pontiac leap forward, throwing him against the steering wheel.

Carefully then, as though it were the action of a calm, collected man, he steered onto the shoulder and braked. Putting the transmission into park, he twisted the light knob so the overhead light went on.

He stared at the envelope, not even wanting to pick it up, much less open it. The car had been locked, all its windows raised. Yet someone had placed the envelope on the passenger's seat.

How?

And who? Veering? Another of his little reality-bending tricks? Chris shook his head angrily. Veering was a wandering mendicant with a crumbling brain, no more. He ignored the fact that Nelson had spoken of Veering. He had to ignore that for now.

Chris sighed and picked up the envelope, turned it over. Blank on both sides, sealed. Letter-size. What was in it? A letter bomb?

He checked the glove compartment and found a flashlight. Turning it on, he held the envelope against the light. No sign of anything suspicious inside. He turned off the flashlight.

Still, he hesitated, sensing, somehow, that whatever was in the envelope was going to change his life even more. Had Gene had it put there while he was asleep? It had to have been Gene. If anyone else had known that he was in the Bide-A-While, they'd have picked him up.

But why not simply slip the envelope underneath the cabin door? Why—?

Fuck it, open it, he told himself. *You're going to mull yourself into a coma.*

Tearing off one end of the envelope, he pulled out a folder. United. A one-way ticket from LAX.

To London.

🔲 Chris stared at the ticket. Simple enough. A one-way ticket from Los Angeles to London. First class. Tomorrow morning. Very simple.

Like the unified field theory.

He had to smile. Not one of amusement, but that of a mountain climber realizing that his rope is just about to shear at twenty thousand feet, and he either screams in mortal dread or remarks, "Aw, shit."

"Aw, shit," Chris said. What *more* could happen to him?

He picked up the envelope and looked inside. There was something else, a folded sheet of paper. He unfolded it and a bill fluttered onto his lap. Picking it up, he stared at Benjamin Franklin's face. One hundred dollars.

He looked at the sheet of paper. A note was typed on it.

For God's sake, get out of the country! Now! I'm deadly serious! Gene.

Chris turned off the interior light and slipped the ticket, bill and note back into the envelope. He placed the envelope on the passenger seat, then pulled down the transmission bar and slowly eased back onto the highway, accelerating to fifty-five miles an hour before he set the cruise control.

Here I am, he thought as the car rolled across the now-dark desert. *Driving sensibly. A law-abiding citizen. Most commendable.*

For a man being swallowed alive by a nightmare.

"*Jesus Christ!*" he yelled. He yelled it three times, each louder than the one before. What in the bloody, goddamn hell was going on?!

He exhaled hard. The situation was becoming more insane all the time. It had started with a missing car. Now—less than twenty-four hours later—he was being told to get out of the country. He didn't know Gene *that* well. Why would Gene pop for a first-class ticket to London?

Was there really any meaning to all of this or was it hideously simple, a lost wager with Veering? Was his reality changing? No matter how he tried to avoid the idea, his mind insisted on returning to the old man in the baseball cap. He heard the tone in Veering's voice as he said, *"I wager the security of your existence against your assumption that you know what's real and what's unreal in your life."*

He began to shiver convulsively and couldn't seem to stop.

✠ It was when he had driven past a coffee shop and saw a highway patrol car parked in front of it that he knew exactly what he had to do with part of the hundred dollar bill.

He was now sitting in the last row of the Trailways bus, eyes closed. Scotty Tensdale's car was parked by the terminal in Yuma. Hopefully, Scotty would get it back in a few days; by the time Chris was in London.

London, he thought. For God's sake, *London*. He'd thought of flying there a hundred times but never under these circumstances.

He'd tried to settle down his brain and take a nap. It didn't work. The sleep ritual at home was too entrenched in his system — a long, hot shower, a good, brain-relaxing read and, presently, unconsciousness for several hours.

The back seat of a bus just didn't make it.

He opened his eyes and looked out at the passing desert. *Déjà vu,* he thought. It was the same view he'd seen from Scotty Tensdale's car early this morning — the silver-cast sand, the dark forms of cactus and desert trees.

Was he really going to get on that plane and fly to London?

He couldn't make up his mind just yet. He was en route to Los Angeles. That was enough for now. Maybe by the time he arrived in Inglewood, he'd have made his decision.

Not that he had a hell of a lot of options. Hand himself in? — that seemed a really bad idea now. Go into hiding — how long would that last if the CIA was onto him?

It had to be the project, he realized.

He found himself nodding. Had to be. It was the only thing that made him special enough to warrant all this attention.

The project was important, there was no doubt of that. To the Pentagon. To national security. If he could solve the problem, God only knows what international ramifications would take place. He'd never really thought about the significance of what he did at Palladian. It had been just a tedious job.

But it was obviously a lot more than that and he was thinking about it now.

Small wonder he'd dreamed about directing numbers in a play. A play whose set had a clock on the wall. Time was running out, Wilson had been clear enough on that. *Chris, we need that answer.* He sighed and closed his eyes again. *Well, you weren't getting that answer from my flagging brain,* he thought. *And God knows you're not going to get it now.*

He opened his eyes as the bus began to slow down.

For a few moments, he stared blankly at the flashing red light ahead.

Then a hand, invisible and cold, slid in between his ribs and got a good hold on his heart. He felt it starting to squeeze, felt his heart straining to beat against the pressure. Dear God, he thought. All his thoughts and plans were pointless now.

He couldn't seem to fill his lungs with air as the bus drew closer to the highway patrol car blocking the lane. *They've got me,* he thought. *It's done.*

He looked around in sudden desperation. No way out. He felt sick with fear. Where would they take him? To highway patrol headquarters? CIA headquarters?

Or were they working in league with Meehan? Would they simply drive him into the desert and put a bullet in his brain?

He flinched and stiffened as the bus braked and the front door opened with a hydraulic hiss.

11

A pair of highway patrolmen came on board and spoke softly to the driver. Chris saw the driver start to look back into the bus. One of the patrolmen said something quickly to him and he turned to the front again.

Chris felt himself pressing back against the seat. There was a throbbing sensation in his right temple that felt like the ticking of a clock. Is all of this really happening? he thought. It seemed unreal and dreamlike.

The two patrolmen started moving up the aisle, checking the seats on either side. There were seventeen passengers; Chris's eyes counted them in a glance. How long would it take them to reach him? What would they say? *You're under arrest?* Would they draw their pistols? He stiffened.

Would they shoot him?

A shiver made his shoulders jerk. They could if they chose to, if they had orders to do it. *He killed a government agent in Tucson this morning,* he heard one of them report. *We had no choice.*

He closed his eyes and waited. He was trapped.

A sudden noise up front made his eyes jump open again.

One of the patrolmen was wrestling with a male passenger—a bulky man in a black jacket sitting on the right side of the bus. The other patrolman came to assist him and they yanked the heavyset man into the aisle. None of them spoke, but only hissed and grunted from the effort of their struggle.

Chris saw the flash of handcuffs and heard them clicking shut on the man's wrists. He was surprised at how soundlessly the other passengers were taking all this. Not one of them did anything but watch in silence as the two patrolmen dragged the man down the aisle, his shoes squeaking on the rubberized floor.

The man was pulled out through the door and Chris saw, through the windshield, the two patrolmen forcing him to their car and bending him inside. A few seconds later, the patrol car drove away, starting back for Yuma.

"Well, folks," the driver said loudly—his voice made Chris twitch, "you just saw the capture of a bank robber."

Chris slumped back, eyes falling shut. Jesus God, he thought. His breath shook badly.

Only after the bus had driven on for several miles did he realize that what had happened had made up his mind for him. He couldn't face that kind of pain again, that kind of terror.

He was going to London.

⌖ The bus arrived in Inglewood at seven in the morning; he had two and a half hours before the flight.

Rising on rubbery legs, Chris walked along the aisle and stepped down to the sidewalk, shivering. It was a cold, foggy morning. He looked up at the dark gray sky, trying not to visualize the airliner taking off into it.

Crossing the floor of the nearly empty terminal, he went into the men's room and relieved himself, then washed his hands and face. He scowled at his reflection in the mirror. He needed a shave; he looked too much like a wanted man.

He went outside and bought some shaving cream and disposable blades at the counter. Carrying them back inside the men's room, he shaved as quickly as he could, considering that he hadn't used a blade for more than ten years. Inevitably, he cut himself a few times, forced to press tiny pieces of toilet tissue on the nicks.

Even so, it was an improvement. Not bad-looking for a mathematician on the run, he thought. His clothes didn't look too good but they'd pass. He checked his watch. He may as well get over to the airport before trying to have breakfast.

He tossed the blades and shaving cream into a waste can, then telephoned for a cab. *I suppose I should have kept them,* he thought as he walked back across the terminal. He couldn't plan that far ahead, though. His brain was stuck in the present.

The cab showed up in fifteen minutes and he got inside, telling the driver that he was flying to London on United and would he take him to the proper terminal. The driver, puffing on a cigar, nodded without a word. A blessing, Chris decided. He was in no condition for a chatty driver.

The ride to the airport took twenty minutes. Chris paid and tipped the driver and walked into the United terminal. Impressive-looking, he thought.

He went directly to the first-class line and placed his ticket on the counter in front of the young woman on duty there. She smiled and said, "Good morning," checked the ticket and asked him if he preferred Smoking or Non-smoking. In first class, what difference does it make? he thought, but told her Non-smoking anyway. She made out a boarding pass and pushed it into the envelope slit.

He was turning away when she said, "Mr. Barton?"

He didn't turn back at first. Was this it? he wondered. Were they going to arrest him now?

Sighing, he turned. "Yes?"

"I have something here for you."

"You do," he murmured.

He watched as she reached beneath the counter and, after a few moments, came up with an envelope. It looked like the one he'd found in the car.

"This was left for you," she said.

"By whom?" he asked.

"I don't know," she said. "I wasn't on duty when it was left."

"I see." He stared at the envelope. What now? he thought. *Ignore previous ticket. You sail to Hong Kong on the morning tide.*

"Oh, Jesus," he mumbled and took the envelope from the young woman. "Thank you," he said.

He walked toward one of the chairs. Another jigsaw piece that wouldn't fit? he wondered. Reaching the chair, he sank down on it wearily and tore open the envelope.

There was a piece of cardboard inside, a locker key Scotch-taped to it.

Chris held it in his right hand, staring at it. A locker. Did it have a bomb inside? Turn the key and *ka-blooey?* The end of C. Barton, Fugitive Mathematician?

He blew out a heavy breath. It was another jigsaw piece. Would the overall picture ever be formed? Right now, he doubted it. He simply couldn't keep up with all the new pieces.

He looked at his watch. Nearing eight. What should he do? Forget the key? Drop it into a waste can, wait to board?

Ten minutes later, he decided. He may as well play this through, use the hand he was being dealt. Standing, he started for the boarding gate. It seemed as though everyone he passed knew who he was and, at any moment, was going to shout, "Hey, stop!" "It's him!" "It's Barton!" "He's the Arizona Agent-Killer!" "Grab him for the CIA!"

The detector buzzed as he went through. He felt himself tighten guiltily, then realized it was the key and dropped it on the plastic tray. This time, he got through without a sound and the man monitoring the machine handed the key back to him.

He rode the escalator to the second floor and walked to the boarding area, then moved around the edge of it until he found the locker. *Locker,* he thought, *a spot you put something in and lock 'er up.* Word derivations were a bane to him.

He stood in front of the locker for ten minutes, wondering whether to open it, his brain a swirl of conflicting theories. All right, they wanted him dead. But why a locker bomb? Their last opportunity before he left the country? Didn't it make more sense that Gene would be behind this? In that case, why not mention it in his note? Had he thought of it after the ticket and note had been delivered?

Finally, to stop the swirling contradictions in his mind, Chris slipped the key into the locker slot and turned it, hunching his shoulders and half-closing his eyes at the last instant in case there was an explosion. Much good it would do if there *was,* he thought.

He released a held-in breath and opened the door. There was an overnight bag inside. He pulled it out and closed the door.

Was there a bomb inside the bag? he wondered suddenly. *Oh, for Christ's sake, you're bomb-happy!* he assailed himself.

He went to the men's room and locked himself inside a booth. Lowering the lid of the toilet he sat down and put the overnight bag on his lap. It was expensive-looking. Nothing but the best for Fugitive Chris, he thought.

He braced himself and pulled open the zipper on top of the bag, thinking, *God, I'll really feel dumb if it explodes* now.

He looked inside the bag. A change of clothes. A sweater, slacks, shirt, underwear, socks, shoes, a warmer jacket than the one he was wearing. Expensive clothes, too. Whoever his guardian angel was—Gene?—he (or she?) was certainly generous.

He felt down through the neatly folded clothes to see what else there was. Toilet articles. He unzipped the case and looked inside. Everything he needed. He blinked in amazement. Two vials as well, prescription: Calan and Vasotec. Whoever was watching over him knew about his hypertension. Mystery on mystery, he thought.

For several moments, sitting there, he felt almost a glow of pleasure. The clothes, the first-class flight to London. This sure was one hell of a lot more intriguing than his life had been for the past five years. He was almost looking forward to this. All he needed now was a svelte Hitchcockian blonde sitting next to him on the plane.

There was more in the bag; a small package that he opened to find himself looking at a bottle of hair dye and a mustache, a tube of spirit gum. "Aw, now, wait a minute," he said, scowling. Play-acting now? A disguise? Jesus God, that was absurd. Still, why was it in there if Gene (he had to be behind this) didn't think it was important?

Chris sighed and shook his head. Then he saw another package on the bottom of the bag and lifted it out, a plastic envelope. It was heavy and he almost dropped it. Snatching at it clumsily before it could fall, he put the overnight bag on the floor and put the plastic envelope on his lap to unzip it.

He stared blankly at what was in the envelope.

Now the picture seemed complete. His life a maddening enigma. Men chasing him. Mysterious events. A flight to London. A change of clothes. A disguise kit.

A pistol.

He stared at it, an expression of distaste on his face. A clip of bullets was wrapped beside it. He had no idea what caliber it was except that it was smaller than a .45. Probably smaller than a .38 as well.

For what? he thought, unable to repress a shudder. What in God's name was he up against? Did Gene actually think he might have to *shoot* someone?

He gasped and almost dropped the pistol as someone pounded on the door.

"Come on, there's people waiting!" said an angry man.

Chris swallowed hard. Sweet Jesus, he thought. It's heart-attack time.

Hastily, he put the pistol back into the plastic envelope, zipped it up and pushed it under the clothes inside the overnight bag. He'd dump the damn thing as soon as he could.

He wondered, for a few moments, how the bag had been brought up to the boarding area. How could it have passed the metal-detector? Another mystery. His brain was swollen with puzzles. He could sit in this booth for a year just analyzing all the questions raised since early this morning.

Forget it, he thought. Just . . . damn, forget it. He unlocked the door and left the booth; there *were* a lot of men waiting. A fat man wearing a red sport coat pushed by him and entered the booth, slamming the door. Sorry, pal, Chris thought. Have a primo b.m.

He made his way to the exit and left the men's room. As he walked into the boarding area, he wondered if he should have stayed in the booth long enough to put on the mustache.

"Oh, that's *ridiculous*," he muttered. Forget about breakfast. He was going to down a couple of drinks so fast, they'd vaporize in his throat.

By the time he reached the bar, he'd changed his mind. His stomach was too empty. Except for a small bag of Fritos in Yuma, he'd had nothing since his mother's house. Two drinks might make him reel. He ordered an Irish coffee and sat at the counter; there were no tables open.

A *mustache,* he thought, making a scoffing noise. He'd look like a Spanish pimp. No, if they were going to pick him up, let it be as himself, and not some character from a spy movie.

Fifteen minutes later, he paid for the Irish coffee and left the bar. He walked over to the gift shop and bought a copy of the *Los Angeles Times* to read on the plane. He wasn't sure whether he wanted to read about Nelson or not—or about himself for that matter, if there was anything about his situation. But he had to know.

Is this what it feels like to be a fugitive from justice? he thought as he crossed the boarding area to his boarding gate. *Fugitive from the law, you mean,* he told himself. Justice had no part in this game. Thank God for Gene, he thought. He didn't know why Gene was being so helpful but bless him for it.

He sat in a corner, waiting quietly until they announced the boarding for his flight, first-class passengers first. Drawing in a deep breath, he stood and moved toward the doorway.

As he drew nearer to it, his heartbeat quickened more and more until he could actually hear it thumping in his ears. Was he going to make it? Was someone on the lookout for him? Did he look completely guilty? It was like a bad dream in which no matter where one hid, one was found.

The woman at the doorway checked his boarding pass, tore the stub off his ticket, smiled and said, "Have a nice flight, Mr. Barton." *God, don't say my name!* he thought in panic.

Anticlimax, he thought next as he walked along the slanting tunnel toward the plane. Entering it, he showed the boarding pass to the stewardess waiting there and she gestured toward the first-class section. "Would you like me to store your bag?" she asked.

"No, thank you, I'll put it under my seat," he told her.

The stewardess in the first-class section showed him to his seat. It was by a window. He slumped down, feeling suddenly exhausted.

"Would you like some champagne?" the stewardess asked.

"Could I have a screwdriver?" he said.

"Of course." She smiled and turned away.

He slid the bag under the seat in front of him, put the folded copy of the *Times* beside him on the seat, then leaned his head back, closing his eyes. Was it really over? he thought.

Over? his mind retorted. *It's barely begun, you idiot. You're on your way to London. Didn't you notice that the ticket was only one way?*

He blew out a long, slow stream of breath. Would he make it to London? Or would the plane explode halfway across the Atlantic? Was that the kind of film this was? Maybe he wasn't the hero at all but some subsidiary character, the poor sap who got it in the first reel.

"Here you are, Mr. Barton," the stewardess said.

Oh, Christ, am I going to be called by my name all the way to England? he thought, opening his eyes. He forced a smile and a "Thank you" as he took the drink.

He took a deep swallow of the screwdriver. He could afford to get a little alcohol inside himself now. He felt at his neck. *As usual, stiff as ye boarde,* he thought.

Groaning softly, he put down the drink and picked up the newspaper.

Nothing different, conflicts and corruptions as always. Disinterested, Chris ran his gaze across the stories.

Until page five. Then, suddenly, he was having trouble with his breath again, the corners of his eyes were tearing. *Oh, my God, my good God,* he thought.

REPORTER SHOT
Gene Wyskart, a reporter
on the *Tucson Herald*, was
killed last night by an
unidentified gunman.

12

Chris put aside the paper and closed his eyes. *I can't go on with this,* he thought. *It's too damn much.* It had been bad enough with Nelson and he hadn't even known the man. Gene had been a friend.

"God," he whispered. "Jesus. *God.*"

"May I move this?" said a man's voice.

Chris opened his eyes and looked to his right. The man in the aisle was smiling cordially. Chris didn't understand what he'd meant, then, abruptly, he saw the newspaper lying on the seat beside his and picked it up. "I'm sorry," he said.

"No problem," the man replied. He sat down and extended his hand. "Jim Basy."

Chris almost knocked over his drink, then raised his hand above it. Basy smiled and shook it briefly. Chris wondered if the man was wondering why he hadn't given his name in return.

Jim Basy was in his forties, wearing gray trousers and gray tweed jacket, a white shirt with a black knit tie. He looked like a successful executive, dark hair neatly trimmed, face cleanly shaven, black shoes polished to a gloss.

Chris winced and reached involuntarily to massage the back of his neck. It was really hurting now.

"Stiff neck?" the man asked.

Chris nodded. "Yeah."

"I have problems with my neck too, sometimes," Basy told him. "I hang upside down for it."

Chris looked at him blankly.

"It's like a trapeze," the man explained. "Gravity helps to separate the neck vertebrae."

"Oh." Chris nodded. The part of him responding to the man was minor. Most of him was sick inside, getting ready to stand and leave the plane, surrender himself.

Putting the newspaper beside him, he reached beneath the seat in front of him and slid out the overnight bag. Picking it up, he began to stand. "You *leaving?*" Basy asked. Chris didn't like his tone and started to edge past him to the aisle, muttering, "Excuse me."

The man's grip on his wrist was like steel.

"I wouldn't do that, Barton," he said.

Chris stared down dumbly at the man. Basy wasn't smiling now. "Sit down," he said.

Chris couldn't move. All he could do was look at the man.

Basy smiled now, a sympathetic smile. "You have to leave the country, Chris," he said.

Chris's legs began to give and Basy braced him up, then helped him back down onto the seat. He took the overnight bag out of Chris's hand and slid it under the seat in front of Chris.

"Now," Basy said. He looked at Chris, his expression one of slight exasperation. "I wasn't supposed to let you know," he said, "but I couldn't let you leave either. Why were you leaving?"

Chris didn't know what to say. After a few moments, he reached to his left and tugged on the folded newspaper. He lay it on Basy's lap, pointing at the article.

Basy winced. "Oh, jeez," he said, "I didn't know that. Poor guy."

"You *know* about him?" Chris demanded, unable to keep the sound of anger from his voice.

"I know you spoke to him and he said he'd help you."

"He *did* help me," Chris said tightly. "He got me the ticket for this flight and that bag there."

"No, we got you the bag," Basy said. "We would have gotten you the ticket, too, if he hadn't done it first."

The vise on his head again. *I'm losing touch,* he thought; *I really am.*

"I was sent to go with you to London," Basy told him. "Help you after you got there."

Chris drew in a long, wavering breath.

"*What's going on?*" he asked.

Basy hesitated, then shrugged. "I can't tell you much," he said. He held up his hand to stop Chris from breaking in. "For the simple reason," he continued, "that I haven't been told that much myself."

"Is it the project?" Chris asked quickly.

"Bottom line? Of course," Basy said. "You're a very important part of it."

"*Me?*" Chris made a scoffing noise. "I'm just a cog."

"Don't underestimate yourself," Basy said grimly. "You know what your contribution means."

Chris shrugged. "Well," he said. "You—" He broke off, looking at Basy with suspicion.

"What?" Basy asked.

"How do I know who you are?" Chris said.

Basy took a billfold from his inside coat pocket and opened it. He pulled out a plastic-covered card and showed it to Chris.

James R. Basy, it read. An operative number. Central Intelligence Agency.

"You know Nelson?" Chris asked uneasily.

"Who?"

Chris told Basy about Meehan and Nelson.

"Well, I never heard of them," Basy said. "But that doesn't mean anything. There are a lot of agents in the CIA."

"All working on my case?" Chris asked edgily.

"No." Basy smiled faintly.

"You don't know then whether—" Chris broke off.

"Whether what?"

"Whether they're really CIA," Chris lied. He'd been about to ask whether Basy knew if Nelson had survived or not. He'd decided, mid-sentence, not to pursue it. If Basy didn't know about Nelson, let it stay that way.

"What about Veering then?" he asked, handing back the card.

"Who?"

Chris couldn't control the groan.

"What's wrong?" Basy asked.

Chris hesitated, then told him about his conversation with Veering. "And Nelson *mentioned* him," he added.

"Well, since I don't know who Nelson is, that doesn't mean a hell of a lot to me," Basy said. He grunted with amusement. "This Veering sounds like quite a nut case though."

"What about the couple in my house?"

"That I know about," Basy replied. "That's how I got involved." He looked around. "Oh, we're leaving," he said.

They didn't speak as the plane backed away from the terminal, then began to taxi along the airfield. Chris tried to convince himself that he was doing the right thing but was unable to do so. Everything seemed wrong to him; distorted, unreal.

After the plane was in the air, Basy spoke to him again. "Okay, we're on our way," he said. "I've been thinking. Those two men you mentioned; I doubt if they really were CIA. Our orders were to keep an eye on what was going on, not move in and get involved."

Chris felt a kind of relief at that. Meehan had been so vicious. Nelson had intended to kill him. He would much prefer to believe that they weren't CIA, that they were—

Were *who*? Foreign agents? They were obviously American. His brain was starting to reel again.

He started to ask Basy a question when the agent said, "I have to use the rest room, I'll be right back." Standing, he moved away.

Chris sank back against the chair. Noticing the drink, he picked it up and took a long swallow. The stewardess came by and asked him if he wanted another and some hors d'oeuvres. He said he would and she moved away.

Chris closed his eyes and tried to form a brief summation in his mind.

It was the project. That was definite. Some kind of cabal taking place against people working on secret military projects. Meehan and Nelson were probably not CIA. Had *they* killed Gene? And why did he have to leave the country?

He eliminated the questions from his summation. He didn't

want to confuse things. The situation seemed to be falling into some kind of order.

Except for Veering. Would Veering ever fit into what was happening?

The stewardess brought him another screwdriver and a small china plate with some crackers and wedges of cheese on it, a tiny knife. "We'll be starting lunch service in a little while," she told him, setting down a pair of menus on Basy's seat.

Chris finished up the first drink and set it aside. He took a sip of the second screwdriver, then made himself a cracker sandwich with Brie cheese. He felt considerably better now. Some kind of pattern was emerging. He always felt better when patterns emerged. Which was why he'd been so unhappy with, and frustrated by, the project for so many months now.

 Fifteen minutes later, he twisted around and looked back toward the rest rooms. He'd read part of the *Times*, finished the crackers, cheese and the second screwdriver and had ordered chicken Kiev for lunch.

Now he was wondering if something was wrong with Basy.

He looked back at the front and tried to push the feeling away. *Goddamn it, don't get started again,* he told himself. *As soon as things start clearing up, you insist on muddying the waters again.* Basy was performing his A.M. ablutions. He had a stomachache and was hunched over on the john. He'd taken a stewardess in there and was bopping her. Who knows? he thought irritably. He's fine though. Fine.

Minutes passed. He finished looking through the *Times* and put it down. He looked out the window at the clouds, at the land below. He tried to feel calm.

It didn't work. Anxiety was trickling slowly through his thoughts. He tried to resist. Relax, he thought. Take it easy. He closed his eyes. Music, he thought. He'd put on the earphones and listen to some classical music.

He looked at his watch. Almost twenty minutes now. He looked toward the back again. A woman was trying to get into one of the rest rooms but it was locked. Is that where Basy is? he wondered.

He swallowed. Could Basy have gone in back of the plane to consult with some other agent? That didn't make sense. Two agents to escort him? Christ, he was Chris Barton, not Albert Einstein.

He tapped his fingers on the seat arm. He couldn't listen to music. Not until Basy was back. *I'm sorry,* he addressed his mind. *He should be back by now. Call me paranoiac if you want to but he should be back by now.*

"Aw, no," he said. It wasn't going to get bad again, was it? It wasn't going to be Veering-time again, was it?

"Mr. Basy?" he imagined the stewardess saying to him. *"I'm sorry, Mr. Barton. There's no Mr. Basy booked next to you. You've been sitting alone since you got on the plane."*

Chris undid his seat belt and stood abruptly, a hard look on his face. Stepping into the aisle, he walked back to the rest rooms. *Both of them will be empty now,* he thought. *And I'll start screaming.*

One of them was still locked. He stared at the word *Occupied.* By what? he thought.

He stood indecisively. Should he knock on the door and ask Basy how he was? What if that woman answered? *You start screaming,* answered his mind.

The stewardess came up to him. "This other one is free, Mr. Barton," she said.

"I know. That's not—"

She looked at him inquiringly.

He swallowed. "Did you . . . see a man go in here before?" he asked, pointing at the locked door.

"Mr. Basy, yes," she answered.

Thank God, he thought. His sound of relief was so obvious that the stewardess looked concerned. "Are you all right?" she asked.

"Yes. Yes," he assured her. *I am now,* he thought.

She smiled and walked away.

He waited for a few moments, then knocked softly on the door.

There was no answer so he knocked again. He leaned in close to ask, "Are you all right, Basy?"

Silence.

Chris shuddered. Oh, God, now what? he thought. He's had a heart attack? He's been poisoned? He's in there, dead?

He hesitated, then knocked more loudly. "Basy?" he asked.

Some people looked around and the stewardess returned. "Is something wrong?" she asked.

"I don't know," he said. "This . . . Mr. Basy was sitting next to me. Then he went to the rest room." He swallowed again. "This was more than twenty minutes ago. Now . . ."

"Yes?" she asked.

"He doesn't answer my knock. I've called his name. I—"

"You think something's wrong."

There it was. He didn't want to speak the words. But there was something wrong.

"Do you know if he has any kind of medical condition?" she asked.

"I don't even *know* the man," he said, aware that he sounded agitated.

"I see," she said.

She turned to the door and knocked on it loudly. "Mr. Basy?"

There was no answer.

"Oh, dear," she said.

"Can't you open the door?" he asked.

"Well . . . yes; I can, but . . . I wouldn't want to embarrass him—"

"Embarrass?" he broke in. "He's not answering. There's *something wrong.*"

He tried to open the door but couldn't.

"It's locked," she said.

Oh, bright, he thought angrily. He was starting to feel dizzy. Was the nightmare starting again?

He pounded on the door with the side of a fist. "Basy!" he shouted.

"Please, Mr. Barton," the stewardess said.

"Well, damn it, *open* it then," he told her.

She stared at him uncertainly. *Goddamn it, open the fucking door!* he wanted to shout. *If you'd been through what I have in the past day, you'd goddamn kick it in!*

The stewardess moved quickly to an overhead bin. Reaching in, she took out an odd-looking tool and brought it back. She used it on the door and reached out to open it. She won't be able to do it, he suddenly thought. Basy's dead body will block the way.

The stewardess opened the door.

"Oh, well, this is peculiar," she said.

Chris felt himself weaving back and forth. He'd never fainted in his life. He felt sure that he was going to faint now.

The rest room was empty.

"I don't undertand this," the stewardess murmured.

You don't undertand it . . . Chris thought. "You . . . *saw* him go in," he said in a shaky voice.

"*Yes.*" She was staring into the empty rest room. "I *did.*"

"Is it possible to lock the door from the outside?"

She looked confused.

"I mean could he have come out, closed the door and locked it from out here?"

"No." She shook her head. "I've never seen it done."

She stepped into the rest room and looked around. She started as though an electric shock had struck her.

Chris stepped in to see what she was looking at. There was something scrawled on the mirror with a Magic Marker. Chris could just make out the writing in the dim light.

7 steps to midnight.

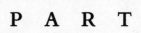

PART

1

He tried not to think as he walked through the terminal. He asked one question: where were the taxis? The man he asked directed him and he went outside. He looked around for the closest cab, then found it unnecessary to signal as one of the small, square black taxis curved in and stopped in front of him, the driver opening the door.

Chris got inside and fell back on the seat. "Park Court Hotel," he said.

"Right away, guv'nor," the driver said. Closing the door, he pulled the cab away from the curb. "American?" he asked.

Chris smiled tiredly. "How d'ya know?" he asked.

"Not difficult," the driver said.

Chris's responding chuckle was barely audible. He put the overnight bag on the floor, stretched out his legs and, groaning softly, closed his eyes. He wished he had a sleeping pill. He'd like to sleep for about a day and a half.

He'd given up the hope that he would wake up in his house and, grinning to himself, think, *Good Jesus, was* that *ever a dream.*

It was all reality, he knew that now. Demented, disjointed, distorted reality but reality nonetheless.

He hadn't slept at all on the flight. Despite exhaustion, his brain would simply not relinquish consciousness. How could it? On top of every other madness he'd been exposed to was Basy's disappearance.

It had been assumed, at first, that Basy was in some other part of the plane. What else could they assume? He'd left the lavatory without being seen and, in leaving, accidentally locked the door behind him. He was no phantom. The stewardess had seen him enter the plane, had spoken to him, had seen him take his place beside Chris. She'd seen him rise and enter the lavatory.

That was the last she saw of him.

Basy wasn't in the plane. It was that simple fact that jarred Chris the most. He'd spoken with the man. Basy was as real as he was. Then he'd vanished into thin air, leaving behind a note scrawled on a mirror.

7 steps to midnight.

"Oh, God," Chris murmured. He shifted uncomfortably on the seat. Problems all had solutions; he'd lived by that tenet, it had never betrayed him. No matter what the problem was, eventually he'd found an answer to it.

Until now.

While they were checking over the plane, he'd sat and waited. What had bothered him most was the continuation of banal details all around him. The serving of the meal. The showing of the movie. The murmuring of people as they spoke. The constant din of the engines. All reality. And, in the midst of it, him, an island of impending madness.

When the stewardess, looking pale, had finally returned to tell him that, no, they were terribly sorry but Mr. Basy was nowhere to be found, Chris had thanked her quietly and politely, then sat staring at the film without seeing or hearing a moment of it.

After a while he'd picked up Basy's overnight bag and checked the contents.

What he found comforted and shocked him simultaneously.

A reservation order in his name for a hotel named the Park Court. An envelope of British money: a half-inch-thick packet of five-pound and one-pound notes. A passport.

His.

He hadn't been able to control the tremor of his hands as he opened it. He'd never had a passport in his life, never dreamed that he would ever have the time to travel overseas. And the photograph. It was undoubtedly him but he couldn't recall ever having it taken.

His head had felt numb as he'd leafed through the pages of the passport. Ah, good, he'd thought dazedly as he looked at the stamps. Chris Barton was obviously a world traveler. Tahiti. Fiji. New Caledonia. Australia. China. *I hope I had a good time,* he'd thought.

He'd closed his eyes abruptly. Jesus Christ. How much more could be endure? Was *anything* what it seemed to be?

For a short while, he'd really entertained the idea that something in his work had caused him to sideslip into an alternate reality. He'd read about it often enough. Was it an actual possibility? Thought lay behind all physical events. Wilbur and Orville thought *flight* and an airplane resulted. Tesla dreamed of alternating current and the world had electricity. Einstein thought $E = Mc^2$ and Hiroshima was obliterated.

Had something in his work created this nightmare?

"Oh, shut up," he muttered. He opened his eyes and looked around. The cab was chugging along an entry road toward a freeway. Do they call them freeways here? he wondered. Expressways? Highways?

He clenched his teeth for a moment and closed his eyes again, determined not to succumb to destructive thinking. There were solid details here; it wasn't all an evanescent mystery. There was the passport; that was real. The money. The hotel reservation. The flight ticket. The overnight bag with clothes and toilet articles, with *medication* for Christ's sake. And the pistol. How real could you get? These were items you could deal with. Items that led one to believe that the mysteries—however inexplicable they seemed at the moment—would eventually be solved.

He had just finished putting the hotel reservation, passport and money into his overnight bag and put Basy's bag back under the seat next to him when a flight officer had shown up to speak to him. One of the pilots? The navigator? There'd been no way of knowing. His name was Captain Blake.

He'd asked Chris questions in a quiet, reassuring voice. Chris imagined that voice over the loudspeaker system, dulcetly informing the passengers that *"This is Captain Blake. We are now plummeting toward the ocean at a horrendous speed and in a few moments, we will all be dead as doornails. Enjoy your flight."*

Blake had asked him what he knew about Basy. *Not much,* Chris had told him. *We spoke a few minutes, nothing specific; then he'd gone to the lavatory to vanish from the face of the earth*—or the face of the sky.

Captain Blake had soon departed, taking Basy's bag with him. *Thank God I looked inside it first,* Chris had thought. . . .

"Here on vacation, guv'?" the driver asked.

Chris's legs retracted and he opened his eyes. "I'm sorry?" he asked.

"Just askin' if you're on vacation," the driver replied.

"Oh," Chris looked blank. "Yes," he said then. "A vacation." The driver smiled. "Have a nice time."

"Thank you," Chris murmured. *I'll have a lovely time,* he thought. *So far it's been just grand.*

He closed his eyes again, wishing he could sleep. Granted, he was accustomed to minimal sleep at home but he had to have *something.*

Home, he thought. Was the other Chris Barton sleeping there at this moment? With Mrs. Barton asleep next to him? *Maureen?*

He grimaced and angrily looked around before closing his eyes once more. *The other Chris Barton my ass,* he thought. *There's only one Chris Barton and it's me.* What name was in the passport, Donald Duck?

❦ He jolted, gasping, as a hand shook his shoulder. Jerking open his eyes, he stared at the man looking at him. It was the taxi driver. "Park Court, guv'nor," he said.

Chris looked around and saw the entrance to the hotel. There was a man in a uniform and top hat waiting on the curb. He rubbed his face and picked up the overnight bag, getting out of the taxi.

"Take your bag, sir?" the doorman asked. He had a bushy mustache and looked like another character from Dickens. Here, it fit.

"That's all right," Chris answered. He had no intention of letting the reality of its contents out of his hands.

He looked at the driver. "How much?" he asked. The man told him.

Chris unzipped the overnight bag and turned away so neither man could see its contents. Reaching into the envelope, he tore off the paper seal and pulled out several five-pound notes. Thank God he'd read that book on European monetary values. He'd never thought it would actually come in handy; he'd only read it out of curiosity.

He paid the driver, tipping him fifteen percent, then gave the doorman a pound note.

"Thank you, sir." The doorman nodded.

Chris went up the short flight of steps and entered the lobby. The desk was to his left. Moving there, he set the overnight bag on the counter and removed the hotel reservation form from it. He felt a moment of icy premonition as he laid it on the counter in front of the clerk. Was he mindlessly letting himself into a trap?

He fought away the apprehension. What choice did he have anyway? So far he was alive and safe. He had to play the hand given to him. There was no apparent alternative.

Anyway, he was too tired to resist.

If it was a trap, it was a damned subtle one. The desk clerk examined the form and smiled, welcoming Chris to the hotel as he gave him a key. Chris thanked him, turned to the right and moved to the elevator. As he pushed the button, he saw a staircase leading down. For several seconds, the wonderment of actually being in a London hotel struck him, not unpleasantly.

He waited until the elevator door slid open, then went inside and pushed the button for the fourth floor.

It made him nervous standing alone in the small elevator as it slowly ascended. He pressed himself against the back wall, imagining Veering suddenly popping into view next to him, smiling and asking, *How do you like it so far?* He shuddered, then snarled without sound. Shape up, he told himself.

The route along the fourth floor hallway was beyond circuitous. It seemed the hotel equivalent of a hedge maze, extending on and on, changing directions, twisting and turning. Chris passed maids and guests entering and leaving rooms. He wanted to stop one of them and ask where the hell he was but didn't have the energy. *This is it,* he thought, *I'm going to spend eternity wandering along a fourth floor corridor in the Park Court Hotel. Someday, they'll find my skeleton in some dusty corner, still gripping the overnight bag with my bony digits.*

Finally, he came to the room and went inside. Locking the door, he leaned back against it with a heavy sigh. If they (whoever "they" might be) were going to try and get him now, they'd have to break in. He had the pistol; he'd make a fight of it.

He snickered at himself. *Sure you would,* he thought. *You're a regular goddamn James Bond.*

Opening his eyes, he moved past the bathroom doorway into the room. There was a low counter to his left with a TV on it, a mirror above that. To his right were a pair of double beds, a table between them, a phone on top of it.

He put the overnight bag on the bed closest to the hall door and walked to the window. There was a park across the street. He saw people ambling along a path, sitting on the grass, a man and woman waiting for a bus. *My God,* he thought, *I'm in* England. *Standing at a hotel window in the city of London!* For a guy who figured he was lucky to get to Las Vegas now and then, he was really on a roll.

He frowned. This was still a nightmare, wasn't it? He grunted. Sure it was. Still, it was rather like a Hitchcock nightmare. Foreign intrigue. Night flight from unknown enemies. He felt— he had to admit it—a little stimulated by it all. *That's because you're safe right now,* his mind reacted. *Let something threatening happen and you'll panic again.*

"Okay, okay," he muttered. "Still . . ." Despite the frightening incidents, he was, at least, far away from that damned office at the plant, that damned computer and the damned project. Half a world distant, in London, living a mystery the like of which he'd only read about before. It *was* stimulating, no other word for it.

He turned and looked at the bed beside him. It was tiring too; hell, exhausting. He crawled onto the bed, pulled a pillow from under the spread and dumped his head on it. *Wait, I have to take off my shoes,* he thought.

He was asleep before he could make a move. There were no dreams. His rest was deep, black and still.

He began to hear music in the distance. At first, he was barely conscious of it. Then his brain began to rise from blackness until it surfaced and he opened his eyes.

He stared at the ceiling, half-awake. The music was clear now; "The Swan" from Saint-Saëns's *Carnival of the Animals*. He looked around groggily.

It was in the room.

Chris sat up with a grunt. A radio on a timer, he thought. He hadn't seen a radio though. Was it part of the TV set? He looked at the TV. The music wasn't coming from there. It was to his left. He looked in that direction.

A small cassette player was lying on the next bed. He stared at it dumbly.

Abruptly then, he sat up fast and looked toward the hall door. The room was empty. Yet someone had come in while he was sleeping and put the cassette player on the bed, turned it on and left.

Chris shuddered, feeling lost again, a helpless victim. No matter how he tried adjusting, the mysteries kept piling up faster than he could handle them. He stared at the cassette player. "The Swan" ended and the Finale of the *Carnival of the Animals* began to play.

He swallowed, then gingerly reached out and pressed the Stop button, flinching as he imagined that, in doing so, he'd detonate a plastic bomb inside the player. He pulled back quickly as though to avoid the explosion.

"Idiot," he muttered then. He looked at the cassette box lying beside the player. There was nothing on it; it was painted solid blue.

After several moments, he sat up and, reaching over, picked up the cassette player. Another flinch as he imagined that, in doing so, he'd pulled a wire that would detonate a bomb beneath the bed.

"Oh, for Christ's sake." He scowled at himself. *You* have *been reading too many goddamn thrillers.*

He examined the cassette player, then started to press the Rewind button. He hesitated. What, if in depressing it, he detonated—?

"*Enough,*" he snarled. He lifted the cover of the player and took out the cassette. It was like the box—painted blue, no printing.

He put the cassette back into the player and, closing the lid, pressed the Rewind button. He stared at the cassette player's window until the wheels stopped turning, then pressed the Play button and the music began.

"Introduction" and "Royal March of the Lion," he thought, consulting memory. He sat listening. Next came "Hens and Cocks," then "Mules"; it was apparently the entire *Carnival.* Next came "Tortoises," he remembered then. "Elephants." "Aquarium," "Personages with Long Ears," "Cuckoo in the Woods," "Aviary," "Pianists," "Fossils." Memory ticked them off. Finally "The Swan" again.

Chris turned off the cassette player and set it aside. Standing, he walked into the bathroom, turned on the light and washed off his face at the sink.

Dried, he went back into the bedroom and sat down on the bed again, picking up the cassette player. Pushing the Eject button, he opened the top and lifted out the cassette, turned it over. "Oh," he said. A slip of paper was Scotch-taped to the cassette; on it, a number printed in black: 1530.

He set down the cassette and put both hands across his face. Jesus God in Heaven, was this ever going to make some sense along the way? Hitchcock it wasn't. Maybe Kafka was behind this story; it seemed more his style.

He stood up, trying to blank his mind. Removing his clothes with deliberate slowness, he left them on the floor and walked naked into the bathroom. He started to pull aside the shower curtain, then drew back his hand, imagining a figure hanging in there. Maybe Janet Leigh crumpled, dead in the bathtub.

"Will you *stop?*" he ordered himself.

He turned and went back into the bedroom. Taking the toilet kit out of the bag, he carried it to the bathroom and unzipped it. He would have preferred that his mystery supplier had added a rechargeable electric razor to the kit, but what the hell. He moistened his face, spread cream on it and shaved with the safety razor, managing to nick himself no more than twice. Not bad, he told himself.

He pulled back the shower curtain; no bodies there. Turning on the water, he waited until it was the right temperature, then stepped inside, pulling the curtain shut again.

A blue cassette, *Carnival of the Animals*. Why blue? Any meaning there? Thirteen sections to the *Carnival*. Seven steps— lucky. Thirteen sections—unlucky. That seemed a nowhere route.

Animals, he thought. Lion. Hens. Cocks. Mules. Tortoises. Elephants. Aquarium. Personages with long ears. Cuckoo. Aviary. Pianists. Fossils. "The Swan." The one that was playing when he woke up. Significance there?

And to top it off—1530. Adds up to nine. That miserable number again. Was it a year? An address? A combination to a safe? A waist measurement?

"Just shut up, will you?" he addressed his mind. He finished showering, got out and dried himself. Now he'd go into the other room and find Veering sitting on the bed. Or Meehan. Or Nelson's corpse. Or a Saint Bernard playing a ukulele.

He went into the other room and took the clothes out of the overnight bag, laying them out on the bed. He put on the underwear, then the shirt (light blue), the slacks (gray flannel), the sweater (dark blue). Nothing but the best, he saw. His benefactor had taste.

He had to have some coffee, he thought as he sat on the bed, putting on his shoes and socks. Maybe some food, maybe not.

Carnival of the Animals. Was he supposed to meet somebody at the zoo?

"Christ, who knows?" He stood and transferred the money and key to his new slacks. Going back into the bathroom, he patted shaving lotion on his face and combed his hair. *Well, I'm dressed like Cary Grant even if I look like someone who's just gone six rounds with a gorilla. 1530,* he thought again. *Thirty is double fifteen. And the next number in that progression is forty-five and I look that old right now.*

🦂 As he started down the corridor, it occurred to him that whoever had put the cassette in his room could just as easily have killed him. So there was beneficence in this to some degree. But why the goddamn mystery? Why not just wake him up and tell him what was going on?

He went down to the lobby and asked the clerk if there was a coffee shop in the hotel. Restaurant downstairs, he was told. He was going to ask what time it was when he saw the clock on the wall, 4:12. It wasn't dark outside and there was activity in the lobby so obviously it was the afternoon. He'd arrived about nine this morning. He'd slept almost seven hours then; that was two nights' sleep for him.

He went downstairs to the restaurant, was seated and given a menu. Before he could ask for immediate coffee, the waitress was gone. Would she bring coffee automatically the way they did in Arizona?

Clearly, they didn't; time passed and nothing happened. He stared out the window at a little courtyard. 1530. Blue. Animals.

7 steps to midnight.

Now there was a real puzzler. What kind of steps? And midnight *when?*

He sighed. He didn't dare let his brain loose on that one yet.

Mercifully, the waitress appeared with a glass of water. She looked familiar. Had he seen her in a British spy film? Was she part of the cabal as well? Would there be a message slipped in his farina? *Beware the one-eyed man?*

"Yes, love," said the waitress, shattering the illusion. She was a plump, blonde, middle-aged waitress, nothing more.

He ordered eggs and bacon, wheat toast, coffee. He was tempted to order a banger too (when in Rome, again) but he didn't know what a banger was even though he'd heard them mentioned endlessly in British films. Maybe it was a stick of dynamite. Not likely, though.

He tried not to think when the waitress left but it was impossible; once jump-started, his brain refused to stall. Which was the problem, of course. He'd kept thinking at the plant and put out nothing but dull repetitions and stupid variations.

He grunted, recalling the dream for a moment. Perfect metaphor. Digits screwing up the performance on his mind-stage. Out of position. Running amok.

He took a sip of water. Tastes awful, he thought. It's drugged. He'd topple over and wake up in Shanghai, manacled to a dungeon wall.

"Yeah, yeah, sure," he mumbled. *Enjoy yourself. 1530. Blue. Animals.*

The waitress brought his bacon, eggs, toast and coffee and he ate, surprised by his appetite. *All right, let's get this thing resolved,* he thought as he ate. It had something to do with creatures and blue was a key. A lion. Hens. Cocks. Mules. Tortoises. Elephants. Fish. Donkeys. Cuckoo birds. Pianists? Fossils. A swan.

"Wait a second." He stopped eating. The simplest answer was the correct one; wasn't that always the case? "The Swan" was the piece that was playing when he woke up. The color blue was essential. So was 1530.

He jarred his chair back and stood. Moving quickly to the waitress, he asked her if there was a public telephone nearby. She told him there was one in the corridor outside the restaurant. He told her he'd be right back and started for the exit.

There was a small directory, attached by a chain to the pay telephone. He picked it up and turned the pages quickly. He found what he was looking for, what would have crushed him if it hadn't been there. But it was. "*Bingo,*" he said. It was the first feeling of controlled triumph he'd felt since all this insanity began.

The Blue Swan/1530 Meredith.

⌘ The first thing he thought as he entered was: *I should have brought the pistol with me.* He reacted against the thought. *Who the hell do I think I am, 007?*

He looked around the dim interior of the pub, wondering why whoever it was had gone to so much trouble to get him here. What if he hadn't figured it out? Would they have gone to Clue #2?

It was odd to see computer games in such an ancient setting, huge overhead beams oiled by the greasy smoke of centuries. He looked at the long counter with hams, beef roasts and chickens on it. Now what? he thought.

He walked past the counter to the bar. He was going to order a screwdriver, then ordered a half-pint of ale. *When in Rome . . .*

He carried the mug to the end of the room. There was a stairway to his left and he ascended it to find an empty, low-ceilinged room with booths, tables and chairs in it, a big unlit fireplace at its far end.

He walked to the end of the shadowy room and sat in a booth, facing front so he could see if anyone came in. He took a sip of ale, grimacing. He wasn't used to room-temperature drinks and the flavor tasted strange to him.

The room was quiet except for the distant sounds from the downstairs pub. Chris took another sip of the ale. It tasted a little better now.

He'd had no trouble finding the pub. After getting the new jacket from his room, he'd left the hotel, asking the doorman where Meredith was. It turned out to be Meredith Way and it was only four blocks from the hotel. The air had been crisply cold and invigorating as he'd walked. He'd kept thinking how incredible it was that three days ago he was in Arizona, immersed in his usual existence. Incredible, the number of things that had happened to him since he'd woken up in his office. It really would be stimulating if it weren't for Gene's death and the possible death of Nelson, of Basy.

He sighed and looked once more toward the stairs. Was it all some monstrous joke? he thought. Was this the end of it? Was he just going to be left here, high and dry?

It couldn't be. Someone would show up. A little man in a bowler hat carrying a black umbrella. Slipping him a sealed envelope. *Plans for the new laser cannon, guv'.*

He frowned. Come on, he thought. He wondered then if he'd made a mistake coming up here. Maybe his contact was searching for him downstairs. Maybe he should go back down.

He tapped his fingers restlessly on the table. Except for the faint sounds of trade going on in the pub below, he might have been sitting in the room of some run-down manor house. Any moment now, a secret panel in the wall would open and a thin, mustachioed man with a stiletto—

He snickered. Stupid, he thought. It *was* vaguely enjoyable though, like something from a mystery-suspense novel. Would his contact be a woman? A slinky Hitchcock blonde? A sloe-eyed redhead? A dark-haired, witchlike—

He tightened as he heard the sound of footsteps on the stairs.

A man came into the room. Chris started. The man *was* little and *was* carrying an umbrella, even though he didn't have a hat on. He was also carrying a mug of ale in his right hand.

Chris wondered what to do. If he signaled to the man and the man turned out to be only a pub customer, he'd feel like an idiot. No need, he told himself. If the man was there to see him, he'd make the overture.

He felt his heartbeat slowly quickening as the man approached. Here it comes, he thought.

The man stopped by the booth. "Barton?" he asked.

Somehow, it seemed an anticlimax. Weren't secret agents supposed to be cagier, use passwords or something? He swallowed quickly. "Yes," he said.

The man sat down across from him and eyed him in silence.

His scrutiny made Chris nervous. The man's face was ferretlike, pocked, discolored. *This was a secret agent?*

Suddenly, the man looked toward the stairway and the way he did it made a chill run up Chris's back. It was the fast glance of a man expecting menace to appear at any moment.

He looked back at Chris. "You found this place all right," he said. "Good."

Chris had to ask. "What was the point of all that? Why not just a note slipped under my door? Come to The Blue Swan on Meredith Way."

"A note anybody could read?" the man responded.

Chris didn't understand that but, before he could ask, the small man chuckled nasally; his teeth were bad, too. "Anyway," he said, "it's Number One. He relishes these little mysteries to test his people."

"I'm not one of his people," Chris said irritably.

"You are now," said the man. Again, he turned his head to look toward the stairs. As he did, the right edge of his jacket shifted and Chris glanced downward, stiffening as he saw the butt of a holstered revolver under the jacket. *Jesus,* he thought. It definitely wasn't fun and games he was involved in. The man's words echoed chillingly in his mind: *You are now.*

He noticed how icy-blue the man's eyes were as he turned back. "I have to go," the man said. He emptied his mug and set it down.

"*Go?*" Chris said. "You just—"

"Crown above H. Tonight," the man broke in. Chris watched, astounded, as the man stood up. "Got that?" he asked. "*Crown above H. Tonight.*"

"Aw, come *on,*" Chris pleaded. "I've been dragged over rocks for almost three days now. Surely, you can tell me something more."

The man's face was hard as he gazed down at Chris. Then it softened with a smile and he patted Chris on the shoulder. "I know it's hard," he said. "It always is at first."

"At *first?*" Chris's voice was agitated.

"You've got a way to go before it's home-sweet-home again."

He started to turn and Chris reached out impulsively to grab his sleeve, wincing as the man coldly looked back at him.

"For God's sake, can't you tell me something more?" he begged.

The man's expression was impassive. "I'll tell you this much," he said. "I've been in this business twenty-seven years and I've never heard Number One's voice shake before."

Chris stared at him.

"He's an icy gent, I'll tell you," said the man. "If *his* voice shakes, there's something mighty dangerous afoot."

"Do you know Veering?" Chris asked.

The man looked surprised. At first, Chris thought it meant that the man *did* know Veering.

Then he saw that the look of surprise had to do with something else.

"My God, they didn't—" started the man.

Chris jerked, as the man's legs suddenly collapsed and he fell against the booth table with a gasp of shock, the look of surprise on his face now one of terrified realization. "*God,*" he said. He couldn't seem to breathe.

Chris stared at him, unable to move. The man reached out a shaking hand and tried to reach the empty mug he'd put down. Then his hand twitched and he knocked the mug onto the wooden bench.

Chris gasped as the man grabbed his jacket; the man's eyes looked glassy now. "Get out," he whispered. "Before they come. *Get out!*"

Abruptly, his hand went limp and he was sliding downward. Chris heard the man's head thump once on the floor, then there was only stillness.

3

This isn't real.

Chris tried hard to believe that but it didn't work. He felt the hardness of the bench against his back and buttocks. The smell of ale and cooked meat in his nostrils.

The pressure of the man's out-flung hand on his foot.

He jerked back his foot and struggled up from the booth, looking fearfully toward the staircase. He tried to avoid looking down at the man but couldn't help inclining his head.

The man's eyes were open; dead man's stare again.

"Oh, Jesus Christ," Chris muttered. He twisted around and headed for the stairs.

He had to lurch against the stairway wall for support as his legs threatened to give way. He drew in deep breaths of the pub-smelling air, then continued down. *Look calm,* he told himself. *You're leaving casually; nothing's wrong.*

He swallowed dryly as he walked along the counter. Was his dread visible? He hoped not. He bumped against a man who cursed at him. He tried to apologize but no sound came from his mouth. All he could think was that, any second now, someone would go up to the room and see the man's dead body crumpled there.

An image flicked across his mind: himself, seven, accidentally locked in a trunk in Uncle Harry's attic; the claustrophobic panic, the sense of smothering, the screams flooding from his throat.

Except for the screams, he felt the same way now. There would be no one to release him from the terrifying darkness this time though.

He was alone.

He pushed out through the doorway and started along the sidewalk with long, fast strides. He walked blindly, with no sense of direction, anxious to put distance between himself and the pub, the dead man in the upstairs room.

Is he dead? he thought abruptly. Was it all a trick? He made an angry, scoffing noise. *Sure, a trick,* he thought. *I'll go back and tickle him until he breaks up, giggling.* "Christ," he muttered.

He walked around a corner, down a block, around another corner, striding as fast as he could without actually running, the sound of his shoes on the sidewalk a rapid clicking. *Why didn't they give me rubber soles on these shoes?* he thought distractedly.

By the time his panic had begun to ease, he was lost.

He stood motionless for several minutes, taking in deep breaths of the cold air, trying to regain control of himself.

There were some young men leaning against the front of a pharmacy at the end of the block. As Chris started walking again, he began to notice them. He didn't know why the sight disturbed him. Maybe it was because anything unknown was disturbing to him right now.

In a way, despite the tremor it gave him, he was not surprised when one of them stepped leisurely from their spot against the pharmacy wall and stood in Chris's path. "Well, what 'ave we 'ere?" the young man said.

Chris looked blankly at the young man's white, blemish-ridden face, his dark lank hair, his eyes were so dark they looked almost black.

"Excuse me," he said then and tried to walk around the young man. The teenager stuck out his arm to block Chris's way. " 'Ere now, mister," he said in a voice that reminded Chris of a Cockney character in *Oliver*, "you in an 'urry t'get somewhere?"

Chris heard the other three teenagers chortling. "Please," he said, "I have to—"

"Please?" the young man interrupted. His feral grin was yellow-toothed. "*Please?* Oh, ain't that sad?" He glanced at his friends. "I b'lieve we 'ave a Yank 'ere, boys. A bleedin' Yank."

Chris closed his eyes a moment. *Control*, he told himself. Then he saw the three other young men moving forward. In a few moments, the four surrounded him. Chris felt his stomach muscles quivering. He couldn't fight them, that was obvious. He couldn't run. He tried to remember some moves from a karate manual he'd read, but his mind remained blank.

"What do you want?" he asked, trying to keep his voice steady. He almost added, *"Money?"* then decided that would be a mistake. His gaze flicked around. Was there no one here to help him? He realized then that he had inadvertently wandered into a rough neighborhood. *Idiot,* he thought. *You should have gotten a cab and gone back to the hotel.*

"What do I want, Yank?" the young man was responding. "More than you 'ave t'give, I 'xpect."

Chris couldn't seem to think. Was this part of the nightmare too? Veering's threat of reality gone askew? Or was it just an accident because he'd walked into the wrong neighborhood?

He shuddered, visualizing his body found tomorrow morning in an alley, stabbed and bloodless.

"All right, if it's money—" he began.

"Gentlemen," a voice said behind him.

Chris and the four teenagers looked around. A man in a black suit, wearing a turban, was approaching them. He was of moderate height with a dark, pleasant-looking face on which a genial smile was fixed. "I believe this man is looking for me."

Chris tightened as the man gripped his arm. "I'm glad I found you," he said. "Would you excuse us?" he said to the teenagers.

The young man who had stopped Chris looked incensed. "What in the bloody 'ell d'you—?"

He broke off with a startled grunt as one of his friends jabbed an elbow into his side. "What are you—?"

"We was only 'aving a lark, friend," his friend interrupted, speaking to the Indian man.

"Ah. A lark," the man replied. His East Indian accent sounded incongruous here, Chris thought. "A lark is always entertaining," he went on, "so long as there is nothing else involved."

He impelled Chris away from the group. "Come along, my friend," he said.

Chris looked at him, perplexed. He began to speak but the Indian murmured. "Say nothing and do not look back." He smiled inscrutably. "That might arouse them," he added.

He steered left at the end of the block. "Best we seek out a well-used thoroughfare," he said.

"What—?"

"—made them let me remove you from their clutch?" The Indian made a faint sound of amusement. "The one who spoke to me, you see—who said that they were only having a lark—is experienced in the ways of the street. He knew that to pursue the matter in a hostile way would prove a detriment to them."

Chris looked at the dark-faced man in confusion.

"I see you do not understand," the man told him. "There is a language of the streets which is conveyed entirely through the eyes though it involves much more. That young man looked into my eyes and knew that it was not a good time to pursue the matter. That it was more advisable to draw back and allow the two of us to move on. Do you see now?"

"Vaguely."

"That will do for now," the Indian said. "Oh, I tell you, sir, those four had mischief in their hearts."

"And knives in their pockets."

The Indian's laugh was musical. "Doubtless that is true as well," he said.

"But I haven't introduced myself," he continued, extending his right hand. "Modi is my name."

His grip was strong enough to make Chris wince a little. "Mr. Modi," he responded. "I'm Chris Barton."

"So pleased to meet you, Mr. Barton," Modi said with a smile.

"I'm pleased to meet you, too," Chris said. "Lord knows what would have happened to me if you hadn't come along."

Modi smiled again. "I am so glad I did," he said. "What were you doing there, if I may ask? It is not the most desirable of neighborhoods."

"I'm lost," Chris told him.

"Ah." Modi nodded. "Perhaps I can restore you to your proper place then."

"I'm staying at the Park Court Hotel," Chris told him.

"Not too far away," the Indian said. "Allow me to guide you there."

"That's very kind of you."

"My pleasure," Mr. Modi said.

They walked in silence for a quarter of a block. Then Chris had to know. "I still don't really understand," he said, "why those four guys backed away so quickly."

"Well," said Mr. Modi. "It is, as I have said, a matter of street awareness. I grew up in Bombay under the most harsh of circumstances. I was as they were and perhaps a little worse. There is a brand of what you might describe as telepathic exchange between people of the streets. Mostly in the eyes as I have indicated. The voice as well, however. And also—far more subtly—a matter of the posture, the manner, the assurance. It is difficult to reduce to words but it is quite apparent to those who know it. One knowledgeable street person knows immediately if another is vulnerable to terrorizing. If not, if the other one is clearly not to be trifled with; the retreat is immediate. They *know*. As that young man knew."

Chris still wasn't sure that he understood. What Modi said seemed almost mystical to him. Which gave him an immediate idea.

"There are a lot of . . . mystical things in India, aren't there?" he said.

"Many," the Indian agreed. "Our culture is rich with them. Not that what I have spoken of is mystical in any way."

They had reached a main thoroughfare now and Modi gently impelled Chris to the left. "This way," he murmured.

Chris nodded. "May I ask you something?"

"You most certainly may," said Modi genially.

Chris drew in a quick breath. "I'm from Arizona."

"Arizona, the United States?" The Indian looked surprised.

"Yes."

"That is very far from where we are," Modi said, impressed.

"Yes, it is." Chris's smile was slightly rueful.

"May I inquire what brings you here?" the Indian asked. "Business? Pleasure?"

"More like enigma," Chris responded.

"*Enigma.*" Modi looked surprised again. "How so?"

Chris hesitated. Could he trust the man? He thrust the thought aside. The man had saved his life. And there was the possibility that he could help further.

"I work in this plant," he began. "Government work."

"I see." Modi nodded.

"The other night—about three days ago—actually it was early morning, after three, I went to the parking lot to drive home and my car was gone."

"So far not too enigmatic," Modi said.

Chris chuckled. "Not so far. But I had to borrow a car and while I was driving home, I picked up a hitchhiker named Veering and got into this insane conversation with him about reality versus unreality."

"Ah-ha." Modi nodded. "I sense the enigma coming."

"He asked if I was willing to wager the security of my existence against the assumption that I knew what was real and what was unreal in my life."

"An unusual wager," Modi said.

"An unusual result," Chris replied. "Assuming," he added quickly, "that everything that's happened to me since I took the wager is connected to it."

"What *has* happened?" Modi asked, sounding intrigued.

Chris told him everything, eliminating Nelson and the man in the pub; he was unwilling to trust the man that far. It was a strange experience to walk along the London thoroughfare in the now darkness, telling the turbaned East Indian what had occurred to him. The more he spoke, though, the better he felt and he realized that it had all been bottled up inside him.

"That's it," he said when he'd told all he wanted. "Here I am in London in this unholy mess and I have no idea whatever why I *am* here."

"Goodness." Mr. Modi shook his head. "An enigma indeed. How may I assist you in the understanding of it?"

"Well." Chris braced himself. He didn't want to plunge into this new world too far but he felt it vital that he ask. "Have you ever experienced—or heard of anyone experiencing—such a mystery? In India, I mean."

It seemed at first as though Modi wasn't going to answer; they walked about fifty yards in silence. Chris began to regret telling the Indian anything of what had happened. The man must think him totally demented.

"May I ask," Modi finally said, "the nature of your work?"

Chris hesitated. It was taboo for him to discuss his work. Still . . . perhaps he could generalize. "I can't tell you exactly," he answered, "but as I said, it's for the government."

"I understand," said Modi, nodding. "What I am getting at, however, is the *nature* of the work. I have no desire for you to mention details which are necessarily confidential. By the nature of your work, I mean . . . how shall I put it?" He paused, then said, "Does it deal with aspects of reality perhaps? With areas that go beyond the merely mechanical into zones of, shall we say, more nebulous reality? Where, perhaps, the senses need be transcended?"

Chris had no answer for that. He thought about it hard. It was true that the areas he'd been dealing with were certainly beyond the senses, nebulous. Still—

"Well, I *am* a mathematician," he said.

"*Ah.*" Modi nodded. "And your work, I much suspect, does not involve adding columns of figures."

Chris smiled. "No."

Modi was silent for almost a minute before he said, "In India, as you have sensed, we are more intimate with concepts of reality and unreality. We know full well that the tissues of what we say is *real* are thin indeed. That they can be torn asunder with more ease than people realize. And if your work—your mathematics— seeks to deal with elements beyond the senses, well . . ." He gestured vaguely. "Perhaps you have—how shall I put it?— *trespassed.*"

Chris felt a chill across his body and knew it wasn't the coldness of the wind. It was a kind of fear he'd never known before. "Have you . . . ever run across anything like this?" he asked.

"This aggravated, no," Modi answered. "Small things. Nothing this . . . grievously perplexing." He sighed. "I can only say, it could well be an aspect of your work. One would have to know its precise nature to analyze it. And I realize that this is not feasible."

Unexpectedly, he smiled. "Well," he said, "at any rate, it certainly is food for thought. How fortunate you have the sort of mind accustomed to analysis. It could make things easier for you. Analyze by all means. Use every skill you possess."

Chris started slightly. That was almost exactly what his mother had said to him.

"Well, this has been most interesting," the Indian said. "And you are now within a block or two of your hotel." He removed a pocket watch from his coat and looked at it. "I have a brief appointment I must attend to. However, it appears to me that we have merely scratched the surface of what you have most aptly described as an enigma. If you would do me the honor of allowing me to take you to supper later—perhaps about nine o'clock—we could pursue it further."

Chris almost accepted, then remembered *Crown above H* (whatever that was). *Tonight.* Should he drop it in favor of a further talk with Modi? No. He'd better not.

"I'm sorry," he said. "I have something on tonight."

"Ah." Modi nodded. "Well, perhaps tomorrow. I will telephone you at your hotel before noon. Perhaps we can lunch together."

"That would be nice," Chris replied.

"Well, here I leave you," Modi said. "You go down this block, turn right and there you are."

"Thank you so much," Chris said, shaking his hand. "You've been very kind."

"No, no, my pleasure," the Indian said. "And, now, good-bye."

"Before you go," Chris said quickly.

Mr. Modi turned back, an inquiring look on his face.

"Do you have any idea what *Crown above H* means?"

"Oh, yes, indeed; it means the Theatre Royal, Haymarket."

"Ah-ha." Chris nodded. "Thank you again."

"Most welcome," Modi said. "Perhaps we will rejoin tomorrow."

Chris watched him walking away, then turned down the block. Jesus, what an afternoon, he thought.

And there was still tonight.

4

When he entered the hotel lobby, he noticed a table near the entrance to a small shop. A man was sitting at it, theater posters on the wall behind him. Impulsively, Chris walked over to him and asked if there was a ticket for him for tonight's performance at the Theatre Royal Haymarket.

The blank look on the man's face was his answer. "I believe they're all sold out," he said.

"Thank you," Chris said. He started to turn toward the shop to buy a newspaper, then realized that a story about the man in The Blue Swan couldn't have been printed so quickly and turned away again. He glanced at the lobby clock as he started for the elevators. 6:12. Adds up to eighteen, eighteen (1 + 8) totals nine, that goddamn number strikes again.

He unlocked the door to his room with trepidation. What was he going to find inside now? An elephant? A corpse? Another cassette?

There was nothing extra in his room, he saw as he turned on the light. Thank God for small favors, he thought. He wondered briefly if he should have gone to supper with Modi. At least it would have been predictable. God knows what would happen if he went to the bloody *Crown above H.* tonight.

He realized that he didn't know what time the play started; he had to assume that there would be a ticket waiting for him at the box office. He called down to the lobby and found out that curtain time was seven-thirty.

Removing his jacket, he sat on the bed, a wave of depression settling over him. Should he really go on with this? he thought.

He could end it simply enough. No matter who or what was behind this, he could terminate all efforts with a simple visit to the nearest police station. He was innocent of any wrongdoing. What could they—?

"Oh, sure," he said. He'd been innocent from the start. That hadn't stopped that man in his house from holding a gun on him. Hadn't stopped Meehan from roughing him up or Nelson from trying to kill him. His "innocence" had prevented nothing from occurring. Jesus God, only three days and there were probably four corpses already. It was James Bond out of Kafka sure as hell.

He lay on his side and drew up his legs, assuming a fetal position. *I'm regressing*, he thought. *Dread is infantilizing me.* Use his skills? "Bullshit," he muttered. He'd be lucky if he could stand up again and go to the bathroom. His work on the project seemed somewhere in another dimension. What had that man said in the pub?

"You've got a way to go before it's home-sweet-home again."

❦ Twenty minutes later, he sat up with a tired groan. Well, what the hell, he thought. What was he going to do, just lie around like a vegetable? That man had died to transmit the message about the play tonight. The least he could do was check it out.

Standing, he walked into the bathroom and washed off his face, almost afraid to look at his reflection in the mirror for fear it would be someone else's face; things seemed to be going in that direction.

Drying his face, he went into the room, picked up the jacket and put it on. Suddenly, it struck him that he hadn't taken his hypertension medicine that day. He got one of each—the white oblong tablet, the little white pill—and washed them down with tap water, making a face at the taste of it.

Then he went downstairs and left the hotel, shivering at the outside air. The jacket was heavy but he still felt a little cold. He asked the doorman to get him a cab and waited inside the lobby until it came. Then he exited quickly, tipped the doorman and got into the taxi.

"Theatre Royal, Haymarket," he told the driver.

"Right you are," the driver said, steering back onto the street. *Now he'll tell me that the play's sold out; I'd better eat with Modi after all.*

Chris made a face. Everything isn't a mystery, he lectured himself. Some things are what they seem.

I hope, he thought.

He closed his eyes and tried to blank his mind. It almost worked until he heard Nelson's words in recollection: *"It's not the first time it's happened."*

The memory made him feel stranger than ever, giving him an image of scientists and mathematicians all over the world immersed in similar enigmas.

Why?

The project, of course. Basy had been clear enough about that. *"Bottom line? Of course."* And then, *"you're a very important part of it."*

That he wasn't sure about. He knew that what he'd been doing was important, yes, but *very* important? That made it sound vital. He'd never considered that before. He had taken it for granted that there were multiple mathematicians everywhere noodling with the turbulence problem, some of them better than he was. The idea that he was so important to the project that he'd become a victim of some international cabal seemed just too farfetched, a lot harder to believe than any plot he'd ever skimmed through, seeking sleep.

One option he'd discard though: giving himself up. Why should he? He hadn't done anything wrong. *Let them find me,* he thought resentfully. *I'm going to see it through.* He smiled to himself. It must be a second wind, he thought, or the dazedness of jet lag, because he felt a kind of pleasure once again at the impending evening. The possibilities were infinite.

At least one more corpse. His mind was a wet blanket on his sense of enjoyment.

"Thanks," he muttered. "Nice of you to suggest it." However, he'd better buy an evening newspaper if he could; see if the man in the pub was mentioned in it.

126

He drifted back into thought.

Did *seven steps to midnight* really mean anything? he wondered.

Seven, the magic number, the lucky number. Age seven—childhood. Double seven—puberty. Triple seven—physical maturity. Quadruple seven—mental maturity.

Anything there?

More likely the connection was to seven years' bad luck and the seven-year itch.

Seventh heaven. Seven seas. The Seven Hills of Rome. Seven Wonders of the World. Seven days in the week. Seven colors in the spectrum. The seven virtues. The seven deadly sins. Seven come eleven.

Chris stirred and opened his eyes. His mind was a runaway again. Put on the brakes, he told himself.

He closed his eyes and tried to nap to still the thoughts. But his mind commenced a search of his work in the previous week to see if he could find a special seven in it. . . . Seven steps leading to a twelve?

◪ "Here we are, sir."

Chris started and opened his eyes. He had drifted off. How long? he wondered. Surely not more than ten or fifteen minutes. "You have the time?" he asked.

"Five minutes to seven," the driver said.

"Thank you." Chris paid him through the opening to the driver's seat, tipping him fifteen percent.

He shivered as he got out of the cab and closed the door. Moving quickly to a theater door, he pulled it open and went inside. People were gathered in groups, conversing; some stood at the ticket windows.

Chris got into one of the lines and when he reached the window, gave his name.

"Tonight, sir?" asked the woman in the cage.

"Yes." He was sure now that there'd be nothing. Well, at least the lobby was warm. He'd sit there for a while before moving on.

"Here we are, sir," the woman said.

Chris looked down in surprise at the small envelope with the ticket protruding from it. *My God, it is here,* he thought. "Thank you," he murmured and picked it up.

What was the purpose of *this?* he wondered as he moved toward the door an usher had pointed out. Something in the play? He didn't even know what play it was. Was someone going to sit behind him, jab a hypodermic in his neck and ask about the project?

"Shit, I need a drink," he told himself. He saw people going down some stairs and followed them. There was no bar in the lobby.

In the lower lobby, he saw a bar and crossed to it. A man was being served ahead of him and he waited until the man had left with a pair of drinks, then ordered a screwdriver.

When the drink was made, he paid for it. On impulse, he bought a chocolate bar as well. *Odd combination that,* his mind observed. *None of your business,* he answered it.

He carried the drink and chocolate bar to a small chair across the lower lobby and sat on it. He took a sip of the drink—not cold, not a single ice cube—then unwrapped the chocolate bar and took a bite.

He stared ahead blankly, wondering if it made any sense to try and analyze further. After all, it seemed as though he didn't really have to do a thing but react. The major steps were being taken for him. Step by step, he was being led somewhere. Were there, in fact, seven steps he had to take to "midnight," to fruition, the beginning of a new mental day?

That had a kind of satisfying logic to it. He'd accept it for now.

He finished the drink and chocolate bar in ten minutes, returned the empty glass to the bar, threw the paper wrapper into a waste can and went upstairs.

The usher led him to his seat and handed him a program. The seat was on the main floor, halfway to the stage, one in from the aisle seat. Not bad, he thought. He grunted. Assuming he was here to see the play, that is.

He looked around the theater after sitting down. Beautiful, he thought. How old was it? It could have been built in the eighteenth century. History in its wood. Sheridan and Congreve sitting for rehearsals. Addison and Fielding watching performances of their plays. Remarkable, he thought.

He checked the program inside its illustrated cardboard folder. *The Little Minister,* he read, smiling. Barrie might have sat in this very seat, watching his beloved Maude Adams perform on the stage. Chris smiled. The theater had an atmosphere that was almost tangible.

Thank God the title of the play hadn't turned out to be *Reality vs. Unreality* or *Veering's Wager.* He wouldn't really have been surprised but he preferred it as it was. Everything is not a mystery, he told himself again.

Well, now what? he wondered. He sighed and closed his eyes. Whatever happens happens, he decided.

He heard the rustle of a woman's dress as she sat down beside him.

He wondered if he should open his eyes and look at her. He felt an aversion to the thought. So long as he kept his eyes closed, he could imagine anything. It was Grace Kelly, Eva Marie Saint, Tippi Hedren. It was Hitchcock's penultimate blonde heroine sitting beside him, waiting to make contact and add a touch of spice to what had so far been more redoubtable than romantic. *Was* it his next contact? What if she were built like a weight lifter? That would end the stimulation for him posthaste.

The more he thought about it, the harder it was to open his eyes. He could visualize Jacqueline Bisset or Jane Seymour sitting there. He could also visualize Hermione Gingold.

"Oh, well," he mumbled and, opening his eyes, looked to his right . . .

. . . into the eyes of the most exquisite female he had ever seen in his life—in personal experience, in films, in magazines, in paintings, anywhere. This was a face beyond belief. He actually felt his mouth falling open and quickly, embarrassedly, shut it, turning to the front again. This had to be a cruel coincidence, he thought. It was impossible that—

"Good evening, Mr. Barton," she said.

Even her voice was perfect.

Oh, my God, he thought. He felt himself go limp. My *God.* This was part of it? This *Venus?* His heartbeat quickened as he turned back to her. "Hello," he said. He could scarcely hear the sound of his voice.

She was smiling now. She held out an ivory hand—*It does, it looks like ivory,* he thought, incredulous—and he took hold of it. Ivory was not this warm, however. He felt a shiver coming on and fought to contain it, releasing her hand.

"My name is Alexsandra with an *s,*" she said.

He stared at her, genuinely speechless. Alexsandra? Finally, he mumbled, "That's—"

"Early Roman," she said. "Not so common anymore."

"No," he said. He couldn't help drawing in a shuddering breath. *Not too common,* he thought. *Dear God.*

She wasn't a Hitchcock blonde. Her hair was a dark chestnut, her eyes green, her skin the shade of alabaster, her red lips—*Jesus God.* Now the story was complete; the Mysterious Beauty had arrived.

"Am I . . . supposed to—" He couldn't speak. "I mean . . . are you my—?" *Spit it out!* he shouted at his tongue. "Was I sent here to meet you?" he blurted.

Her smile, the twinkle in her eyes, absolutely captivated him. "That's right," she said.

He was about to ask more about her when his spoilsport Cotton Mather-like mind demanded that he ask, "The man in The Blue Swan . . ."

Her expression was suddenly grave. "Yes," she said.

He drew in a quivering breath. "He's dead?"

"Oh, no," she said. "Badly drugged, in hospital; but not dead."

"Thank God," he said, realizing how the incident had been weighing on him. He stared at her for several moments, then added, "Did he—say anything?"

"He regained consciousness for only a few moments," she answered. "Long enough to say he didn't know what had happened to you."

"My God, he'd just been drugged, maybe poisoned, and he was thinking of *me*?" Chris looked astounded.

"You were his assignment," she said.

He wasn't sure it was enough of an explanation for him but clearly it was for her, she said it so matter-of-factly.

"What *did* happen to you?" she asked.

"I panicked and ran," he said. "Lost track of where I was and got lost."

"Ah." She nodded. "But you managed to get back to the hotel."

"With help," he said.

"Help?"

He told her about Mr. Modi's assistance. She only nodded, adding briefly, "Well, if he does call you tomorrow, best say you're busy. I'm sure he's a very nice man but you really can't afford to discuss your situation any further with a stranger."

"What *is* my situation?" he asked, regretting the slightly belligerent tone in his voice unable to restrain it.

"Haven't you been told anything?" she asked in surprise.

"I was told by a CIA man that what's happening to me is not unique."

"That's right. You're not the only scientist or mathematician to be rescued."

"From *what*?" he demanded.

"Probable death," she answered. "They can't afford to have your replacement revealed by you."

"But . . ." Chris looked confused and aggravated. "How can he be my replacement? He doesn't even *look* like me."

"That's true in your case," she said. "And we don't know why. In every other case, the replacement was identical."

Chris groaned. "This makes no sense," he said. "They could have killed me first and then replaced me if that's what they wanted to do."

She nodded. "We know that. But they did what they did so they must have had a reason."

"Why *me*?" he asked.

"You're being modest," she said. "You're fully aware of how important you are to the project."

He opened his mouth to ask her something, then closed it as another question superseded it. "Is there some kind of—reciprocal cooperation between our countries?"

"Of course," she said.

He sighed heavily. "I'm confused," he said.

"Of course you are." She smiled and put her hand on his. "Just remember that the key to it is your work on the project."

Somehow, to hear about the project again cast a pall over his meeting with this lovely woman. He wouldn't have thought that possible a minute ago.

"What's wrong?" she asked. He wasn't very good at veiling his emotions.

"Oh . . ." He shrugged. "All this talk about the project—not to mention my possible death—has taken the . . . well, the romance out of our meeting."

"Romance?" She looked as though she didn't understand what he was saying. "There's nothing remotely romantic about any of this, Mr. Barton."

He sighed again. "I guess there isn't."

He noticed a ring on the finger of her left hand, still lying on his. "Interesting," he said to change the subject.

"Early Roman," she said, an odd tone in her voice. Chris looked at its crest—a lettered square with two winged angels supporting it.

He looked up into her eyes. "Does Veering have anything to do with all this?"

"Who?"

Oh, God. He felt like groaning. "Veering," he said.

"I don't know the name."

"A CIA man told me that he did."

She looked blank.

"Nelson?" he asked. "CIA?"

"You must understand," she told him. "Whatever happened to you before you arrived in England, we know nothing about it. Except for the basic situation, of course."

He started to reply when Alexsandra abruptly looked past him, her features tightening.

"What is it?" he asked.

She looked back at him. "I'm sorry," she said. "I thought I saw someone I knew."

"Someone you aren't crazy about, from the expression on your face," he told her.

She smiled. "No, it was nothing."

"Can we—?" He broke off as the theater lights began to dim. Oh, damn, he thought.

In the darkness, he felt her face draw close to his, smelled her perfume and the sweetness of her breath.

"We'll talk about this during intermission," she whispered.

"All right." He nodded.

"In the meantime—"

"Yes?"

"Be prepared for anything," she told him.

5

It was agony to sit beside her, watching the first act of the play. Well, not exactly watching, he thought. His eyes were facing the stage, but his concentration was on the seat to his right, on Alexsandra.

Was it possible she was as beautiful as he recalled? Already, doubts were creeping in. No woman could be that exquisite. And a *spy* as well? For God's sake, where was the logic? This was Ian Fleming country, not Chris Barton's.

He wanted to reach over and take her hand in his. Impossible, of course. Her tone had been critical when she'd told him there was nothing remotely romantic about all of this.

He closed his eyes. Why were they sitting here anyway? The contact had been made. Surely, the play was irrelevant now. Why didn't they just leave and go somewhere to talk? Why wait for intermission?

Unless . . .

He felt a delicate chill on the nape of his neck. Had she lied to him? *Was* there someone watching them?

Was something bad about to happen again?

He twisted restlessly. It couldn't be. Not again. There'd been too much. He couldn't handle any more. He was suffering from overload.

Chris drew in a deep, tremulous breath and opened his eyes. He wanted to look at her again, verify her beauty, hell, her very presence. But Veering had done a job on him. He wasn't able to look. What if he did and saw, instead of Alexsandra, an old lady with a shopping bag on her lap?

Modi was right. The tissue of reality seemed paper-thin right now. No assessment of reasonable percentages could account for all the things that had occurred to him since he had woken up in his office, planning to drive home and get some sleep. He might turn and see the seat completely empty and be faced with the probability that Alexsandra had been nothing more than a hallucination.

He had to know.

He turned his head. As he did, she turned hers and they exchanged a look. In the light from the stage, she looked more wonderful than ever.

She smiled at him. He hoped he smiled back but wasn't sure he had the presence of mind.

Then he was looking toward the stage again. One thing, at least, was clear.

Alexsandra was real and he was already in love with her.

After the first-act curtain, he quickly turned to look at her again. Before he could say a word, she asked, "Would you buy me an ice cream, Chris?"

A double reaction hit him: her addressing him by his first name, and, in light of everything that was going on, the banality of her request for ice cream. He couldn't help but snort in amusement.

"What?" she asked.

"Nothing." He shook his head. "Where do I—?"

"Downstairs."

"All right." He pushed up. "I'll be right back."

"Good."

He hated to walk away from her. He almost felt as though, in doing so, he'd rend the tissue and she'd be gone from his reality. *Oh, this has been a dandy period of time,* he thought. And would it ever end?

He made his way to the stairs and descended them, edged in toward a table where a woman was selling ice cream in cups. When he reached the table, he bought one and started back for the stairs, wondering what was going to happen after the play. A romantic tryst in her apartment? He doubted that. It wasn't that she wasn't friendly. But romance? It seemed removed from her bailiwick.

What was the next step in this bizarre adventure, then? In spite of his ongoing uneasiness, he was curious to know.

When he returned to the seats, Alexsandra was gone.

Oh, now, don't get started, he ordered his mind. *The lady has gone to the powder room, period.*

He sat with the cup of ice cream in his hand, knowing that his brain would not be satisfied with such an obvious explanation. Not after what had been occurring since . . .

The powder room? Indeed. More likely she had left him. *More* likely she'd been grabbed, abducted. Maybe she'd been murdered. *Shut up!* He tried to still his mind.

More likely she had never existed in the first place.

He groaned. "Come back," he murmured. This could only be resolved by her return.

When she didn't come back, he began to think that it was more Veering-do.

He looked around uneasily. This wasn't Veering. It was the project and the plot against him, whatever it was. *Had* she seen someone she knew and was she meeting with him or her at this very moment?

The question was (and he remembered vividly the look of dismay on her face when she'd glanced past him), was the person dangerous to her?

He looked down at the ice-cream cup. It would melt soon. *Like my self-control,* he thought.

He put the cup on the floor. Now what? he asked himself. Act Two of *The Little Minister*?

"No way," he muttered. If she wasn't back by the curtain, he was out of here.

When the lights began to dim, he stood quickly, moved into the aisle and started for the lobby; he had no intention of getting further involved in Barrie's machinations.

He took the precaution of going downstairs again to ask the

woman at the ice cream table (who was just cleaning up) to check the ladies' lounge and see if Alexsandra (no, sorry, he didn't know her last name) was in there. He knew the answer before the woman came out, gesturing negatively. "Thank you," he murmured and turned back toward the stairs.

As he crossed the lobby, his imagination, intent on mischief, saw multiple threats waiting outside for him: four toughs armed with steel bars; Meehan with an Uzi; Nelson's or Basy's ghost, hovering above the sidewalk; Veering smiling at him wickedly, chortling, "So. We meet again, Dr. Barton."

There was no one waiting outside. He shivered as he stepped into the cold wind. Jesus, what a comedown, he thought. The evening had started off with a meeting with the most exquisite woman he had ever seen. Was it going to end now with a cab ride back to the hotel and an hour or so of telly-viewing before he slept? That wasn't very—

The roar of the engine behind him was so unexpected that he jumped in shock. Twisting around, he saw a Jaguar coupe zoom over to the curb, the squeal of its sliding tires making him wince. The driver on the right leaned over so quickly to fling open the door, he couldn't make out who it was.

Then the figure straightened up and he caught his breath. It was Alexsandra, a look of alarm on her face. "Get in!" she cried.

For a moment, he was frozen, staring at her. Then his head jerked to the right as a movement down the block caught his eye—a long, black car picking up speed, headed straight for the Jaguar. "Get in!" Alexsandra shouted.

Chris lurched toward the car and flung himself inside. Before he had a chance to close the door, the Jaguar was accelerating from the curb, engine howling. "Jesus!" he cried. Reaching out, he grabbed at the handle and pulled the door shut, looking quickly at Alexsandra. Her face was tight with concentration as she slammed the gearshift around its box, clutching rapidly, increasing the Jaguar's speed as quickly as she could. Chris's gaze jumped to the speedometer; the needle was already almost to sixty. Jesus Christ, he thought.

He twisted around to look out through the back window.

"They're behind us," she told him.

He looked back at her. She was still exquisite but the grim expression on her face undid the beauty. She might have been a hardened race-car driver the way she drove, her right hand and feet a blur as she shifted gears with incredible speed, the Jaguar shooting down the street, the sound of its engine like the snarling of a huge cat.

Reaching the end of the block, Alexsandra downshifted suddenly and cornered with amazing skill; he tried to stay erect but found himself unable to as centrifugal force pushed him toward her. "Buckle up," she snapped, startling him with the coldness of her tone. Without a word, he reached across his shoulder for the harness as the Jaguar picked up speed, shooting around a car in its path. He'd never been driven so fast in his life. Another first, he thought numbly, looking across his shoulder again in time to see the headlights of the black car as it sped around the corner, yawed temporarily, then came straight-on once again.

"Who *is* it?" he asked, sounding breathless.

Alexsandra didn't answer. Looking back at her, he saw that she had time only for driving, her lips pressed hard in a red gash, her unblinking eyes focused on the street ahead as the Jaguar bulleted along, steering rapidly around one car after another. *My God, it's Mr. Toad's Wild Ride,* he thought, uncertain as to whether he was turned on or terrified.

Where are the police? he wondered as she downshifted at the next street, cornering with astounding speed again. What kept the car from skidding? he wondered in awe. It was like a crazy dream: the sporadic roar and howl of the engine; the shifting of his body as she needled through the traffic at high speed; the flash of lights in his eyes; her beside him, driving like a madwoman; the car behind them, pursuing. He closed his eyes for several moments. *Is this really happening?*

He swallowed hard; his throat felt parched. "There *was* somebody in the theater then," he tried again.

She didn't answer.

"Alexsandra?" he asked.

"Yes! Yes!" she cried, her sharp tone making him wince. She

muttered something to herself he couldn't really hear; it sounded like, "But *how?*" She floored the gas pedal and the Jaguar shot along an empty stretch, opening its lead over the black car. Chris clutched out at the dashboard for support as she braked and downshifted blurringly, making a right turn at the next corner.

"Won't the police—?" he started.

"*Don't count on it,*" she cut him off. He grimaced, teeth bared, looking at her. In the dashboard glow, he saw how tense she looked and felt a chill envelope him. *My God, she's* terrified, he thought. The realization stunned him.

The black car chasing them was death.

Another corner, a screech of tires; Alexsandra's right hand was slamming at the gearshift, her left foot jarring in and out at the clutch, her right foot flooring the gas pedal again, the Jaguar leaping forward with a maddened engine-howl.

They almost hit a taxi pulling out of an alley; only Alexsandra's instantaneous jerking of the steering wheel prevented it. The taxi driver honked in rage. "Sorry, mate," she muttered.

Chris looked back and saw the taxi jarring to a front-dipping stop as the black car sped around it. *Now he's really pissed,* he thought.

At the next corner, Alexsandra turned right. He saw her look into the rearview mirror and twisted around again. The black car hadn't made the corner yet. Abruptly, she turned left into a narrow alley. Chris hissed involuntarily, positive that she was going to hit the building wall to her right; in fact, he thought he heard the rasping of its fenders on the brick.

He realized then that she had done it calculatedly, knowing that the larger black car would have a hard time making it through the narrow alley. His fingers whitely gripped the dashboard as the Jaguar shot along the alley, the wall on each side seeming no more than a few inches away from the car. Despite this, Alexsandra kept the gas pedal nearly floored. He didn't want to know how fast they were going but his eyes swung frantically to the speedometer anyway. Eighty-two. *Oh, God,* he thought, *we're doomed.* The walls of the dark alley were flying by so fast it was as though they were hurtling through a tunnel.

Then, abruptly, it was over. Reaching the next street, she shrieked into a right turn, and skidded to the left, adjusting with frantic but skilled precision until she had the Jaguar under control again.

Suddenly, she turned to the right again and Chris gasped, thinking she had cracked and was steering into a building. He closed his eyes, hunching his shoulders for the impact, then felt the car sharply nose down and he opened his eyes again. The Jaguar was shooting down an inclined driveway to an underground garage.

Alexsandra braked and made a sharp left turn, then braked again and turned in sharply for the wall.

The car stopped hard, throwing him forward until the harness caught him. Alexsandra's hand snapped forward and in a single movement, switched off the engine and the lights.

They sat in silent blackness, breathing hard. Then both were mutely rigid as, out in the street, they heard the black car speed by, the sound of its motor fading off in moments.

"What—?" he started.

"*Shh,*" she said.

He looked at where she was sitting but couldn't even make out her silhouette, it was so dark. Seconds went by.

"Right," she said then.

Turning on the engine and headlights, she backed up fast, turning; she braked, accelerated to the driveway, then quickly drove up it, slowing to a crawl before she reached the street. She nosed the Jaguar out, eyes searching down the block.

"Right," she said again and throwing the transmission into first, made a fast left turn and accelerated up the block.

"Why are you—?"

"They'll be back to check," she cut him off again.

She turned left at the corner, then right down another alley two blocks down, and pulled into a covered parking slot behind a building, switching off the lights and engine once again. "This should be all right," she said. She drew in a long, rasping breath and held it in, then released it slowly. "*God,*" she said.

"Who was in that car?" he asked, appalled by the thinness of his voice.

"No one you'd want to meet," she said.

"Alexsandra." His voice was stronger now, demanding.

"I don't *know* who they are," she said. "I only know they want you."

He was going to ask *"For what?"* then didn't have to. Clearly, what they wanted was what he had collected in his brainpan.

He made a faint scoffing sound. "Little do they know how jumbled it all is," he said.

"What is?" she asked.

"The contents of my brain; I presume that's what they want," he answered coolly, put off by her distant behavior.

"That's what they want all right," she agreed. "The contents of your brain are certainly in big demand. What in God's name do you *have* in there?"

She cut him off before he could reply. "Never mind, it's not my place to know." She drew in another heavy breath. "The less I know, the better."

They sat in silence for a few moments. Then, trying to ease the tension between them, Chris said, "What *are* you, a race driver?"

She laughed softly. "Just my training," she answered.

"Are you . . . a spy?" he asked.

Another soft laugh. "Too dramatic a description," she told him. "I work for the government."

A government agent, he thought. It *was* that kind of story: Le Carre, Fleming, Follett, et al.

As he pondered, all the tension that had gripped him during the chase suddenly relaxed and he was super-conscious of her by his side: he could smell the delicate aroma of her perfume; see, in his mind's eye, her magnificent face. In spy novels, men and women kissed at moments like this, after emergencies had been dealt with.

"Alexsandra?"

"Yes?" she said.

He leaned over to kiss her.

As he did, she turned to look out the window and he bumped his nose on the back of her head. "*Ow,*" he muttered.

She turned back. "Was that you?" she asked.

He rubbed his nose, feeling like an idiot. Some romantic moment, that.

"You all right?" she asked.

"Yeah, sure."

"What did you do?"

He sighed. "I tried, totally ineptly, to kiss you," he said in disgust.

"Oh." Was that a stifled laugh? No doubt, he thought.

"I'm sorry," she said.

Leaning over, she put a hand on each of his cheeks and planted a gentle kiss on his nose. "There," she said.

"Thanks," he mumbled. He felt absurd.

"I don't think we'd better take you back to your hotel tonight," she said.

He felt his heartbeat catch.

"They may know that's where you're staying."

"Oh. Yes." He exhaled wearily. Goodbye romance again, he thought. Then he recalled. "But the clothes, the passport. The gun."

"The *gun?*" she said, incredulous. "They gave you a *gun?*"

"After what happened tonight, I think I need one."

"Mmm." She didn't sound convinced. "The rest we can replace by morning," she told him.

"The passport too?" he asked, impressed.

"No problem."

"Listen," he said, "do you know anything about the man who vanished from the plane I was on?"

"*Vanished?*" He could tell from her tone that she didn't know.

"Do you know what *seven steps to midnight* means?" he asked.

She repeated the words in a way that told him she didn't know that either.

"My God," he muttered. "All I have is questions. Not a single answer."

"You have the only answer you need right now." Her voice was grave. "Your work is important enough for a lot of people to want to know about it."

"They wouldn't be so curious if they knew how much trouble I've been having with it," he responded.

She patted his arm. "You'll figure it out," she told him.

Then she looked around and made a sound of decision. "We'd best be off again," she said.

6

The Bond-Tellier Hotel looked like a clone of the Park Court. The same portico-type entrance, the same doorman standing in front with the long coat and high hat—did they make them from a mold? The same polite smile and tip of the hat as the doorman said, "Good evening, Miss Claudius."

Claudius? he thought as he went up the steps beside her to the lobby door. *Alexsandra Claudius?* Or was she simply part of the overall nonreality of this experience? Everything seemed suspicious, since Veering. True, she'd done nothing that seemed to contradict her words. It was just the frame of mind he was acquiring. Her name had jarred it into operation once again. He just wasn't sure he could safely trust anyone at present.

Alexsandra (*was* it her name?) nodded at the desk clerk as they crossed the lobby toward the elevators. The lobby walls were fashioned of dark paneling, buffed to a glow. The floor was made of tiling and the furniture was oversize—Victorian-style chairs and sofas.

Chris found himself shaking his head in disbelief. Incredulity was almost a constant state of mind these days. It was virtually impossible for him to assimilate the number of changes in his life that had taken place since he'd found that his car was missing from the parking lot. There was just no way of discovering a pattern to it all—a condition he always found disconcerting since the four words he spoke most often in his life were *"What does it mean?"*

They entered the lift where the operator smiled at Alexsandra and said, "Good evening." *Fancy,* Chris thought; *I had to push buttons at the old Park Court.*

"Claudius, eh?" he murmured, looking at her. In the dimly lit interior, she looked more beautiful than ever.

"That's right." She smiled at him.

He was going to say more, but let it go. If she wasn't what she seemed, there'd be no advantage to indicate suspicion on his part.

They said no more as the lift glided up its cables to the sixth floor. The operator said, "Good night," as did Alexsandra. Then it was just the two of them, walking along a thickly carpeted hallway. The walls were paneled here as well. *Prestige hotel,* he thought.

Alexsandra stopped at a door with 634 on it in brass numerals. Removing a key from her purse, she unlocked and opened the door, reaching inside to switch on an overhead light.

This is a hotel room? he thought, bedazzled, as he entered. A brief glimpse of an almost full-size living room gave him pause. It looked more like a Park Avenue apartment, for Christ's sake. Surely secret agents couldn't afford such accommodations.

"Quite a place," he said.

"If you're wondering how I can afford it, I can't," she told him as though she'd read his mind. "I'm only here while I'm on this assignment."

"I see." He nodded, looking around the foyer as she closed the door.

He saw the painting then, and caught his breath.

It was very old, the paint faded and cracked—a portrait of a Roman noblewoman standing in a courtyard. She was wearing a diaphanous white robe, her dark hair plaited, lying across her left shoulder. She was radiantly lovely.

She was Alexsandra.

"Now, wait a minute," he said. "How can that be?"

She laughed softly. "It isn't me," she said.

"But it *is.*"

"I'll admit the resemblance is striking," she said.

"*Striking?*" he said. "It's *you.*"

"No." She shook her head, smiling.

"And what's it doing in a hotel suite?"

"It doesn't belong to the hotel," she replied. "I have a few personal belongings to make it feel like home while I'm here. This is one of them."

"Where did you get it?"

"A man I used to go with found it in an antique store in Rome and was so struck by the resemblance that he bought it for me."

He stared at the painting, still amazed. "That's your face all right."

"Maybe I'm a descendant or something," she said.

He nodded. "That could be." He rotated his head, grimacing.

"What is it?" she asked.

"Oh . . ." He hated to mention it, it was so goddamn unromantic. *Well, hell,* he thought. "My neck is stiff. Occupational hazard for mathematicians."

"Come inside," she said, taking him by the hand. She led him into the living room and turned on a lamp. He whistled softly, looking around. "You government agents are well taken care of," he said.

"My usual accommodations are far more Spartan," she told him. "It just so happened this was all they had available and my supervisor experienced a moment of highly atypical generosity."

She pointed at a chair. "Sit."

Chris did and she moved behind the chair. He winced, making a sound of pain as her fingers began to knead the back of his neck. "It'll hurt at first," she said.

"That's what my mother says," he responded.

"Does she massage your neck?"

"On those rare occasions when I see her," he answered. He hissed, wincing as her fingers dug in more strongly.

"I'm sorry," she murmured.

"No, no, keep it up," he said. "No pain, no gain."

Alexsandra laughed softly.

"How long have you been here?" Chris asked.

"A few weeks," she said.

He looked confused. "But I've only been in this mess about three days."

"There are several other things I've been working on," she said. "They only put me onto your situation this morning."

"My situation," he muttered. His neck was starting to feel better now and he closed his eyes. "To repeat: What *is* my situation?"

"We're working on it," she answered. "Do you mind telling me a few of the details? I was given precious little information and it would help if I knew something about it."

As the kneading of her strong fingers continued on the back of his neck, then his neck and shoulder joints, Chris gave her a digest version of the mystery: the car, Veering, the couple in his house, Meehan and Nelson, Gene, the airline ticket, the overnight bag in the LAX locker, Basy's disappearance.

"Good Lord, you *have* been put through the wringer, haven't you?" she said when he was finished.

"Somewhat," he agreed. "The question still remaining: *Why?*"

"Well, as I told you," she said, "it's obviously connected to your work. As to why some of those things happened, I have *no* idea. The Veering thing, for instance. It seems . . . well, not a part of it at all."

"But Nelson got angry that I didn't mention Veering and then tried to kill me."

"Curiouser and curiouser," she murmured.

Chris made a sound of pained amusement, remembering his mother had said that. "Exactly what I thought," he told her. He momentarily wondered why he'd told her so much. If he didn't think he could trust her . . .

Well, obviously, he *did* trust her for whatever reason—her reassuring personality, her alluring appearance or his own emotional vulnerability. He was so alone and harassed that falling in love, especially with so beautiful a woman, was practically *de rigueur*.

He started involuntarily as her fingers were removed from his neck. "What?" he muttered, opening his eyes.

"I have to call my supervisor," she told him. "Let him know what happened tonight. Please excuse me."

He looked around, wincing as he felt it in his neck. Standing, he turned to see her walking toward the bedroom doorway. She glanced back and smiled at him. "I'll only be a few moments," she said.

She went inside the bedroom and closed the door. *Should that bother me?* he wondered. Now he'd have no idea what she was going to tell her supervisor, or indeed, if she was going to call her supervisor in the first place, or if she even *had* a supervisor.

"Oh, come on," he muttered, frowning at himself. He had to trust *someone* or he'd lose his mind. He needed an anchor. Without one, he'd be all at sea.

He ambled around the room, looking at the refined and expensive furnishings, looking out the window at the glittering vista of London (*London, for God's sake!*), then, finally, walking back into the foyer to gaze once more at the painting.

The portrait threw him off again. It wasn't just a resemblance. He could swear that Alexsandra had posed for the painting.

He shook it off. That is patently impossible, he told himself. How many times had he looked at a photograph taken in the 1800s and thought *That looks exactly like . . .* whoever the photograph resembled.

Why should this be different?

Because, he realized, he was in an agitated state of mind, involved in an ongoing mystery. No wonder his imagination was making this portrait a part of that mystery.

He turned away and went back into the living room. Problem solved, he thought.

Unless, his brain needled, Alexsandra did not come out of the bedroom. Unless he'd go in there presently and find nothing but an untenanted room; unless, like Basy, she'd have disappeared and he'd be back in the nightmare again.

He was getting ready to enter the bedroom, nerves steeled for the worst, when Alexsandra came out.

She'd removed her coat and jacket and he now noticed the thrust of her breasts against the pale beige sweater she was wearing. *It's too much,* said his mind. He couldn't prevent an expression of antic disbelief.

"What is it?" she asked with a tentative smile.

"Oh . . ." He didn't know exactly how to put it. Then he plunged in. *Why not?* he thought. "It all seems so insane," he told her. "Like a Hitchcock movie."

"Does it?" Her smile was no longer tentative.

"*Does* it!" He shook his head. "The dull mathematician finds himself suddenly embroiled in an international conspiracy of some kind? Suddenly, from an Arizona tract house, he finds himself in a gorgeous London flat with an even more gorgeous government agent who has just eluded God-knows-who in a high-speed car chase? Yes, my dear. That is your standard suspense plot . . ." He couldn't finish for chuckling.

She smiled at him, then repressed the smile into a look of mock distress. "I'm sorry you think it's standard," she said.

Now, he thought. *Now is the moment.* He should walk over to her, put his arms around her, kiss her hard.

"Are you hungry?" Alexsandra asked.

Shit, he thought.

He got a look of surprise on his face, then said, "My God, I *am,*" he said.

"Come in the kitchen then," she said, turning away.

"I'm following," he said.

"And thank you for calling me gorgeous," she said across her shoulder.

"What else could anyone call you?" he asked.

"Thank you," she responded.

"You *do* see that this whole thing smacks of exotic fiction," he said.

Her sigh was not a happy one. "Would that it were," she said, the tone in her voice making him shiver unexpectedly. He remembered then that Gene was dead, Nelson too, in all likelihood, Basy probably. It certainly took the exotic edge off the situation.

The kitchen was small but well appointed. Alexsandra gestured toward a chair and Chris sat down, looking at her as she crossed to the refrigerator and opened it. *She moves gracefully too,* he thought. Was there *nothing* wrong with her? How could any female be so perfect?

"How about some caviar and finely chopped onions and eggs on biscuits?" she asked. "Some chilled white wine?"

He laughed aloud. "Is that how spies eat over here?"

She smiled as she took the plates from the refrigerator. "I'm not a spy," she said. "And, actually, this is here compliments of the hotel."

"Remind me to stay here next time I'm involved in an enigma," he said.

She kept smiling as she took the wine from the refrigerator and set it on the table with the plates of caviar and chopped egg and onion. She got a box of biscuits, a plate, knife and a crystal wine glass and set them down in front of him. "There."

"Nothing for you?" he asked.

"I ate just before we met at the theater," she told him. "However . . ." She got a second wine glass for herself and sat across from him at the table.

Chris picked up the bottle, pulled out the cork (a little of the wine had already been drunk), and poured some in her glass, then his. Putting down the bottle, he picked up his glass and held it out to her in a toast. "To the one enjoyable feature of this highly unenjoyable experience," he said.

She clinked her glass against his and they each took a sip of the pale white wine.

"Good," he said. "Dijon LaFitte Chardonnay, 1973."

"Are you—?" She glanced at the bottle.

"Showing off," he finished. "I read it on the label as I poured."

They exchanged a smile, then she gestured at the plates. "Eat," she said.

He nodded and spread some caviar and chopped eggs and onions on a biscuit. *Caviar and wine in London with a goddess,* he thought. It really was difficult to comprehend.

He took a bite of the biscuit and spread. "Mmm," he said. "Delicious." He hadn't realized how hungry he was. "Tell me something," he said.

"Surely."

"Why the blue cassette box? *The Carnival of the Animals?*"

"I beg your pardon?"

"You don't know about it?" he asked.

"I'm afraid not." She looked perplexed.

He told her about waking up to find the cassette player and the blue cassette box. How he finally came to realize that he was supposed to go to The Blue Swan.

"Then that man in the pub—" he continued.

"Williams," she told him.

"Uh-huh. He told me *Crown over H* and I had to figure that out, too. Wouldn't it have been a lot simpler to just put a note under the door of my hotel room telling me there was a ticket waiting for me at the Theatre Royal Haymarket?"

"Undoubtedly," she said, laughing. "My supervisor *does* move in mysterious ways now and then."

"Williams said that 'Number One' relishes these little mysteries."

"He does." She shook her head with a smile. "I imagine he gets fed up with the stupefying boredom of what we typically do. So, when he gets a chance to have a little fun . . ."

"Fun?" He wasn't sure of that.

"For *him*," she said. "Especially with a Yank."

Chris grunted. *Must be a weird guy,* he thought. He finished the biscuit and took a sip of wine, then spread caviar on another biscuit.

"What's his name?" he asked.

"My supervisor? Mr. Raymond. That's what we call him anyway. It might not be his real name."

"You live with enigmas, too," he said, taking a bite of the second biscuit.

"Indeed." She looked a bit discomfited. "Such as what I'm going to do with you tomorrow."

He felt a tremor of uneasiness at that. "What do you mean?" he asked.

"Well, obviously, you can't go back to your hotel. I don't think Mr. Raymond will want you to stay here. We'll have to find a place."

"Uh . . ." He.didn't know how to put it. "Is there a . . . plan? I mean—why am I in England? Am I staying here?"

"That remains to be seen," she answered. "As to why you're here—for protection, of course. Until this conspiracy or whatever it is is sorted out." She clucked. "Whatever you do, it must be bloody important."

He sighed. "I never thought it was." He gestured vaguely. "Well, that's not exactly true. I guess space defense is important."

"You don't have to tell me anything," she cautioned. "It's none of my business."

"I know," he said. "I'm not about to give you formulas."

"No, don't," she said. "The less I know, the less anyone can find out from me."

That sounded ominous, he thought. He looked at her gravely. "I wouldn't want to put you in any danger," he said.

"You won't," she assured him.

He decided that he'd better tell her nothing. It probably wouldn't make sense to her anyway.

"Does it bother you to work in a field where—people get killed?" he asked uneasily.

"Well, of course it bothers me," she replied. "It really doesn't happen all that often though. What's going on with you is rather more advanced, as these things go."

He nodded. That didn't make him feel particularly good. He ate a third biscuit spread with caviar, chopped egg and onion, and washed it down with the chilled white wine. As he did, he looked across the table at Alexsandra. What was going to happen now? he wondered. In James Bond novels, bed always followed peril. *Didn't* it?

Somehow, he didn't think it would tonight.

He was unable to repress a sudden yawn. "Oh, dear," he said.

"Tired?"

"I shouldn't be," he said. "I took a nap earlier today and I'm not used to getting that much sleep."

"Don't forget jet lag," she told him.

"Oh, that's right." He yawned again. "I'm sorry," he said.

"Why don't you lie down on the sofa for a while," she suggested.

He thought about it momentarily. "Good idea," he said then.

"Had enough to eat?" she asked.

He nodded. "I think so. Thank you."

They got up and walked into the living room and Chris sat down on the sofa. "Lie down," she said.

"Okay." He took off his shoes and stretched out. "Here," she said, putting a pillow under his head.

"Thank you," he said. He took her hand impulsively. "Thank you for saving my life, too," he told her.

She smiled. "It may not have been all that dramatic," she said, "but you're welcome."

Again on impulse, he kissed the back of her hand. "Could you sit beside me for a while?" he asked, amazed at his own temerity. He'd never have been able to do such a thing at home. Maybe it was the unreality of it all.

"All right," she said. "Ease over a little."

He moved in against the sofa back, then turned half onto his left side and pressed against the back to give her room. Alexsandra sat beside him, smiling down at him. He groaned as he yawned again. "It's not the company, I promise you," he said.

He studied her face for a few moments, then said, "You *are* exquisite, you know."

She smiled, not replying. Then she leaned over and kissed him lightly. The soft warmth of her lips made him draw in a sudden breath.

She sat up again, looking at him with a faint smile.

"Alexsandra," he said.

"Yes?"

"Would you do it again?"

She made a soft sound of amusement, then leaned over again and kissed him a little more firmly. He felt the yielding pressure of her left breast against his side as she did. He put his arms around her and she pressed her cheek next to his. "Oh, God," he said.

"You sound so unhappy," she said.

"I am," he responded. "To be with you like this and be as sleepy as I am is pure hell."

Alexsandra drew away from him and he released her. She smiled down at him. His eyelids were getting heavier now.

"I want to know about you," he murmured, "where you were born, what schools you went to, how you got into government work, if you feel toward me one one-hundredth of the way I feel toward you."

She stroked his cheek gently and he felt her ring on his skin. Just before he slipped away, it came to him.

The woman in the painting was wearing the same ring.

7

So many times, in dreams, he had been conscious of the fact that he was dreaming. The more bizarre the dreams, the more his mind had thought, in essence, *Well, it doesn't matter anyway, I know this is a dream.*

This dream was different.

He was in Rome; not today's Rome, but Rome of the Caesars. He felt as though he had literally time-traveled there; he kept thinking to himself *I'm actually here.*

How long it went on, he wasn't sure. He wished that he could film it or, at the very least, take notes.

He tried to tell some people he met how remarkable this was for him but they replied in Latin. *Did they really speak it conversationally?* he thought in amazement.

He saw men in chariots riding by. Women in robes. Children playing. Soldiers.

And the buildings! They were marvelous, white marble with graceful columns. He saw Roman numerals on them; construction dates he supposed, or dedication dates.

Then he was in a less populated street. It was lined with pine trees; *The Pines of Rome,* he thought. He was moving toward a house. Opening a gate and entering a courtyard.

The woman was on the other side of it, standing by a sparkling fountain.

It's her, he thought.

He moved across the courtyard. Except for the splashing of water in the fountain, there was no sound. *It is her,* he told himself. He recognized the robe, the hair arrangement. And there was a ring on her finger he felt sure was the ring he'd seen.

But how can she be here? he thought. *Unless,* his mind explained, *this is another Alexsandra.* An ancient relative. A former life. *No, that's ridiculous,* he thought. *I don't believe in that.*

He reached her and put his hand on her shoulder. She turned.

"I'm glad you've come," she said.

"It *is* you." He gazed at her beautiful face. "Alexsandra."

He put his arms around her and felt her arms embrace him. Her body was warm against his; he could feel the soft pressure of her breasts against his chest.

"I love you," he said.

"And I love you," she whispered. "You are mine at last."

He began to wonder what she meant by that but then they were kissing and he couldn't think. He felt her warm lips moving under his, the tightness of her embrace.

Then her cheek was pressed to his. "I mustn't lose you again," she whispered breathlessly. "Say that you—"

She stopped and, suddenly, she was cold and lifeless in his arms.

He drew back to look at her.

And cried out, horrified.

He was holding a corpse in his arms. Her face was white, her eyes staring sightlessly. Her body weighed down his arms.

"No," he muttered.

He felt a wave of horror rushing over him as she began to moult before his eyes, her features turning gray, skin crumpling, cheekbones showing through as flesh decayed and slipped from them.

With a scream, he flung her away and, turning, ran toward what appeared to be a tunnel. *I won't look back,* he told himself. Terror-stricken, he hurled himself into the tunnel and ran along it. It smelled damp and fetid. *Get me out of here!* he thought.

He turned a corner, staggering to a halt.

There were four slabs lying just in front of him.

On each was a body.

He wanted to turn and retreat. But he knew that Alexsandra's corpse was that way and he couldn't bear the thought of seeing it again.

If he could edge past the slabs, not look at the bodies.

He pressed his back against the cold, wet wall and began to shift along it, trying to keep his eyes from the bodies. He couldn't though. He felt compelled to look.

The first body, naked, was Gene's. His flesh was bluish purple, his eyes staring. "Oh, God," Chris murmured.

The next body was Nelson's; he was naked too. There was a jagged, blood-rimmed hole in his stomach. Chris clenched his teeth, shuddering. *This has to be a dream,* his mind insisted. But he couldn't make himself believe it this time.

The next body was that of Basy. He was naked, his eyes closed, his face white. *This is where you went,* Chris thought. He looked at the last body.

And froze in place.

It was Veering.

He wasn't naked but was wearing the outfit he'd had on when Chris picked him up on the highway—even the baseball cap on his head.

Is it really him? the question came. Look. Make certain.

He edged closer to the slab and leaned over. The light here wasn't clear. He had to make sure—

He gasped, choking, as Veering's right hand shot up, grabbing at his jacket. Veering's eyes popped open, and the old man leered at him, a toothy grin drawing back his lips. "We meet again," he said.

Chris couldn't speak. He could scarcely breathe. He tried to pull away from Veering but didn't have the strength. He stared down at the grinning old man.

"*Are you enjoying the wager?*" Veering asked.

Chris could only utter sounds of dread as he tried to pull free.

Veering's face grew hard. "You aren't going to get away," he snarled. "Face it, Barton. That's the way things are. You may as well accept it."

He jerked Chris down until their faces were no more than several inches apart.

"Now listen to me," Veering said. "Time is running out. You hear? Reality is dissipating for you. You have one chance to survive and one chance only. *Use your mind.* You hear?!" he shouted in Chris's face. "*Think or die!*"

Darkness seemed to rush up at Chris like an ocean wave. It broke across him, swallowing him, pulling him down and down. He thought he heard himself screaming as he tumbled head over heels in blackness, unable to breathe.

🜚 He jolted awake. *I'm screaming!* he thought.

He looked around in panic. He was still in Alexsandra's living room. And he wasn't screaming. The shrill sound had focused itself into the ringing of a telephone.

He rubbed his eyes, trying to alert his mind. *Jesus, what a dream,* he thought.

The phone kept ringing. He looked around groggily. *Why doesn't she answer it?* he wondered.

"Alexsandra?!" He tried to call out but his throat was dry. The crusty sound that emerged was more like a wheezing gargle.

Maybe she's gone out, his brain provided.

Thanks for waking up, he thought. He sat up and looked at the telephone on the table next to the sofa. *Well, for Christ's sake, why don't you give up?* he sent a mental message to the caller.

Not received, he finally realized. And obviously Alexsandra was out. What should he do? Answer it? It might get him into even more trouble.

He stared at the ringing telephone. Was it possible that she would be calling him?

He grimaced at the continued ringing. *Stop. Enough!* he thought and, reaching out, snatched up the handset. He didn't speak but held it to his ear.

A man's voice, pleasantly polite, said, "Your limousine is here, Mr. Barton."

He stared at the receiver as though it were an artifact from Mars. Then he spoke into the mouthpiece. "What?"

"Your limousine is here."

My limousine. Chris felt half-uneasy, half-amused. More insanity.

"Thank you," he told the man and put the handset down on its base.

"Your limousine is here," he muttered. Jesus Christ, *now what?* Had she sent it to have him taken to a safe place?

"Alexsandra?" he called out again.

No answer. If she was here, she wasn't speaking to him.

Well, obviously she wasn't here. He picked up the handset again.

"Front desk," said the man.

"This is Mr. —" He broke off, then said, "This is room 634. *Suite 634.*"

"Yes, sir?"

"Did you just call me to tell me that a limousine is here?"

"Yes, I did, sir."

"Did Miss Claudius order it?"

"Who, Sir?"

"Miss Alexsandra Claudius," he said. "The woman living in this suite."

The man's silence was like a cold blade being pushed into his stomach. *Don't say it,* he thought pleadingly.

"I'm sorry, sir. I don't quite understand," the man said.

Chris forced a calmness to his voice he didn't feel.

"Listen," he said, "I was brought here last night by a young woman named Alexsandra Claudius. The desk clerk knew her. She had a key to this suite. She said she'd been here for a few weeks. Are you telling me there's no one by that name here?"

"I . . . only have your signature on the register, sir."

Don't crack, Chris thought. "Who paid the bill?" he asked.

"You did, sir, with cash."

"I see. Thank you." Chris put down the handset and sat staring across the room.

Is this what going insane feels like? he wondered. He seemed to recall thinking that before.

The wager, he thought. There seemed no escaping it. The tissue of reality was tearing again.

He sat in silence, trying not to think. Thinking was getting him nowhere. Every time he came up with one answer, two more questions appeared.

He twitched as the telephone rang again. Turning his head, he looked at it. Now what?

He sighed defeatedly. Whoever was behind this, they were wearing him down. He picked up the handset. "Yes?" he asked.

"Will you be coming down for your limousine, sir?"

Chris's voice was expressionless as he answered, "Sure. Why not?"

He hung up and stood. Walking into the bedroom, he checked the closets and bureaus.

All empty.

"What else?" he muttered.

He started back for the living room, then stopped midstride. *Now wait a minute*, he thought angrily. *No one's going to tell me I was not in here last night with Alexsandra. Do they think I'm a moron? She was in the theater, she drove me in a high-speed chase, she drank some wine with me and—*

The thought broke off as he moved into the living room, toward the kitchen.

The crackers, caviar, chopped eggs and onions were still on the table. The bottle of white wine.

And one glass.

He turned away and closed his eyes. *I will not believe this*, he told the unknown. *You cannot make me believe this. I know this woman exists.* For God's sake, he still had the tactile memory of her kiss!

"All right, all right," he muttered. What was the alternative to what he remembered?

He had come to this hotel on his own. Signed the register, paid in cash and had come up to this suite. Eaten alone in the kitchen, then had fallen asleep on the sofa because he had to rise this morning to be picked up by a limousine.

"Bullshit!" he shouted.

"Let's get out of here," he said. "The limo waits without." His voice assumed a burlesque comic's nasal twang as he added, "Without what?" tipping the ash from an invisible cigar.

He washed off his face in the bathroom, combed his hair, then went into the living room, got his jacket and started for the foyer. *What about my overnight bag?* he thought. *My clothes, my passport, my medication, my pistol?* He sighed heavily. *God will provide,* he told himself.

He stopped at the foyer door, hesitated, then turned around.

It was hardly a surprise to see another painting on the wall.

Okay, he thought, amazed at how calm he felt. *Someone's playing pranks on me. Why? Who know? Except to rattle me, of course.* Well, they weren't going to rattle him.

He left the suite and started along the corridor, thinking about his dream. Where did that fit in to all this? Or did it fit in? Did anything fit in? Or was he running barefoot over a gigantic jigsaw puzzle in which none of the pieces fit together?

"Fuck it," he muttered. He could only resist so long. He had to go along with this mystery, impenetrable though it was and might always prove to be . . .

"No!" he snapped. *Just give me time,* he thought. He'd figure it out. He always figured out problems. *"Think or die,"* Veering had told him in his dream. All right, goddamn it, he *would.* But not right now. In time, in time. Right now he'd better drift with the current. Later on, he'd swim to shore.

The only thing he really needed at the moment was his medication.

✸ Crossing the lobby, he glanced at the desk clerk to see if there was any furtive avoidance of eye contact.

The man was busy signing up a guest.

He'd thought, on the lift-ride down, of storming to the desk and ranting about Alexsandra, the night clerk, the door key, etc. He'd given up the idea before reaching the lobby. A scheme this carefully fabricated wouldn't likely fall before a few shouted accusations.

As he left the hotel and saw the black limousine parked by the curb, he had a perverse inclination to ignore it and walk down the street. What would the driver do? Follow him? Call his boss for instructions?

He stopped on the bottom step of the hotel and looked around, taking in a deep breath of the cold air. Make him wait, he thought, really foul him up by going back into the hotel for breakfast.

No. He had to go along with this. He'd never find out what was going on if he tried to solve it all by himself.

The driver was wearing a uniform, standing by the back door, waiting. *Still life with limo,* Chris thought. *I don't move, he doesn't move.*

Sighing, he went down the last step and headed for the car. The driver opened the door for him. "Good morning, sir," he said.

Yeah, yeah, Chris thought. *Now you'll tell me you're my Uncle Charlie.*

Bending over, he stepped into the large back area of the limousine and sat down on the leather seat, wincing at its coldness. *The least you could do is warm the goddamn seat,* he thought. *I'm not accustomed to such shoddy treatment.*

He grinned to himself as the driver, having closed the door, circled the limo and slipped behind the steering wheel. *Home, James,* Chris had an urge to tell him.

Then he saw the basket on the floor and picked it up, setting it down beside him on the seat. He raised its cover.

God, he thought.

A thermos jug, no doubt filled with hot coffee. A cup and plate and silver knife. A package of small croissants (still warm), two pats of wrapped butter and a tiny jar of strawberry jam. A most accommodating nightmare, he thought.

He looked up as the engine started and the driver pulled away from the curb. Should he inquire where they were going? No, the hell with it. "Surprise me," he mumbled. The driver wouldn't have told him anyway.

As he breakfasted on warm croissants spread with butter and strawberry jam, washed down with hot coffee, he noticed the small suitcase on the floor. A bomb? he thought. Feed him breakfast, then blow him to bits? One less mathematician to worry about.

He looked at the suitcase as he ate and drank. Assuming that it wasn't a replacement of the things he'd had in the overnight bag, what could it be? He didn't think it was a bomb. Basy's head perhaps? Too gross. A computer? Pads and pencils? A disassembled rifle for assassination? A dwarf who'd leap out at him, wrestle him from the car and drag him down a manhole where they'd descend together to the fairy kingdom?

"Yeah, that must be it," he said. It made the most sense.

Groaning softly, he continued to eat, thinking about Alexsandra's ring. There were two possibilities. Her friend had found not only the painting but the ring from the painting in the Rome antique store. Which, odds-wise, came out somewhere in the neighborhood of several million to one.

It was the same ring though; he felt sure of that. Or had Alexsandra inherited it? Was that her great-great (God knew how far back it might get) grandmother? What were the odds of her friend finding a painting like that? About several million to one, again.

Which meant, of course, that in some bizarre way, Alexsandra *was* that woman.

"Come *on*," he muttered irritably. This was *thinking?* He almost wished he had some paper and pencils so he could immerse his thoroughly muddled brain in something simple like a large distortion equation. This kind of thinking wasn't getting him anywhere.

He finished eating, put the cup, plate, knife, paper and jar back into the basket and set it on the floor. *That was good,* he thought.

He picked up the suitcase, undid the clasp and opened it.

At least something was consistent here. He looked at the contents, nodding. Clothes, again of the finest quality. A toilet case. No gun.

And medication. "Ah," he said. A *most* accommodating nightmare.

As he took his tab and pill (a small bar across from him provided water to wash them down with), it occurred to him that, actually, except for Veering and what seemed to be his effects, the situation was not impossible to decipher. His work was important to the space defense program; he accepted that now. Some conspiracy was trying to damage his work in that program and he was being protected from it.

It was the mixture of that understandable conspiracy with Veering's wager that disturbed him. It was impossible to see how there could possibly be a connection between them. If only Nelson hadn't mentioned Veering, indicating that there *was* a connection.

He realized suddenly that he had made a bad assumption back at the hotel. Opening closets and bureau drawers in the bedroom, he had assumed that all of Alexsandra's clothes had been removed. It was just as logical to assume that they had never been there in the first place.

Simple enough, then, to remove evidence of her having been in the suite. Take down the painting, wash the wine glass. *Voilà.* No Alexsandra.

He looked around abruptly. He hadn't noticed before where they were headed. Now it was evident.

Out of the city.

Chris grimaced. *So much for my visit to Merry Olde London,* he thought. He shook his head. *Guess I won't be having lunch with Mr. Modi,* he thought. He tried to find amusement in that but had some difficulty doing so, considering that he had no idea where he was being taken.

8

Suddenly, the limousine began to pick up speed, accelerating rapidly. Chris started to ask the driver why, then realized that he could not communicate with the man; a glass partition was separating them. He looked around for a speaker he could use.

There wasn't any.

"Well, for Christ's sake—" He began to lean forward to rap on the window when he saw the driver glancing quickly at the rearview mirror.

Twisting around, Chris looked out through the back window. They were being followed by a black sedan.

There was no question that the sedan was following, because the faster the limousine went, the more the sedan picked up speed.

He was being chased again.

At first he couldn't think, he felt so dumbfounded. *Who's after me now? The same people as last night?*

The limousine skidded slightly as it made a curve at high speed. Chris fell to his left, then pushed himself up quickly. He looked at the driver and felt a sudden chill as he saw the man speaking into a hand microphone. He couldn't see the driver's face or hear his voice but his impression was that the man's demeanor was one of total urgency. He saw the man toss aside the microphone and grab the steering wheel with both hands again. The limousine surged forward, raking around a curve with a squeal of tires.

Chris grabbed on to a strap and held himself tightly, sucked in a rasping breath of air. He looked across his shoulder and saw the black sedan still following, a little farther back now but coming on fast. *Dear God,* he thought. *What if they catch us? What will they do to me?*

He cried out, stunned, as something cracked against the back window, grazing it. *Jesus God, they're* shooting *at us!* he thought in horror. He could see that the window was bulletproof but flung himself to the left as another loud crack hit the glass. *God,* he thought, *you could read about something like this a thousand times and never be prepared for the terrifying impact of it actually happening.*

He clung to the seat with clawing hands, his face a mask of dread. *It's real,* he thought. It was all his brain could summon. *Jesus God, it's* real.

Even holding on, he was unprepared for the sharp right turn the driver made and, losing his grip, tumbled sideways. Rolling, he collided with the door, gasping in pain, then scrambled to his knees. What was happening *now?*

He gasped again as the limousine skidded to a halt. Rising in frightened shock, he looked at the driver, then across his right shoulder as the limousine backed up suddenly, pulling behind a high hedge. Chris was flung back as the driver braked hard. He bumped his side against the seat, crying out in startled alarm.

Twisting around, he saw the driver looking toward his left. Chris shuddered as the man abruptly raised what looked like a .45 automatic, as though preparing to fire. "*Jesus,*" Chris muttered. He was back in the nightmare again.

Now he looked in the same direction, hearing the roar of the sedan's engine as it sped by. Almost instantly, the sound was gone.

His gaze jumped to the driver as the man pushed out and lunged to the back door, jerking it open. "*Out,*" he said.

Chris stared at him dumbly.

"Come on!" the driver snarled.

Reaching in, he grabbed Chris by the arm and yanked him toward the opening. "Look out!" Chris cried.

The man paid no attention, dragging Chris from the limousine, then hauling him to his feet; the man looked afraid and furious at once. Letting go of Chris, he leaned into the limousine and jerked out the suitcase. Tossing it on the ground, he reached inside his jacket and pulled out a white envelope.

He held it out to Chris, then, when Chris could only stare at him, flung the envelope on top of the suitcase.

"What am I—?" Chris started.

"*Stay here till you know they're gone,*" the driver interrupted. Slamming shut the rear door of the limousine, he lunged toward the front.

"What am I supposed to—?!" Chris broke off, stunned as the driver threw himself behind the steering wheel, slammed the door shut and pulled out past the hedge and back onto the road, turning in the opposite direction from the way he'd been driving. Chris heard the big car roar away, accelerating quickly.

"God Almighty." Chris stood motionless, unable to think. He felt bruised all over from being flung around in the back of the limo.

Now what? The man said stay here till—

He stiffened, catching his breath as he heard the sound of a car coming. He looked toward the hedge and, in a few moments, saw a dark blur speeding by. Obviously, the driver of the black sedan knew that he'd been tricked and had doubled back. If he caught the limousine now, it would only be the driver who got taken. He now knew why the man had left him behind.

Chris looked down at the envelope then; it was still on top of the suitcase. Bending over, he picked it up and tore it open at one end, slipping out what was inside.

A one-way ticket for the Hovercraft at Dover. Time: Four o'clock this afternoon.

Destination: Calais, France.

❧ The Hovercraft waiting room was huge and high-ceilinged; voices of waiting passengers rang out echoingly in the large open area. The jarring sounds made Chris wince as he entered, closing the small umbrella he'd found in the suitcase.

Far across the waiting room, he saw a food counter and some

tables and chairs. His stomach rumbled; he hadn't had a thing to eat since his modest breakfast in the limousine. *Meals are certainly erratic on this adventure,* he thought. He scowled. "Adventure?" he muttered.

He shrugged. Well, it was as much of an adventure as he could expect in his lifetime. He just hoped he'd see the end of it alive. If he did, he'd certainly be happy to confine all future adventures to the novels on his bedside table.

After a short hesitation, he set the suitcase and umbrella by an empty table. He'd have to assume that the suitcase would be safe; he couldn't very well carry it and a tray of food at the same time.

As he stood in line, he wondered what would happen if the suitcase was snatched. Would they replace it again? He felt a perverse desire to deliberately lose it just to find out what would happen. The thought of aggravating "them" was vaguely satisfying. Granted, they were watching over him. Still, the hush-hush insanity of it all irritated him.

Reaching the counter, he bought some scrambled eggs, white bread and coffee. He carried the tray to the table and sat down. The suitcase was still there: *Wonder of wonders,* he thought. He took a sip of coffee, making a face. *Yow,* he thought. *That'll keep me awake for a while. Like a year.*

As he ate, he reviewed his trip here.

He'd had to walk a long way, constantly on the lookout for the possibility of the black sedan coming back, before the truck had stopped to give him a ride. Fortunately, it had not begun to rain until he was riding.

At one point, as the lorry neared Dover, a helicopter had flashed by overhead. *God, they're chasing me by air now,* he'd thought, actually believing it until it struck him how absurd the notion was.

Almost as absurd as his suspicion of the lorry driver had been, once the man had begun to question him about his work. It took him a good half-hour before he discarded the paranoiac fancy and spoke openly with the man, joking and laughing with him.

He started to think about Alexsandra. Would he ever see her again? It seemed unlikely, if he was going to France. Where would it all end? Who was going to meet him in Calais and where were they going to take him next? To some mountain eyrie in Switzerland where all the "replaced" mathematicians were sequestered to work on their individual projects? Now there was a really absurd notion.

Alexsandra, he thought. He visualized her face as best he could, trying to remember how she'd felt last night, her soft lips, her body against his, as they kissed. Was it really possible he'd never see her again? Was last night to be a single, isolated, golden page in his book of memories? The idea made him feel a sense of gloom as he ate eggs and bread and washed it down with the bitter coffee.

He had to force the idea out of his head; he didn't want to think about it. Instead, he tried to summate what he'd been through. It was a need his mind had, to encapsulate all prior information.

One. Someone wanted to interfere with his work. They had tried to replace him. Now they were chasing him. To kidnap or kill him? No way of knowing.

Two. Someone was protecting him. They'd taken him from the United States. Now he was going to France. And then? No way of knowing.

Three. Veering's wager was a part of it; how, he had no idea. It was the wild card in the hand he'd been dealt. He had to hold it with no way of knowing its value.

He took out the Hovercraft ticket and examined it. The reservation was attached to it. He'd noticed people lined up at a reservation window. His had already been made, for the four o'clock sail—or was it flight?

What would "they" have done if he hadn't made it on time? *Had* the lorry driver been one of them, dispatched to pick him up after the emergency call from the limousine driver? Again, that seemed farfetched. They weren't omnipotent, surely, couldn't be. They couldn't readjust for every unexpected incident, every single failure in their game plan. No, if he'd missed this sail (flight?) he'd have had to try and take the next one.

Or what? he wondered.

What would "they" do if he refused to play the game? If he went to the nearest hotel, booked a room and stayed there for a week, or so, reading? Would they find out he'd done it? Sneak into his room by night, chloroform him and pack him off to France anyway?

Shit, he thought. If he tried to calculate probability factors on what might happen, he'd need a computer.

Anyway, he had to go on. He vividly remembered the utter dread he'd experienced in the limousine when the black sedan was chasing them. He had no intention of booking a room and waiting. If "they" could find him, so could the others. He shuddered at the image of waking up in the dead of night and peering down the barrel of a pistol, just before the explosion sent a bullet into his brain.

He heard a noise outside the building and, draining his coffee cup, stood with the suitcase and walked to a window.

He was impressed. He'd seen photographs of Hovercrafts, but viewed up close, the craft made a startling sight. It looked like a rectangular building, constructed on a black foundation. On its roof were four immense propeller units painted red.

It was literally floating in off the water, jets of air bearing it slowly across the concrete landing pad—*if that's what it's called,* he thought. How could those same jets elevate it off the water? It seemed impossible.

Passengers were already clustering around the entrance doors. Chris slowly edged in among them. In spite of his apprehension, he felt a renewed sense of excitement at what was happening. The next stage of his journey (all right, hell, *adventure* then) was about to begin.

He visualized meeting Alexsandra again. Paris—surely he *had* to go to Paris. A surge of violin music. The sight of her approaching. Running toward one another like a couple in a TV commercial. The wind blowing through her hair. Coming together. Their great embrace, their lingering kiss.

Sure, thirty days. Next case, he mocked himself. She was an agent. She'd done her job. The assignment was over. She was on to something else. He'd never see her again.

"Oh, shut up," he muttered to his cynical brain. A woman next to him glanced over, eyebrows raised. He started to apologize, then let it go.

Reaching the gate, he went outside and started across the windswept tarmac, toward the Hovercraft. It looked really huge now, like some vehicle from outer space. It was difficult to comprehend how such a giant structure could float over water. But then he still found it hard to believe that a 747 could get off the ground, even knowing the science of it.

He followed the line of passengers up a flight of steps, ascending slowly, yawning as he did. His eyelids felt a little heavy. No surprise there. He'd done a lot of walking today, not to mention the ongoing stress, continuing jet lag and many months of non-rest. Even black bilious coffee wasn't strong enough to resist all that.

The cabin resembled that of an airliner except that the windows were rectangular and curtained in white. There were three seats on either side of the aisle, each outer seat with a yellow pad drawn down over its back, the middle seat with a white pad.

Chris stopped at a row about halfway down the cabin. The interior was so spacious that the crowd of passengers had thinned out; there was no one in the rows in front of or behind him.

Chris slid his suitcase into the overhead rack and sat in the window seat. His eyelids felt heavier now. He doubted if even the glaring overhead fluorescent light fixtures would keep him awake. Too bad, he thought. He'd enjoy watching the channel-crossing. Twenty-one miles, he recalled. Incredible that Germany hadn't made it across in World War II. He remembered a film in which Nazis on the shoreline of France looked through a telescope at the English coast. They had been that close; it was mind-boggling.

He leaned his head back with a tired sigh, eyes closing. Just a nap, he thought.

The shuddering of the Hovercraft as the bottom jets began firing air startled him awake. He felt groggy but he did want to watch this part, anyway. He leaned in close to the window, pushing aside the curtain to see. He smiled as he felt the entire structure slowly rising from the tarmac. Too much, he thought.

The Hovercraft, still shuddering, began to edge slowly toward the channel. Chris looked at the water ahead. It was very rough. Would the Hovercraft be affected by that? He got motion sickness very easily. *Some hero I am,* he thought. *High blood pressure. Motion sickness. Half-asleep. Ready for anything, folks,* he thought. *Bring on the bad guys. I'll bore them to death.*

Now the Hovercraft was starting to move out over the water. Chris grinned sleepily, seeing a cloud of air-blown water flaring out from underneath the lower edge of the craft. By God, the damn thing was actually floating above the water!

He chuckled to himself. Considering the intricacy of the work he did, it was amusing that the Hovercraft impressed him so. *Shows you how much I get around,* he thought. *A helicopter ride would probably blow my mind.*

Completely above the rough channel water now, the Hovercraft began to pick up speed. Well, hell, it *is* impressive, Chris thought. Flying across the water at a height of nine or ten feet, supported by columns of air? And moving how much faster than a boat? Five times? Chris grunted, smiling. Unbelievable, he thought.

Then his eyes would not stay open and his head slumped back. He heard the muffled roaring of the jets below. *Just rest your eyes a while,* he told himself. Mom always said that. He made a faint noise. *Mom,* he thought. He had to try and get in touch with her, let her know he was all right.

He felt his brain turning over backwards, slipping into darkness. Yet he still felt the shuddering of the Hovercraft, heard the sound of the jets. Was he asleep or awake? Or halfway in between?

He heard a voice. He thought he heard it anyway; he wasn't sure. The voice was muttering something. He couldn't make out the words. It wasn't a pleasant voice. It had a harsh edge to it, a bullying quality.

Finally, he heard what it said:

"You don't seem to know that time is of the essence," said the voice, accusingly.

Chris winced as he felt a light slap on his left cheek. He

grunted. Jesus, how could this be a dream? He'd never felt a sensation like this in a dream; had he?

"Who are you?" he mumbled.

He hissed as he felt another slap on his cheek, this time harder.

"Now listen to me," the man's voice said coldly. "I'm going to tell you once and no more. Get it right or next time you'll be sorry."

Chris shivered, feeling cold. Was that a dream sensation? He couldn't believe it somehow. He still heard the air jets below, felt the shaking of the Hovercraft. *I'm* not *asleep,* he thought in sudden dread.

I'm drugged.

"Do you know what reality slippage is?" the man's voice asked.

"What?"

Chris gasped as his cheek was slapped again.

"I said *listen* to me, damn it," the man's voice told him angrily. "Reality slippage. Do you understand? *Reality slippage.*"

"I don't know what that is," Chris said, frightened. He braced himself for another slap, which didn't come.

"It's what's happening to you," the man's voice said. "It's happening to everyone who's working on the turbulence problem. You understand?"

"Yes." Chris drew back unconsciously, fearing another slap.

"Dozens of you losing touch with reality. You *understand?*"

Chris cried out softly as his cheek was slapped again, harder yet. "Don't," he pleaded.

"Then *listen* to me," snarled the man. "You made it worse by wagering. *Do you understand?*"

Chris caught his breath in shock.

"Veering?" he whispered.

"*What?*"

"Veering?" he repeated, more loudly.

"Yes, *Veering,*" the man's voice said, as though through clenched teeth.

Another unexpected slap made Chris sob chokingly.

"Finish your work before the slippage is complete," the man's voice said. He sounded as though he were repressing utter fury.

"But how—?"

Chris broke off, crying out, as his cheek was slapped again.

"Do you *want* to be replaced?" the man's voice demanded. "Do you want it all to end? Do you want to lose touch with reality? Give up your mind?"

Chris had his left hand up before his face to stop the slaps. He now knew that he wasn't asleep. The coffee, he thought suddenly. The bitterness.

He stiffened as he felt the man's face so close to his that the warmth of the man's breath was on his lips.

"I tell you this and only once," the man said slowly. *"It's now only six steps to midnight."*

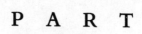

PART

1

Faintly, distantly, he heard the laughter of a woman. *It's her*, he thought. *But why laughing? And with such hysteria?*

Chris opened his eyes and looked up at a ceiling. He was in a bed, lying on his back, a pillow underneath his head. *Now where?* he thought. *And how long had he been sleeping?*

The woman was still laughing, though he could barely hear it now. It wasn't Alexsandra, couldn't be. He turned his head to the right.

Windows. Gray outside. Was that a filmy drizzle falling? *Where the hell am I?* he thought. Pushing up on an elbow, he looked around.

A hotel room.

He slid his legs over the mattress and dropped them across the edge. Sitting up, facing the windows, he tried to recall the last thing that had happened to him.

Remembrance came immediately. The Hovercraft. The stinging slaps across his left cheek. The voice. *"Dozens of you losing touch with reality. You understand?"*

No, Mister, I don't, he thought. *Not a bit of it.*

Except that the man had mentioned the wager. And verified that it was Veering. What else had he said? Chris put his left hand over his eyes, retreating to that moment to hear the man's voice telling him *"It's happening to everyone who's working on the turbulence problem."*

6 steps to midnight.

Chris lowered his hand and blinked, focusing on the windows. He tried to stand but wavered, feeling dizzy. Drugged, he remembered now. Goddamn it, he'd been drugged again! What did he have to do, go without food and drink to prevent it from happening?

He stood motionless, arms outstretched as though he were standing on a tightrope, trying not to topple off. Easy, he told himself. How had they done it this time? It had to have been the coffee in the Hovercraft waiting room. It had tasted vile, as he recalled.

He groaned and shook his right hand as though to brush away confusion. There were just too many things to grasp.

He looked around. That woman was still laughing, a little more loudly now. She was in the next room obviously. What the hell was she laughing at? Who the hell was she *with*, a troupe of stand-up comics? Or was she chained naked to a bed, with a feather-wielding sadist hovering above her? *Just shut up, lady,* he thought.

Clenching his teeth, he walked slowly to the nearest window and looked out, blinked. "Jesus," he muttered.

Off in the distance, looking ghostlike in the mist, was the Eiffel Tower.

He breathed deeply and slowly, a faint, humorless smile drawing back his lips. He remembered wondering, on the Hovercraft, if he'd see Alexsandra again and thinking that "surely" he had to go to Paris.

"Well, I have," he murmured. Another deep breath released. "But for what?"

He looked at the courtyard below. There was a design on its paving that resembled dark blue sine waves on a gray background. There were benches down there, small trees. Chris lifted his gaze again and stared at the specter-like tower. Paris, he thought. My God, *Paris*.

Turning abruptly—he had to lean against the window frame as a momentary wave of dizziness fogged over him—he looked at the room.

There was his bag again, lying on a table. Whoever was behind all this was certainly efficient.

He checked his watch and saw that it was still the same day, just past three o'clock. *How I do get around* he thought without amusement.

He moved to a bureau and stared at his reflection in the mirror above it. He *looked* drugged, for Christ's sake, punchy as hell. He ran his right hand through plastered-down hair. In the next room, the woman's laughter escalated suddenly. She sounds demented, he thought. The feather-wielding madman must be tickling into high gear.

He looked over at a small desk with a telephone on it. There was a yellow card lying next to the telephone and, stepping over to the desk, he picked up the card.

Mme/Mlle/M Barton was on the top line of the card, his name printed in ink. *No. de chambre 729*; the seven had a line through it. *Date de partre*—blank. When was he scheduled to leave? Or *was* he going to leave? Was this the end of the line? A modest *pensione* in Paris, supplies to do his work with an assumed *nom?* He scowled. The notion was ridiculous.

He looked at the card again. It folded in the middle. He turned down the top half and saw the words *Bienvenu au Paris Penta Hôtel.*

"Okay," he said. "I'm here. What's next on the agenda? An ascent up Mont Blanc? A shoot-out in a Bavarian castle? A race . . .?"

"Fuck it," he muttered. He had to come back to earth. Seeing a coffeemaker on the wall, he moved to it and lifted off the pot. Carrying it into the bathroom, he filled it with water. Was the water drugged? he wondered. He frowned at himself. Sure, they piped it just to this room. Come on, Barton. Get real.

But when he carried the pot back to the coffeemaker and slid it back into place, he found himself fingering the packet of coffee. Now *that* could be drugged. He turned it over and over in his hand.

"God," he muttered finally. He tossed the packet onto the desk. *Forget the coffee,* he thought. *I'd love some but I'm not—repeat, not—going to surrender my brain to these bastards again.* He had a strong feeling that the packet of coffee was legitimate. But after what he'd been through, he simply wasn't willing to take a chance on it.

He opened the bag and checked its interior. Everything looked the same. He examined some of the contents, then dropped them back into place. Sighing, he sat on the bed. "All right, *quo vadis* now?" he muttered. Was Robert Ludlum in the next room, dreaming up more complications for him? Was that why that woman was laughing so hysterically?

The woman stopped laughing at that moment. Chris waited, listening, but there was only silence now. Had she left the room with Robert? he thought. Or died from the tickling?

He sat, shoulders slumped, looking toward the window. He couldn't see the tower from where he was, only the gray sky, the near-invisible drizzle. *I love Paris in the winter when it drizzles,* sang some murky-voiced chanteuse in his head. Except it wasn't winter, it was June.

Reality slippage, he thought.

Was there really such a thing? Was that what Veering was talking about when he presented his wager?

Chris scowled and tried to blank his mind. Looking around, he saw a pad and pencil on the bedside table. *Le crayon est sur la table,* he thought.

"Finish your work before the slippage is complete," he remembered the man saying. *Well, I'm* sorry, *Mister, but it's not that easy to finish my work,* he thought angrily. *I have a few problems—*

His legs jerked in spasmodically as the telephone rang.

It made a different ringing sound, like British telephones did, Chris thought. More strident, more demanding.

Should he answer it? Go along with the next step, the next ride? He sighed. He had a strong urge to leave the room, go down and see if he could somehow book the next flight to Phoenix. He stared indecisively at the phone as it kept ringing loudly.

I can't, he thought finally. He still didn't know what was really going on. And he wasn't brought all this distance on a lark. Death had taken place. This was hard reality.

Standing, he moved to the telephone and, even though he felt like a pawn again, lifted the handset from its cradle and raised it to his head. "Yes?"

"Chris, it's Alexsandra."

He started, tensing. "Where *are* you?" he asked.

"Meet me outside Sacré-Cœur, Montmartre," she told him. "*Right away.*"

"What's *happening*—?"

He broke off, staring at the earpiece in disbelief. She'd hung up on him.

His heartbeat had quickened again. "Goddamn, *now* what?" he muttered with nervous anger. The anger diminished quickly when he thought about seeing her again. It was absurd—it had been entirely too brief, too rapid—but he *was* in love with her. "Well, why not?" he demanded. Everything else was insane. Why not that?

Sacré-Cœur, he thought. Wasn't that a church, a cathedral? Montmartre. A section of Paris?

He stood immobile for a few seconds, trying to organize himself. Abruptly, then, he went into the bathroom, washed off his face and combed his hair.

Returning to the bedroom, he changed shirts. He was about to slip on his jacket when he realized that he hadn't called his mother yet. He knew she'd be worried by now, maybe frantic.

The question was, would "they" pay a long-distance telephone charge?

"Try," he told himself. Picking up the handset, he gave the hotel operator his mother's number.

No problem. Less than a minute later, he was listening to the sound of her telephone ringing.

She wasn't home. He had to leave a message on her answering machine. He didn't tell her where he was; he felt a sense of caution about that. "I'm okay though," he told her. "I'll get in touch with you again as soon as I can. Love you."

As he left the room and started down the corridor—the room key had been lying on the table next to his bag—he felt inside his jacket pocket to find a clump of bills in the right-hand pocket. Taking them out, he looked at them. Somehow, he was not the least surprised to see that "they" had substituted French currency for British.

"They think of everything," he said.

Except enlightening him.

🎴 It had taken him nearly half an hour to get a taxi; there was a line of waiting guests in front of the hotel. Not very fiction-like, he'd thought. In a book or movie, the hero leaves his room—boom, he's in a taxicab en route to further perils. Not like real life, even with the doorman ordering for him. He had no choice but to wait impatiently, anxious to be with Alexsandra again.

When he finally settled back on the seat of the cab and told the driver where he wanted to go, the driver nodded, saying, "You are *Americain?*"

Chris looked at him suspiciously. *I know I'm being paranoid,* he thought, *but after everything that's happened . . .*

"*Monsieur?*"

Chris swallowed, not knowing what to say. He forced suspicion away then. For Christ's sake, he couldn't be *surrounded* by spies. Were they so goddamn cunning they could time the taxis perfectly, making sure he got the very one with agent X-9 driving it? *Come on,* he chided himself. "I'm sorry, what did you say?" he asked.

"*Monsieur* is *Americain?*"

"How did you know?"

"Your accent," the driver said. Chris felt like an idiot. What else? he thought. He nodded.

"From California?"

Chris couldn't help grinning. "Why do you think that?"

"Just curious," the driver said. "I plan to move to California one day."

"Uh-huh." Chris leaned to the left as the driver made an abrupt turn and started driving past rows of colorful old buildings. "Offices?" Chris asked him.

"Residential," the driver said.

Chris nodded.

"Oh, *merde*," the driver muttered.

Chris repressed a smile. Looking ahead, he saw a traffic jam waiting.

"No, we will bypass this," the driver said. Signaling, he made a right turn and picked up speed. At the end of the block, he made a fast left turn; Chris saw the street sign: Boulevard Maurice Barres. To his right, he saw a park.

"Bois de Boulogne," the driver told him.

"Mmm-*hmm*." Chris nodded again, looking at the people on the sidewalk. Two were walking small dogs; a woman in furs and high heels and a squat, midle-aged man wearing a black trench-coat and beret, a cigarette dangling from a corner of his mouth.

Chris glanced to the front as movement caught his eye. Pedestrians were crossing in front of the traffic, leaping to safety like frantic ballet dancers. Chris watched in awe. None of the vehicles slowed down for an instant. Amazing the street wasn't littered with bodies, he thought.

He twisted his head to the right. "Is that a *camel?*" he asked in surprise.

"Indeed," the driver said. "That is the Jardin d'Acclimatation. A zoo. Children love it. Many animals, many rides. Also the Grand Maison des Poupées—a doll museum. Some wonderful antique dolls."

"I see," Chris said. If the man is a spy, he thought, he certainly is a chatty one.

The taxi reached a traffic circle now. The driver seemed to floor his accelerator; Chris had to clutch at the seat to keep from falling over. The circle was jammed with speeding, honking cars and taxicabs. Jesus God, he thought, what is this, a training course for Le Mans?

Suddenly, the taxi shot off to the right as though flung off by centrifugal force. To Chris's right now was what looked like the skyscrapered downtown of any major city. "La Defense," he thought he heard the driver say. He looked in wonderment at a huge building built like a square arch, windows spaced around its perimeter.

"The Arc de La Défense," the driver said. "A modern version

of the Arc de Triomphe. If you look through it, you'll see the Arc de Triomphe further down."

Chris looked but missed it. Abruptly, then, the taxicab was speeding onto an expressway. "La Périphérique," the driver told him. From the word periphery? Chris wondered. *The external boundary of an area,* the dictionary definition floated up into his mind.

He closed his eyes. There was nothing visible now but a wall on either side. *Great,* he thought. *Here I am in gay Paris—well, scratch that adjective the way things are today—okay, in chic, romantic Paris and what do I have to look at? A pair of gray walls.*

He drifted into thought. The thing that bothered him most about all this, he recognized, was its lack of meaning. The one thing his mind craved in any situation was the one thing he couldn't find in this one. Sure, he had the basics: his work, his replacement, his assisted flight. But what was *behind* it all? Who was against him? Who was helping him?

He grimaced and shook his head. Once again, the complication of Veering's wager threw him off. Every time it seemed as though this situation might conceivably be analyzed, the wager threw a wrench into the works.

He opened his eyes, feeling the taxi ease to the right. A sign ahead read Porte de Clignancourt.

As the taxi shot off the expressway, Chris could see the city again. Somehow, they'd climbed without his noticing or feeling it, for now Paris lay far below. *Montmartre,* he thought. *Martre* he didn't know, but *mont* meant mountain and it certainly seemed as though they were on a mountain here. It was still hazy, though the drizzle had stopped, but he could see, he estimated, twenty miles or more across the city. Another angle on the ghostlike tower. Would he have a chance to visit it? he wondered.

There was a church to his right. "Notre Dame de Clignancourt," the driver said. "Incidentally, this is not a neighbourhood to walk in after dark. *Monsieur* should leave before then."

Up ahead, Chris saw what he assumed was Sacré-Cœur, its many cupolas topped by a huge dome that looked as though it were made of sugar icing. "Is that—?" he started, pointing.

"Sacré-Cœur," the driver said, nodding. He pulled the taxi over to the curb and braked hard.

Chris paid the bill, tipping the man fifteen percent; it took him a moment or two to recall the value of French currency. Then he got out of the cab and it was driven off at high speed. *So much for my spy theory,* Chris thought.

He stood motionless, looking across Paris. The vista was awesome. In addition to the Eiffel Tower, he could see the curving Seine River, La Défense, the Arc de Triomphe and what he took to be the gothic extravagance of Notre-Dame Cathedral.

He looked around then. Where was he supposed to meet Alexsandra? All she'd said was Sacré-Cœur. She hadn't indicated whether she'd meet him inside the church or not.

"Well—" he said.

He started, gasping, as a hand clamped hard on his right shoulder. Jerking around, both hands raised to defend himself, he saw a tall man glaring at him, an expression of furious agitation on his face.

"For God's sake!" the man said, sounding breathless. "*What the hell are you doing up here?*"

2

"**W**hat—?" Chris began.

He winced as the man grabbed his arm and started forcing him along the sidewalk. "Come *on,*" the man said irritably. "We can't just stand here." He spoke with a French accent.

Chris tried to pull free. "What are you—?"

"*Not now,*" the man interrupted. "Just move. *Move.*" Chris felt a chill across his back as the man looked around, head snapping from side to side, his expression one of apprehension.

"Who *are* you?" Chris demanded.

"Down these steps. *Vite, vite.*" The man's fingers gouged at Chris's arm as they started down the steps. Below, Chris saw an open area crowded with artists and tourists, some having sketches made of themselves, others purchasing silhouettes scissored from black paper.

He tried to pull away. "You're hurting me," he snapped.

"They will hurt you far more if they get their hands on you," the man said curtly. Chris shuddered at his words. *They?*

He said no more as the man hurried him across the area; a sign identified it as the Place du Tertre. Chris stumbled on the cobblestone paving and the man pulled him upright again. It made Chris grimace involuntarily to see the way the man kept looking around as though searching for pursuers.

Abruptly, then, he turned Chris into a café, past the outside tables. Leading Chris to the back of the inside room, he had him sit in a booth. He pointed at a side door. "Remember that," he said.

He slid in across from Chris and looked at him as though he

couldn't understand what was wrong with him. "I'd like to know what in the hell you are doing here," he said. "If I hadn't caught sight of you leaving the hotel in that taxi, you'd be here alone."

Chris swallowed nervously. "What's going on?" he asked, his voice thin.

"This is what I am asking *you*," the man said sharply.

Chris stared at the man, afraid to trust him. The man was pale with a thin, black mustache, his hair dark and lank. He wore a black leather jacket and a red shirt.

"*Well?*" he demanded.

"I—" Chris broke off as the waiter approached them.

"*Messieurs?*"

"Uh . . . *Pastis pour moi, s'il vous plaît,*" the man told him. He looked at Chris.

"What's that?" Chris asked.

"Licorice. Like Ouzo," the man told him. He looked irritated at Chris's lack of decision. "*Citronnade,*" he said quickly, gesturing toward Chris.

"*Oui. Un moment.*" The waiter turned away.

Chris started to speak but the man cut him off. "Why did you leave the hotel?" he asked. "You were supposed to stay there."

Chris tightened angrily. "How the hell was I supposed to know what to do?" he demanded. He now believed that the man was on his side, though.

"But why Montmartre?" asked the man.

"I was telephoned."

"By whom?"

"Uh . . . I don't know if you know her. Her name is Alexsandra Claudius."

"Who is she?" the man asked.

"She helped me in London," Chris said.

"Well, I wouldn't know her, then," the man replied. "But she would not have told you to go to Montmartre."

"*I heard her voice.*"

"You haven't heard of voice changers?" the man asked irritably.

"Oh, my God," Chris murmured. He *had* heard about them; read about them anyway: special integrated circuits on a telephone that could disguise a voice, even change the sound of a man's voice to that of a woman.

"I see that you know what I am talking about," the man observed.

"Yes, I do. But . . . *why?*"

"To lure you here, of course," the man replied, leaning to his left to look toward the front of the café. "I think we are safe," he said, leaning back. "Better we stay inside for a while though."

"You . . . don't know who this woman is," Chris persisted.

"No—but that is no surprise," the man said. "If your relationship with her was in London . . ." He gestured vaguely.

"Who called me, then?" Chris asked.

"The less you know, the better," the man replied.

"Oh . . . God," Chris muttered. Alexsandra had said the same thing. He was getting damn sick of all this secrecy.

The waiter brought their drinks and set them down. Chris's was a glass with an inch of what looked like lemon juice, and a carafe of water. "Put some sugar in it," the man told him. "It will be less sour."

Yeah, sure, that's what I'm really worried about right now, Chris thought, *sour lemonade.* Abruptly—irrationally, it seemed—he wondered if he had taken his hypertension medication that day. He had, hadn't he? In London? He felt a wave of mental dizziness overwhelm him. London this morning, Paris this afternoon. And three short days ago, Arizona.

"We'll have to put you in a different hotel now," the man said, sounding put-upon. "Obviously, they found out where you were."

"Who the hell is *'they'?*" Chris asked in a low, resentful voice.

The man only shook his head.

"All right, then, if they knew I was in the hotel, why didn't they just come and *get* me there?"

"Because they knew we were watching you," the man said as though answering the foolish question of a child.

"*Will you please tell me what's going on?*" Chris asked almost pleadingly. "I keep getting shunted from place to place and never—"

The man raised a hand to silence Chris. "I only know," he said, "that I was assigned to keep an eye on you while you were at the Penta Hotel."

"Of course," Chris responded. *You were only following orders.* He poured some water into the lemon juice and took a sip, face curling up at the taste. "*Jesus,*" he mumbled.

"A little sugar," suggested the man.

Chris lifted the teaspoon off the table and picked up a little sugar with it. "Can you tell me if I'm to stay in Paris?" he asked.

He thought at first that his question had, for some inexplicable reason, startled the man. Then, suddenly, he realized that the man was looking past him, features stiffening. Chris twisted around, breath catching as he saw two men approaching the booth, their faces dark, their clothes Middle Eastern.

"*Get out of here,*" the man said quickly. "Use the side door."

Before Chris could respond, the man was pushing to his feet. Chris saw the two strange men break into a run. Abruptly, the man was facing them. To Chris's startlement, he saw that his carafe of water was in the man's right hand; with a blur of movement, the man was swinging it at one of the men.

The Middle Easterner tried to avoid the blow but only managed to dodge enough to have the bottle shatter on the area between his shoulder and neck; blood sprang from the slash in crimson drops. The Middle Easterner's legs buckled and he stumbled to one side, crashing into a table and knocking it over. The man and woman who had been sitting there sprang back in their chairs, the woman losing balance and falling back against another table with a cry of fright. Dishes, cups and glasses shattered noisily.

Chris's gaze leaped to the second Middle Eastern man. He blinked, as—magically, it seemed—a long, thin knife blade shot up from the man's right hand. The tall man leaped at him and grabbed at his right wrist, their shoes squeaking on the tile floor as they wrestled. The tall man glanced at Chris, his face distorted. "*Go!*" he shouted.

Catching his breath, Chris slid from the booth and lunged for the side door. As he did, he looked aside and made a sound of horror as he saw the Middle Easterner driving his knife blade straight into the tall man's chest. His face a mask of dread, Chris yanked open the side door and ran outside; as he did, he heard another crash of dishes in the café, people screaming.

Heart pounding, he turned left and started racing along a narrow alley, almost knocking down an old man trudging toward him. "*Dieu!*" The old man shrank aside, bumping hard against the brick wall of a building, a stunned expression on his face. Chris rushed by him, heard the old man shouting after him. "*Connard!*"

He reached an intersection in the alley, slowing down enough to turn right. He glanced back, tensing, frightened, as he saw the Middle Eastern man pursuing him, lips drawn back from crooked teeth, giving him a fierce and animal-like appearance. *God!* Chris thought. The adventure wasn't stimulating now. He was terrified.

The bottoms of his shoes made tiny singing noises on the paving as he ran, already panting for breath. He looked ahead in desperation, with no idea what to do. If he just kept running, the man would surely overtake him. To die in a Paris alley with a knife thrust in his back? It seemed a nightmare beyond belief and yet there might be only seconds before it happened.

"*No,*" he muttered, trying to pick up speed. But he was not in good condition; his job had only required sitting and thinking. Inadequate breath was burning in his lungs, a stitch beginning to stab at his left side. He wouldn't be able to run much longer.

He raked around another corner and, on impulse, dashed into a small café, almost knocking down a waiter carrying a tray of glasses. "Aiee! *Fais gaffe!*" the waiter snarled at him. Chris kept running, reaching a narrow corridor. Should he lock himself inside the men's room, climb out a window? What if there *was* no window? He kept running and slammed through two swinging, shuttered doors into the kitchen. He'd go out the back door, try to—

He staggered to a halt, with a stricken expression. There was no back door.

He was trapped.

It isn't true. His mind rejected what was happening. Such things did not take place. His life in total jeopardy? The probability of violent death? He was only thirty-seven years old, for Christ's sake!

Chris looked back across the swinging doors and saw the Middle Eastern man come striding into the café; there was no sign of the knife now. Chris stepped back against the wall, heart jolting. *My God, what do I do?* he thought. His gaze jumped around and, seeing a knife rack on the wall, he stepped over to it, pulling out a long carving knife. *You're insane!* he heard his mind protest. *You don't know how to defend yourself with a knife!*

"Hey! *Vas-y! Bouge ton cul!*" a voice snapped behind him.

He whirled and saw a florid heavyset man in white cook's garb glaring at him. Chris stared at him blankly, then winced as the cook advanced on him. He glanced aside to see if the Middle Easterner was coming in. He wasn't.

The cook pulled the knife from Chris's hand, returned it to its rack and gestured toward the corridor. "*Qu'est-ce que tu fous?*" he growled.

"*Pardon,*" Chris murmured, looking toward the swinging doors again. The Middle Easterner was still not coming in; what did that mean?

He edged to the doors and peered across the one on his left. He felt his stomach muscles jerking spasmodically. The man was sitting at a table, waiting for him. Apparently, he was not inclined to face a repetition of what had happened in the other café.

The other café, Chris thought, grimacing in pain. Was the tall man lying dead there, his blood running over the tile floor? Where were the police whistles, the pursuit?

He jerked around with a hiss as the cook grabbed him by the shoulder. He didn't really hear what the cook said, he was so agitated, but clearly the man wanted him out of his kitchen.

"*S'il vous plaît,*" he muttered.

"*S'il vous plaît, mon cul,*" the cook responded in a surly voice. He held open one of the swinging doors. "*Vas-y!*"

Chris could only gape at him. *I can't go out there,* he thought. *I'll be killed.* He shuddered. He had to do something to save himself. *Come* on! he thought. *You're supposed to have a brain! Use it!*

The cook grabbed him by the arm and, suddenly, Chris yanked free, face distorting as he snarled, "*Va te faire foutre!*"

Apparently, he had remembered correctly from the book on French profanity he'd once read because the cook looked startled and intimidated, backing off. *Now don't retreat,* Chris ordered himself. He made a hostile gesture with his right hand as though waving back the cook. The heavy, red-faced man drew back several steps. Obviously, he was a bully with no real confidence, Chris decided.

He glanced across the swinging door again. *Goddamn the man!* he thought in sudden fury. He was actually having a drink while waiting for Chris to come out of the kitchen, not even looking in that direction.

Chris turned back. Think! he screamed at his mind.

Night of the Ninja, the memory sprang up.

Would it work here?

He drew in shuddering breath. What other choice did he have? It was that or death.

He looked around quickly and saw a dark raincoat and a hat hanging on a wall peg. With an abrupt movement, he pulled them down.

The cook started forward, and Christ twisted around, forcing a glare to his face. "*On ne bouge plus,*" he said in a low, menacing voice. The cook backed off again, looked shocked.

Chris glanced across the swinging doors again. The Middle Easterner was gazing out at the street. *Bastard,* he thought.

Moving quickly, he pushed through the swinging doors and, pulling open the door to the men's washroom, stepped inside and locked the door behind him, heart jolting heavily again. What was this doing to his blood pressure? he wondered. *What the hell difference does that make?* he thought angrily. *A knife blade in my heart will kill me a lot faster than hypertension.*

All right, all right, he told himself. *Do it.*

Hastily, he pulled on the dark raincoat and hat. He'd have to move fast before the cook said something to the waiter and his hoped-for ploy was undone before it started.

Thank God the man who owned the coat—the cook, the waiter?—was bigger than him. He buttoned it to the neck, then stopped and ran the fingers of his right hand over the wall behind the toilet. A health inspector would go crazy in this place, he thought as he rubbed oily grime on his face, looking into the small wall mirror.

He had to rub the wall behind the toilet twice more before he had enough grime smeared onto his face to cover all of it. He then tore off pieces of toilet paper and stuffed them into his mouth, bulging out his cheeks. It had worked in the novel but would it work in real life? It seemed improbable to him.

He looked at his reflection analytically. Well, he *did* look different, there was no doubt of that. He felt something in the pocket of the raincoat and pulled out a glasses case. *Good,* he thought. He slid the glasses free and put them on. That helped even more.

He drew in a deep, bracing breath. *Now or never, Barton,* he thought.

Opening the door, he stepped into the corridor, glancing toward the kitchen. The cook, thank God, was still there, looking across the swinging doors, an expression of fear on his face.

Chris shuffled into the café, slumping over. *Yes,* he thought as the idea came to him. He started to act like a man beset by stomach gas. He belched loudly, kept moving, shoulders hunched, a look of discomfort on his face. The Middle Easterner glanced at him and turned away. *My God, it's working!* Chris thought exultantly. He forced himself to belch again.

Seconds later, he was walking casually along the street, leaving the café behind. For a few minutes, he felt sure that the man would realize he'd been tricked, that Chris had walked by him, ineptly disguised.

Amazingly, it didn't happen. Once, Chris even stopped and got down on one knee to retie a shoe, glancing back to see if the Middle Easterner was after him. He wasn't. Where was the man from? he wondered as he stood to continue on. Egypt? Iran? Libya? He had no way of knowing.

Unexpectedly, a laugh tore back his lips. By God, it had worked, he thought. *Night of the Ninja*, for Christ's sake! Who would have believed it?!

A few minutes later, he was able to hail a taxicab. At first, he didn't know what to tell the driver. Then he realized that he had little choice. He had to go back to the Penta Hotel in hope that someone would pick him up there, take him to safety. At the very least, he had to pick up his bag and find safety himself.

He slumped back against the seat and closed his eyes as reaction set in. Had he really done it? The memory seemed farfetched, unbelievable.

Then gloom set in again. The pleasure of his escape had already faded. He was still in Paris, still caught in the web of what was happening to him.

At any moment, he could be pounced on again.

3

At the last minute, Chris decided to tell the driver to let him off down the street from the hotel. Better to come walking up in this disguise, he thought. Inept as it was, it would call less attention to him if he entered the hotel on foot.

He paid the driver and started walking down the block, hunching over again. It was dark now. Anyone watching for him should be thrown off a little more by the lack of visibility.

No one even glanced at him as he entered the hotel. He walked, using the shuffle again, across the lobby and stood in front of the elevators. A cluster of Japanese tourists were standing there. When the elevator doors opened, they charged in before the occupants—also mostly Japanese tourists—could get out. *Banzai,* Chris thought as he shouldered himself in among them. He couldn't resist working up a belch as the door slid shut. He pretended he didn't see their looks of distaste.

He stood in silence to the seventh floor, managing to raise another belch as he exited. "Par*don,*" he said as though pardoning himself was the last thing in the world he had in mind.

He walked to his room and listened at the door to hear if there were any sounds inside. When there was nothing, he turned the key in its lock and, bracing himself for a possible struggle, and shoved the door open so hard it banged against the wall.

There was no one in the room that he could see. Leaving the door ajar, he edged forward and peered cautiously into the bathroom. It was empty.

As fast as he could, he tossed his discarded clothes into the bag and zipped it shut, then started for the door. A thought occurred to him and, closing the door, he moved to the telephone, picking up the handset.

"*Operatrice*," a woman's voice said.

"This is Room 729," Chris said. "Are there any messages for me?"

There was a pause before the woman said, "*Oui, monsieur.* An Alexsandra Claudius left a message."

Chris tightened. They were after him again.

"She said that, upon your return, to please meet her in the hotel bar."

He shuddered; he'd walked right by the entrance to the bar.

He thanked the operator and hung up. Quickly, he picked up his bag and moved to the door, hesitated before jerking it open. There was no one in the corridor.

Closing the door behind him, he strode hurriedly to the elevator and pushed the button. He'd have to pass the bar one more time, he thought. The idea chilled him. Who was in there? More Middle Easterners waiting with concealed knives? "Jesus," he muttered.

Another ride down with a group of Japanese tourists. This time, he didn't play the part of the gas-ridden man but they edged away from him anyway. His nose curled as he sniffed. It was the grime he'd smeared on his face; it had the definite aroma of a toilet.

He braced himself for the onslaught as the elevator reached the lobby floor. The doors slid open and he lunged out determinedly, prepared for collision. There was only one Japanese couple standing outside; they shrank away from him in alarm as he came charging from the elevator. *Great*, he thought, looking around nervously. *That's what you need to do, call attention to yourself.*

He had to force himself not to hurry across the lobby. He visualized what he must look like, a ridiculous sight at best, his so-called disguise stupidly transparent.

But he made the front door with no one exiting the bar to challenge him. There was a line of guests outside again, waiting for taxis; he wouldn't stand on line this time. He shambled away from the hotel and started along the sidewalk.

As he walked, an unexpected wave of depression swept over him. What in the name of God was he supposed to do now? The only possibility he could come up with was to hire a cab to the airport and return to Arizona. What else was there?

He was trying in vain to make up his mind as he walked when a car quickly pulled over to the curb and braked beside him. His head jerked around and he looked at it with dread. Inside the car, a figure leaned over from the driver's seat and shoved open the passenger door.

Chris gaped in disbelief.

"Get in," said Alexsandra.

He stood immobile, staring at her.

"*Quickly,* Chris," she told him.

Twitching, he bent over and tossed his bag on the backseat, then slid onto the passenger seat and reached for the door handle. Before the door was shut, Alexsandra was accelerating quickly into the street.

He looked at her in grateful wonderment. "I didn't think I'd ever see you again," he said.

She reached out and squeezed his arm. "I'm here," she told him.

The sound of her voice made something break inside him. The involuntary sound he made was something between a gasp and a sob.

"Are you all right?" she asked in concern.

"I've been through a bit," he said.

"I want to hear all about it," she said, "but let me get us somewhere safe first." She was looking into the rearview mirror as she spoke.

"Oh, God, don't tell me we're being followed," he said.

"I don't think so," she said. "But I want to be sure."

The car sped down beneath an overpass. As it did, Chris glanced aside and saw enough of his reflection in the window glass to make him start. "Wait a minute," he said.

"What is it?" she asked.

"*How did you know it was me?*" For a moment, he had the wild suspicion that she was in league with the Middle Easterner, who had finally realized that it had been him passing in disguise and had let her know about it.

"I didn't at first," she was saying. "I was parked by the hotel, hoping you'd come back; I'd been told you went to Montmartre."

"That man," Chris said impulsively.

"What man?" she asked.

"The one who met me there. The one who got stabbed. I thought you might know if he's alive or not."

He could see from the way she looked at him that all of this was news to her. "My God, what have you been through?" she murmured.

He started to tell her but she stopped him again, telling him she wanted to get them someplace safe before they spoke. *Is there* someplace safe? he wondered bitterly.

"Anyway, I was waiting for you to come back to the hotel," she continued. "I actually looked at you and didn't recognize you. What made you do that to yourself? No, don't tell me," she went on quickly, frowning at herself. "I can't concentrate yet."

"But how *did* you recognize me?" he demanded.

"I didn't," she said. "I recognized the bag you were carrying. Then I took a closer look, driving along behind you."

Chris fell silent after that. Now don't start being suspicious of *her* as well, he told himself. Wasn't the nightmare bad enough without adding that?

After several moments, he took off the hat and glasses, withdrew the soggy toilet paper from inside his cheeks and put it in the floor wastebasket. Unbuttoning the raincoat, he took out his handkerchief and started wiping the grime off his face. "Yes, please," said Alexsandra, glancing over.

"Smells bad, doesn't it?" he said.

"Atrocious."

He hadn't paid attention to where she was driving. The first thing he became conscious of was greenery surrounding them.

"The park?" he asked. He couldn't keep a trace of uneasiness from his voice. Anything could happen in a park, he thought.

She nodded at his question, then drove another ten minutes before turning into a cul-de-sac and braking the car. In spite of himself, Chris tensed as though preparing to defend himself.

She only turned to face him and returned his gaze. The sight of her undid his caution. He felt a surge of need for her and started leaning forward.

"Wait," she said.

He tensed again as she picked up her purse and opened it, expecting her to take out a pistol and shoot him.

She removed a packet of tissues and, pulling one free, began to rub it over his face, grimacing slightly as she did. "What did you put on it?" she asked.

"Some stuff off a wall behind a toilet," he said.

"Oh, God." She exhaled, grimacing. "What made you do that?"

He hesitated, then decided that he had to trust her, he simply couldn't function any longer if he didn't. He told her about the phone call that had taken him to Montmartre, the tall man accosting him, the two Middle Eastern men (he got the impression that her reaction to that was one of alarmed surprise, but he wasn't sure and didn't pursue it), the tall man being stabbed, his flight from the café and escape after disguising himself.

"That was very ingenious of you," she said. "Where did you get the idea?"

"From a novel," he told her sheepishly.

Her laugh was a soft, explosive sound. "A *novel?*"

"What about that man? Can you find out if he's alive?"

She nodded as she continued wiping off his face, wetting the tissues with her tongue. "I'll find out," she told him.

He kept staring at her as she finished cleaning off his face. Memory had not erred. She looked as marvelous as ever. He had to trust her; he just had to.

She put the last tissue in the wastebasket and gazed back at him. "There, that's better," she said. She looked at him with sympathy. "You've had such a terrible time. I'm so sorry."

Leaning forward, she put a hand on each side of his face and kissed him gently.

"I'm happy you're safe," she told him, drawing back.

"Alexsandra." He could barely speak her name.

Abruptly, they were in each other's arms, lips pressed together.

"I can't help it, I love you, I'm sorry," he murmured breathlessly, holding on to her as hard as he could, his cheek against hers, his eyes closed. *Trust* her! his mind commanded.

"Why sorry?" she asked.

"I don't know," he said. "I just . . . thought you might not want to hear it."

She drew back and looked at him with a gentle smile, stroking back his hair. "You're wong," she told him. She sighed. "I've tried very hard to get you out of my mind. It wasn't easy."

"But you succeeded," he said sadly.

That enchanting half-smile. "Who said that?" she murmured.

She was in his arms again, holding him firmly, her lips demanding as much as his.

Suddenly, she pulled away. "*Oh. No,*" she murmured, sounding almost unhappy.

"*What?*"

She rubbed her face as though she felt dizzy. "We're in so deep," she said. "There's so much to do yet."

"What has that got to do with—?"

'There's no time, love, no *time,*" she interrupted. She did sound unhappy now.

He looked at her hungrily. "Just let me hold you again."

She hesitated, then was in his arms once more. They clung to each other, cheeks pressed together. "I wish you could love me," he said.

"What makes you think I don't?"

Seconds later, she pulled away from their passionate kiss. "We have to go," she said, looking around uneasily. "I just don't feel safe here."

He swallowed, nodding.

"Are you hungry?" she asked.

It seemed an odd question to ask at that moment, he thought. He realized then that he *was* hungry; did danger increase his appetite or something? "I . . . guess I am," he admitted.

"All right." She started the engine. "I'll take you someplace safe to eat."

"What, a restaurant on top of the Eiffel Tower?" he asked.

"No." She smiled a little as she started the car forward. "Better than that."

⌘ Harp music softly playing something by Fauré. A glass-topped boat gliding slowly along the Seine. The illuminated Eiffel Tower framed against a dark sky. Candlelight reflected glitteringly on crystal glasses. The most beautiful, exciting woman he had ever known sitting across from him.

It should have been heaven.

But as soon as they'd been seated, Alexsandra had asked him about the two men on Montmartre. "You said they looked Middle Eastern," she reminded him.

"As far as I could tell," he said. "What country, I have no idea."

"You're certain they were Middle Eastern though."

"Well, I've never seen men like that except in the movies," he said. "They weren't wearing fezzes or anything but they looked Middle Eastern to me."

She nodded, looking worried. "I hope to God it isn't him," she said under her breath as though speaking to herself.

"*Him?*"

"He's Middle Eastern; no one knows for sure what country he was born in. He's a billionaire and very powerful." She winced. "And probably quite mad."

He looked at her, appalled. "That's wonderful," he said. "Now I'm involved with a madman."

"Let's hope it isn't him," she said.

"Yes, let's," he agreed. "What's his name?"

"We don't know his real name. He's called Cabal."

"As in 'conspiracy'?"

She nodded.

He shook his head with a groan. "I don't see how I could have been any worse off if I'd stayed in Arizona."

"You could have been," was all she said. "There *was* the replacement problem, you know."

The replacement problem, he thought. How polite a phrase for the plot that had flung him into this ordeal.

He looked out the window toward a huge domed building on the left. He wondered what it was, but didn't have the energy to ask.

He turned back to her. She was gazing at him with a look of compassion. "I know it's difficult," she said.

"Do you know anything about the man who spoke to me on the Hovercraft?" he asked.

"The Hovercraft?"

He saw immediately that she didn't know about him. Was there *anyone* who knew *everything* about what was happening? Veering? Or was the wager something separate from all the rest?

"What did the man say?" she asked.

He told her how the man had slapped him, told him about reality slippage and how he'd better finish up his work before he was a victim of it.

"Reality slippage?" she asked. "What's that?"

"Your guess is as good as mine," he said. "Although my reality has sure been slipping in the past few days."

"Did he say anything else?" she asked.

"Yeah," he told her. "He said that it was *six* steps to midnight now."

He wondered if she had any idea how helpless he felt, seeing the look on her face that clearly told him that she had no knowledge of anything he'd just told her.

"I don't know who it was." She verified his fear. "I only know that you were picked up at Le Havre and taken to Paris. I was ordered to follow."

"Ordered," he said quietly.

She smiled at him. "That doesn't mean I'm unhappy about it."

He nodded, only half-convinced. "I'm so confused," he said.

Before they'd boarded the boat, Alexsandra had gone to make a telephone call. He hadn't asked her what it was about. He did now.

She looked at him gravely. "The man," she said. "Maret. He's dead."

4

"**O**h, Jesus God." Chris lowered his head, grimacing. "He died to save my life, then."

"It was his profession, Chris," she said. "He knew the risks. You shouldn't feel guilty about it."

He looked up quickly. Was it possible that she was really so cold-blooded?

Her expression gave him the answer. There was pity in it, regret. "It's a terrible business," she said. "You can go on for years with nothing really violent occurring. Then, suddenly, it all erupts at once."

"Why do you do it, then?" he asked.

She didn't answer at first. He wasn't sure she was going to answer. Then she sighed. "It came over me gradually," she said. "At first, it was nothing more than office work for the government. Then some field work. Years going by. Then more difficult assignments, more difficult training for those assignments. And before I knew it—" She gestured haplessly. "I suppose if I'd known, from the start, exactly what I was getting into, I might not have done it. But . . . as I say, it came over me gradually. Does that make sense?"

He nodded. "Sure." Of course it made sense. Wasn't that how most things happened?

He looked out the window again. They were sitting in the front of the boat, a view of either riverbank available to them. To his left, he saw the floodlit top of an obelisk that looked Egyptian. *Place de la Concorde,* he thought.

He looked back, trying to smile. "What *is* this boat?" he asked.

"One of the Bateaux-Mouches," she said.

"What does that mean?"

"A small passenger boat, I think," she told him.

She leaned forward abruptly, reaching across the table. He hesitated, then put his right hand in hers.

"Listen, my dear," she said. "I'm going to do whatever I can to get you out of this."

"How can you?" he asked. "It's so damn complicated."

"I will though," she promised. "I'll take you out of it."

"Where, to the moon?" he asked, smiling faintly.

She hesitated, then said, "I'd take you to my secret island if I could."

"Where's that?"

"In the Pacific."

"You *own* it?"

"No." She made an amused sound. "Nobody knows about it though. Only islanders live there. I found it years ago. I've gone there six times now and I've had it in the back of my mind that, someday, I'm just going to chuck it all and slip away, unnoticed— disappear forever. Go native. Walk the beaches. Catch fish. Turn primitive."

"Take me with you when you do," he said.

"Wouldn't you miss your work?"

"I don't think so," he answered. "All I'm doing is contributing to the troubles of the world anyway."

She was silent for several moments. Then she smiled at him and he knew, once more, how much he was in love with her.

Until she squeezed his hand and he felt her ring.

The moment clouded instantly and he watched her hand as she drew back and picked up one of the tall, white menus. He thought about the painting and the dream. The ring was real though. It was not the figment of a painting or a dream. He felt a coldness in himself. Why did things keep changing? he thought. Why couldn't anything remain the same?

She looked over at him. "I'll interpret the menu for you, if you want," she said.

He picked it up and looked at the black printing. It was all in French.

The waiter came up to the table and Chris, glancing up at him, acquired an immediate dislike of the man; he was plump, his hair combed into an extravagant pompadour, his eyelids heavy, a look of superiority printed on his features.

If Alexsandra noticed this, she gave no indication of it, ordering a bottle of wine in a polite tone of voice. Her selection, Chris observed, seemed to fill the waiter's Gallic heart with scorn, the most fragmentary of snide smiles drawing back his thick lips as though he was thinking, *You really intend to drink that piss?*

While waiting for the menu, they talked about Paris and the garden of the Tuileries the boat was passing. Then the waiter returned and something about the man's expression added to the tension Chris already felt. As the waiter pulled the cork and handed it to him with a supercilious smile, Chris's face became hard. *"Pensez-vous vraiment que je vais le renifler?"* he asked in a contemptuous tone.

The waiter blinked, obviously taken aback by Chris's perfect French. Chris lifted the cork in front of the waiter and added, coldly, *"Le bouchon est ni mouillé, ni moelleux."*

"Monsieur?" There was a hint of fluster in the waiter's voice.

"Apparemment, la bouteille n'a pas été inclinée comme il se doit." Chris snapped, aware that Alexsandra was gaping at him.

"Monsieur, je—" the waiter began, protesting mildly.

Chris cut him off. *"De l'air a pénétré a l'interieur et a oxidé le vin."* He tossed the cork onto the table and waved away the bottle in distaste. The intimidated waiter carried it off.

Chris looked at Alexsandra. Her mouth was hanging open. Suddenly aware of it, she closed it. *"What was that?"* she asked incredulously.

"A little French," he said.

"A *little*?" She stared at him in amazement. "You spoke it like a native."

"I took a course once," he said, grinning. "And I have a good memory."

She couldn't seem to get over it. "You must be a genius."

He chuckled, embarrassed. "No," he said.

She shook her head, still impressed. "What did you *say* to him?"

"Uh . . . let's see if I can remember. I . . . asked him first if he really thought I was going to sniff the cork; obviously that's what he expected me to do. Then I told him that the cork was . . . not wet, not flexible, that *apparently*—I gave him a shot on that word—the bottle hadn't been properly stored and air had gotten into it and oxidized the wine." He grinned. "I think I impressed him."

"You positively decimated him," she said in an awed voice. "I can't get over it."

"Shucks, ma'am, 'twarn't nuthin'."

"I think you *are* a genius," she said. "Tell me about yourself."

"Oh . . . it's not that interesting."

"Please," she said.

"Well . . ." He hesitated. "Okay, the *Reader's Digest* version, then. I was born in Tucson. My father died when I was three. My mother is a college teacher—English. She raised my sister and me in a learning atmosphere. I started reading at five. We were taken to concerts, plays, lectures, museums. When I showed an aptitude for mathematics, she enrolled me in a special school. She used to—"

He broke off as the waiter returned with another bottle of wine. Trying to ignore Alexsandra's lowered head and repressed amusement, Chris again assumed the icily haughty expression and, when the waiter poured him a half-inch of wine to taste, he ran it around in his mouth, then sucked in a hissing breath of air, lips pursed, the way he'd once seen an expert do it at a wine-tasting contect. He made a sound as though to say, *well, I guess it will have to do since you obviously have nothing better.*

As the waiter began to pour, Chris spoke to him irritably. "*Ne remplissez pas le verre a plus d'un tiers, s'il vous plaît,*" he said. "*Je voudrais que le bouquet se developpe de lui-même.*"

"*Oui, Monsieur, absolument,*" the waiter replied, sounding totally cowed now.

After he'd left, the bottled-up laughter in Alexsandra burst out and she looked at Chris in delight. "What did you tell him now?" she asked.

"Not to fill the glass more than a third full; that I wanted the bouquet to develop on its own."

"You must be a wine connoisseur."

He made a scoffing noise. "Not at all," he said. "It's just a good memory."

She raised her glass of wine and held it out toward him. "To your incredible memory," she said.

He held out his glass. "To whatever fate put us together."

They gazed at each other for a few moments, then Alexsandra drew in a quick breath, as though restoring herself, and took a sip of the wine. She looked at him inquiringly as he took a sip of his. "Is it good?" she asked.

"God, *I* dunno," he said. "All I ever drink is Diet Coke."

Her laughter enchanted him. He tried hard to put from his mind any uncertainty about her, because, whatever else he felt, he was hopelessly in love with her.

"You were telling me about yourself," she said.

"Oh." He mock-scowled. "Not very interesting."

"*Very* interesting," she disagreed.

"Well . . . okay. I'll get through it as quickly as I can. My mother used to fill our house with guests—throw little mental soirées, I guess you'd call them. My uncle Harry came a lot; he's a pretty well-known physicist. Teachers. Educators. Writers. Musicians. Even politicians. My sister and I were always welcome, even when we were little kids. They treated us like equals."

"That must have been exhilarating," Alexsandra said.

"Intellectually, sure," he conceded. "I drank it all up. That, in addition to my early reading and my mother's tutoring, helped me to graduate from grade school at eleven, high school at fourteen, earn my first bachelor's degree at seventeen."

"You *are* a genius, aren't you?" she said, that look on her face again.

"No, no." He didn't want her to think of him that way. "I'm pretty good at mathematics, that's all. I have that kind of brain."

"How many degrees do you *have?*"

"Oh . . . three or four." He suppressed a smile. "Actually, you should be addressing me as *Dr.* Barton," he told her. "But if you do," he added quickly, "I'll dive through this window and swim back to the dock."

They smiled at each other. He was feeling better now. The wine on his empty stomach had helped, blurring away the hard edges. Now he was starting to feel the way he wanted to when they'd first gotten on the boat. The harp music and the gliding glass Bateau-Mouche, the lighted city of Paris and the candlelight illuminating Alexsandra's stunning face added up to the proper sum—a relaxed, romantic peace. He took another sip of wine, then poured each of them a second glassful.

"Won't the waiter see that you're not making it only one-third full?" she teased.

"Screw him," he muttered, smiling crookedly.

When the waiter returned and took their order, Chris thoroughly confused him by pretending that he couldn't read a word of the menu and let Alexsandra carefully translate for him.

"That'll give him something to think about," he said as the waiter left.

"Now he won't know *what* to think," she said, laughing.

"I have a confession," he told her. "That stuff about the wine came from a scene in a mystery novel; the hero does that to a nasty waiter. *Murder by the Numbers.* Jessica Wayne."

"I'm still amazed," she said.

He looked at her intently. The glow of the wine inside his head gave him the courage to ask impulsively, "Where did you get that ring?" He had to know.

"This?" she held up her left hand. "I liked it so much in the painting, I had a copy made."

Oh, for God's sake, he thought; he felt disgusted with himself. How simple could it be? He reached across the table impulsively. She gave him her right hand and he kissed it lingeringly, then looked up, smiling, at her.

"I feel a lot better," he told her.

★　★　★

✸ "Tell me what you do, Chris," she said.

The dinner had been sumptuous, the conversation warmly intimate. She'd told him about her childhood in England, her family and her education. He'd managed to put from his mind the things that had been happening to him since it had all begun that night at the plant.

The blurring at the edges of vision and thought had lessened as they ate. Now her question brought it all back and he felt a sense of keen regret about that. He was sorry she'd asked.

"I thought you didn't want to know," he said.

"I didn't before, but now I'm curious. It must really be important to justify everything that's happened to you." She looked at him in silence. "You don't have to tell me if you don't want to," she said, her tone a little hurt.

"Oh . . ." He looked pained. "I don't mind telling you. It's just . . . I've been having such a good time, I hate to go back to it."

"I'm sorry," she said. "I didn't mean to spoil things."

He sighed. "Okay." Picking up the glass, he swallowed the last of his wine. "What do I do?" he said. "I try to find an answer to the turbulence problem."

"What's that?"

"It has to do with lasers," he explained. "They don't propagate—transmit, that is—through the atmosphere because of turbulence, which is a kind of distortion in the atmosphere that prevents the laser from delivering enough energy to destroy a target."

"A target," she repeated.

His smile was rueful. "I told you that all I'm doing is contributing to the troubles of the world."

"Doesn't that bother you?" she asked.

"To quote a lovely young woman I know: 'It came over me gradually.'"

She sighed. "Touché," she murmured.

"Anyway, that's what I work on," he continued. "I try to set up theoretical equations, in what we think tankers call 'an analytically tractable form,' then do the calculations on a computer."

"I don't really know what that means," she said, "but . . . Well, have you had success?"

"A lot of it," he said. He made a face. "Up to a point. Then I ran out of steam. I haven't done anything useful for some time now." He made a sound of derisive amusement. "Which makes this whole damn thing ridiculous. If whoever's behind it really knew how lame my work has been for the past few months, they wouldn't have bothered."

"Well, obviously, they don't feel that way," she said. "What you're working on must still be regarded by them as very important."

"What I'm working on, sure." He nodded. "What I've been doing with that work lately . . . forget it."

He glanced out the window, then back at her, then did a violent double take. "*My God,*" he muttered, a spastic chill making him wrench in the chair.

"What is it?" she asked in alarm.

He pointed out the window. "Do you . . . see—?"

She turned her head. "The Statue of Liberty, you mean?"

He looked at her with relief and astonishment. "You can see it?" he asked.

"Of course," she said with a perplexed smile. "I don't understand."

"Well." He swallowed dryly. "The last I heard, it was in New York Harbor and considerably bigger."

Her smile brightened. "This is a copy given to Paris by the American colony here," she told him.

He drew in a tremulous breath and closed his eyes. *For a moment there* . . . he thought. He shuddered uncontrollably. "Jesus," he said.

"Why did the sight of it shock you so?" she asked, perplexed again.

"It made me think about reality slippage," he told her.

"Oh." She nodded, understanding. "And about that wager, I imagine; that man."

"Veering. Yes, that too." He managed to force a smile. "Know enough about what I do now?" he asked.

"All I'll ever know, I guess," she said, amused, "since I didn't understand a word of it."

"Except for 'targets,'" he reminded her.

Her smile faded. "Except for that," she said.

As they stepped off the boat onto the *embarcadère*, Chris put his right arm over her shoulders. "In the midst of all this insanity," he said, "I hope you don't mind that I've fallen in love with you."

She didn't look at him. "You know I don't mind," she said. "I feel the same but . . ." Her voice trailed off.

"But?"

She sighed unhappily. "It simply isn't possible right now."

"Why?" he asked. "Just because my life's a nightmare? Just because people want to replace me or kill me or both?"

Her laugh was not one of pleasure. "Oh, Chris," she said. He felt her arm slide firmly around his waist. "I wish it could be."

"Can't we go to your island?"

She looked at him worriedly. "You won't mention that to anyone, will you?" she asked.

"To whom?" he asked, smiling. "Who do I know beside you that isn't out to get me?"

"I'm so sorry for what you're going through," she told him. "I *am* going to try and get you out of it. Until that time though . . ."

He nodded. "Okay. Until that time. As long as you know I love you. As long as I know you feel the same."

They had reached her car now and, turning to him, Alexsandra pressed hard against him, her arms tightly around him. "I feel the same," she said.

Her lips moved hungrily to his and, for those seconds, he felt nothing but impassioned joy.

But then she was whispering, "Just remember. Whatever happens . . . whatever you find out . . . I didn't know I was going to love you."

He tried to ask her what she meant but she had abruptly pulled away from him to unlock the car door; before he could speak, she'd gotten inside. A sense of cold anxiety inside him, he walked around the car and, as she unlocked the other door, slid in beside her. "What did you *mean* by that?" he asked.

There was a rustling in the backseat. Both of them gasped and jerked around as two dark figures loomed behind them. Suddenly, Chris felt hands grabbing at him and a cloth forced across his mouth and nose, a hideous acrid smell lancing into his nostrils. He tried to pull the cloth away but the man who held it was too strong. Chris caught a glimpse of Alexsandra struggling with the other man, a cloth across her face as well.

The last thing he heard was her pitiful cry. "No, don't!"

Then darkness swallowed him.

5

He twisted uncomfortably, clenching his teeth; his neck felt stiff and achy. *Damn,* he thought and opened his eyes.

He was still in the car.

Automatically, he looked toward the other seat, wincing as he stretched his neck muscles.

Alexsandra was gone.

What else? he though with unexpected fury. He twisted around to look at the backseat. Except for his bag, it was empty.

"Goddamn it!" he raged. *Here we fucking go again!* Drugged and taken someplace else, drugged and taken someplace else, drugged and taken someplace else! He was sick and tired of it! Sick and tired of being treated like a goddamn puppet!

He kneaded at the back of his neck, grimacing as he looked around.

At first, he thought the car was parked in the Bois de Boulogne again. Then his gaze elevated and he saw that there were no buildings anywhere in sight; all he could see were trees and meadows. He was in the country somewhere. Where—in France? he thought bitterly. Or was it Austria, Germany, Switzerland, England again?

It could be anywhere.

He rolled down the window and drew in deep breaths, trying to rid his nostrils and throat of the sickening aftertaste; chloroform, no doubt, he thought. But administered by whom? The Middle Easterners? That made no sense. They wanted him dead, didn't they?

A *third* group then?

"Oh . . . God!" He pounded a fist down on the seat, hissing at the flare of pain it caused in the back of his neck. Groaning, he kneaded at it with both hands, trying to relax the muscles.

While he was doing it, he saw two objects on the driver's seat, one a small box, the other a small cassette player. Now what? he thought angrily. Another goddamn composition to interpret the address of some house hidden in the fucking titles?

He exhaled heavily. "Well, *screw you,*" he addressed whoever had put the objects there beside him. He wasn't going to play this goddamn game anymore, be led around by the nose mentally. *No way.*

He got out of the car and paced along the side of the two-lane road. The air was a little chilly, making him shiver. He looked at a small truck as it rattled by. The back of it was loaded with potatoes. Farm country, he thought. He continued pacing, breathing deeply.

He checked his pockets. The money was gone, which meant that he couldn't drive back to Paris—or whatever major city he was near—and try to get an airline ticket to . . .

The thought faded. He couldn't do that anyway, remembering the horrible sound in Alexsandra's voice as she'd cried, *"No, don't!"*

He had to know where she was, if she was safe.

With a surrendering groan, he returned to the car and got back in. Picking up the box, he opened it.

Inside, lying on a crumpled tissue, was Alexsandra's ring.

He picked it up and looked at it, abruptly feeling sick as he saw that it couldn't possibly be a copy—at least not one that she'd had made. It was far too old. He closed his eyes. Why did she have it in her possession? And how could she be in that painting? Would she tell him that was a copy too?

He opened his eyes and looked at the small cassette player. He didn't really want to hear what was on it. He wanted to hurl the ring into the meadow the car was parked by, then go home. He was in way over his head, he knew that. He just couldn't handle it anymore.

Reaching out, he pressed the Play button.

"In the glove compartment is an envelope with a train ticket in it," a man's voice said. "You will drive in the direction the car is pointed until you reach the next town. There you will park the car at the train station, leaving the keys inside, and board the first train to Lucerne, Switzerland. A man will meet you there. He will take the ring and give you back the woman."

Chris started, tensing, as he heard Alexsandra's voice on the player. "Please do it, Chris," she said. "I have to tell you—"

She broke off and there was a sound of scuffling. "*Please*," she said.

There were more sounds as though Alexsandra was being dragged away. A door slammed. Then the man's voice said, "If you fail to take the ring to Lucerne, the woman will come to considerable harm." His voice, already harsh, made Chris wince as it added, malignantly, "Don't doubt it for a moment, Barton."

He kept listening but there was no more. He finally reached down and turned off the player.

Opening the glove-compartment lid, he removed a bulky envelope from inside the compartment. It contained the train ticket, some Swiss currency and a passport.

He opened the passport and looked at it. The same photograph of him was in it. But now his name was Wallace Brewster and he was from Oklahoma City. He'd traveled to England, Scotland, Wales and Ireland, Italy, Greece.

Chris put a hand across his eyes. How much more of this could he endure? he thought.

He shivered. Had he actually thought, however briefly, that this experience was stimulating, romantic? "Sure," he muttered. "As romantic as a funeral."

He lowered his hand and glared at the cassette player. "I'll tell you what I'm going to do," he told the faceless man. "I'm not going to fucking Lucerne. I'm not taking the ring to anybody. I'm heading for the nearest police station where I'm going to turn myself in and—"

The vow broke off. He sighed wearily. *No, I'm not,* he thought. He couldn't turn his back on Alexsandra.

"Lucerne," he muttered, dismally.

🕸 He kept swallowing dryly, trying to clear his throat as he drove. He'd almost gagged on the Calan and Vasotec when he swallowed them without water.

His bag was still the same except that his former passport was gone. *Naturally,* he'd thought with sardonic acceptance. *I'm not Chris Barton anymore. I'm Wallace Brewster.* What did he do for a living now? Plumbing? Distribution? Pornography?

The countryside he drove through was stunning. He'd read that the French landscape was beautiful. That was an understatement. Maybe it was because he was from Arizona, but the vivid shades of green in the trees, the bushes, the grass looked so much richer than anything he'd ever seen before; no wonder so many famous French artists had used nature for their model.

A pity he could take no pleasure from it.

Fifteen minutes later, he was in the town; he went by the name sign too rapidly to see what it read. It started with P, that was all he knew.

The railroad station was on the road he was driving along. Steering the car into a parking area in front of the wooden station house, he got out with his bag, leaving the key in the ignition; it felt odd to do that even though he couldn't care less what happened to the car. The name of the town was Prienne.

Entering the waiting room, he walked to the ticket window and asked, in French, when the next train to Lucerne was due. An hour and forty minutes, he was told. He nodded, then asked if there was a café nearby. The man said there was one several blocks farther along the road.

Chris thanked him and left the station. He'd momentarily thought of asking if he could leave his bag with the man, then decided that, the way things were going, he'd do best to keep it in his possession.

He got back into the car and drove down the road to the café. Parking beside it, he locked his bag in the trunk and went inside.

He ordered orange juice, croissants, butter, jam and coffee and sat down with the food. Interesting, he thought—perhaps offensive was a better word—how regularly his appetite reclaimed its place in his attention. No matter what went wrong—now it was Alexsandra's safety—he got hungry. He felt guilty for the almost voracious manner in which he drained the glass of orange juice, tore off pieces of croissant, thickly spread them with butter and jam, and wolfed them down, following each swallow with a sip of the strong, black coffee. *I should be drinking decaf,* he thought, but he felt as though he needed some caffeine at the moment.

Eating, he recalled his vow to watch everything he ate and drank from now on. He hesitated briefly, then decided that he had to stop thinking, like a paranoiac, that everything he ingested was drugged. All right, they'd sent him to the railroad station. They couldn't possibly have foreseen that he was going to get some breakfast in this particular café.

With that, he continued eating.

As he chewed on the warm, crusty croissants—the strawberry jam and butter on them tasted delicious—he was surprised to note that his brain, uncoerced, had begun to think about the project. That's insane, he reacted. Unless, of course, he'd been away from it long enough, his attention distracted by other—albeit traumatic—circumstances and had therefore "rested" his mind.

Amused, he let his mind have its way. That was how it functioned best. He would consciously "stand back" and let it generate on its own. Numbers and symbols fluttered across the screen of his awareness. He often visualized his brain as a computer screen operated by his subconscious. Or was it his superconscious? Whatever it was, when things were clicking and the "computer" was on, he had only to watch—sometimes bedazzled, even amused—as the formulas appeared on the screen as though entered by his autonomous operator.

X_m **both** a_x **(s,y,z).** He "saw" the symbols. The words *scattering effect.* More symbols: I_x **(x,y,z).** More words: *due to significant extinction.* More symbols, more equations.

"Wait a second," he muttered, superimposing his will on the "readout." "Run through that again."

The screen flickered backwards like a VCR picture being rewound while played. He reviewed the numbers and symbols. Interesting, he thought. He'd never noticed that before.

He looked around, returning to the quiet café, empty except for himself and an old man sitting by the window, sipping on a glass of wine.

Abruptly, he stood and walked to the kitchen entrance, asking the man if he could borrow a pencil. The man gave him one and he returned to the table, sitting down again. *Forgive me,* he thought, turning over the menu. Well, it was obviously typed up daily, he saw; it was hardly as though he were desecrating the ultra-fancy menu on the Bateau-Mouche.

He turned his mind-computer on again and started transcribing the equations appearing on its "screen." If people only knew, he thought randomly, how simple it was when the "computer" was working on its own. Of course, it didn't matter how the answers came, they were still coming from his brain; though, on some occasions, he felt more like an amanuensis than a mathematician.

The world around him disappeared as the top of his pencil skidded rapidly across the paper. Yes, he thought, nodding to himself, unaware that he was doing so. Steady state clearance zone (**for times t$\geq$ [d(x)]/u**).

He'd forgotten the croissants and coffee; they grew cold as he worked, totally absorbed.

Until he reached a point where the screen began to flicker and the formulas repeated themselves. "Damn," he muttered. He was back in the café again, himself, Chris Barton, fallible human being—not Chris Barton, secretary for the flowing dictates of his inner mind.

He read over what he'd written. Not too bad, he thought. A hell of a lot better than the fumbling efforts he'd been putting out for the past two months. At least there was some insight here, some originality.

But nowhere near an answer.

He checked his watch and shook his head. It was incredible.

He was always impressed by the vanishing of time when he worked. Lucky for him he *had* reached that glitch, the computer faltering. Otherwise, he might have been sitting here until dark. As it was, the train would be arriving in thirty-two minutes; he must have been in a trance for almost an hour. It *is* like a psychic trance, he thought. They popped off and disincarnates flowed through them, or so they claimed.

He popped off and equations flowed through him, the source of which was no more apparent than the source of a psychic's results. He stared at the back of the menu, wondering whether, under the circumstances, he should take the time to commit it to memory. It would take a concentrated effort but, eventually, it might be safer doing that than having everything laid out in black and white on a piece of paper. If he was in danger—and who could doubt it now?—his main protection would certainly be in having all the answers buried in his mind.

🕉 Parking by the station, he saw that he still had twenty-five minutes before the train was due.

Leaving the bag locked in the trunk, he decided to take a short stroll through the town. Crossing the road, he started up a street resembling an alley, four-story buildings on each side. The street angled steeply upward and it seemed as though the mustard-colored buildings on each side were leaning toward him, threatening to topple.

There was no one in the street. His footsteps made faint ringing noises on the stone pavement. He passed what must have been, at one time, a garden behind a wrought-iron fence. It was here now, as though its soil had died, its nutrients vampired by centuries of growth.

At the corner was an archway of stone with a heavy barred gate in it. The grimy, faded brown stone reminded Chris of the dream he'd had about Alexsandra: the courtyard, her waiting for him in a pale white Roman gown.

He shivered, wincing. Drop it, he told himself. There's enough going on without that.

He started walking along another narrow street; this one angled downward. Don't get lost now, he told himself. He looked around uneasily. Where were all the people? Was it Sunday or something? He thought about it. As a matter of fact, it was; the shops were all closed. The residents were probably in church or at home.

He stopped beside a shop and looked in its windows. They were filled with what appeared to be artificial flower arrangements. What are those for? he wondered. He stepped back and looked up at the sign. Across the tops of the windows, dark letters on a white background, were the words *Fleurs Artificielles/Croix* on the left-hand window, *Céramiques/Plaques* on the right. That wasn't much help. He stepped back a little more and looked at the sign above the windows, faded gold letters on a black background: *Articles Funéraires.*

"*Oh, God,*" he muttered, repelled. He turned away and started walking along the street again, then froze in his tracks.

Far down the block, a young woman in a pale white gown was looking at him.

Chris felt his shoulders jerk. He stared at the woman. She was too far away for him to see her features but she looked, to him, like—

"No," he said. He shook his head. He wasn't going to let this happen to him. Reality slippage, his mind whispered perversely. "*No,*" he said, resisting it.

The woman left the street and disappeared.

Suddenly—he couldn't stop himself—he was running down the angled street, moving faster and faster. He didn't want to know and yet he had to.

He reached the place where the woman had disappeared; it was an archway into an empty, shadowed courtyard. He hesitated for a few moments, then found himself moving into the courtyard. All the doors there were locked except for one; it stood ajar in a building with a wall that was stained and cracked, its second-story windows covered by grime, some of their panes broken.

Chris moved to the doorway and looked inside. There was a narrow stairway leading to the second floor. He drew in shaking breath. Don't go up, he thought. But it was as though another's will controlled his own. Moving through the open doorway, he started up the steps, which creaked beneath his weight. The stairwell smelled of something foul, something rotten. He tried to make himself go back but couldn't.

"Alexsandra?" he called abruptly, the sharp sound of his voice in the narrow stairwell making him start. Go back, he pleaded with himself. *Don't do this.*

At the head of the stairs, there was a doorway to his right. He moved through it into an open room. There was broken glass strewn across the floor; it crunched beneath his shoes. The room was empty except for what appeared to be a very old armoire, its finish gone, its doors cracked and sagging on their hinges.

He found himself moving toward it, trying again, in vain, to stop. He didn't want to do this. Why couldn't he stop? He imagined spectral hands pushing at his back, forcing him forward. The glass shards kept crunching underneath his tread. He drew in laboring breath. The smell was awful. It was the smell of death, he thought, shuddering.

He stopped in front of the armoire, knowing that he had to open it. He visualized seeing the dead woman inside, the one he had embraced in his dream, white-faced, staring. *Stop it, that's insane!* he ranted at his mind.

He watched his hand slowly reach forward for the handle of one of the doors. *Don't!* screamed his mind.

He pulled open the door.

And drew back, chilled, his heartbeat quickening.

There was one item of clothing hanging inside.

An old, white, rotting dress.

"Oh, no," he murmured weakly. It was a coincidence; it had to be.

He couldn't take his eyes off the dress. He knew that if he touched it, it would crumble into dust. It couldn't be the same dress from the painting, from his dream. The same dress the woman was wearing when he followed her into the courtyard.

He had to leave.

He turned to go back to the doorway and gasped in horror, recoiling, feeling his heart leap in his chest.

He couldn't breathe. He stood frozen in the empty, fetid-smelling room, staring at the words scrawled jaggedly above the doorway.

5 steps to midnight.

6

I t's going faster, he thought. The idea frightened him. Bad enough he had no idea what *steps to midnight* meant. Now the words—were they warnings?—were accelerating.

What in the name of God was going to happen at midnight? And midnight *when?* Today? Tomorrow?

He shivered, refocusing his eyes to stare at the passing countryside. The only sound he heard was the rhythmic clacking of wheels on the railroad tracks.

He looked around the train car. It was not crowded with passengers; he counted nine. The car was modern, sterile in appearance, its seats hard, made of wood, metal and brown plastic. There were overhead luggage racks but he had the bag beside him on the seat, one hand holding on to it as though he feared someone might try to grab it from him.

He looked out through the window again. His throat felt terribly dry; he needed a drink. He drew in trembling breath.

In fleeing from the room, he'd tripped and almost fallen down the steep flight of steps, catching on to the banister at the last second. Maybe it would have been better if he'd fallen and been knocked unconscious, even—he genuinely felt it at the moment—been killed.

He shivered again, uncontrollably. How could that woman know he'd follow her into the courtyard? How did she know he'd go up to that room, see those words above the doorway? Who had put them there? And what had happened to the woman? God, who *was* the woman?

He closed his eyes. He'd tried, in vain, to shut down thinking since he'd boarded the train. It was impossible though. His brain kept spinning a web of unnerving fancies.

Had Veering been, in fact, not merely an annoying hitchhiker, but a harbinger of something truly awful? Had his wager been authentic and, in accepting it so offhandedly, had Chris plunged himself into its nightmarish consequences? What other explanation for these outlandish things happening to him but that the fabric of reality in his existence had been torn apart?

He grimaced scowlingly. And yet so much of it made perfect sense. The turbulence project, his replacement, his assisted flight to Europe, the perils he'd been exposed to—all of these seemed real and feasible, albeit terrifying.

It was the rest of it . . .

He was beginning to feel more odd with every passing day, his mind an increasing turmoil of anxieties. How long could he go on like this? Something had to snap finally; but when?

Maddeningly, a segment of equation floated through his mind like a bubble. *Fuck off!* he screamed at it. The bubble popped and vanished. He glared out at the field.

And saw—

He felt as though he'd just been plunged into a vat of ice water.

Far across the field stood the figure of a woman.

Wearing a pale white gown.

Chris felt tears of dread spring into his eyes. *I'm going mad,* he thought; *I really am.* It's her, it's Alexsandra. She wasn't a real woman at all. She belonged in ancient Rome, yet there she was; standing in that field, watching the train.

Looking at him, he knew.

A sudden wave of nausea flooded his stomach and, lurching to his feet, he weaved along the aisle as quickly as he could, heading for the men's washroom. *Don't leave the bag!* a voice warned urgently, but he couldn't stop. *God, don't be occupied!* he thought as he neared the washroom door.

He slammed the door behind himself and locked it, turning just in time; the contents of his stomach burst from his mouth as he bent over the toilet, bracing himself against the wall with one hand. A spasm of repeating nausea hit him and he bent over more, body jerking as he vomited.

As in a tear-blurred dream, he saw his new passport—he'd slipped it into his shirt pocket to make sure it was safe—drop into the toilet and out the hole through which he saw tracks rushing by, and disappear. "No!" he wheezed. Now he had no identity! He was nothing but a nameless body, throwing up his guts on a train to Lucerne, Switzerland. He *did* feel unreal now. It would not surprise him, if in straightening up, he cast no reflection in the mirror above the sink.

At last, his stomach felt empty and, taking in a deep breath, he stood, avoiding the sight of the mirror, turning on the faucet and washing off his lips, then face, with cold water, rinsing out his mouth.

At last he raised his eyes and stared at the reflection of his dripping features. *Thank God, I recognize myself,* he thought. *I'm still Chris Barton.*

Or was he? When the train arrived at Lucerne, would Meehan and Nelson be there to apprehend him? Would his mother be there and his sister and Alexsandra and the man and woman from his house, all pointing at him and shouting, *"Arrest that man? He's an impostor!"*?

His fingertips felt numb. *I'm really going,* he thought; *I'm falling apart.* He'd never been so disoriented in his life. Was that the wager at work? Was that what was happening? Step by step, was he losing touch with himself? In four more steps would he be undone completely? Was that what those words meant?

After a while, his pulse slowed down—he checked his wrist to make sure—and, opening the washroom door, he went out, half-expecting to see someone sitting in his seat, the dead agent from Montmartre maybe, that wouldn't have surprised him.

The seat was still unoccupied. To his surprise, the bag was there as well, untouched. His smile was devoid of amusement, as he imagined the bag having turned into a sheep playing a violin; he wouldn't have been surprised by that either. He would merely have sat down beside it and requested one chorus of "The Swan."

He closed his eyes. All right, he thought; enough. *Enough.* He wasn't going to go on like this. When he got to Lucerne, he was going to turn himself in; they'd probably arrest him for not having a passport anyway. Let the police take over, he thought. Whoever had chloroformed him must have been insane to expect him to deliver the ring to Lucerne. He felt uncomfortable with guilt about failing Alexsandra, but it was simply more than he could handle. Anyway, *was* there really an Alexsandra? Or had he been keeping company with a ghost?

He opened his button-down jacket pocket—You couldn't keep the passport in there, could you, idiot?! he snapped at himself—and took out the tissue-wrapped ring.

He turned the ring over and over in his hands. If it wasn't a ring from ancient Rome, it was certainly a perfect copy of one, he thought. He felt queasy handling it, considering what it might be—the ring of a dead woman. He wished that he *were* psychic so he could psychometrize it, maybe get some kind of answer to the dark enigma of her.

He looked more closely at the ring. There seemed to be a line around the top of it. Does it open? he thought. He tried to press his index fingernail into the line to see. At first, nothing happened. Abruptly, then, the ring top jumped up on a tiny hinge. There was something in a small receptacle inside. Chris lifted the ring and held it close to his eyes, trying to see what the something was.

A square of microfilm.

◈ "*Lucerne!*" the conductor shouted.

Chris twitched so hard, the square of microfilm flew out of its receptacle and fluttered to his lap.

Hastily, he picked it up and put it back inside the ring, pressing down the top until it clicked shut.

Now what? he wondered.

Every time insanity seemed on the verge of claiming him, a touch of harsh reality brought him back.

This had nothing to do with Veering or the wager. This was factual.

Someone wanted him to bring this square of microfilm to Lucerne.

Was Alexsandra even involved? he thought. Or had that been just another lie, another ruse to get him here?

He sat motionless, watching the outskirts of the city drift by. Microfilm.

So he was back to spies again. Agents. Military secrets. Something to do with his work? No way of knowing.

All he could be sure of was that he was not supposed to know about the microfilm.

But now he did.

Did that change things?

He'd have to wait and see.

At least there was a semblance of relief occurring now. All was not reality slippage—whatever that was. He looked at the city passing by. *Did* this change things? Should he alter his plan?

When the train stopped, he picked up the bag and walked along the aisle to the exit. Stepping down onto the platform, he followed the other passengers toward the station. He still didn't have his passport, of course. They weren't going to like that.

They didn't.

When he reached the exit gate and told the uniformed man there that he'd dropped his passport into the toilet on the train, the man looked at him with obvious suspicion. "Into ze toilet," he repeated dubiously.

"I was sick—throwing up," Chris told him. "The passport was in this pocket." He tapped the shirt pocket. "It slipped out and fell into the toilet, onto the tracks outside. There was nothing I could do, it happened so fast."

The man nodded, hooded eyes regarding Chris balefully. "You have other identification?" he asked.

"No, I don't; I'm sorry," Chris answered.

"What is your name?" the man asked.

Chris wondered what name he should give the man. If the passport was somehow found, he'd have to be Wallace Brewster. If he said he was Chris Barton, he'd be in even deeper trouble then. Not even considering the fact that a number of people might be on the lookout for Chris Barton.

"Well?" the man asked impatiently.

"Wallace Brewster," Chris said.

"Well, Mr. Brewster, I'm sorry but I can't let you into Switzerland with no identification." The man raised his arm and signaled to someone.

Chris looked to that direction, tensing as he saw a policeman approaching. Now's the time, he told himself. Tell the policeman the truth and end this goddamn rollercoaster ride. Whatever else might happen, he would at least be able to enjoy the relief of surrendering responsibility. Under the circumstances, he wasn't at all sure he was up to any further responsibility for himself.

The railroad official said something in German to the policeman. Oh, that's right, Chris thought; there *is* no Swiss language—they speak German, French or Italian. *So what?* his mind retorted. What difference does that make?

"You are American?" the policeman asked. He sounded to Chris like some actor portraying a Nazi officer in a World War II movie.

"Yes," Chris said.

"I will have to take you to the police station for a while," the policeman said, pronouncing his *w*'s like *v*'s, his *v* like an *f*, his *th* like *z*. Chris nodded at him. "Fine," he said. This really was the time to end it. When they started questioning him, he'd lay it all out—tell them who he really was and what had been happening to him. He'd ask for their assistance.

"We should be able to discover some way of establishing your identification so that you can proceed with your trip," the policeman reassured him. He sounded kind, immediately undoing the Nazi image.

"Thank you." Chris nodded again. *That's what I want, all right,* he thought; *to proceed with my wonderful trip.*

"So," the policeman said, pronouncing it *"Zo."* He gestured toward the station exit.

Chris walked beside him across the waiting room. He was

beginning to suffer an increasing sense of guilt now. What if he was wrong about Alexsandra? At this moment, his notions about her seemed infantile. She was a real woman, for God's sake; he'd held her in his arms, kissed her. She might be in real danger if he didn't deliver the ring.

He frowned. Deliver it to *whom?* he thought. *A man will meet you there,* the voice on the cassette had told him. What man? Was he watching Chris at this very moment being led away by a policeman? Why in God's name had they given him the ring with the microfilm in it anyway? *Because no one would stop you,* the answer came; *you could carry the ring into Switzerland without questioning.*

He made a scornful snorting noise that made the policeman glance at him. Well, he *had* been stopped and he was on his way to being questioned right now. So much for their dandy plan, if that's what it had been.

"There is nothing at all in your bag which might identify you?" the policeman asked.

"No." Chris shook his head.

"How are you traveling then?" the policeman asked. "You have no credit cards?"

"Only cash," Chris answered.

"That is very risky," the policeman said. "I find it odd that you would do that."

Not as odd as the story you're going to be hearing soon, Chris thought.

"What do you have in the bag then?" the policeman asked.

Thank God I don't have a gun anymore, Chris thought with sudden relief. "Clothes," he said. "A toilet kit. Some medication."

"You are ill?"

"Hypertension," Chris replied.

"Oh, yes." The policeman nodded again. "What sort of work are you in?"

Subtle police interrogation? Chris wondered. He thrust aside the thought. What the hell, he might as well get started on the truth, he decided. "I'm a mathematician."

"*Are* you?" the policeman said as they left the station and walked out onto the sidewalk. He sounded impressed. "What sort of mathematics? You teach?"

He is *interrogating me,* Christ thought; *he's suspicious.* He hesitated, then, once again, decided that he'd do better to stick to the truth. "No, I work for the government," he said.

"Ah. Of *your* country?" the policeman asked.

"Of course."

"What sort of work?"

Chris tried to repress the irritation he was beginning to feel. "I'm not permitted to discuss that," he answered.

"Ah-*ha*." The policeman sounded impressed again. "Military secrets?"

Chris tried not to smile. "Something like that," he answered.

"Interesting." The policeman kept nodding. "That is very interesting."

He opened the door on the passenger side of the police car and Chris got in, holding the bag on his lap. He felt more and more strange doing this. There was something wrong in submitting, he thought. Alexsandra had probably saved his life in London. He had no reason not to help her; he shouldn't be giving in like this. If she was really in danger . . .

How could he possibly be sure that she wasn't?

And you're in love *with her?* he thought condemningly. The guilt was getting more severe with each passing moment. *You're a coward,* said a voice in his mind. He wanted to lash back at it but couldn't.

The policeman was in the car now, starting the engine. He signaled with his left arm, then slowly pulled out into the flow of traffic.

"So; you dropped your passport into the toilet," he said.

"I didn't *drop* it in, it fell in accidentally," Chris responded, a little tensely. He didn't like the implication that he'd done it on purpose.

"Of course," the policeman said.

Chris drew in a long, deep breath. *My God,* he thought; *if the man can't even believe that, what the hell will his reaction—and those of his fellow policemen—be when I tell him what's been happening to me in the past six days?* They might all decide that he was insane and have him committed for observation. Suddenly, the idea of giving up and seeking their help didn't seem quite so promising. He could, in fact, end up worse off than ever.

But what could he do about it now?

The answer came with startling suddenness.

The policeman had turned the car into a narrow side street and was a quarter of the way down the block when they saw the car ahead.

It was turned across the two lanes of the street, its driver's door open, a man's body sprawled motionless on the pavement. "*Gott'n'immel*," the policeman muttered, braking fast. Throwing open his door, he jumped out and started running toward the body. *No,* Chris thought. He didn't know why he thought it, but he knew that there was something wrong.

His feeling was immediately validated as a second man jumped out from behind the other car and sprayed something into the policeman's face. Chris caught his breath as the policeman stumbled to one side and collapsed to the pavement as though shot. The sprawled man quickly got up and he and the other man turned toward the police car.

They started toward it on a run.

7

For an instant Christ sat frozen, staring at the two men running toward him—one short, bulky and blond (the one who had been lying on the pavement), the other tall and slender with black hair.

Then, jerking with reactive movement, he yanked up the door handle and shouldered the door open, lurching to his feet, the bag in his left hand; somehow he knew he couldn't leave it. Twisting around, he started fleeing up the street.

"Don't run!" one of the men shouted. Wincing, Chris picked up speed, racing along the pavement. He leaped onto the sidewalk and ran as fast as he could. An approaching man, seeing his charging approach, ducked to the right, a startled look on his face as Chris rushed by. At least they couldn't shoot at him, Chris thought. There were pedestrians; two women now came walking toward him. Like the man, they reacted with alarm to his charge and separated, one banging against a storefront window, the other jumping into the street. They shouted at him angrily in German as he sprinted by.

Just ahead, he saw an opening and, impulsively, raked around a building edge and started running up an alley, thinking *God, don't let it be blocked!*

It wasn't. Far down the narrow passageway, he caught sight of traffic and pedestrians on the next street. He glanced across his shoulder and saw the two men racing into the alley. *I have to dump the bag!* he thought in desperation; it was holding him back. *You need it though!* his mind cried back. He sucked in air with a wheezing sound and tried to ignore the weight of the bag pulling down his left arm. Running hard, he shifted the bag to his right hand, losing impetus for a few moments as he swerved and almost grazed the building to his right.

At the next street, he made a wide turn onto the sidewalk, almost bumping into a street lamppost; he pushed off it with his left hand. There were more pedestrians here. Would he be better off stopping and remaining in their midst? He dropped the notion instantly; the men would grab him anyway, he was sure of that. He was breathing through his teeth now as he dodged past walking men and women; most of them were forced to dodge aside to avoid collision, their expressions stunned or angry, their voiced reactions either astounded or infuriated.

Impulsively, he dashed into the street. A car jolted to a halt bare inches from him, brakes shrieking. He heard a muffled shout inside the car, a curse in French. He ignored it, jumping up onto the curb again, glancing back once more. The men were close behind, their expressions grimly intent. He wasn't going to outrun them, that was obvious. He'd have to do something else to elude them.

He wheeled around another building edge and started running down an alley toward the next street, wracking his brain for an idea, something he might have read in a novel or *something*. He couldn't keep this up much longer. Already he was losing breath, the bag beginning to feel like an anvil dragging down his body.

He gasped in shock as a figure emerged from a doorway, a man carrying a large cardboard carton. Chris couldn't stop. "Look out!" he cried, slamming into the man head-on and knocking him back. The man went floundering to his right, lost balance and began to topple over. Chris veered as quickly as he could and just missed tripping over the man, who cursed at him violently in German as he crashed against a building wall, then went sprawling into the alley.

It was a momentary break for Chris. As he reached the next street and looked back, he saw the man leaping to his feet as though to pursue him. The two men were also unable to avoid the man and collided with him sharply, all three tumbling down onto the cobblestone paving; it would have been funny if the situation had been different. There was no time for amusement though. Briefly relieved, Chris turned onto the next street and raced along the sidewalk, causing pedestrians to scatter. He had to stop soon. A stitch was starting to jab at his left side. Why hadn't he jogged in the mornings the way he had always intended to? *Damn* it!

First, the bag, he thought. He reached another alley and glancing back, saw that the two men hadn't reached the street yet. A burst of harsh elation struck him as he darted into the alley. There was a fence to his right, a sign on it reading LI-TAI-PE/ Fine Dining. Swinging the bag, he tossed it over the fence, still running. The release of the weight gave him a momentary illusion of lightness and he sprang forward rapidly. *Now* he'd outdistance them! They weren't going to get him now, goddamn them!

Another street. He recoiled and leaped back as a small car almost ran him down. The driver honked his horn, his face behind the windshield a twisted mask of rage. Chris kept running, heading back in the direction he'd been running from on the last street.

All right, he decided; he'd have to try it. There was no way he could keep on running; the illusory lightness was already gone, his legs were becoming leaden. Looking back, he saw the men emerging from the alley, looking around to see where he was.

The instant they spotted him, Chris lunged into a building doorway. His footsteps echoed in the narrow, low-ceilinged hall as he ran. *Dear God, let there be a back door!* he thought in panic.

There was and reaching it, Chris pulled it open. An alley stretched ahead of him, extending to the next street.

Leaving the door ajar, he quickly turned back to the staircase and lunged up two steps at a time, flinging himself around the corner at the first landing, wincing in pain as he crashed against the wall.

He stood there, panting, one hand pressed across his mouth. Below, he heard the two men come rushing into the building and pound along the hallway. Then the sound of their running footsteps outside the building, fading down the alley. Jesus Christ, it *worked,* he thought, incredulous.

Dragging in a lungful of air, he thudded down the stairs and looked around the edge of the back doorway. The two men were just turning onto the next street. *Now,* Chris thought. He ran back to the front entrance and onto the sidewalk. They'd know soon enough that they'd been tricked and would double-back. He had to hide from them.

He ran back to the alley and turned into it. Reaching the fence where he'd ditched his bag, he stopped. Abruptly, he jumped up and grabbed the top of it. His shoes scraped on the wood as he tried to use his feet to climb; mostly he had to pull himself up with his arms. He managed to flop one leg over the fence and, using it for leverage, hauled his body to the top and rolled over.

He fell into a yard filled with debris. Crashing down onto a wooden crate and shattering it, he grunted in pain at the impact. Then he half lay, half sat, his back against the fence, trying to recapture breath. His bag lay nearby. He nodded, smiling faintly. In spite of the pain, he felt a kind of strange dark pleasure with himself. He'd gotten away from the bastards!

Then he recalled, again, that the man he was supposed to meet had been at the railroad station. There was no way of contacting the man now.

He was adrift in Lucerne.

His footsteps sounded hollowly on the aged wood as he trudged inside the covered Chapel Bridge, crossing its diagonal length toward another part of the city. He looked out to his right at the huge octagonal stone tower beside the bridge, wondering what it was.

His gaze elevated now to the paintings on the timber ceiling of the bridge; obviously scenes from Lucerne's historical past, he thought. As he gazed at them, he heard the rushing current of the river against the supports of the ancient bridge.

He looked down again, sighing. He had no idea what to do or where to go. Utterly on his own now, he felt helpless. He remembered once, as a boy, being lost in Phoenix when he'd accidentally wandered off while shopping with his mother. This feeling was akin to that—a kind of black dread, a sense of sick vulnerability. One grew older, he thought, but never escaped the built-in fears of childhood.

It was just past five o'clock, the sun descending toward the distant mountain peaks. Lucerne was a truly lovely city, he thought. Too bad he wasn't in the mood to appreciate its colorful charm—the deep blue sky above it, the green-clad hills surrounding it, the immense blue lake seen in all directions, the spectacular mountain peaks. If he were here as a simple tourist, he'd be enjoying it completely. As it was, he could only worry about Alexsandra and about himself.

Reaching the other side of the bridge, he started along the riverfront street, looking around. For *what?* he asked himself. What the hell was he supposed to do now? He couldn't just wander around indefinitely.

Suddenly, he realized how tired and achy he was; that run had sapped his energy and strained his muscles. He had to sit down and have a cup of coffee, maybe a sandwich. *God help me, I'm* hungry *again,* he thought guiltily. *Well,* fuck *it,* he reacted. *I'm not James Bond and never will be. I'm just a poor sap of a mathematician lost in a maze.* If he *was* a secret agent, he'd probably eat so much to relieve nervous tension that he could be portrayed not by Sean Connery but by Dom DeLuise.

He stopped at the first café he came to, started to sit at an outside table, then decided that was a bad idea. Obviously, those two men would still be looking for him, whoever they were (he hadn't even addressed that question yet). He couldn't take the risk of their spotting him by chance. He went inside and took a booth in the back where he could keep an eye on the street. When the waiter came to take his order, he asked for water, coffee and a ham sandwich, then, sighing, leaned his head back against the paneled wall and closed his eyes.

All right, who *were* those men? he thought. They weren't Middle Easterners, that was clear. Did that mean they represented yet *another* group involved in this dilemma? God almighty, he thought, is there no *end* to these groups? He couldn't keep them all accounted for in his mind. There had been the ones in Arizona— the man and woman in his house, Meehan and Nelson; not even considering Veering. There had been Basy on the airliner. The man in The Blue Swan, and Alexsandra, presumably working for the same organization. The ones who'd chased him and Alexsandra by car when he'd left the theater. The ones who'd chased the limousine the next morning. The man on the Hovercraft. The Middle Easterners on Montmartre. The men who had chloroformed Alexsandra and him after they'd left the Bateau-Mouche. Now these two in Lucerne. How did they all fit together?

Or *did* they fit together? Was it all just part of an ongoing madness of the lost wager with Veering?

"Oh, stop," he muttered, trying hard to blank his mind. His head felt numb. And all this because of the turbulence problem? He simply couldn't believe it. There had to be more.

The waiter brought the sandwich, coffee and water and, while he started in on them—were *they* drugged too? he wondered, then shunted aside the idea with a scowling snarl—he placed the bag on the booth seat beside him and, opening it, went through its contents carefully, looking in every clothing pocket, every fold, every inch of the bag's interior.

There was nothing. Chris sighed wearily, chewing on the sandwich. What could he hope to do anyway? he thought. Without a passport, his freedom was obviously limited. Sooner or later, he'd be picked up by the police. Once again, he wondered if that wouldn't be the best thing to do after all. What options had he left?

The answer came as he removed the money from his pocket and started unpeeling bills to pay the check.

On the second bill below the surface, there were small words linked across its top.

If trouble at station, Tyrol Inn, 8 P.M.

He looked at his watch. It was several minutes past six. What was he supposed to do until eight? Get a hotel room? That seemed inadvisable. For all he knew, he'd be in Tokyo by tomorrow morning.

He ordered a piece of apple pie and more coffee, then sat staring across the dim interior of the café, out through the cottage-type windows at the street. The café was quiet, nearly empty; it was probably a dead period between afternoon and evening patronage.

The waiter brought the pie and coffee and Chris forked a bite of pie into his mouth, washing it down with a sip of coffee. *What do I do?* he thought. He wasn't used to minutes of mental inactivity, much less hours; it simply wasn't part of his makeup to relax and do nothing.

All right, he thought. At least it would kill some time. Unbuttoning the top pocket of his jacket, he eased out the folded menu, opened it and ran his gaze across the notations. Yes, it *was* a new approach, he saw; minor but definitely innovative. He wondered where it might lead.

He signaled to the waiter and asked to borrow a pencil. For the want of a nail, he thought as the waiter went to get him the pencil. What if he was unable to get pencils when he needed them? Would all his unreleased ideas dry up? He wished that he had a laptop computer; that would really be helpful right now.

"Oh, well," he murmured. He thanked the waiter for the pencil, then examined the menu. It was in a pseudo-leather binder. He looked around, then put it down on the seat of the booth and, slowly, tore out one of the pages. *Two years, menu desecration,* he imagined a judge's sepulchral voice.

It would be nice if the man on the Hovercraft had been right in telling him that he might be able to go home if he finished his work. It didn't exactly make sense under the circumstances but it was inviting.

That was his last conscious thought as his concentration dipped into the formula and all conceivable variations. He began scribbling numbers and symbols on the back of the page, the machinery of his brain turned solely to the problem at hand. As always, everything vanished—the environment, his identity. He became, in essence, a computer devoid of personality, a thinking device. Figures seemed to appear from the pencil point as though the pencil was a conduit between his brain and the paper—or a tube of numerical and symbol-laden toothpaste that he was quickly squeezing onto the paper. He felt no conscious connection to the rapidly appearing lines of mathematics. It was as though they came from a source other than his brain.

When he reached the bottom of the sheet, he blinked with the sensation of emerging from a trance; he always came out of successful productivity like that. Looking up, he saw to his surprise that it was dark outside. Oh, God, he thought. What time was it?

He checked his watch in alarm, then made a sound of appreciative amusement. It was a quarter to eight. His mind seemed to have that capacity as well, to retain a subconscious alarm system which protected him from missing valuable appointments. It was not the first time this had happened.

He hastily ran his gaze over the sheet, nodding. Even better, he thought; possibly closer to the answer. He looked at the two sheets of equations. Did he dare keep them as they were? There wasn't time at the moment but, when there was, it would be better if he committed all of this to memory. God forbid anyone got their hands on these sheets. Not that they were exactly the open sesame to the turbulence problem. But an imaginative mathematician would be able to see where he was headed and travel further along the theoretical track. He nodded to himself. He *would* memorize it later. It would be decidedly safer.

Folding the menu pages, he slid them into his jacket pocket and buttoned it shut. There, he thought. He felt a trifle guilty for having completely forgotten about Alexsandra while in the throes of concentration. Still, he felt a kind of pleasure too. He'd been bumbling over this area of the formula for too damn long. It made him feel good to see a glimmer of light in the fog.

He paid the bill and asked the waiter where the Tyrol Inn was. It was located only a few blocks away, he was told. He left the café and turned left, heading toward the lake. The lighted street looked charming to him and, once more, he regretfully thought how much he could enjoy being in Switzerland if he didn't have this menace hanging over him. To be a tourist here with Alexsandra on his arm; that would really be perfect.

Dream or no dream.

* * *

Halfway to the Tyrol Inn, an idea occurred to him and he stopped in a dark alley for a few minutes. Play it safe, he told himself. He reached the Tyrol Inn at three minutes to eight; good timing, he thought. He went inside, wincing at the blast of noise that hit him from the crowded interior. Why was the meeting set for here? he wondered. Was it because the more crowded a place, the safer it was? That had a kind of perverse logic to it.

The hostess led him to a small table for two far in the back of the inn and handed him a menu. *Jesus, do I have to eat again?* Chris thought. *That shouldn't be so difficult for you,* his mind rejoined; *you get hungry every time the clock ticks.*

The waiter came and he ordered a stein of beer and a sausage sandwich; he probably wouldn't eat it, but he felt that he should order something.

While he waited for the beer and the sandwich to arrive—and whoever was going to show up (would they know him by sight?)—he watched the woman entertainer on the platform far across the room. She was dressed in a gaudy peasant outfit, her molten blond hair hanging down in two fat pigtails, singing a song that Chris assumed was meant to be an imitation of a bird. Either that or the woman's voice was hideously high-pitched and peeplike.

The audience enjoyed it greatly though, applauding thunderously when she was finished, whistling and cheering, stamping their shoes and pounding steins on the shellac-thick tables; obviously stein-pounding was a long tradition here, Chris thought. The woman smiled, revealing two gold teeth, then curtsied cutely and ran from the platform to be replaced by a burly man with a large handlebar mustache, wearing lederhosen, carrying a horn so huge it had to be propped on one leg like a giant telescope.

The noises that burst from the mouth of the horn were so piercing that they made Chris catch his breath. *Jesus Christ,* he thought; what was the horn designed for, calling sheep ten miles away? Signaling aircraft?

The waiter brought the stein of beer and sandwich and dumped them down on the table, turning away hurriedly. Chris grimaced at the continuing horn blasts as he took a sip of beer. It tasted good, rich and flavorful. Too bad he had to drink it to the ear-splitting accompaniment of that horn from hell.

He was just sighing with relief as the man completed his deafening solo—even the cheering, whistling, shoe- and stein-stomping sounded easier on the ears—when a young, brown-haired man came over to the table and sat across from him.

Chris looked intently at the man, wondering if he'd been directed to this table because the inn was so crowded or if this was the man he was supposed to meet at the railroad station. The man was in his thirties from the look of him, stern, imposing and thoroughly Germanic in appearance, and smiling at him.

Then the man reached beneath his jacket, making Chris stiffen guardedly. The man's smile widened as though he knew what Chris was fearing. Instead of a weapon though, he removed a key attached to a dark plastic tag and dropped it on the table in front of Chris. "There," he said.

Chris looked at the key.

"You will find your lady in that room," the man told him, his German accent extreme.

"Is she all right?" Chris asked.

"Perfectly," the man replied. "And now, if you would be so kind."

"How do I know she's really there?" Chris demanded.

"You must take my word for it," the man said. "The ring, please."

Chris reached into his side jacket pocket and removed the ring. He set it on the table in front of the man, who snatched it up. "Thank you," the man said, nodding once. He immediately stood and walked across the crowded interior, exiting into the night. *Thank God he thinks I'm an idiot,* Chris thought.

The moment the man was gone, Chris put a bill on the table to pay the check and quickly got up, carrying his bag. Crossing to the entrance, he went outside and looked in both directions. The man was already out of sight. He'd be back soon enough. As soon as he opened the ring.

He stopped a passing woman to inquire where the Bernerhof Hotel was; the name was on the tag. She told him and he turned back toward the Chapel Bridge.

His running footsteps echoed hollowly inside the covered bridge as he rushed across the river, turned left onto the Bahnhofstrasse, then right at the first street he came to. His heart was pounding from the exertion, his breath laboring. He kept running though, down the block and into the hotel entrance.

When the elevator failed to appear soon enough, he turned to the stairs and pelted up them two steps at a time. He was panting by the time he reached the room on the third floor. Hastily, he slipped the key into the lock and opened the door. The room was dark. He felt around for the light switch, found it and flicked it up quickly.

It didn't surprise him to see that the room was empty.

8

"**Y**ou son of a bitch," he muttered.

He glared at the room. Looked toward the dark bathroom. Shivered as a dreadful notion struck him. Walked hesitantly to the bathroom doorway and, reaching in, switched on the light.

The sound he made was one of deep relief. He'd suddenly imagined Alexsandra crumpled in the bathrub, dead; strangled, slashed, shot, whatever.

"For Christ's sake," he said, angry at himself. *You read too goddamn many thrillers. Grow up.*

Drawing in a long, restoring breath, he walked over to the bed and sank down on it with a groan. They'd be here soon enough; maybe just one of them. Which would it be? The man who'd taken the ring? The tall, black-haired one? The short, bulky man with blond hair? He didn't relish the idea of seeing either of them again, but he had to know where Alexsandra was.

He started, gasping, at the sudden crashing noise. The door flew open, its latch kicked apart. The bulky, blond man lurched into the room, his expression one of fury. "What the hell do you think you're doing?" he demanded.

Chris swallowed quickly, trying to keep his voice controlled as he answered, "The deal was the ring for the woman. You have the ring, I don't have—"

"I don't have what was *inside* the ring!" the man interrupted.

Chris stood up; felt his legs shaking. "I don't have the woman either" he said.

Skin pulled taut across the man's face as he started forward. Chris drew back, bracing himself. The man reached for him and Chris slapped aside his hand. "You want the micro-film, you—"

He broke off as the man reached out again and grabbed him by the shoulder. His head snapped aside as the man slapped him hard across the left cheek. "Damn it!" he cried.

The man drew back his hand to slap again and Chris wrenched free of his grip, falling back toward the bed. The bulky man lunged forward and fell across him, clutching at his throat. "Where is the film?" he demanded savagely.

Chris jerked up both legs, his right knee catching the man full in the groin. With a startled cry of pain, the man let go of Chris and stood up, features distended as he clutched as his testicles. Chris shoved himself up and shouldered the man as hard as he could, knocking him back against an armoire standing by the wall; he heard the paneling crack as the man backed hard into its door.

For an instant, Chris was going to run for the hall and try to escape. Then he realized that if he did, he'd still be in the dark about Alexsandra and, impulsively—had he seen the move in a film, read about it in a novel?—he flung himself at the man; crossed his wrists and grabbed the collar of the man's jacket, yanking it together chokingly. "*Where is the woman?*"

His advantage ended in a second. The man was frighteningly strong, reaching up to jerk Chris's hands free, then shoving him away. Chris floundered backward, crashed against the bed and started to fall, grabbing on to the mattress to stay on his feet.

To his surprise, the man didn't charge but remained leaning against the armoire, face white, teeth bared in a grimace of pain.

"We *told* you," he muttered. "She's all right. You can speak to her on the telephone."

A rush of fury inflamed Chris. "Goddamn it, I don't want to talk to her on the telephone! I want to see her! Where *is* she?!"

The man drew in a rasping breath. "Paris," he said.

"Paris?!" Chris stared at him, appalled. "I was told to come *here* if I wanted to save her!"

The man winced, still gingerly rubbing at his testicles. "We must have that film," he said. "It is essential that you give us the film."

"You don't get it until—"

Chris broke off with a shudder, staring at the pistol the man had pulled from his pocket. "Wait a second," he murmured.

"I have no time for this shit," the man's voice crowded out his. "Give me the film or die."

Chris drew in a long, shaking breath. "If I die," he was aghast to hear himself say, "you never get the film. It's not here," he added quickly, seeing the man's face tighten. "I've hidden it and, until I see her personally, it *stays* hidden. So go ahead and shoot."

What the fuck are you saying?! screamed a frantic voice in his mind. *This isn't a goddamn story, Barton! The bullets in that gun are real!*

The blond man straightened up now, fingering a line of sweat from his upper lip. He moved across the rug to Chris and grabbed him by the right arm. Suddenly, the muzzle of the pistol was shoved beneath his chin, forcing back his head.

"Where is the film?" the man asked gutturally. "You tell me now or your brains are on the ceiling."

Chris felt frozen, unable to respond. *I'm going to die,* he thought. The idea seemed inconceivable.

He grimaced and made a sound of dread as the man cocked the hammer of the pistol. "Now," the man said.

"I haven't *got* it here!" Chris was astonished at the amount of anger still in his voice. It was as though he were two men simultaneously—one blank with utter, mindless terror, the other like a stubborn madman.

"Where *is* it?" the man snarled.

"I *told* you! *Hidden!*" he cried out faintly as he felt the pistol jammed up harder against the bottom of his chin. *I'm committing suicide,* he thought.

"Stop that," said a voice from across the room.

The pistol was pulled from under Chris's chin and he turned toward the doorway.

The tall man with black hair was standing there, looking across the room in disgust. "Are you insane?" he asked.

For a moment, Chris thought the man was speaking to him.

Then the blond man was muttering, truculently, "He won't say where the film is."

"So you were going to blow his brains out; wonderful," the tall man said. "Brilliant, Karl. You always were a brilliant man."

"Well, what do you expect?!" the bulky man responded angrily.

"From you, obviously nothing," the other man said. "Get out of here and wait in the car."

Chris looked quickly at the blond man as he tapped Chris painfully on the chest with a rigid index finger. "You're a lucky man," the man said through clenched teeth.

He stood motionless as the blond man walked back across the room and went into the corridor, closing the door behind him; it thumped against its frame, the latch unable to close.

Suddenly, Chris's legs began to vibrate and felt as though they were made of rubber. Wavering back to the bed, he slumped down with a faint groan. "Jesus God," he murmured.

"You *should* look unnerved," the tall man said, approaching him. "You're fortunate that I decided to come up. Karl is not the most benign of men."

That's the understatement of the week, Chris thought, still shaken.

The man sat down beside him on the bed. "Listen," he said. He patted Chris on the leg. "Barton."

Chris looked at him in surprise. It was not unlikely that the man would know him by name but it still startled him a little.

"You're only making things difficult for yourself," the man said. His tone was kindly. Good cop, bad cop, Chris thought. That he'd read about *ad infinitum*. The bad cop softens up the victim with intimidation, even threats of death. The good cop stops what's going on and manages to wheedle information through benevolence.

"We really need that microfilm," the man told him. "It's of no value to you obviously. Where is it?"

Chris struggled to regain control. He sensed that he had an advantage. The man couldn't kill him because he needed the microfilm. Thank God he'd had the suspicious foresight to remove it from the ring and hide it in that alley.

He swallowed dryly, then spoke. "You're wrong," he said. "It *is* of value to me. I'm supposed to get the woman in exchange for it."

"The woman is fine," the man said irritably. "I can let you talk to her on the—"

"*That isn't good enough*," Chris cut him off angrily. Goddamn them anyway! They put a gun to his head, then expect him to give in to quiet reason? Fuck them!

"Listen to me, Chris," the man said quietly. "We *must* have that film."

"And I must have Alexsandra," Chris replied, his voice equally quiet.

The man made a sighing sound. "You're frustrating me," he said. "You don't know what you're involved in. Get out of it while you can. *Give us the film*."

"In return for Alexsandra," Chris said.

"She's in Paris!" the man snapped angrily.

"Then bring her here," Chris told him.

The man regarded him with hooded eyes. "I suppose there's no point in searching your bag."

"I'm not stupid," Chris replied.

"No, you're not. Far from it, I now see."

The man seemed to reach a decision. He stood and looked down at Chris. "All right," he said. "Find out how to get to Mount Pilatus. Go there in the morning. We'll be waiting for you. You give us the film, we give you Alexsandra."

Chris stared at him. It sounded too simple, the man too easily agreeable. He swallowed again; *God,* his throat felt dry. Well, he had no choice, he realized. He'd gotten a concession from the man, at least it seemed as though he had. Of course, they'd try to follow him when he went to get the film; he'd have to be careful about that.

"Well?" the man asked, features hardening.

"All right." Chris nodded. "I'll be there at ten tomorrow morning. Is it near here?"

"You'll find it," the man replied. He looked at Chris in silence for a few moments, then said, "Are you sure you won't give us the film if you can speak to her on the telephone? It would be a lot simpler."

"I want to see her in person," Chris told him.

The man frowned. "All right," he said. "Ten o'clock tomorrow morning then. Mount Pilatus."

Chris tensed as the man reached down and grabbed his jacket collar, pulling him up a little. He noticed suddenly how dead-looking the man's eyes were.

"You'd better have that film with you," the man said. "You try another trick and I'll let Karl have his way with you." He jerked at the collar, making Chris wince. "Karl likes to kill," he said. "He enjoys it."

"I'll have the film," Chris said.

The man nodded and left, closing the door behind him.

Chris shivered violently. God Almighty, he thought. He'd just gone through a scene the likes of which he'd only read about in make-believe thrillers. A gun jammed up beneath his chin, his life in jeopardy, a deal made under stress to regain a kidnapped woman.

Such things really happen, he thought, staggered by the realization.

It felt as though his strength had drained into the mattress. He had to sit heavily for almost twenty minutes before he could summon the energy to rise.

He got himself a drink of water—emptying the glass three times—then went downstairs and told the clerk that someone had broken in the door of his room and could he have another?

The clerk was suspicious and Chris had to accompany him to the room before the man would believe him.

Ten minutes later, he was in another room. He locked the door behind him, bolted it. His habit of taking a long, hot shower before retiring had to go tonight. He dropped the bag beside the bed and, sitting on it, crawled onto the mattress, dropping his head on the down-filled comforter covering the pillows.

He had never gone to sleep so fast.

Pilatus is 7,000 feet above sea level with a magnificent panoramic view.

It was just past eight A.M. and Chris was having breakfast in the hotel restaurant, looking at a pamphlet he'd found in a rack beside the lobby counter.

He'd been amazed at how well he'd slept. After what he'd gone through, he would have expected a night of sleepless anxiety. Instead, he'd never moved, waking up groggily at seven-thirty; another useful capacity of his brain, a built-in wake-up call.

The proud rock pyramid of Mount Pilatus is the characteristic feature of Lucerne. The summit can be reached in two different ways.

He checked his watch. He'd leave about quarter of nine to get the film.

The scenery can be admired at ease from the spacious terraces of the well-appointed restaurants on the summit of Pilatus. The Hotels Pilatus-Kulm and Bellevue are heated throughout—

His eyes moved to the last descriptive sentence in the paragraph, which was repeated in German, Italian and French. Interesting, he thought, that the first paragraph in the pamphlet was in English.

An excursion up Mount Pilatus is a valuable contribution to happy memories of a holiday in Switzerland.

Right, he thought. It's been a lovely holiday. Replete with happy memories.

"Christ," he muttered. He folded the pamphlet back up and slipped it into his jacket pocket.

Two minutes later, he had paid the bill and was walking out of the hotel with his bag; he hadn't checked to see if the hotel bill was paid. He assumed that it was, but he'd be damned if he was going to pay it if it hadn't been.

He walked down the block and turned left at the Bahnhofstrasse, heading toward the covered bridge. Were they watching him? he wondered. He had to remain alert to that or everything could fall through. Was it possible that they had lied about bringing Alexsandra here, planning to grab him when he picked up the film? He tried to avoid the thought.

He started across the Chapel Bridge, thinking how bizarre it was that, never even having been out of Arizona before, he was crossing this historic bridge in Lucerne, Switzerland, for the third time in less than a day. Not to mention his having been in both London and Paris in the past week; he still couldn't take that in.

When he reached the other side of the bridge, he stopped and kneeled to retie a shoelace. As he did, he glanced around as surreptitiously as he could. If anyone was following him, he wasn't clever enough to notice it. Sighing, he stood back up and moved through a narrow street to the Kapellgasse.

He stopped in front of a gift shop and glanced in both directions as he pretended to look in the window. Still he could spot no sign of anyone.

He started to turn away, then entered the shop impulsively as an idea occurred to him.

He purchased a small cigarette lighter and had the man in the shop put fluid into it for him. He tried it out five times, spinning the wheel. It worked each time.

He was about to pay for the lighter when he decided to buy a Swiss army knife too. He felt a little foolish as he slipped it into his jacket pocket, with its double blade, saw, scissors, screwdriver, bottle opener, can opener, magnifying glass and all. *What are you going to do, defend yourself with it?* a mind-voice razzed him. *Go fuck yourself,* he answered it. *I want a Swiss army knife, period.*

Leaving the shop, he walked along the street until he reached the alley he'd stopped at the night before, on his way to the Tyrol Inn. Again, he looked around, obviously this time, making no attempt to be covert. If there was anyone after him, he was invisible, Chris decided.

Entering the alley, he walked down it until he came to the loose brick he'd found in the building wall. Easing it out, he removed the microfilm he'd wrapped and double-wrapped in a piece of tissue.

When he turned back toward the Kapellgasse, he saw Karl waiting for him at the end of the alley.

Jesus Christ, he thought. He almost felt admiration. How had the man been able to track him without ever revealing himself?

He stood immobile, wondering if he should turn and run. Immediately, he decided against it. The bag was still too heavy to run with. And he was tired of running.

He bristled as Karl gestured casually for him to approach.

When he didn't move, Karl started toward him.

Chris set down his bag and removed the tissue from the square of microfilm. He held up the film with the thumb and index finger of his left hand.

With his right, he flicked the wheel of the cigarette lighter and held the flame beneath the film.

Karl jolted to a halt, a look of panic on his face. "For God's sake, don't burn it!" he cried.

"Then get out of my way," Chris told him.

Karl stood motionless, glaring at him.

"*Now,*" Chris said. He raised the flame toward the square of film.

"All *right,* all *right.*" Karl turned quickly and walked back to the Kapellgasse.

Chris picked up the bag with the free fingers of his right hand and started forward.

When he reached the street, he looked at Karl, who stood some seven paces from him.

"If the woman isn't waiting for me, I'll burn it anyway," he said.

Karl said nothing. Jesus God, Chris thought in dread, does that mean she *isn't* there? That all this was a waste of time?

He braced himself. He had to go there anyway and find out.

He started backing along the street, his gaze fixed on Karl. Once it seemed as though the bulky man was starting forward and Chris flicked on the lighter again. "I'll *do* it!" he threatened. Two women passing by glanced at him in frowning surprise.

Karl remained motionless then and, turning, Chris broke into a run along the street, weaving his way through the walking people. He'd already inquired, at the hotel, where the dock was.

As he ran, he looked back. Karl had not moved. He stood watching Chris, a cold expression on his face. *He'd* really *like to blow my brains out now,* Chris thought.

To his surprise, the idea actually amused him.

9

The white steamship glided across the dark blue Lake of Lucerne, headed for Alpnachstad. Chris sat inside the lower deck cabin, gazing out the window at the passing city. Far off in the distance, he could see the peak of Mount Pilatus partially covered with snow; it was an impressive sight. All he could think of was Alexsandra though, and whether this was going to be a wasted trip. Simple enough for them to lie to him, planning to get the film when he went for it.

Well, that had failed. What would they try next? Was there someone else beside Karl waiting for him on top of Mount Pilatus? Hoping to take a second crack at wresting the film from him? By God, he *would* burn the damn thing if they'd lied to him and Alexsandra wasn't there; a possibility that seemed more likely the more he thought about it.

And if she wasn't there and he burned the film, what then? His bargaining chip would also be consumed with the flames. Why wouldn't they just do away with him then?

He shuddered and looked around the cabin as though for some suspicious move. There were few people in the cabin, most of them outside on the upper decks. Chris swallowed dryly. Any one of the men nearby could lunge at him and get the film before he could burn it. He had the cigarette lighter in his right hand, but he couldn't very well spend the entire trip holding the square of film poised for igniting; it was in his shirt pocket. Hopefully, he could remove it quickly if the need arose.

He sighed and looked back outside again. Was there anything he could do right now to help matters?

Memorize your work, the answer came.

Did he dare take out the two folded menu pages and begin to stare at them intently? Wouldn't that put him off guard? What if there *was* someone in the cabin waiting for an opportunity to jump him? They'd get his work, too.

Jesus God, he thought; he was back to full-time paranoia. Everyone around him was a suspect; his world was crowded with a legion of plotters.

He tapped the fingers of his left hand on his leg, trying to make up his mind.

The indecision proved unnecessary.

"Oh, my goodness," he heard a man's voice say. Its melodious lilt made him recognize the man before he turned to see Mr. Modi starting to sit down beside him, smiling with delight. "Is this not a marvelous coincidence?" the East Indian said.

Chris had been on the verge of jerking the film from his pocket when he checked himself. He smiled at Modi as though equally delighted to see him. "Well, I'll be damned," he said. "It *is* a marvelous coincidence."

Coincidence, my ass, he thought.

He tensed himself, to shove Modi away if the East Indian made a move at him; the fingers of his right hand tightened on the cigarette lighter.

"How have you been?" Modi asked, extending his right hand.

Even though he knew it could be a mistake, Chris automatically shifted the lighter to his left hand and gripped at Modi's hand with his right. "Fine," he said.

If it was a trap, it was a damned subtle one, he saw, for Modi only squeezed his hand once, then withdrew his own hand, still beaming. The East Indian shook his head wonderingly. "I just cannot believe this," he said. "I might well be part of your reality wager gone amiss. This is so strange."

"Yes, isn't it?" Chris pretended to agree.

"What on earth are you doing in Switzerland?" Modi asked. "One day I come upon you in a lesser neighborhood of London. The next I find you in a steamship in Lucerne. Incredible."

His expression suddenly went serious as though he'd just

remembered something grim. "Oh," he said. "Is this another twist in your peculiar plight?"

My peculiar plight? Chris thought. *You know exactly why I'm here, you bastard.* He smiled. "Well, I'm still on the run," he said, trying to sound amused.

"If I can be of any service," Modi said. His voice was so sincere that, for several moments, Chris thought himself unworthy for doubting the man.

Then logic intervened. A coincidence that Modi was on this very boat at this particular time? Hardly. He was a mathematician, for Christ's sake. The odds against this being coincidental were astronomical, and unacceptable. Where Modi fit into this labyrinthine picture, he had no idea. That he *was* a part of it was obvious.

He felt himself tensing as Modi regarded him in silence, his smile cryptic. Finally, Modi spoke. "I can see that you do not—how is it that you phrase it in your country?—'buy' that this is truly a coincidence."

Stunned, Chris braced himself to move, to push the East Indian away, retrieve the film for burning or lunge for the doorway and throw both film and papers into the lake. Unnerving possibilities crowded his mind: Modi was aligned, somehow, with Karl and the other man; he was part of the group that had gone after him at Montmartre. It seemed least likely that he was associated, in some unknown way, with Alexsandra.

He waited tensely.

"Am I correct in this perception?" Modi asked.

Chris swallowed. "Perhaps."

Modi smiled with amusement. "Then you must suspect, as well, that our 'coincidental' meeting in London was, also, no such thing."

Chris felt nervous and confused by Modi's casual manner. He drew in a tremulous breath. One more piece to fit in. The jigsaw puzzle was unsettling again.

"You look dismayed," Modi said. Chris shivered as the East Indian patted his arm. "Please do not be; you are perfectly safe with me. I am, in fact, a representative of someone who demands that you come to no harm."

He was going to ask if Modi worked with Alexsandra, then changed his mind. He felt dazed with bewilderment. *I can't handle this,* he thought; *it's too damn complicated.*

Still, he had to know something. "Why is everyone so interested in me?"

"Oh, surely that is clear to you," Modi answered with a tone of mild chastising. "You are a very valuable commodity."

"*Commodity?*" Chris drew away from Modi with an unconscious movement.

"A poor choice of a word," the East Indian said apologetically; "I amend it to *a very valuable human being.*"

"Because of my work," Chris said.

"Well, naturally," Modi responded. "What you do is of utmost concern to many people."

What am I caught up in? Chris thought. Once more, he was hyperconscious of the folded papers in his pocket. If he was able to find the time to memorize what he had scrawled on them, he'd burn them. And if it came down to it, he'd burn them even if there wasn't time for memorization. Better he lost that work than had it fall into the wrong hands.

"All right, now what?" he asked.

Modi gestured casually. "You will, I assume, proceed to your business on Mount Pilatus whatever it may be and I—"

"*How do you know I'm going there?*" Chris demanded.

Modi chuckled, his smile confusingly benevolent. "It is the only place you *could* be going, riding this boat to Alpnachstad."

Chris felt foolish. He wanted to counter Modi and regain some kind of advantage but couldn't think of what to say or do.

Then he thought of asking, "Who do you work for?"

"Ah, that I am not permitted to divulge," Modi said as though the refusal grieved him. "I can only reassure you that, as long as you are in my presence, you are completely safe."

Chris wanted to believe him. He wanted to believe *somebody.* Still, Modi had turned out to be not merely the good savior from London, but a man more darkly involved in Chris's affairs. How could he trust Modi any more than anyone else right now?

"I'd *like* to trust you," he said.

"Oh, please do," Modi said. "I wish only that you get through all this turmoil totally unscathed."

"All *what* turmoil, Mr. Modi?" Chris demanded in a low, taut voice.

"Why, the nightmare you have obviously been suffering through," Modi replied.

An answer but not an answer, Chris thought. He looked at the East Indian in silence. Modi looked so damned concerned for him, it comforted and infuriated him at the same time.

"All that talk about . . . the *mystical* things in India," Chris said resentfully, "that was bullshit, wasn't it?"

"Oh, no." Modi looked genuinely distressed. "These things are part and parcel of existence in my land. I would not have you—how do you say it?—'lump' that together with the rest of it. Reality is a shifting and confounding phenomenon. Never think otherwise. Your life will be the worse for it if you deny the truth of that."

Chris slumped back against the seat. At this moment, he knew, if Modi chose to, he could, with the least of effort, remove the cigarette lighter from his hand, the film from his shirt pocket and the folded papers from his jacket pocket.

At this moment, he felt helpless.

🔲 When the boat docked at Alpnachstad, Chris walked beside Modi as they went down the gangplank and moved across the road to the cog-railway station.

"Your party is waiting for you on Pilatus?" Modi asked.

Chris looked at him suspiciously but Modi only smiled. "It was my assumption that, under the circumstances in which you are involved, you are not traveling to the top of a seven-thousand-foot mountain merely to sightsee."

Chris exhaled tiredly. "I don't know if anyone's there," he admitted. Why try to deceive the man anyway? he thought. For all he knew, Modi already knew exactly why he was going to Pilatus. "Do *you* know?" he asked.

"No, not at all," Modi replied. He sounded so damned sincere,

Chris thought, it was maddening. "I have no idea why you are ascending to the peak. I am, as you might say it, only 'tagging' along to keep the peace."

"Yeah," Chris said glumly. He felt like a pawn in Modi's hands. Still, he had to continue with this. If Alexsandra *was* up there, he couldn't very well not go up to find out.

To make any decision at all gave him a sense of relief and the breath he had held in shuddered out of him. Okay, that's the plan, he told himself, trying not to face the obvious fact that it was little, if any, plan at all.

"The summit is clearly visible today," Modi commented, sounding nonchalant. "It is said that when Pilate hides his head, sunshine below will spread. Conversely, when Pilate's head is bare—as it is this morning—of rain beware." He made a sound of amusement. "So it is said anyway," he went on. "The mountain is named after Pontius Pilate, of course. It is also said that his ghost walks those heights. If so, it is probably because of guilt, wouldn't you say?"

Chris barely heard the offhanded words. He had to pull himself together, he was thinking. If he was going to get away from Modi when they reached the top, he'd have to think of something good. Benign or not, the East Indian obviously represented a group that had nothing to do with Alexsandra's organization; he didn't know why he was so sure of that, but he was. Neither did it seem likely that he represented the Middle Eastern group—they had been immediately violent toward him. Nor did he seem to be allied with Karl and the other man; if he were, he'd had ample opportunity to get the film.

Dear God, how many different groups *were* involved? he wondered again. And here he'd always assumed that his work was of marginal interest at best.

How little I know, he thought.

"Please; allow me to carry your bag," Modi said abruptly, startling him. "It looks quite heavy."

"No, that's—" Chris got no further as the East Indian took the bag from him. *Don't let him do that!* a voice screamed warningly in his mind. But there was nothing he could do about it. Modi seemed in total control. The notion of starting a scuffle with him seemed out of the question. Was the East Indian applying some kind of hypnosis to him? Chris wondered.

Oh, shut the fuck up, ordered his brain.

Still, his mind had to allow, there was the lingering mystery of what Modi knew. Was he aware of the microfilm and what had happened to Chris since he'd arrived in Lucerne? Lucerne, hell, since he'd left Modi that afternoon in London? *Reality slippage,* the thought drifted across his brain.

He was almost ready to believe it.

He watched like a child observing a parent as Modi walked over to the ticket office. Somehow, it seemed appropriate, if mad, that the East Indian should pay admission for him. When Modi returned with a pair of tickets, he only mumbled, "Thank you."

"Oh, it is my pleasure," Modi said. "Come, let us get our seats."

They started toward the red car on the angled track; it was the size of a small trolley car, Chris saw.

"This is the steepest cogwheel railway in the world," Modi told him like a cheerful tour guide. "Gradients of a one-foot rise every two feet are not uncommon. It takes about half an hour to reach the top."

Chris looked ahead as they took their seats in the car. *Oh, my God,* he thought; any kind of height made him nervous and the track ahead sloped upward at an angle that looked to be at least forty-five degrees. It wasn't enough that he had to worry about what Modi might or might not do, what might or might not happen when he reached the top. He also had to endure this nightmare ride to the peak of Pilatus.

He swallowed dryly, grimacing in dread.

"Oh, it is perfectly safe, I guarantee you," Modi told him, looking over. "I think you will find the ride most intriguing."

Sure, Chris thought, until the chain breaks and the little red trolley car that couldn't goes plummeting backward down the slope at two hundred miles an hour until it reaches the end of the track.

He stiffened as the engineer came in and started the car.

Immediately, it hitched forward and began to climb the steep incline. Chris caught his breath.

"It really is quite safe," Modi reassured him.

Why should I believe you? Chris thought angrily. Modi was just another spy, albeit smoother than the rest he'd met. Except for Alexsandra, of course—assuming that she *was* a spy and not a figment of his imagination.

He glanced over at Modi and was surprised to see that the East Indian's eyes were closed. *Sure of yourself, aren't you?* he thought. Well, why not? What could he do to Modi at this point? Set him on fire with his little cigarette lighter? Pry off the top of his head with his Swiss army knife's can opener?

He looked across his shoulder, grimacing as he saw how high the railway car had already ascended; he could see for miles across the countryside, see the dock and steamer far below. Turning back, he did what he could to blur the focus of his eyes. Better he didn't look.

He glanced at Modi again. Was the man really asleep or only feigning it? He waited for several minutes, then, very slowly, reached down to unbutton his jacket pocket. Eyes fixed on Modi, he removed the two folded menu sheets and opened them with one hand so that his body wouldn't stir.

It seemed to him his mind had never worked so fast as he raced his gaze across the equations and formulas he'd penciled down. He had to memorize them in five-second bites, eyes shifting constantly to Modi to make sure that the East Indian was still asleep. How could the man be so casual under these circumstances? he wondered. It gave him a sense of what the East Indian's temperament was really like: action when needed, relaxation in between. A sound way to proceed and one that Chris was incapable of practicing.

In less than two minutes, he had the contents of one menu sheet committed to memory. He closed his eyes and brought up the readout on his mental computer, saw the page clearly. There, it was programmed now; he could bring it up at will.

Using the same procedure—five seconds on the sheet, one to glance at Modi—he memorized the second sheet. This time, he could see—with pleasure he could not deny, despite the tension of the moment—that one sheet led inexorably to the next, the concepts blending, the first equations like parents to the latter ones.

Done, he thought. He closed his eyes again and brought up the sheet for viewing. *Good.* He flipped the image to the first sheet again, nodding. There it was. Not everything, of course. He still had a way to go. But like a traveler on a new road, he knew where he was going now and that only steps and time separated him from his destination. *7 steps to midnight?* his mind inquired. He scowled away the question.

Now. He looked at Modi. If the East Indian wasn't napping, he certainly was giving a precise imitation of it.

He turned very slowly, inching around until his back was half turned away from Modi.

Then, refolding the sheets, he began to tear them in half, tearing the halves in half, the quarters in half. He tore and tore until he had to separate the pieces because they were too thick to tear all at once.

When the two sheets had been reduced to confetti, he began to drizzle pieces of them out the window of the car. If Modi had sat on the aisle to prevent him from trying to bolt, it had worked in Chris's favor with regard to the papers. He felt a weight slowly rising from his back as more and more pieces fluttered away. He knew that the couple sitting behind them was watching him, probably with disapproval. He didn't care. In a few minutes, the pieces were all gone and he had eliminated at least one major source of tension.

Once more, he closed his eyes and reviewed a mental playback of the two pages. Perfect. He smiled. Now let anyone try to get what he'd done so far.

Wait, he thought suddenly. What if someone administered scopolamine to him? Wouldn't he just blurt out all of it? He made a despairing face. Had he done all this for nothing?

No, he thought irritably. It was still better than—

He jolted, opening his eyes as the car made a rattling sound.

He reacted in surprise, seeing a herd of gray cows thinly spread out on a green, flowered slope, their heads lowered as they grazed. He grunted softly at the sight.

"A scene of great tranquility," Modi said.

Chris turned quickly to look at him. *Had* the East Indian pretended to be asleep all this time? What would the point of that have been if, in doing so, he'd allowed Chris to get rid of those sheets? He had to assume that Modi really had been napping. "Yes," he replied.

Modi looked at his pocket watch. "Well, we are almost halfway there."

Chris nodded, feeling another sense of deep relief that he'd gotten rid of those sheets without Modi knowing.

"Still nervous?" Modi asked.

"I'm getting used to it," Chris replied.

He looked ahead. There were patches of snow visible now, the green slopes becoming rocky and stark in appearance. He looked up as far as possible. The slope was so steep that he could see only blue sky ahead. He swallowed, pressed back against the seat by the extreme angle of the car. What was waiting for him up there? he wondered.

He glanced at Modi. The East Indian had his eyes shut again.

He stared at the man. Modi was not bad looking; his features were cleanly cut, his skin an interesting, bronzelike shade. Chris looked at the white turban on Modi's head, then back at his face. He remained confused by the East Indian.

Even asleep, Modi's expression was benevolent.

As the car clanked up the final slope toward the top, Chris wondered if this was the place they'd shot the James Bond film *On Her Majesty's Secret Service*. Fitting, if it were, he thought.

He looked at Modi. The East Indian's eyes were open again; he smiled at Chris. "See how easy that was?" he said.

"Yes." Chris hesitated, then said, "Mr. Modi, I don't know if you're planning to stay with me up here, but I'll have to ask you not to. If anyone is with me, the person I'm supposed to meet won't approach me." He had no idea if that was true, but it sounded logical.

"I see." Modi nodded. "Well. I have no desire to hinder you in any way. I will, of course, remain some distance from you, maintaining the attitude of a stranger. If you don't mind, however, I do feel it advisable that I keep an eye on you, however distant. I am quite sincere in my wish to see that you remain safe."

Chris nodded. "Thank you." There was no point in arguing with the man, he thought. With distance between them, he'd have a better chance of eluding Modi completely.

The car leveled at the top, entering a covered area beside a circular, three-story structure that Chris took to be the Hotel Pilatus-Kulm. The car jarred to a halt and he followed Modi outside; he'd grabbed the bag before the East Indian could offer to carry it. For all he knew, the man would offer to watch it while Chris searched for the person he was there to meet. He wasn't going to give Modi an opportunity to do that.

He shivered as they stepped outside into the cold, thin air. "*Wow*," he muttered.

"Yes, the air is very chill and thin at this altitude," Modi said. "I will be sitting on that railed balcony in front of the Bellevue Hotel," he continued without looking at Chris. He strode away as if they were strangers. Chris felt another sensation of relief as the East Indian walked off. *Now*, he thought. He looked around.

Was Alexsandra really here?

He looked at the hotel Modi was walking toward. It was more traditional in design, rectangular, three stories high. Was he supposed to go there to meet whoever he was intended to meet?

He stopped for a few moments to take out the square of film and hold it in his left hand, along with the bag; the cigarette lighter he held in his right hand again. He mustn't lose caution now. If they hadn't really brought Alexsandra here, he'd make damn sure they didn't get the film. They might kill him for doing it, but then they might have every intention of killing him anyway.

He'd try the Hotel Pilatus-Kulm first, he decided. Entering the lobby, he crossed to the desk and asked if there was a message for him. There wasn't. He sighed heavily. Is anything ever easy? he thought. Now what? Was anyone watching him as he stood there?

He looked around the lobby, braced for someone to approach him. When a portly man in a gray suit quickly got up from a chair and walked toward him, he tensed, prepared to drop the bag and burn the film if necessary.

When the portly man walked past him, cursing in German under his breath, Chris relaxed in spite of his disappointment.

He went and looked inside the bar, then the restaurant, standing in the entrance of each long enough for anyone to catch sight of him if they were looking. Both bar and restaurant were crowded but no one did more than glance at him in disinterest and he was not approached.

Which leaves me where? he thought. Should he go up to each hotel corridor and search? That made no sense. Why were they being so evasive about this? Did they want the God-damn film or not? He'd come here as requested. Why hadn't there been someone at the railway platform, waiting to accost him?

"No such luck," he muttered.

His idea that checking the hotel corridors would be a waste of time proved to be exactly that—a lot of trudging with the heavy bag, resulting in nothing. He took the elevator down from the third floor and stepped into the lobby again. Should he sit there? he wondered, give whoever was supposed to meet him time to—

He brushed aside the thought. If someone had really been on the lookout for him they would certainly have found him by now.

He left the hotel and circled around it to the left. As he did, he saw a red cable-car glide into view. He shuddered at the sight. *You are definitely not going down in one of those,* he told himself.

To the right of the cable-car structure, he saw a railing and gingerly moved there. There was no one around as he approached the railing. "*God,*" he murmured. The view of Lake Lucerne was staggering, its deep blue vastness curving around the craggy headland the boat had passed on its way to Alpnachstad. He lifted his gaze. White-clad mountains as far as the eye could see. What had he read in that pamphlet? *An unrivalled panorama of the alpine region.* "You can say that again," he murmured.

He was just turning away from the railing when he saw the body.

At first, he thought it was someone resting. He could not conceive that it could be anything else.

Then he saw the body wasn't just lying there, it was sprawled. And, as he drew closer, feeling as though some magnetic force was pulling him in, he made a faint sound of revulsion, seeing a puddle of blood around the body. He froze in his tracks, staring at it.

It was the tall, dark-haired man who'd told him last night to come up here.

He twisted around with a gasp, gaping at the man approaching him.

The man was Middle Eastern and Chris recognized him as the one who'd chased him in Montmartre.

He shuddered as the man took something from his pocket. Suddenly, a long, thin knife blade shot out from its handle, glinting in the sunlight. *No,* Chris thought. It wasn't possible, it couldn't be. To have it end like *this?*

He backed off, nerveless fingers dropping the frame of microfilm. The man paid no attention to it. He isn't here for the film, Chris thought in unbelieving horror. *He's here to kill me.*

Where are all the people?! a voice cried out in his mind. How could something like this happen when there were so many people around? He drew up the bag in front of him as though to block the knife thrust. He knew it wouldn't help, but did it anyway. *I'm going to die,* he thought incredulously. Why was he unable to believe it when it was so obvious now, so close?

Well, not without a fight, he thought, muscles tensing. Goddamn it, not without a fight. He dropped the cigarette lighter and grabbed onto the bag handle with both hands, preparing to swing it at the man when he attacked.

Abruptly, someone ran around the circular buidling, headed

for the Middle Easterner. Chris glanced aside; he saw that it was Modi. Incredibly, he looked unarmed.

A flurry of activity took place in front of him: the Middle Easterner whirled to face Modi, lunging at him with the knife blade; Modi agilely sidestepped, then, with a movement so rapid that Chris could barely follow it, chopped at the Middle Easterner's neck with the edge of his right hand, fingers stiff and rigid; the attacking man made a hollow sound of shock and, stumbling forward, collapsed onto the deck.

Modi looked at Chris, his expression hard. "Go! Leave!" he snapped, pointing. "Take that ramp! The cable cars are just below!"

Without a word, Chris broke into a run in that direction; immediately, the thinness of the air made him labor. Glancing back, he saw the Middle Easterner trying to get up; then Modi chopped the man behind the neck, and he dropped, face first, onto the concrete.

Chris wasn't conscious of racing down the ramp, or his sprinting entrance into the cable-car waiting room. Panting, he rushed to the ticket booth and quickly bought a ticket, leaving his change behind. A car was just about to leave and he rushed across the platform, heaving in the bag, then diving in himself, wheezing with breath.

He cried out, recoiling as someone leaped into the car with him. He fell back across a seat, then, gasping, looked at her as though she truly were a ghost.

"Alexsandra," he said, his voice barely audible.

Then she was in his arms and they were clinging tightly to each other as the cable car swung out across the deepest void Chris had ever seen in his life. Hastily, he pressed his face into her hair; one visual shock at a time, he thought. He had her back, that was all that mattered now.

"Thank God you're safe," she said.

He tightened his grip on her, deeply breathing in the perfumed smell of her hair. "I thought they'd lied to me."

"No," she said; she sounded breathless too. "We were waiting

. to meet you when a Middle Eastern man came up behind us with a gun and took us to the other side of the hotel. Harris jumped him and told me to go after you."

"Harris?" he asked. "The dark-haired man?"

She nodded. "Did you see him?" she asked.

"Yes." He grimaced. "He's dead."

"*Dead.*" She looked at him in shock.

"The Middle Easterner must have stabbed him, he went after me with a knife. He's the one who chased me in Paris."

"My God," she said, looking at him with dread. "How did you get away from him? I saw you come running into the cable-car station and was just able to catch up with you."

"I didn't get away from him, I was helped," he said.

"Helped?" She looked startled.

Quickly, he told her about Modi. "You know who he is?" he asked.

"No, I don't," she said quietly. "I don't like it either."

"But he saved my life." Chris looked at her in disbelief.

"*Why,* Chris?" she asked him. "Why is he involved in this?"

He stared at her in confusion. "He told me to go, to leave. Told me where the cable cars were."

She tensed and looked back at the car far behind them. "You've been followed, then," she said.

"*Alexsandra,*" he said, protesting.

"Do you think he'd just let you go, after everything he's done?" she said, turning back to him. "He followed you here all the way from London; how, I have no idea. You think he doesn't *want* something from you?"

He had no answer; he knew she was right. Whoever Modi worked for wanted access to his work. How could he have forgotten that?

"We've got to get you out of Lucerne," she said.

He groaned softly. "To where?" he asked.

He wasn't sure he'd heard her answer correctly. "*Where?*"

"Venice," she repeated.

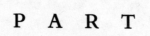

PART

1

Chris opened his eyes to find himself looking toward a large open window about six feet away. He felt a damp pillowcase against his cheek and he made a face. Sitting up, he dropped his legs over the edge of the bed.

Gray, he thought.

The very air seemed gray and laden with moisture; he could almost feel the weight of it on his skin. It was a warm moisture, and there was a thicker, wet smell in the air, a smell of age and rot.

Pushing to his feet, he crossed to the window. Both casements had been cranked out all the way, the pale white curtains stirring in a feeble breeze.

The room overlooked an alley-like street. He could see now that it was raining; a thin, mistlike curtain of it was descending so slowly, it seemed to defy gravity. Unreal, he thought.

His lips drew back in a soundless snarl. Don't start *that* again, he ordered himself.

The floor felt damp beneath his feet and he looked down. His clothes were on, but his shoes and socks had been removed. He vaguely recalled Alexsandra doing that as he had fallen asleep on the bed.

He turned to look at the room. Where was she? Had she disappeared yet one more time?

There was a piece of paper on his bedside table. He walked there to pick it up.

Be back in a little while. Don't leave the room. —A.

He read the note a second time. *Yes ma'am,* he thought glumly. *Anything you say. Where the hell would I go, anyway?*

He dropped the note on the bed and, sitting down, pulled on his shoes and socks. He rubbed a hand across his cheeks. *Need a shave,* he thought. But with what?

Blowing out a heavy breath, he stood and returned to the window.

The paving of the alley-like street was about six feet below the windowsill. Across the way, about twenty feet distant, was either another hotel or an apartment house, wall and windows rising so high that he couldn't see the roof. He checked his watch; it was 3:27. How long had he slept? he wondered. The train trip from Lucerne had been exhausting. He'd barely made it to the hotel.

One of the windows across the way had a light in it. He saw a man inside the room, sitting in his underwear, reading a newspaper and sipping at a glass of wine. Was he a spy? Chris thought. He shook that off, irritably. *Come on, Barton,* he told himself. *Everybody in the world isn't a spy. Even though it seems that way sometimes.*

He looked down at the shop windows on the street, the cafés with furniture outside, glistening and dripping from the rain. This is *Venice?* he thought. Where were the canals? Even when they'd arrived last night—early this morning, actually—he hadn't seen a canal. Unless that arcing footbridge they'd walked over had crossed a canal. But immediately after crossing it, they'd been walking along a dark, muggy street; probably the one he was looking at now.

He turned and gazed at the bed, noticing now that the other side of it appeared rumpled as well. She'd slept *beside* him? Good God, he thought. He shook his head, a pained smile on his lips. Here he'd been desperately wanting to go to bed with Alexsandra ever since he'd met her. Now, it appeared, he'd done so and hadn't even known about it.

✪ As he stood in the bathroom, relieving himself, it occurred to him that gray was the ideal color (or lack therof) to describe the way he felt.

Whatever stimulation he'd experienced before had completely faded now, the "adventure" reduced to a dismaying progression of different places, different people, different deaths.

He felt a sense of weighty depression settling on him. Was this nightmare ever going to end? He'd tried to maintain a sense of humor about it, but it had become impossible to do that now. The characters in novels he'd read seemed able to accept death easily, blithely moving on to the next suspenseful incident.

To actually see it happen was a different story altogether. The memory of the murdered man on Mount Pilatus would be with him for a long time.

He gazed at his reflection in the mirror hanging above the sink. *Still me,* he thought; *barely.* He was beginning to get a definite sense of what "reality slippage" might actually be. He shivered convulsively. This has got to end, he thought.

But how?

Finish your work before the slippage is complete, he heard the words of the man in the Hovercraft in his mind.

He stared at his reflection in the mirror. Was that the answer? Something about it seemed persuasive. If he were able to complete his work, keep it all in his head, with nothing down on paper, wouldn't he be in some kind of bargaining position with whoever was behind all this?

There was nothing else to hold on to.

Hastily, he dried his face and hands and ran water into a glass. Returning to the bedroom, he took the two vials of medication from his pocket and swallowed his Calan and Vasotec. Thank God he hadn't left the vials in his hotel room in Lucerne. As it was he had no belongings again. Would "they" provide him with *another* bag of clothes, a passport—?

A look of confusion gripped his features.

How could Alexsandra have gotten him into Italy without a passport? They'd arrested him in Lucerne when he hadn't had one.

He clenched his teeth in aggravation. Another goddamn mystery, he thought.

He didn't want to get caught up in the muddle of trying to figure things out again. Putting the vials back in his jacket pocket, he turned toward what looked like a writing table, and was pleased to see a bowl of fruit on it. He was hungry. *Again,* he thought, amazed.

Sitting at the table, he pushed aside the bowl of fruit and opened the top drawer. "At last," he muttered. Something was going right for a change. There was stationery in the drawer, a ballpoint pen. He saw that he was in the Hotel Adrian.

He lifted out the sheets of paper and the pen and laid them on the table. Then, as he allowed his eyes to go out of focus, once more staring inwardly to summon up the readouts on his mental computer, he idly picked up an orange and began to peel it.

He grunted, jolting as he saw what looked like blood dribbling across his palm. "Jesus," he muttered, staring at his hand, the first "computer readout" vanishing from his mind. Blood from an orange?

He realized then, with a labored swallow, that it must be some kind of orange he'd never seen before, possibly indigenous to Italy. He slowly exhaled, imagining that a screwdriver made with the juice of these oranges would look like a Bloody Mary.

He cleaned off his hand with his handkerchief and set the orange aside. As he mentally drifted inward again, he started eating grapes from the bowl. The computer screen flickered on in his brain and he began retrieving information, nodding without realizing that he was doing so. It was there, he saw. Maybe not the total picture. The basic path though. He only had to walk along it now and observe the countryside attentively.

He began to scribble the last part of the final readout onto paper, then continued with it, gaze fixed on the array of formulaic figures spilling across the sheet as though by magic. *Yes,* the analyzer in his brain observed. No doubt about it.

He was almost there.

🃏 He started on the chair, twisting around, the calculations in his brain evaporating instantaneously.

Alexsandra was standing by the door, looking at him.

He knew from the moment he saw her that something was wrong.

"What is it?" he asked.

She didn't respond, but stood immobile, gazing at him.

"What *is* it?" he repeated, urgently now.

Again, no answer. Instead, she walked across the room and, reaching down, picked up the sheet of paper. He tensed for a moment before he realized that the figures couldn't possibly have any meaning to her. Unless it turned out that she was an advanced mathematical theoretician, and he didn't think she was.

"So," she said, a grim smile drawing back her lips. "This is what it's all about?"

He wasn't sure what she meant by that, but didn't ask. He watched as she shook her head, the somber smile fixed to her lips.

"Difficult to believe," she said, "now that I see it here on paper." She looked at him. "How many people can it kill?" she asked.

He tightened at the question. "I'm not trying—" he began.

"It *can* kill people," she interrupted. "That *is* the idea, isn't it?"

He didn't answer at first. *Well, yes,* he thought defensively. *That isn't what I have in mind though, while I'm trying to—*

The thought vanished as she put down the paper and turned away. "You don't have to answer," she said. "It's none of my business."

He stared at her as she walked to the window.

What is wrong? he thought. She'd sounded so bitter, so condemning.

He stood and walked over to her. She was gazing out the window just as he had. As he reached her, he heard a deep sigh falling from her lips.

"What *is* it, Alexsandra?" he asked. He wanted to hold her, but something in her manner kept him from it.

At first, she said nothing. He heard the sound of her swallowing, dryly. "Look how gray it is outside," she murmured. He winced a little. His exact reaction, earlier. Did *that* mean something?

She turned to face him and he tensed to see tears glistening in her eyes. He took hold of her arms. "*What is it?*" he asked, pleading.

Without a word, she slipped her arms around him and kissed him hard. Somehow it struck him as a farewell kiss. The notion made him shudder.

She drew back then and gazed into his eyes. "I love you, Chris."

He was going to respond with pleasure when she added, "But I can't do anything to help you."

He felt a chill sinking into his stomach. "What do you mean?" he asked.

"I've spoken to my supervisor," she said. "I asked if there was some way of getting you back to your own country. Some way of getting you away from Europe."

When she didn't continue, he spoke for her. "He said no?" he asked.

"It has to go on," she told him.

"For how long?" he asked uneasily.

She shook her head. "I don't know," she said. "He doesn't know. He's following orders too."

"My God, how can I be *that important?*' he said angrily. "I'm just a cog in a goddamn wheel."

"No." She shook her head. "You know that isn't true. What you're working on is most important to your government." The grave smile once again. "Or should I say your *Pentagon?*"

"Why are you so accusatory?" he demanded. "Aren't we both in the same business?"

"No." She shook her head again. "This is the first time I've ever had anything to do with something like this."

She pressed against him once more, tightly holding onto him.

"I'm sorry," she said. "We have to go. There's something I've got to show you. You and I are almost finished now."

He tried to get her to explain what she'd meant by that, but she wouldn't do it; she only crossed to the door and opened it. He asked if he shouldn't shave first and she responded with a mordant smile.

He hesitated, then quickly moved to the writing table, picked up the paper and memorized what he'd written on it. Then, taking the sheet into the bathroom, he tore it up and flushed it down the toilet. She waited for him by the door, saying nothing.

They walked downstairs to the hotel lobby and out into the street. The rain was so fine that Chris could scarcely feel it on his head.

Five minutes later, they were sitting in a covered boat (Alexsandra called it a Vaporetto), moving along the Grand Canal. Chris almost felt guilty since he couldn't appreciate the remarkable building they passed, the bottom floors of which were at water level. But it was Paris all over again, with his inability to enjoy anything because of the circumstances.

He barely glanced at the exotic antiquity of the Rialto Bridge as the Vaporetto glided beneath it. All he could think about was Alexsandra and what she intended to show him. He remembered how unhappy she'd sounded in the car after they'd eaten on the Bateau-Mouche. It was far worse now. There seemed to be such a depth of embittered sorrow in her. He wanted to know why more than anything, but she seemed entirely cut off from him; he had no idea whatsoever what he could say to end her dark isolation.

Despite the sense of gloom her presence—and the overcast weather—forced on him, he couldn't help feeling a thrill of historical awe as he saw the green-capped tower of the Campanile above the building tops ahead. *St. Mark's Square,* he thought. He was actually there.

The Vaporetto drew over to its landing dock and Alexsandra stood up. Chris followed her ashore. *My God,* he thought. *There it is.*

Even though he'd seen the square in movies and in photographs, he was still unprepared for the impact of it. The towering Campanile bell tower was made of brick, a gilded angel statue on its peak. There were the arches, architraves and crowning statues of the Renaissance-era library. The clock tower with its figures of two Moors on top, poised to strike the hours. The immense rectangular structure of the Doge's Palace with its porticoes and loggia at the bottom, its massive walls above. Most impressive of all, the extraordinary St. Mark's Basilica with its combination of

Byzantine, Romanesque and Gothic architecture—the great balcony of its main facade, the upper lunettes with their stunning mosaics. Looking at the church, Chris was struck by the fact that its overall form was that of a giant altar.

He glanced at Alexsandra as she took him by the hand and led him toward the Doge's Palace. He had to break the silence between them, with anything.

"How did you get me into Italy without a passport?" he asked.

"That wasn't a problem," she answered quietly. "We have people everywhere."

She sounded so disappointed that he simply had to know why. "What's *wrong?*" he asked. "Please. Tell me."

For several moments, it seemed as though she was about to tell him. He could see that she wanted to, that not telling him was painful to her.

But then, with a tightening of her lips, she said nothing, and only drew him toward the entrance of the palace. Porta Della Carta, he remembered it was called. Goddamn memory, he thought, disgusted by it. Once something was rooted in his head, it never left.

They started up a staircase rising from the first-floor loggia. Scala d'Oro, he thought. The Golden Staircase. It was aptly named. The stairway shone with a golden redolence, the stuccowork, mosaics and bas-reliefs of its arched ceiling leafed with glowing gold.

He lost track of the rooms they passed through. The Doge's Apartment. The Square Drawing Room. The Room of the Four Doors. Alexsandra clearly had no interest in them, nor was she taking him to see them. She had something else in mind. Wondering what it was, Chris was in a state of nervous apprehension. He was thinking of the wager now. Their movement through the palace had an air of unreality about it. Somehow, he knew, some kind of answer was coming and he dreaded it.

The Hall of the Collegium. The Hall of the Pregadi. The Hall of the Council of Ten. Sumptuous and immense. Richly decorated. Paintings on the walls and ceilings. Hall after hall after hall.

Their footsteps ticking faintly on the hardwood floors. Her hand holding his; cold now.

At last, she stopped. They were in the Hall of the Maggior Consiglio, more than one hundred and fifty feet long, seventy-five feet wide and fifty feet high, a completely open space with window apertures reaching high up the walls. Gray lights, filtering through the window glass, created a strange, funereal kind of illumination.

Alexsandra was looking up at a painting on the wall. Chris raised his eyes to it.

And felt himself turn to stone.

The painting he had seen in her hotel room in London had only been a segment of this painting.

A painting of ancient Rome.

In its lower right corner stood Alexsandra in her pale white gown.

"It *is* me, Robert," she whispered.

2

He'd been unable to speak until now. He had little recollection of walking here. What she'd told him must have stunned him so intensely that he'd lost all track of time and place. They had to have gone back through those many halls, had to have descended the Golden Staircase and left the Doge's Palace, crossed the square to this café and sat at a table underneath the roof.

Yet only in the last few seconds had Chris been conscious of himself, realizing that he was clutching a glass of wine in his right hand. Heard her telling him to drink some more and seen her watching him with almost pitying sadness as he had drunk.

Now, finally, he'd spoken one word.

"How?"

She spoke oddly, as though the revelation was of little import to her despite its incredible content. Her tone was monotonous, devoid of conviction, her face virtually without expression. It was as though the impact of her history had gouged away her insides, leaving her hollow and emotionless.

"I don't know who my real parents are," she said. "I was raised by a couple from London. He was a history teacher, she an artist. They were living in Rome while he was on sabbatical. One day, they found me wandering on their property; I was seven.

"They tried to find my parents but they couldn't. Finally, unable to locate any relatives at all, they decided to adopt me, took me back to England and raised me as their child."

She hesitated, staring sightlessly, then drew in a long, slow breath and continued:

"When I'd been living with them for a year or so, they said

that I began to tell them that my name was Alexsandra—I'd never given them a name before. They'd called me Celia after my father's mother. I insisted that my name was Alexsandra though, and they agreed to call me that.

"I began to show a fascination with ancient Rome. I read everything I could about it and begged them to take me to museums where I could see artifacts from ancient Rome."

She stoped again and Chris wondered if she was finished. Then she went on.

"When I was twelve, they took me back to Rome. They said that I became extremely agitated. I insisted that they take me to certain areas of the city. When they did, I wept and told them that it all looked different to me. I became so distraught that they had to take me back to the hotel and call for a doctor to see me.

"That night I had a fever of one hundred and four and kept insisting that I had to go to the catacombs of S. Callisto. I tried to get out of bed to go there myself. Then I fainted.

"They brought me back to England and it took six months for me to recover.

"I never forgot that trip to Rome but I managed to live a more or less normal life. Even when that man gave me the painting and the ring—"

"I thought you said the ring was a reproduction," he interrupted.

"Did I?" she said offhandedly. "No. He gave it to me." She swallowed. "And brought it all back." She put her left hand across her eyes. "It's been with me ever since."

"Have you . . . gone back to Rome?" he asked.

She shook her head. "I'm afraid to," she answered.

"But if you went to those catacombs—" he started.

"God forbid," she said. "I could never go there. I'd be terrified of what I'd find."

"What could you find?" he asked.

She shuddered. "Myself," she whispered.

Chris stared at her blankly. It had all come back to him now too, sitting here in the grayness, the rain misting down outside, the buildings in the square spectral-looking in the fading light, listening to her story—it had brought back everything in an icy rush of memories.

Veering's wager. The couple in his house. His panicked flight. Leaving Nelson in the desert. Fleeing to Los Angeles. The flight to London, the discovery of Gene's death followed by Basy's disappearance.

7 steps to midnight.

The Blue Swan and the agent's collapse. Modi and the threatening teenagers. The theater and Alexsandra, the breath-stopping car chase. His first exposure to the painting and the ring. Alexsandra's disappearance and the car pursuit. The Hovercraft ride and the man (*Had* it been Veering?) slapping him and telling him about reality slippage.

6 steps to midnight.

Then Paris. The agent's death on Montmartre and Chris's escape from the agent's killers. His reunion with Alexsandra and their dinner on the Bateau-Mouche. The two men waiting in her car. His walk in that small French town and what had seemed to be Alexsandra in the white dress. The old building with the rotted dress inside.

5 steps to midnight.

Lucerne and the two men chasing him; the microfilm. The trip up Mount Pilatus, Modi reappearing. Another agent dying, Modi rescuing him. Alexsandra again.

All ending here with her strangely chilling account. Never had he felt so close to unreality in his life. If Veering were to sit down at the table at this moment and ask him what he thought about the wager now, he wouldn't hesitate a moment before telling Veering that he knew he'd lost it. There was no way in the world that he could find an explanation for the things that had occurred to him in the past week. He could only accept them at face value now.

A face of utter bafflement.

She lowered her hand and looked at him somberly.

"We have to go," she said.

"Why did you say that you and I are almost finished now?" he asked.

"Because we are," she answered. "Once you're out of Venice, we'll never see each other again."

"*No.*" He felt a sense of anger, not at her but at whatever made her speak those words. "*Why?* Why shouldn't we see each other again?"

"Because my assignment ends here," she said. "It was supposed to end in Paris but you kept it going by insisting I be brought to Lucerne."

"Oh, God." He looked around as though for some escape from all this lunacy. "*I don't understand what's going on.*" He looked at her tensely. "I'm totally confused and lost and maddened, Alexsandra. All I can hold on to—other than my work—is you. You can't just leave me like this."

Tears started down her cheeks. "Oh, Chris," she said; she sounded desolate. "I don't *want* to leave you. All I want to do is get you out of all this. But I can't."

"Why?!" he demanded, conscious of how loud his voice had become, that people at nearby tables were looking at him. "You're not making sense! Why do you have to leave me?!"

She seemed on the verge of telling him, leaning across the table, her expression tight. Her lips began to move as though words were formed though they remained soundless.

Then, with a convulsive groan, she shoved back her chair and stood.

"We have to go," she told him, almost angrily.

He slumped back, glaring at her. "You go," he said. "Just leave me here. I'll manage to—"

"Chris, *please,*" she begged, leaning over close to him. "How many times do I have to tell you? Your life is in danger. If Cabal locates you, *you're a dead man.* Now, for God's sake, get up and let's go!"

Instantly, resistance drained from him. He was afraid again; he simply couldn't doubt that she was telling him the truth. Standing shakily, he moved beside her as she started walking, tightly holding on to his right arm. The rain had stopped, he noticed, though it was still overcast, close to darkness.

They were almost to the Vaporetto dock when Alexsandra suddenly steered him from it. "What are you doing?" he asked.

"I have to speak to you," she said.

He looked at her intent expression. Was she finally going to tell him what had been going on—at least since London? He walked beside her anxiously. She was heading toward a group of gondolas.

As they neared the pier, he could hear water slapping against it, the gondolas shifting from side to side in the current. One of the oarsmen jumped to the pier. "Down the Grand Canal, past Marco Polo's house and under the Bridge of Sighs. Fifty thousand lire," he blurted in heavily accented English.

"All right," Alexsandra muttered.

"Fifty thousand?" Chris whispered as she drew him toward the long black gondola.

"Forty dollars," she murmured. He grimaced. Of course, he thought. He knew that.

The oarsman helped Alexsandra into the pitching gondola and Chris stepped in behind her, almost losing his balance. Why were they doing this? he wondered as he clumsily dropped onto the plastic cushion beside her. The water seemed terribly rough to be riding in a gondola.

The oarsman quickly moved to the stern of the gondola and, picking up his long pole, stepped up onto his platform and slid the pole into the water, backing the gondola away from the pier. Chris winced at its heavy rocking. He wasn't in the mood for a swim in the Grand Canal; he remembered once reading how badly Katherine Hepburn's eyes had become infected when she'd fallen into this water while filming a scene.

Bracing his feet and tightly holding on to the gunwale with one hand, he nervously looked back at St. Mark's Square. Now that the rain had stopped, there were a few more tourists evident, strolling around, examining bookstalls under an awning.

He felt himself go rigid as his eyes locked onto the shadowy figure of a man standing in a doorway, apparently looking toward the water. For several moments, he felt positive that it was

Veering—the man was the same size, dressed similarly, with what looked to Chris like a baseball cap on his head.

He twitched sharply as Alexsandra asked him, "What are you looking at?"

For a number of seconds, Chris had the impression that his lungs had no air in them, that they'd collapsed and he was just about to suffocate.

"Chris?"

He made a wheezing noise as he felt himself sucking in air. Dear God, he thought. He had never felt so removed from reality as he did at this moment, sitting in this black, rocking gondola in Venice, eyes fixed on the receding figure of the man who had to be—

He fought it off; he had to or he would completely lose control. How could it possibly be Veering? It hadn't been him on the Hovercraft and it wasn't him now. Veering was a deranged hitchhiker in Arizona, nothing more. He had to rid himself of this insane brooding about the wager. The wager was nonsense, utter nonsense. He had to believe that.

"Chris, what *is* it?"

He swallowed, tearing his gaze from the distant figure of the man. "Nothing," he said. "I'm just . . ." He shook his head. "All those things coming at me one after the other. I'm getting paranoiac, or I'm there already."

She grasped both of his hands with hers; he was startled by how strong she was. "I'm so sorry," she said. "So sorry, love, for what they're doing to you."

He swallowed again, with greater difficulty now. "It ain't been easy," he admitted.

"Chris." She pressed against him suddenly, arms around him, clinging to him. He put his arms around her and held her as tightly as he could. *It's the only constant left,* he thought, *my love for her and*—he prayed that it was genuine—*her love for me.*

He looked out at St. Mark's Basin as the gondola turned. There was a liner anchored there, its cabins lit. All the way across the channel he could see the looming spires and tower of the church on St. George Island. Once more, in spite of the fear that ate at him, he experienced a twinge of regret that he was unable to enjoy this fabled city as a simple tourist. But, of course, that was impossible.

The gondola was being propelled along the shore now, St. Mark's Square to their right. He saw a restaurant ahead, some of the more brave diners already eating outside by candlelight. He watched them as the oarsman guided the gondola toward a side canal.

The moment it entered the canal, sound and light fell away in an instant and the surface of the water became almost completely smooth. He heard the water lapping at the gondola's sides, the only sound he could hear. Abruptly, he felt uneasy, his imagination needled by the heavy silence and darkness between the buildings on each side. A perfect place for murder; his brain distressed him with the image. A blow to the head with the pole, his body dumped into the foul-smelling water, not to rise until—

He fought it off, angrily grimacing at himself. *For Christ's sake, Barton, aren't things bad enough as they are?* He exhaled in relief as he saw another gondola approaching theirs. Small candles were burning on its prow; their own gondola was dark. He saw the approaching gondola glide beneath a dark footbridge, along the side of a dark building directly on the canal. As it passed them, he saw a young couple in the middle seat, embracing and kissing passionately.

"I wish to God we had nothing else on *our* minds but that," he murmured.

"Oh . . ." She drew back, looing at him intently. As the gondola moved past a small café, he saw, in its dim light, a glistening of tears in her eyes.

"Oh . . ." He said it in the same way, pained, despairing.

Then their lips were pressing together, and he could taste the sweetness of her breath in his mouth.

"I love you, Chris. I love you so," she whispered.

"I love you too," he said. "It's the one thing I'm holding on to right now."

They kissed again. Again. Again. Dear God, how he wanted her, he thought.

Then, breathless, she was quietly holding on to him.

The silence was oppressive; Chris swallowed, broke it willfully. "Why are all the buildings dark?" he asked the oarsman, feeling idiotic even as he spoke, sure that the man had only one phrase in his vocabulary, the one he'd used to sell his services.

"People on vacation," said the oarsman.

Chris drew in a deep, faltering breath. The smell was so awful, he thought. He'd take long vacations if he lived here.

Had Alexsandra fallen asleep? She was so quiet. The silence disturbed Chris again.

"How deep is the water?" he asked, saying the first thing that came to mind.

"Five, six feet," the oarsman answered. "Deeper in winter. Piazza St. Marco sometimes knee-deep. Build wooden walks for people."

Chris made a polite, impressed sound. That was more information than he'd thought to ask for.

Another gondola passed them now, a larger one with eight passengers in it. There was barely enough room for the two gondolas to pass each other. The oarsman was singing "La Paloma" and the passengers were chatting, laughing.

The other gondola moved away and the heavy silence fell again. The canal was dark and felt airless to him, humid. That terrible smell of rot in the air. Shadows of people walking in dark alleys. Chris clung to Alexsandra, the sense of unreality returning. He was riding through the darkness in a black gondola with a woman obsessed by ancient Rome; he felt at once frightened and enamored of her. How much longer could his mind cope with these dark contradictions?

The only sound now was the faint slapping of the water against the gondola. Chris had to hear her voice again; her silence was beginning to unnerve him.

"Alexsandra?" he said.

She drew away from him and, in the darkness, he could see her looking at him, hear the straining of her breath.

"What *is* it?" he pleaded.

"I can't," she said. "I just can't do it."

"Do *what?*"

"I can't let this go on," she said. "I have to—" She broke off as a faint illumination suddenly fell on the gondola and he saw her gaze move out past him. He began to turn. Alexsandra tried to stop him. "*Don't,*" she said. "Don't look."

But it was too late. He was staring at the wall of a building the gondola was passing. Crude words had been scrawled there so hurriedly that the white paint had dribbled downward toward the water.

4 steps to midnight.

3

Chris felt as though his body had been turned to stone. His gaze transfixed on the letters, the only sensation of life he felt was the heavy thudding of his heartbeat.

He jerked around as Alexsandra cried out, "No!"

He gazed at her. She'd fallen forward, a look of shock on her face.

Chris leaned down suddenly to see what had happened to her. There was a popping noise behind him and a buzzing past his ear as though a giant bee were zooming by. Twisting around with a gasp, he looked up at the oarsman. The man was pointing what looked like an air pistol at him. Chris stiffened, waiting to be hit.

Abruptly then, the man jolted with a faint cry of pain and started toppling forward. Chris gasped as he saw the handle of a knife protruding from his back. The oarsman collapsed to the bottom of the gondola and, glancing up in dread, Chris saw the dark figure of a man standing at the dead end of an alley behind them. The man whirled and disappeared.

Chris gasped again as Alexsandra's hand clutched at his shirt. He looked at her dumbly. Her eyes were glazed, she drew in rasping breath through gritted teeth.

"Chris," she muttered. "Run."

He felt completely helpless, staring at her.

"*Run!*" she whispered. "Save yourself!"

"I can't leave—"

He broke off, catching his breath in shock as she slumped back, her eyes falling shut.

"Oh, my God." He rubbed a shaking hand across his cheek. It isn't true, he thought. *It can't be true.* He murmured her name as he tried to feel for her pulse beat in her neck. But his fingers were too numb and shaking. "*Alexsandra,*" he murmured.

He cried out in startled terror as someone leaped into the gondola and grabbed him. Yanking himself around, he had a fleeting impression of a dark-faced man glaring down at him, of fingers digging into his shoulders.

He moved without thinking; fear and rage combined to produce a violent twist and shove that flung the man away from him. He heard a sickening thud as the man's head struck the canal wall. Suddenly, the man had slumped unconscious across the gunwale of the gondola.

Running footsteps. Chris looked up to see another man racing down an alley toward him. He looked around in desperation. There was an alley on the other side of the canal.

He moved without thinking, sure that Alexsandra had been killed. Stumbling across the gondola, he stepped up on the gunwale and leaped, slamming onto his knees on the cobblestone paving. He heard another popping noise behind him and a chunk of mortar on a nearby building wall exploded out. "Jesus Christ!" he muttered. Scrambling to his feet, he started running up the alley.

Another popping sound from behind. Chris cried out as a searing pain ripped through his right forearm. He clutched at the arm spasmodically. Then, as another bullet whined off the paving, ricocheting off a building wall just ahead, he ran faster, mouth open, gasping at the warm, heavy air.

He glanced back and saw the man clambering rapidly across the gondola and jumping to this side of the canal. Sucking in breath, teeth clenched, Chris tried to run faster. It felt as though his right forearm had been set on fire, the hot pain was so agonizing. A wave of dizziness swept over him and, for several moments, he was sure that he was going to fall. *No!* he thought.

He knew he couldn't outrun the man. His mind raced frantically through his file of novel memories. Hero chased by killer, then: alley with side alley. It seemed as though the answer sprang into his mind. He knew it was his only chance.

Skidding around the corner of a building, he jarred to a halt, trying not to breathe so loud. He heard the running footsteps of the man approaching and braced himself. *Now or never, Barton,* said a faint voice in his mind.

The instant the man began to turn the corner, Chris charged sideways at him, ramming him as hard as he could with his left shoulder and knocking him back; the pain in his right forearm flared so sharply that he cried out uncontrollably. The man went floundering back and crashed against a building wall. He started to recover but Chris kicked out at him as violently as he could.

He'd never in his life even imagined actually kicking a man in the testicles: In books and movies, such a kick was somehow associated with humor. There was nothing humorous about it though. The man's mouth opened wide in a wheezing cry, his expression suddenly one of total agony. Chris had to force himself to grab the man's right arm and slam the hand against the brick wall of the building. The pistol clattered to the cobblestone paving and the man began to slump. Chris turned and started blindly running to escape.

The moment he did, he saw the two men coming at him.

Suddenly, he couldn't breathe. The fiery pain in his arm began to shoot into his shoulder and neck. Darkness pressed at his eyes again. He tried to fight it but was unable to do so. Stumbling, he fell against a building to his right. The explosion of pain in his arm began to cloud his brain.

Then darkness swallowed him.

🜨 *"There is no time left,"* the voice whispered.

Chris stirred, a faint groan in his throat.

"You can run no longer," the voice continued. "You are at the end of the road. Now is the time for you to discover all the answers. *Now.*"

As he jerked up with a startled gasp, Chris thought he heard running footsteps receding from him. His eyelids fluttered, then lifted and he stared ahead blankly. His right forearm was throbbing.

There was a wall of stone and mortar across from him, very old. Light filtered down from above like gray mist. He shivered. The air was chilled. He became aware that he was sitting on cold stone and struggled to his feet, hissing at the pain in his arm as he used his right hand to push up. His arm was bandaged, he saw.

He looked around dazedly. Where *was* he?

Then abruptly he looked down. He'd been holding a slip of paper in his left hand and, in standing, he'd let go of it so that it fluttered to the floor. He stared down at it, afraid to see what it was.

Then, after several moments, he braced himself and, bending over, picked up the scrap of paper. It was the size of a business card.

He closed his eyes for several moments, the flaring pain in his arm making him wince and hiss. Then he looked at the slip of paper.

There were words printed on it. Using his left hand, he raised the slip to the light, glancing upward to see that the gray illumination came from an overhead shaft; far above, he saw what looked to be the sky.

He peered closely at the slip of paper then.

Pontifica Commissions/Di archeologic Sacra was printed at the top with a symbol on each side of the words, a dove with a garland in its beak on the left, what looked like an anchor on the right.

Below that were words printed in darker, thicker letters.

Biglietto D'ingresso/alle Catacombe/Di S. Callisto.

Chris shuddered violently, his fingers twitching, dropping the slip again.

He was in a Roman catacomb, an underground cemetery.

The one Alexsandra had insisted that her foster parents take her to see.

It was completely back now, the sense of total unreality. The wager *had* been lost; he knew that. There was no way he could cope with this. He was ready to be put away at last, his mind undone.

A movement at his left caught the corners of his eyes and he jerked around.

He stared in breathless silence at the figure at the far end of the tunnel-like corridor.

Standing in deep shadows was a woman in a pale white gown. Her, he thought. Her ghost. She'd never been real.

He felt as though his mind was being slowly crushed in by a tightening clamp.

Her, he thought again. *Alexsandra.*

He had to know.

He started walking toward her, hearing the faint scuffing sound his shoes made on the stone floor of the tunnel. The figure didn't move. It *was* her. He could see it clearly now. She was staring at him, waiting for him. Her figure wavered. Chris drew in choking breath.

He could see right through her.

He stopped and leaned against the stone wall, eyes closed, body wracked by shivers. The pain in his arm was a dull ache that pulsed like a heartbeat.

When he opened his eyes again, she was gone.

Chris swallowed dryly, staring at the place where she'd been standing. Why was she gone now? he wondered.

He spoke her name aloud, unnerved by the stricken sound of his voice.

There was no response and she did not appear again.

He pushed away from the wall and continued down the corridor. He held himself tightly, expecting, at any moment, her ghost to reappear.

When he reached the spot where she'd been standing, he looked to his left and saw an open crypt.

The same gray light filtered down from above.

A sarcophagus stood across from him, built against the back wall.

Chris moved inside the crypt, unable to hold back. It has to go all the way, he thought. The voice had been right. Now *was* the time for him to discover all the answers.

He stopped. There were faded words on the wall above the

sarcophagus. Carved in stone innumerable centuries ago. He had studied Latin from a textbook once, and, slowly, he deciphered the meaning of the words.

While the Kingdom of Heaven carries off her chosen soul, this revered tomb encloses the mortal remains of the good lady—

"—*Alexsandra,*" he whispered.

He couldn't hold himself back. It was as though a magnet drew him forward to the sarcophagus.

He stared down through the thick plate glass.

All that remained were brownish fragments of bone and gray dust. He leaned down closer, his heartbeat slow and heavy.

The ring was there, encircling what was left of her finger. . . .

At first he thought that someone else was moaning in the tomb.

Then he realized that it was coming from his own throat as he backed off from the sarcophagus, whirled, and found himself confronted by two men in black.

He stood frozen for an instant, staring at them as they started for him. Then, something wild and dark erupted in his mind and with a savage cry, he leaped at them.

Grabbing one, he hurled him aside; the man staggered, off balance, against a wall. The second man threw his right arm around Chris's neck and jerked it tight. Pain shot through Chris's right arm as he elbowed the man in the side. The man's arm loosened and he gasped in startlement.

Then something smashed on Chris's head and blackness leaped up from the floor, enveloping his brain. He fought against it, blinking rapidly, swinging out blindly at the air. The dark fog thinned and he could see the second man about to hit him on the head again with the barrel of an automatic. Rearing back, he lost his balance and began to fall.

He landed on the elbow of his right arm, screaming at the burst of pain. Shadows poured across his brain again as he writhed in agony on the cold stone floor.

He gasped as the two men grabbed him beneath the arms and

hauled him to his feet. He tried to resist but couldn't. There was no strength left in him.

Drifting in and out of consciousness, he felt himself being half walked, half dragged from the tomb and along a corridor, up a curving staircase of stone and out into gloomy daylight.

He tried to struggle again but couldn't, hissing as one of the men twisted back his right arm. Darkness pulsed across him once more. He tried to think, to be aware, but there was no way. He stared at a line of pines that seemed to stretch into infinity. *The Pines of Rome,* his mind thought dully.

Then he was being dragged toward a towering brick structure, through its open doorway and up a long, curving flight of wooden steps. "Who *are* you?" he muttered dazedly.

The men said nothing. He could hear their heavy breathing as they dragged him up the steps. The climb seemed to take hours.

Then he was being pulled into a darkened room with narrow lancet windows. The two men let go of his arms and he felt himself falling. He cried out as his knees hit the hard wood floor, then strained to keep from falling any farther, wavering in the dimly lit room, sucking fitfully at the air, which smelled of old dust.

"So this is our genius," said a man's voice, sounding icily amused.

Chris raised his head and blinked laboriously. As the cloudiness lifted from his sight, he saw a heavy man looming over him. He couldn't make out the man's features because it was too shadowy in the room. He could only see a bulky form, a dark suit and a white shirt, a fez on the man's head.

"I'm glad to meet you finally," the man told Chris. "You have been no end of trouble to me."

Chris swallowed with effort, coughing weakly. "What d'you want?" he mumbled.

"Primarily your death," the man replied. Chris shuddered at the casual sound in his voice.

"Why? What have I—?"

Chris broke off as the man gestured. He felt himself being abruptly grabbed beneath the arms again and roughly yanked up to his feet. He groaned at the pain in his right arm, his vision clouding again.

"That hurts, I suppose," the man said. "Your own fault for resisting in Venice."

"What d'you—?"

"Be still," the man told him. "As I said, my primary desire where you're concerned is to see you dead. If you are dead, you can no longer do your work. That's clear to you, of course."

Chris stared at the man. In the gray light from the windows, he could see the man's face now.

It was broad and pockmarked, with heavy-lidded eyes, and lips as thin as knife blades; across the man's forehead was a long white scar. It was the most inhuman face Chris had ever seen.

"My advisers tell me it would be more profitable, however, if I possessed the information locked up in that singular skull of yours." The man smiled coldly. "Unless, of course, this strenuous activity has knocked it from your mind. Has it, Mr. Barton?"

He knows who I am was all Chris could think.

"Let us see what still remains," the man said.

Chris saw him reach down and noticed that the man was holding a cassette recorder in his hand. There was a clicking sound on the recorder and a small red light blinked on.

"Now," the man said, "I would like you to explain your project. Do not hesitate to enumerate mathematical details which none of us here—except you, of course—will understand. I have people working for me who *will* understand."

Chris stared at the man in stricken silence. *I'm going to die,* he thought.

"Please. Don't hesitate," the man instructed him. "If I can get the information on this problem—what do you call it . . . turbulence?—I can sell that information for enormous sums of money. There are many buyers, many governments who would be happy to acquire such information. Please. Begin."

Chris stared at the man dumbly, trying to think. Was there any way at all of getting out of this?

"*I do not enjoy waiting,*" the heavy man told him.

Chris swallowed. His throat felt completely dry. "I—" He

cleared his throat. "My work is written down on papers. I hid them in my hotel room in Venice."

He broke off with a cry of pain as the heavy man slapped him so violently across the cheek that his head snapped sideways, a pain shooting up his neck like an electric shock.

"If you insist on lying, we will kill you straightaway," the man informed him.

"I—"

"We know about your comprehensive memory." The man cut him off. "You would leave nothing on paper, you are not that stupid. Now, begin to speak into this recorder. My last warning."

"But it's too complicated to just dictate—" Chris began.

His voice stopped and he drew in a long, gasping breath as the two men shoved him to one of the lancet windows and began to cram him through the opening.

"Wait!" he cried.

He felt the two men grab his legs and lift his feet from the floor.

"No!" Chris froze in their grip, his features distended by terror.

Then he was hanging head-down, staring in shock at the ground far below.

Chris drew in rasping breath, his heartbeat quickening.

"Is your heart beginning to beat quite rapidly?" the man's voice drifted down to him. "That is called *chamade*, Mr. Barton— the drumbeat which signals the moment of surrender. Are you ready to surrender yet? Or would you prefer to plummet down and crack your skull like egg?"

"If I die, you have no formula!" Chris yelled at him, appalled to hear fury in his voice, knowing it was madness.

"And no one else has it either," the man said; he actually sounded amused. "Least of all, your filthy government. And I shall have to find some other worthy formula to sell. Perhaps a finer nerve gas."

God, Chris thought.

"One more opportunity," he heard the man say. The calmness of his tone made Chris's skin grow cold.

Suddenly, there was a muffled voice inside. He couldn't hear what it said. He kept staring in horror at the long fall beneath him.

"Drop him," the heavy man ordered.

The muffled voice spoke again as Chris closed his eyes abruptly, preparing to die.

"I said—!"

The heavy man's voice was cut off by a crashing pistol shot. Chris tried to grip at the rough brick siding of the tower but couldn't get hold of anything. He drew in a hissing breath, still convinced that he was going to die.

Then, to his amazement, he felt himself being hauled back up. His right arm raked across the brick wall, making him cry out at the flare of pain.

Now he was being pulled back into the tower room, the grip on him released as he reached a standing position.

He fell back against the wall, breathing hard, and stared at the man across the room who held a pistol in his hand.

"A good thing that I came no later," Modi observed with a faint smile.

Chris stared at him incredulously, then glanced down at the floor.

The heavy man was lying there, a pool of blood slowly expanding around him.

"Go down the stairs, Mr. Barton," Modi instructed quietly. "I will follow."

Chris said nothing, but crossed the room and walked past Modi. As he did, he glanced back and saw the two men in black regarding Modi with hatred.

"Mr. Barton," Modi said.

Chris stopped and looked around. Modi was holding a ring of ignition keys in his raised left hand. He tossed them backward and they jingled to the floor in front of Chris.

"My car is a gray Mercedes coupe," Modi told him. "Unlock it and get inside. I will be with you momentarily."

Chris gulped and, bending over, scooped up the keys with his left hand. Turning abruptly, he left the room and started to descend the winding wooden steps.

He was halfway down when there was a sudden crashing noise above, a single pistol report, then another crashing.

"Run!" he heard Modi shout.

Chris bit his teeth together hard and started down the steps as quickly as he could, shoes clattering on the wood.

He had reached the bottom and was lunging out the door when something dark came hurtling down from above and hit the ground violently, making him recoil with a breathless cry.

He froze, mutely gaping down at Modi's dead face, the East Indian's expression one of dazed surprise.

Then he heard the two men rushing down the steps and, catching his breath, he broke into a run along the entry path to the tower. Glancing around, he saw a gray Mercedes coupe parked about thirty yards down the tree-lined road. Another car, a black Jaguar, was parked behind it.

His right arm began to throb as he sprinted along the road, shoes pounding on the hard dirt surface. He looked across his shoulder just as the two men came running from the tower, eyes searching for him. One of them pointed at Chris as they dashed for the road.

Turning back, his teeth still clenched, panting, Chris tried to run faster despite the pain in his arm.

Now he was at the Mercedes, fumbling with the keys. *Jesus, why did he lock it?!* he thought in a panic. His hand was shaking badly as he tried to slip the correct key into the door lock. He glanced aside. The men were getting closer. One began to raise his right arm, pointing a pistol.

Suddenly, the key slid into its slot. Chris twisted it and jerked open the door. Bending over, he practically flung himself into the driver's seat, expecting, at any second, to hear the back window exploding inward from the impact of a bullet.

He cried out as he automatically used his right hand to slide the ignition key in and turn it. The motor started instantly and, throwing the transmission into gear, Chris jammed his foot down on the gas pedal. The Mercedes leaped forward so abruptly that he almost lost control of the steering wheel.

Then he held it tightly with his left hand, his right hand barely gripping the rim as the coupe picked up speed, roaring down the road. He glanced up at the rearview mirror. The men had tried to catch him on foot. Now, seeing him drive off, they were turning back to the Jaguar.

Where am I supposed to go? he thought. He had no idea whatsoever where he was except that he felt certain it was Rome. He looked ahead. In the distance, he saw a cluster of low brick buildings built around a courtyard. He couldn't go that way! he thought in sudden dread. He'd be trapped.

There was a side road just ahead. He began to brake, then downshifted quickly, and raked around the corner, shifting up again. He shot a glance to his right. The Jaguar was close behind. Could he possibly outrun them? He wished to God Alexsandra was driving—

The thought evaporated. Alexsandra was a ghost, a heap of bone and dust. He snarled without a sound. *It's all insane!* he thought. *None of it makes any sense!*

"*No,*" he muttered. Ahead was another building with a covered gateway leading into its courtyard. He looked around desperately. Was that a right turn up ahead? It had to be or he was finished.

Again, he had to brake. The Jaguar was only twenty yards behind him now. He downshifted again and turned the corner of the high-walled building, tires squealing loudly.

"Oh, my God!" He gaped at the heavy metal gate just ahead, blocking the narrow road he was on. In seconds, the Mercedes would crash into it.

He had no idea what made the page appear in front of his frightened mental gaze, but suddenly it was there, as clear as if it were hanging in the air directly before is eyes—*Ninja 1990* was the book (he'd read it a while back), page 65.

His feet and hands became a blur of movement as he followed its instruction. Throwing the transmission into neutral, he turned the steering wheel sharply to the left, at the same instant jerking the emergency brake into place, locking the rear wheels.

Instantly, the car began to rotate, quickly, its rear wheels leading. Chris waited a second, then released the emergency brake, threw the transmission into low gear and jammed the gas pedal to the floor. By now, the Mercedes had spun around 180 degrees and was leaping forward in the opposite direction. The maneuver—which had totally astonished him—had taken less than five seconds.

He saw the Jaguar flying past him, the sides of the two cars almost scraping as they passed each other. A moment later, he heard the grinding impact of the Jaguar as it hit the gate, then exploded. He looked into the rearview mirror to see a ball of fire enveloping the wrecked car. He winced at the sight.

Then he was turning left again, heading for the tree-lined road. Reaching it in seconds, he turned left and started back toward the tower.

At first, he didn't know what was causing the noise above—a spasmodic, roaring sound. He pressed down on the accelerator and the Mercedes picked up speed.

He started in shock as the helicopter roared across the tree tops, passing him. It wheeled around and hovered just above the road. Chris thought he heard a voice. He lowered the window.

"Pull over, Chris. It's finished now," the voice instructed him through a loudspeaker.

He didn't know what to do. Was he to meekly surrender now, after all he'd been through? But then, the helicopter might be armed with machine guns, it occurred to him.

"Pull over now," the voice said firmly.

Chris slowed the car down and steered over to the shoulder of the road. He braked the car and waited, suddenly feeling very tired and very beaten.

He watched as the helicopter settled down in the field to his right like a gigantic insect. There was a white star on the helicopter's side. It was an American military vehicle.

The blades slowed down. The door of the helicopter opened and a man jumped out. As he approached the car, Chris stared at him incredulously. He had to blink hard to make sure his eyes were working right.

The man was Wilson.

4

The helicopter had flown directly to Heathrow Airport where they'd helped Chris across the tarmac to a private waiting room. There, Wilson had left him with a nurse and doctor who had attended to his arm, cleaning and bandaging the wound. It had started to become infected and the doctor gave him an injection which he said was an antibiotic. Chris hadn't questioned him—he was even too dazed to speak—though he was immediately convinced that the injection was a drug and that, after a period of unconsciousness, he'd wake up somewhere in Africa, Russia, the Far East.

It hadn't been a drug though. It slowly sank in that the shot had been exactly what the doctor said it was. *I'm not used to things being what people say they are,* Chris had thought.

He'd asked the doctor and nurse if they knew anything about Alexsandra but they didn't know what he was talking about. *No wonder,* he'd thought. *I'm asking about someone who'd never really existed anyway. How could they possibly know about her?*

After they'd treated him, they gave him a sandwich and a cup of tea. He'd barely touched them as a wave of drowsiness had overcome him and he started slipping away. It had been at that moment that he was most convinced he'd been drugged again.

An hour later, Wilson had woken him and they'd left the waiting room, walking out to a Learjet. *Are we going back in this?* Chris had wondered. Then he'd asked.

"You're entitled," Wilson had told him.

Now they were inside the jet, the door was closed and they were sitting across from each other in luxurious armchairs as the jet taxied down the runway, then picked up speed and soared into the air. Chris looked out the window. *Alexsandra,* he thought, torn between the hope that she really existed somewhere down there and the dark conviction that she'd never been real from the start. It defied logic to believe that; she'd felt completely real. Still . . .

He looked at Wilson.

"Are you feeling better?" Wilson asked.

"Yes, thank you," he said, his tone lifeless. He cleared his throat slowly. "Do you know what's happened to me in the last seven days?" he asked. *7 steps to midnight,* he thought. Was there any connection?

He hadn't heard Wilson's answer. "Sorry?" he murmured.

"Of course I know," Wilson repeated. "I was in charge of it."

Chris stared at him. Wilson was in *charge* of it?

That seemed the most insane reality of all.

"What do you mean?" he asked.

"If you weren't so modest you might have figured it out," Wilson explained. "But you've never seemed to have the slightest inkling of how important you are to the project. How absolutely indispensable."

I should be feeling pleasure at this praise, Chris thought. *Why don't I?*

"I can see that you're still not sure of it," Wilson continued. "Just take my word for it, Chris. Without you working on the turbulence problem it would have taken years more to reach the point we're at now.

"Unfortunately, your brain was in a rut, tired, stagnating. We needed something to break up the logjam in your thinking."

"Are you telling me—?" Chris began, a sudden sound of appalled disbelief in his voice.

"Let me finish," Wilson interrupted. "Then I'll answer any question you want to ask."

Chris stared at him. He couldn't be saying—

"We consulted a well-known psychologist," Wilson went on,

"head of his department at a famous Ivy League university in New England. We asked him what we could do to get you out of the rut you were in.

"He examined your psychological profile and told us that he thought there was a possibility. A remote one, but a possibility.

"Noting that you devoured a huge variety of action, suspense, espionage, science-fiction and occult novels, he suggested—"

"You're telling me it was all a *trick?*" Chris demanded. He felt cold fury rising in his gorge.

"Well, we thought it was," Wilson answered. "Unfortunately, it got more complicated than that."

"At any rate," Wilson continued, "this psychologist suggested that we contrive to involve you in what seemed to be a real adventure the like of which you'd only read about. He felt that, in this way, your mind might be stimulated in a fresh way and be able to—"

"*You're telling me it was all a trick?*" Chris repeated sharply.

"I *told* you, Chris," Wilson replied. "It became more complicated than that."

Chris slumped back against the chair, stonily looking at Wilson. *I've been a dupe,* he thought. *A pathetic dupe.*

"Do you want to hear about this or not?" Wilson asked.

Chris wearily exhaled and gestured with his right hand as though to say *Sure, why not? Rub in the salt as deeply as you can.*

"The psychologist discussed it with a committee," Wilson said.

"A *committee,*" Chris muttered in disgust.

Wilson looked at him in silence for a few moments, then went on.

"They decided that you needed certain outside stresses which would divert attention from your work. Intriguing stresses, the sort you read about."

Gotcha, Chris thought. *Do go on.*

Wilson took a folded sheet of paper from his inside jacket pocket and, unfolding it, began to read.

"What is required is that the patient's environment—with its attitudes and rigidities of personality—be discarded and the patient be placed in a less enforced and restrictive environment in order to re-open his creative channels."

Chris said nothing. He only gazed at Wilson, his expression flat.

"So they devised a scenario," Wilson went on. "The disappearing car. The couple in your house. They thought it would be more intriguing if the man looked exactly like you but we couldn't find or produce a duplicate on short notice, so we let it go. They thought it might be more provocative if he didn't look exactly like you anyway."

"And Veering?" Chris asked.

Was that a smile on Wilson's lips? "Ah, yes, Veering," he said. He was amused, Chris thought, tightening.

He reacted as Wilson picked up a telephone receiver and pushed a button on its base. Wilson listened for a moment, then spoke, "You can come back now."

Chris twisted around and looked toward the front of the cabin. A door there was opening.

He tensed involuntarily as he saw the man approaching.

Veering.

He shivered, watching as the small man neared him. The old clothes and the baseball cap were gone, replaced by an expensive three-piece suit.

"This is Dr. Albert Veering of the Princeton Psychology Department." Wilson introduced the man.

"I know how angry you must feel," Veering said. "Betrayed. Cheated. But, believe me, it *was* necessary if your mental state was to be improved."

Chris didn't want to speak to the man but he had to know: "Why all the unreality shit?" he asked.

There was a faint stirring of Veering's lips as he repressed a smile. "Simple," he said. "You're too intelligent a young man. You would have begun to see through the overall artifice if it had been confined to an espionage adventure. It was my suggestion that we add the larger dimension of the wager in order to give your intellect more to cope with."

"I see." Chris's eyes were dead as he regarded Veering. "And that included Rome, and Alexsandra?"

"It did," Veering answered. "A recognition of your taste for novels dealing with the occult and the supernatural."

"I see." Chris's voice was barely audible. He felt a heavy weight in his chest and stomach and couldn't tell if it was rage or sickened despair. "I presume, then, that Alexsandra isn't her real name."

"Her real name is, I believe, Jane Malcolm." Veering told him.

It was rage he felt; he knew that now. Rage at being made to look like a total fool. At being made so vulnerable. At being terrified again and again.

"At any rate," Veering continued, "exclusive of that, the remainder of the 'adventure' was relatively simple—"

"Except for the complications," Wilson broke in.

"Yes." Veering nodded gravely. "They were most unfortunate."

What complications? Chris wondered. He felt too bound up with resentful fury to ask.

"The initial mysteries were, as I say, relatively simple to orchestrate," Veering told him. "The missing car, the couple and the changes in your house. The two so-called agents. Unfortunately, the first one had a rather vile temper, not to mention an old knee injury incurred while playing football. He disliked you intensely and rather overplayed his part."

"Speaking of overplaying the part—?" Wilson began, amused.

"Yes," said Veering with a smile, "The other agent, Nelson, didn't dislike you but he did have some difficulty getting you to wrestle him for the gun and 'kill' him."

"*Twice?*" Chris asked.

"That's what Mr. Wilson meant about overplaying," Veering said. "Nelson—" He turned to Wilson. "That *is* his name, isn't it?"

"Carter," Wilson replied.

"Ah." Veering nodded. "Well, at any rate, the man apparently does quite a bit of work in little theaters. He's a real ham. Couldn't get himself offstage, as it were."

Wilson chuckled. "Served him right to break his shoulder bone when he fell from the car."

Glad you two are enjoying this, Chris thought. Thank God he didn't have a gun in his hand right now.

"Of course there were contingencies all along the line," Veering went on. "Nothing was left to chance. If you hadn't picked me up on the highway, or if you hadn't believed that you were responsible for Nelson's—Carter's—death, we would have have had an alternate method to get you on that flight to London. That was a must."

Chris felt cold and empty now. He wanted to be out of there but obviously that was impossible. And his brain persisted in being curious.

"What about my sister?" he asked. "My mother?"

"That wasn't your sister you spoke to," Veering said. "We had a cut-in line to her telephone. We didn't tell your sister or your mother what we were planning to do, on the logical assumption that they probably would have refused to help. As it turned out, your mother's behavior was most helpful to us."

So they made a fool of her too, Chris thought. He could not recall ever experiencing such poisonous hatred before.

"And Gene Wyskart?" he asked.

Veering got a grim expression on his face. "That was where the complications began," he said.

"What are you talking about?" Chris asked.

"We didn't realize, at first, that there was an information leak in the project," Wilson told him. "Your friend Wyskart was actually the one who found out about it. After he'd agreed to help us, he phoned some insiders he knew in Washington and they found out that at least one group already knew you were coming to London and was preparing to pick you up there. Wyskart tried to stop you before you left, the group got wind of it and killed him, to make sure you'd leave the United States."

"*You knew it wasn't all your game then,*" Chris said.

"The word was out before your bus reached California," Wilson said.

Chris leaned forward in his chair. "*And you let me go anyway?*"

"We were into it too deeply by then," Wilson told him. "Moreover, the need was still there—to get your mind operational again."

"Even though my life might not be," Chris responded.

"We took the risk that we'd be able to protect you," Wilson said coolly. "And we *did* have our British and French allies to help. Since they'd share the benefit of the turbulence solution, they were more than willing to—"

"In essence then, my friend Gene died so you could play a trick on me," Chris interrupted.

"That isn't the way I'd put it," Wilson said.

"He wasn't the only one to die, Mr. Barton," Veering added.

Chris answered through clenching teeth. "I *know* that," he said. "I *saw* them die."

"If we'd known how bad it was going to get, we would, of course, have terminated the project," Veering said.

Chris looked at the little man. *The project,* he thought. Veering might have been discussing an unsuccessful chess game.

"So the game went on," Chris said. "The tickets and money left on my car seat. The overnight bag in the airport locker. The man on the airplane. What happened to him anyway; was the bathroom rigged?"

"Of course," Wilson answered.

Chris nodded, smiling coldly. "So I got to London and you had me taken to a hotel."

"As a matter of fact, the taxi that was supposed to pick you up was bypassed by a regular cab. It was fortunate you weren't picked up by one of the groups waiting for you."

"Yes, fortunate," Chris said. "So what then? The cassette in my room, my Blue Swan adventure? Was that man really drugged?"

"He was," Wilson said. "Probably by Modi or one of his associates."

"Who *was* Modi anyway?" Chris asked. He didn't want to keep talking with these two bastards but curiosity kept him at it.

"We don't have all the details," Wilson said, "but, apparently, there were *two* groups after you. Modi worked for one, Cabal headed the other. The first group was interested primarily in what you knew. The second group was only interested in killing you— until Cabal realized, toward the end, the value of what you knew. His group was the one that chased you in London, and outside of it; you were, of course, in our limousine."

"The dream I had in that hotel suite," Chris said.

"Not a dream," Veering told him. "Induced by drugs and suggestion. To embellish your experience."

"Thanks, that was good of you," Chris replied. "I suppose you were the one who slapped me on the Hovercraft as well."

"I was." Veering nodded.

Chris smiled bitterly. "You had it all figured out, didn't you? A little evening in the theater, a high-speed chase with a gorgeous female agent . . ."

"The chase was genuine, as I've said," Wilson replied. "She saved your life."

"And added romance to my little adventure, of course," Chris said.

"Unfortunately—" Veering began.

"*Unfortunately?*" Chris broke in. "Hell, it was perfect. Even the two groups added to the game. Of course, they might have ended the game by killing me but what the hell."

"Chris—" Wilson started.

"So on it went." Chris cut him off. "Romantic Paris. Reunion with the mysterious Alexsandra. Sorry I almost fouled things up by not following the plot you'd arranged and going to Montmartre by mistake. Losing my passport on the train, refusing to give up the microfilm in Lucerne. What was on it anyway, a shot of Sleeping Beauty's castle?"

"No, as a matter of fact, it was quite valuable," Veering told him. "The agent who was supposed to carry it to Lucerne was the man who got killed in that restaurant at Montmartre. There was no immediate replacement for him, so it was decided, on the spur of the moment, to use you instead, incorporate the microfilm into your adventure."

"And the ring was already hollow, right?" Chris said.

"No, we had to work on that while you were unconscious in the car," Wilson said.

"And where was *she* unconscious?" Chris asked.

"In a Paris hotel room," Wilson answered. "We thought she'd completed her assignment. Until you demanded that she be brought to Lucerne."

"Sorry I wasn't playing the game right," Chris said. "I'm really not used to being a spy though. My apologies." He didn't really care that Wilson's face grew hard as he spoke. "I really screwed it up in Lucerne, didn't I?"

"You could have gotten yourself killed as well," Wilson told him. "The man who picked up the ring made the mistake of assuming that you were too naive to give it to him without the microfilm inside. Then when the other agent broke into the room you were in and you kicked him in the balls . . . Well, let's just say that it was fortunate his partner came into the room when he did. Otherwise, the 'project' might have ended right there. And by someone working for *us*." He made an amused sound. "And you thought Meehan's temper was bad. Sorry, *Applegate's* temper."

Chris slumped back in the chair. "And where is 'Alexsandra' now?" he asked with a scornful smile.

"You mustn't be too hard on her," Veering said. "If it wasn't for her, you might still be in Europe."

Chris tightened. "What do you mean?"

"She tried to talk us out of continuing with the project from the moment she knew it was more involved than we'd planned— although she didn't know, of course, exactly what our plan *was*— when she had to drive you to safety that first night in London and we had to make abrupt rearrangements to put you in another hotel.

"If there'd been time, we probably would have removed her from the operation as soon as she expressed doubt about it. But by then, too many details of the operation involved her.

"By the time you'd reached Venice, though, it was clear that we had to accelerate the project and get you out of Europe, in the hope that your brain had been stimulated enough by all the things that had happened to you by then to have made it all worthwhile."

Worthwhile, Chris thought, remembering the look on Alexsandra's (Jane's) face when, looking at his sheet of figures in the Venice hotel room, she'd said, *"So, this is what it's all about?"*

"Unfortunately, it became apparent to us that Jane Malcolm was unable to withhold information any longer," Veering said. "She was on the verge of telling you everything when our man— the gondolier—put a tranquilizer dart into her."

"Where is she now?" Chris asked.

"In London," Veering said. "Perfectly well. Questions?"

Chris just looked at him, feeling almost apathetic now.

"What if I'd just given myself up from the start?" he asked.

"Our psychological profile on you indicated that you wouldn't," Veering said. "That was discussed most carefully before the operation was approved."

"Mm-hmm." Chris nodded. "And 'seven steps to midnight'?"

"Designed to instill a sense of urgency in what was happening," Veering answered. He smiled again; he *was* amused, the son of a bitch! "Unfortunately, we ran out of time after Venice. Rome was a nightmare for all of us—leaving you in the catacombs to see that projected figure, that tomb wth Alexsandra's 'remains' inside. Cabal's group complicated everything. We had to end it then and there. Otherwise, we would have utilized the psychological pressures of steps three, two and one as well."

Chris nodded again. "And how many people died in order for this little game to take place?"

"Listen, Chris."

Chris turned to look at Wilson. He'd never seen such an expression on Wilson's face before; it was one of total dispassion. "If you're looking for remorse or an apology, forget it," Wilson told him. "We didn't create this venture as a lark. It was—it is— deadly serious.

"If what happened to you stimulated your brain enough to enable you to complete your project, it was worth *any* price because it will help make the United States invulnerable to surprise enemy attack.

"The solution of the turbulence problem will provide the ultimate force multiplier to the Star Wars system—or, for that matter, to any military system.

"By the year 2032, there'll be three nuclear-powered space battle stations in geo-synchronous orbit around the earth. These orbital fortresses are essential to the defense of our country. And the turbulence formula is the keystone to that plan.

"If you think the nation's problems are over because the cold war with Russia is over, you're naively mistaken. The race for space defense will continue. So don't, for an instant, think that what we did with you was wasted time or money—*or* lives.

"Your country needs that formula and needs it now," Wilson finished coldly. "That we went to all the trouble we did should make that perfectly obvious.

"The 'game,' as you call it, was completely justified, no matter what the consequences were. You understand?"

Chris answered quietly.

"I understand," he said.

5

The jet had landed in Tucson just past six P.M. A car had been waiting there to pick up Chris, another for Wilson and Veering. Although Chris had napped on the flight, Wilson had told him he'd be driven home so he could get a full night's sleep before returning to work. Obviously, Wilson knew, somehow, that he'd been working on the program during his "adventure" in Europe.

He'd been driven home by an Army sergeant and let off at his house. For a few moments he'd almost expected to find the couple still there. But of course they were gone and the alterations to his house had been eliminated.

He'd taken a long, hot shower, trying to keep the bandage on his arm dry. Then he'd put on a clean pair of pajamas and gotten into bed. He automatically reached for a book to read before sleeping, but at the last second, he winced and went rigid. *No, thank you,* he thought. He felt as though he'd never touch one of the damn things again.

It took him more than two hours to fall asleep, his brain a maelstrom of painful recollections, the worst having to do with Alexsandra. *Pardon me,* he'd thought, *Jane Malcolm.* Not quite so evocative a name. But then, of course, "Alexsandra" had been the idea from the start, probably Veering's.

The bastards.

Sometime after three A.M., he woke up to go to the bathroom. While he was standing by the toilet in the front bathroom, he glanced outside.

The car was still there. Inside it, he could see the glowing tip of a cigarette.

Clearly, they were not about to let him out of their sight.

🜨 Four days had gone by.

Now he was finishing up his work on the turbulence problem.

He typed in the last few lines of the formula, then turned off the computer. The screen went dark and, standing, he stretched. *Finis,* he thought.

He sighed and cleared his throat, then took the disc from the computer and added it to the others in the box. Picking up the box, he walked to the door of the office and opened it.

Sergeant Akins was waiting there as always, a .45 belted to his waist. He looked at Chris inquiringly.

"I'm bringing this to Mr. Wilson," Chris told him.

"Yes, sir." The sergeant nodded once.

He walked beside Chris along the corridor until they reached Wilson's office, then waited outside for Chris to return.

"Chris!" Wilson looked at him with eager anticipation as he came in. "You *have* it?"

Chris held out the box as he crossed the office. He laid it on Wilson's desk.

"*Finished?*" Wilson asked.

Chris nodded.

"That's amazing," Wilson said. "You had all of it in your head?"

"Yes." Chris nodded again.

"The boys at the Pentagon are going to be very happy to hear about this," Wilson told him.

"The boys," Chris murmured.

Wilson chuckled. "We're all boys," he said. "The playing field is a lot bigger now, that's all."

Chris smiled. "I understand."

Wilson tapped the box. "I wonder if you appreciate what you've done here," he said.

"I think I do," Chris answered.

Wilson came around the desk and shook his hand firm.

"The nation is in your debt," he said.

Chris smiled again. "Thank you." He exhaled wearily. "I'd like to go home now, if you don't mind."

"Take the rest of the week off," Wilson said expansively. "You're entitled."

Sergeant Akins drove him home and Chris went inside his house. He knew that Akins would remain there for the next six hours or so, then be replaced. They weren't going to leave him alone for a moment now.

Not until the program checked out anyway.

Chris left the drapes and blinds open as he made himself some supper. He watched television while he ate, flipping channels until he found a program devoid of the slightest element of suspense or mystery. He finally settled for a cable shopper's program. He stared at it almost blindly for several hours before turning it off.

At ten P.M., he went into the bedroom and took off his clothes. He showered and put on his pajamas, then got into bed. Was Akins watching every move? Not likely. His schedule was, as before, boringly similar night after night.

He picked up a novel and, opening it, stared at it for an hour or so, turning the pages in a regular pattern.

It was just past 11:15 when he turned out the lights.

He lay there for about ten minutes, then got up.

Remaining in the shadows, he took off his pajamas and got dressed, putting boots on his feet. He slipped on a jacket and moved across the bedroom, staying in the shadows.

He went into the family room and, unlocking the glass door, slid it open enough to edge through to the patio.

Keeping the house between him and the street—he looked back periodically to make sure he was moving in a straight line— he headed out across the desert. He was very glad now that he'd bought a house on the edge of the development.

It made his escape a lot easier.

He walked quickly across the desert, boots crunching on the sand. He could have done this two days ago, but he had had to wait for a new moon so the desert would be dark. He'd stalled for several days before completing the program on his computer.

He removed the compass from his pocket and looked at its luminescent face.

Dead on, he saw.

❂ The car was parked on the side of the dirt road, exactly where he expected it to be. *Pays to phone a professional (from an untapped booth),* he thought, smiling to himself.

He opened the door on the passenger side and got in.

They held each other in silence for more than a minute before she spoke.

"I was afraid you wouldn't come," she murmured. "I thought I'd dreamed your telephone call."

"There's only one thing you have to be afraid of," he said.

"What's that?"

"That it's going to take me a hell of a long time to start calling you Jane."

She drew back and smiled at him. Stroked his cheek. "It seems so far away now," she said. "Thank God."

She kissed him and they clung to one another for a long time.

Then, finally, she said, "We should leave."

"Let's do it."

She kissed him again, then started the motor and started driving toward the highway with the lights out.

"You don't think they'll know you've gone?" she asked.

"Not until morning. The good sergeant saw me getting into my pajamas, climbing into bed and reading for an hour before turning out the light."

"A spy novel?" she asked, amused.

"Robert Ludlum."

She laughed, delighted. "Perfect," she said. She looked at

him. "You tricked them most professionally," she said with praise.

"I was primed for it after what I went through," he answered.

She looked at him in concern. "You *do* know that I tried to get you out of it."

"I know." He leaned over and kissed her on the cheek. "Everything's fine."

She sighed in relief, then said, "You also know this flight is going to cost us a *lot* of money. But it's the only way. We can't take the chance of taking a commercial flight."

"What about the pilot of the private plane?" he asked, repressing a smile. "Do we kill him afterward?"

"He's a chum," she said. "We've worked together many times in the past. Our secret will be safe with him."

He smiled, feeling happy for the first time since he'd been with her in France.

"Am I going to like your island?" he asked.

"You're going to love it," she answered.

She turned onto the highway now and, turning on the headlights, pushed down hard on the gas pedal. The car surged forward.

"Chris?" she said.

"What?"

"Did you . . . finish your program?"

"I had to," he said. "They'd never relax their surveillance of me until I did."

"I see." Her tone was soft, deflated.

Chris chuckled.

"What is it?" she asked, looking at him in surprise.

"We'll have a perfect tan before they locate the piece of the equation that fouls up everything," he said.

His smile faded.

"They'll have to figure out how to destroy the world without my help," he added.

She was smiling happily now; there was a glistening in her eyes. "I'm so glad," she said.

"By the way," he told her, "one promise."

"Anything," she answered.

"If you ever buy me books for my birthday or Christmas, make sure they're picture books, will you?"

She reached over and squeezed his leg.

"It's going to be a long, long time before you have a chance to read again," she said.